I0782218

MATT SPIKE AGAINST THE AMAZON SAUCER WOMEN FROM VENUS

OR *MODERN LOVE*

From the case files of Matt Spike, P.I.

By R.E. SOHL

Curious Corvid

PUBLISHING

*L*ong ago, before recorded history, the shamans of the various tribes of humanity discovered, quite by accident, how to manipulate the fabric of reality using magic. They created a civilization that spanned the globe, using magic to accomplish many of the things we do today through technology.

In time there arose two warring factions of magic users who vied for the domination of the planet, this was the **Great Magic War,** a terrible conflict which destroyed their civilization and nearly wiped out the human race. It was a time when many monsters and beasts that are only thought of as legend really walked the Earth.

This war only came to an end when one wizard, Thoth, created a magic item that made it impossible to cast spells for miles around it, this was the **Orb of Thoth.** It was then given to a clan of Assassins, who used it to breach the defenses of the magic users on both sides of the war and kill their leaders in their sleep. They left a warning for the remaining magic users: end the war and use your powers to rebuild civilization, or face the same fate as your leaders.

The two factions of magic users then divided the world between them, one group, which became known as the "**Temple of the Old Gods**" dominated Europe and Africa (and in time the Americas as well), while the other group, "**The Order of the Golden Path**", asserted its influence from the Middle East and India all the way across Asia to the islands of the Pacific. Only these two groups were allowed to practice the most potent and effective kinds of magic, constantly under the watchful eye of the Assassins, who maintained the peace through their control of the Orb of Thoth. These three groups came to call themselves the **Guilds,** and in time they were joined by other influential groups that were accepted into their ranks. Together, they rebuilt human civilization into one that was more dependent on technology than magic. In time, the Guilds relinquished much of their control over humanity, content merely to continue to collect tribute from the nations they had helped create.

In 1995, this balance was upset. The corrupt leader of the Temple of the Old Gods sought to destroy the other Guilds and set up a televangelist as a false Second Coming of Christ, plotting to use magic to fake his miracles and rule the world through him. They gained control of the Orb of Thoth, framed the Order of the Golden Path for *trying to start a new Magic War by stealing it, and when the assembled armies of the Guilds and the Golden Path were all in one place, they destroyed them all, or so they thought. Little did they know that the televangelist, and a wizard named Dexter Sinister were planning on double crossing them, secretly creating an Orb of their own. They planned to use it to slaughter the remaining members of the Temple of the Old Gods so they wouldn't have to share power with them.*

*In the end, the plot was foiled thanks to the help of a Private Eye named **Matt Spike** and his friends **Naomi** (who would go on to become a history professor and his wife) and **Randy** (who would someday become a wizard and a detective himself) who had all gotten mixed up in the situation. In the end, the Orb of Thoth was lost in space, but the **Orb of Sinister** remained, and was secretly entrusted to Matt Spike and Naomi to make sure that its power could never be abused again. To help him in this task, Matt was given a powerful sword, the **Vermilion Avenger**, that could cut through anything, fly and which he could control with his mind, and also a suit of futuristic armor. Naomi would also get some special weapons of her own on a subsequent adventure, a magic ring that created a force field around her, and the flaming sword of an angel.*

*For 25 years, Matt and Naomi acted as the **Guardians of the Orb**, and through their association with the Guilds, encountered a variety of strange menaces, these are their stories....*

PROLOGUE

Their world was dying.

So it was with great interest that they looked at the first images from their latest probe as it emerged from the other end of the portal and began its first detailed survey of the planet, which they called Tulienel in their language. A planet which just might be their best hope for survival. A holographic image of a beautiful, blue marble of a planet illuminated the otherwise dimly lit control room.

The Supreme Leader looked upon this image with great pride, aware of the many naysayers from the other Nations that had mocked them, and had said that this moment would never come, that their plan was just a silly dream.

If only they could see us now! The Supreme Leader thought, *They'd eat those foolish words!*

They hadn't believed that it was even possible for them to open a portal to another era, let alone one that was so stable. It hadn't been easy, it had taken them a long time and many failures before they finally found an era where the fabric of space/time was malleable enough to allow them to create a stable portal big enough for such a large probe to pass through. This era was much farther in the future than they had ever penetrated before. Hopefully Tulienel would still be as hospitable in this time period as it had proven to be the last time they had scanned it millions of years earlier. If it wasn't, then this whole enterprise would be in vain. This was the only era they could ever possibly send a colony ship to.

The probe was still quite far from Tulienel, as it was just breaking away from the pull of that world's sole satellite, but already the probe's finely tuned complement of sensors were gathering an astonishing amount of data on the planet it was hurtling towards and relaying it back through the portal. There was a palpable, electric excitement in the air as the technicians running the mission quickly worked to analyze the incoming data stream with the help of their computers.

"Atmosphere is confirmed as breathable!" one of the technicians reported breathlessly.

"The planet is virtually teeming with life!" another one added.

"Hopefully not with intelligent life!" The Supreme Leader said warily.

"Actually.... about that...." said the nearest technician.

"*What*? What are you picking up? Out with it!" The Supreme Leader commanded impatiently.

"We're reading multiple signals from the surface, they appear to be transmissions."

"Perhaps they're of a natural origin?" The Supreme Leader inquired hopefully. It wasn't an unreasonable suggestion. A variety of celestial bodies and other naturally occurring phenomena created radio busts and other kinds of signals which could easily be mistaken for a communications signal from an intelligent civilization. There had been many such false alarms in the past.

"Doubtful. There's also signs of heavy industrialization in the atmosphere."

The Leader cursed profusely. This was something that hadn't been foreseen. Were all their years of hard work to now be in vain? Would they now suddenly reverse course after coming so tantalizingly close to their goal? It was unthinkable! They had already done what many people considered being impossible just by getting their probe this far. They had pierced the very fabric of time and space to reach this moment. Surely this latest obstacle was nothing compared to that?

"Can you make any sense of these 'transmissions'?" The Supreme Leader asked.

"I believe I can display the visuals."

"Do it!" ordered the Supreme Leader urgently.

The image of planet Tulienel was replaced by a bewildering number of images, thousands of them now flooded the room.

"They look just like us!" an astonished technician gasped.

Indeed they did. The aliens had two arms, two legs, two eyes, two ears and a single nose and mouth. What were the odds? Yet, was it really so unusual? It was an efficient form. There were many examples in their own world of a species being wiped out, only to have another, similar species evolve again from a different source. Why couldn't such a thing happen on another planet? Perhaps there was even something of themselves in those creatures? Maybe a meteorite from their world carried some microbes to this world and evolved from there? The possibilities were endless.

"Not quite. They appear to have two sexes," another one observed. Pointing to one image of a man and a woman in a romantic embrace about to kiss.

The Supreme Leader was particularly fascinated by this series of images, only not in a good way. A look of distaste marred the otherwise noble, statuesque features of the Supreme Leader.

"Sexual reproduction? *Disgusting*! These creatures are clearly little better than animals!"

"But animals don't create broadcasts like these. Surely we must now abandon the planned colonization?"

The Supreme Leader laughed.

It was not a happy sound.

"Abandon the plan? *Never!* We might need to modify it, yes, but what is the alternative? To leave our world behind and foolishly hope that nothing goes wrong with our ships while we spend the next thousand plus years trying to reach the next hospitable world? We've already seen that those ships will prove to be nothing more than the tombs for our people, forever lost, alone and forgotten tumbling through the cold void. Or we could live on one of the other moons or planets in our system deep underground or in environment domes, never again able to feel the touch of natural sunlight upon our faces, or the stirring of a cool breeze against our skin, prisoners in our own cities! These are not true alternatives! We will not allow ourselves to be diminished like that! *This* is the only way!"

There was an uncomfortable silence for a few moments.

"But what of these natives? You wouldn't have us enslave them, would you?" A nervous technician finally asked.

"Of course not! We're not *monsters*, are we?" The Supreme Leader purred.

"We shall simply have to find a way to eliminate them all. It's the only *humane* solution. That world obviously isn't big enough for the both of us!"

The technicians looked at each other with worried expressions on their faces, but what could they do? The word of the Supreme Leader was law.

"We will cleanse this world of these creatures which infest it and claim it for ourselves – for the glory of Pfoff!" The Leader declared.

"For the glory of Pfoff!" The others repeated with slightly less enthusiasm than the Supreme Leader would've hoped for, but it was of little consequence.

In time, they would all have to accept the wisdom of this decision. It was the only way for their civilization to continue with its dignity intact, to preserve their cherished way of life without compromise. The Supreme Leader took no delight in the prospect of destroying this species, even if they clung to some obviously savage ways of reproduction. It was merely an unfortunate fact that they had what the leader's people needed.

It was them or us.

The Supreme Leader had no doubts about which side must prevail.

"In an early year of a decade not too long before our own
The human race suddenly encountered a deadly
Threat to its very existence
And this terrifying enemy surfaced
As such enemies often do
In the seemingly most innocent and unlikely of places"
—Prologue from Little Shop of Horrors

CHAPTER 1:
SIGN OF THE TIMES

Matt Spike was stuck in traffic again.

He had nobody else to blame but himself for it. He felt vaguely idiotic and irresponsible for even attempting to drive into the city in this kind of weather. Was it really such a surprise that he should find himself in this predicament?

Last night, a blizzard had dumped several inches of snow all along the Northeast, all the way up to Canada. They hadn't experienced it as severely in NJ and NY as they had in New England, but it had still been severe enough to temporarily shut down the major airports in the city until this morning.

However, despite the weather, neither of the two events that now brought him and his family to head for Manhattan had been canceled, so here they were, braving the elements on the Jersey Turnpike to try and reach the Lincoln Tunnel. Actually, it hadn't been all that bad until recently. The roads had been cleared overnight and traffic had been pretty light, then it had all slowed down to a crawl. Matt couldn't quite tell what the holdup was from his current vantage point, but he assumed that there was some kind of an accident on the road up ahead of them.

He was currently stuck in the car with his wife, Naomi, his fifteen-year-old daughter Autumn, and a five-year-old boy named Paul who had been living with them for the past year. Paul was like family, a term which Matt applied rather loosely to anyone he was close to. He was the son of people that Matt certainly *felt* were as good as family, maybe even better than some of the people he really was related to.

His father was Matt's partner in his detective agency, Randy. Paul's mother was Penny, Matt's receptionist/office manager. Matt thought of those two like they were the younger brother and sister that he never had,having grown up as an only child. Both of the boy's parents also happened to be in a rock band together, which was called "the Mystery Smiths", a band that had been on tour for the better part of the past year. Today was the final show of their tour; Matt and Naomi had been taking care of the child while his parents traveled the world, and tonight he would finally be reunited with them.

Paul idolized his parents. It was easy to see why, they were both rock stars, albeit moderately successful ones who still had to maintain their day jobs. While they had a loyal fan base, they were far from being household names, at least in this country (although they *were* wildly popular in Japan and Norway). Not only that, but the kid thought that they were superheroes. This is because when they became parents, Randy and Penny decided to make their act more "family friendly". Their music had never been particularly edgy or serious to begin with, so this wasn't all that difficult of a transition to make.

To that end, they created a narrative for their band that they were not only musicians, but also crime fighting mystery solvers. This led them to starring in a short lived live action TV series in which the band fought against a variety of intentionally cheesy menaces, at least until the show was canceled after just one year because the fledgling cable network that carried it had gone under. Despite the fact that it had been explained to Paul many times that his parents were not *actually* super heroes and that was all just part of the act, he still stubbornly clung to the belief.

It didn't help matters much that the kid's dad was not only a bona fide licensed Private Investigator, but that he was also a powerful wizard (yes, you read this right, this is one of *those* kinds of stories where magic is real, although most people aren't aware of it) a fact that had been played up in the TV show, where his character was called "the Magic Man." Try convincing a kid that their dad isn't a superhero when he not only plays a wizard on TV, but can do real magic too. Kids at that age already think their parents can do virtually anything, the trouble was that Paul's parents *really* could.

In fact Paul was currently amusing himself by watching a DVD of his parent's show on the player in the backseat of their SUV. Matt knew the episode well, it was the one featuring "Cownan the Bullbarian", a Minotaur from another dimension that is accidentally sucked into our world when Magic Man defies the vegetarian diet that he's been put on by Mystery Queen (Penny's character) and tries to conjure up the biggest hamburger in the world. Upon learning that cows are eaten in our world, Cownan begins attacking fast-food restaurants and busting up the joints until he is finally captured and returned to his home by the Mystery Smiths. Matt thought the pro-vegetarian messaging in this episode (which was all Penny's idea) was a bit heavy-handed and preachy at times, which was unusual for the series, which usually mocked the fact that many of the cartoons from the 1980's like "GI Joe" and "Masters of the Universe" tried to tack on morals or safety messages at the end of each episode by including their own often silly and nonsensical moral lessons. Matt supposed that it was also possible to interpret the episode as a parody of the excesses of some of the more militant members of the "meat is murder" crowd too, which was part of the genius of the show.

Randy, for his part, was not a vegetarian. When asked about it he would just shrug his shoulders and say something like "Life feeds on life. Just because animals have eyes and can look at you, people value animal life more." To him, plant life was just as precious, perhaps even more so. The abilities he had developed over time as a wizard had attuned him to the fact that plants were incredibly vital, alive in ways that most people could only guess at. However, he could appreciate how eating plants was probably better for the environment, but beyond that, he didn't see it as any more or less morally superior.

Paul had inherited his mother's vegetarianism, which had been a bit of a challenge at first when he moved in with Matt, but Naomi, who enjoyed cooking had risen the task and learned how to craft vegetarian dishes that even a devoted carnivore like Matt had been forced to admit "weren't too bad", which was high praise indeed from someone like Matt when it came to that kind of cuisine.

Soon, it would be time to return Paul to his parents for good. Matt would miss having the kid around every day. He had been like a breath of fresh air in the house; kids could be a lot of fun at that age, and he missed having kids that young around. His own son, Joe, was in his early twenties now and living the life of a starving artist in Greenwich Village, or at least he would be if it wasn't for him and Naomi constantly giving him money so he could keep his dreams alive. They had plenty of money, so they didn't really mind supporting him like that. It bothered Joe more than it bothered them to keep asking for funds. Recently, he'd managed to actually sell a few paintings, so his requests had become less frequent. Both of his kids were artistic, with Joe working in more traditional mediums, and Autumn preferring to create her art digitally. He didn't know where all this talent came from. Neither he nor Naomi could draw so much as a stick figure. Matt and Naomi weren't completely without artistic talent, but it wasn't expressed visually, Matt passed his spare time writing detective novels that were vaguely based on his cases, and Naomi had her cooking and her own writing which was more academic than Matt's fictional efforts.

The plan was for the whole family to attend the final concert of the Mystery Smiths' tour tonight and hand Paul back over to his parents. Autumn would spend the weekend with her brother. In the meantime, Matt and Naomi would attend ECPIC (East Coast Private Investigators Conference), which was a convention for Private Investigators that was also happening this weekend. Matt rarely bothered to attend these conventions anymore, but since it was happening the same weekend that the Mystery Smiths' tour was wrapping up, he thought it might be fun to check it out. Matt and Naomi also hoped to take this weekend as a rare opportunity for a little alone time together, just a few days before Valentine's Day.

At the convention, they'd also meet up with Kevin Scott, a young man who worked as a junior investigator at Matt's agency. He didn't have a PI license yet, but he could still work on cases under the agency's license and in doing so, was gaining valuable experience towards getting his own someday. Kevin would rendezvous with them at the hotel where the convention was being held, which was also where they were staying this weekend. Kevin was taking a NJ transit train into the city.

As the traffic continued to crawl along at a snail's pace, Matt was now beginning to wish that he'd done the same thing.

Well, if you have to be stuck in a car, you could do worse than to be stuck in one with the people you love, he thought. At times like this, he liked to reflect on how lonely his life had been back in his early twenties, when he was living in the city while he was in college, and how different it was now. A supportive network of friends and family surrounded him and even though they drove him crazy sometimes, he was truly grateful for them. He tried to maintain an upbeat attitude by admiring the beauty of the snow covered landscape, which had somehow managed to transform the usually unpleasant industrial wasteland that dominated the view from the Turnpike in this part of Jersey into a wintry wonderland. *That's the real magic - finding the beauty in all the ugliness of the world.* He thought. It was an attitude he'd picked up from Paul's dad, Randy, who lived in the moment and always seemed to find the goodness in every situation, no matter how fucked up things might be. He saw a lot of that same mentality reflected in Paul's placid, accepting way of surfing through the ups and downs of life.

Finally, whatever obstruction had been holding up, the traffic seemed to have been cleared up. Matt never found out what it had been exactly that had been holding them up. That annoyed the part of his mind that didn't like loose ends and dangling mysteries, but he told himself to just relax and be grateful that they were at long last back on their way again. As they moved along down the highway, Matt caught sight of a billboard off to the side of the road, which had him suddenly feeling all grumpy and irritated again.

The billboard featured a meteor flying across it and it read "2012 let's talk about it" with the name of the website for some obscure church in the bottom corner. The meteor part was actually sort of impressive, being a three-dimensional object fastened to one end of the sign, with its trail being a painting. He wondered how much money, time and effort had been wasted in creating something that was as awesome as it was stupid and now, was also dated and unintentionally hilarious. Here they all were in February 2013 and the world was still here, just as terrifying and amazing as it ever was.

Matt didn't understand why everyone seemed so eager for the world to end. He supposed that they were, for some reason, convinced that the new world which would arise to replace it would inevitably be better. He guessed people didn't see how it could be much worse than it already was, but it wasn't all that hard for him to imagine that it really could be much, much worse.

Why did they assume we had already reached our lowest point as a species? That there was nowhere left to go but up? No, Matt was much happier to stick with what we already had and try to build a better world on the foundation of all that prior experience than he was to see the whole thing burn down and possibly degenerate into who knows what.

He knew that many of the people who were so fervently hoping for an end to this world were doing so because they had faith that God or whatever would whip up a better one for them, but Matt had actually met a few Gods once and he hadn't been particularly impressed with them. He preferred to place his faith in his own wits and in his friends and family.

"When are they gonna take down those stupid things?" He grumbled. "December 21st was a few months ago now, and everyone is just fine!" December 21st, 2012 being the prophesied date for the end of the world.

If the whole 2012 apocalypse thing irritated Matt, it positively infuriated his wife Naomi, who was a professor with a doctorate in world history. She couldn't help but launch into a now familiar speech on the topic that everyone in the car had heard different variations of on multiple occasions over the course of the past year. Matt should've realized that by complaining aloud, he'd trigger such a response. Truth to tell, although he found her repetition of such facts tiresome at times, he also sort of liked it when she showed off her knowledge like this. He always found brainy women to be impossibly sexy. That's why he'd married the brainiest woman he could find.

"It was all based on a bunch of bullshit." She began in her naturally blunt and refreshingly unprofessional way before smoothly transitioning into full academic mode "There's absolutely no evidence that the ancient Maya regarded the end of the 13th b'ak'tun as being the end of the world. It's purely an invention of misguided 20th century scholars, Christian apocalyptic ideas being superimposed onto a culture that wasn't obsessed with the end of the world so much as it was with maintaining the continuity of the current one. Then of course, you had tons of New Age authors and everyone else jumping on the bandwagon to try and make a buck off of all the hysteria."

Autumn, who up until now had her face buried in her phone, suddenly looked up from the screen and wrinkled her nose. "Ugh. Mom, not *this* again! We've heard it all a million times before!" Being the daughter of a university professor meant that she frequently had to endure *literal* lectures from her mother.

Naomi sniffed in exaggerated indignation. "I'm just trying to bring a little enlightenment to the masses and this is the thanks I get?"

"I like learning new things, Auntie Naomi," Paul piped up.

Autumn's eyes narrowed.

"Nobody asked you, Turnip!" She said, calling him by the nickname his vegetarian diet had earned him. Autumn liked Paul, over the course of the past year she'd learned to maybe even love him like a little brother, but sometimes, like right now, she also thought that he was something of an insufferable little suck-up.

"See, at least someone appreciates the light of wisdom!" Naomi said approvingly.

Matt knew enough by now to stay out of such family skirmishes unless they got out of hand, and that not stirring things further was the best way to make sure that they remained manageable.

Naomi's lecture wasn't quite over yet. "This entire mindset that the world has an end is flawed. The end of one civilization's history is often the beginning of another. Even if there were no more people, the natural world would go on and keep on changing and evolving. The world and the universe will go on and on, with or without us."

"Alrighty then! And on that bright and cheerful note…," Matt commented dryly.

Naomi laughed, a bright, musical sound. "Sorry, I didn't mean to bring everybody down. it's just that the end of the world isn't exactly the most uplifting of subjects, y'know?"

"Quite," Matt agreed.

The rest of the ride into the city was fairly uneventful, although Paul was impressed with the Lincoln Tunnel, as it was the first time he'd been in it. Well, at least so far as he was capable of remembering. Naomi usually carried some Dramamine with her when she had to ride in a car being driven by Matt because even at 43, he still drove like someone who just got his license. He especially had a tendency to take corners too quickly, which wreaked havoc with her intestines. She was happy to report though, that on this occasion, (thanks no doubt to the bad weather and children in the vehicle) he was showing remarkable restraint and driving more responsibly than he normally did.

The Dramamine stayed in her purse.

CHAPTER 2:
AN UNCONVENTIONAL CONVENTION

They'd left early enough that day that even with the traffic delays they'd encountered along the route, they still arrived well before check-in at the hotel. The hotel they were staying at was the "Grand Royale Imperial", a once swanky location that had seen better days. It was located only a few blocks down from the United Nations Headquarters, and in its heyday had once been a favorite destination for many visiting foreign dignitaries. Unfortunately, the construction of newer, more modern hotels nearby had slowly sucked away much of its revenue and today it was on life support, mostly sustained by the business that conventions like the ECPIC brought in.

They met Kevin in the lobby, where he'd been waiting for them, and he helped carry their bags up to their room (much to the chagrin of the bellhop). Once they got up to their room, Matt carefully placed the Orb of Sinister in the hotel safe. The Orb was a powerful magical item that made it impossible to cast a spell for miles around it. Years ago, Matt and Naomi had been entrusted with being the Guardians of the Orb by a group of secret societies called the Guilds, who paid them handsomely for their efforts. This was one reason why Matt and his family almost never had to really worry much about money. That, plus the fact Matt's detective agency had grown into quite a lucrative business over the years, and Naomi was also quite well paid by the university. These days, the Orb was fitted with a motion sensor and miniature camera. Matt and Naomi had an app on their phones that alerted them if the Orb was moved and allowed them to see and record what the camera detected at any time.

Coffee fueled Matt. It was his lifeblood. As soon as the orb was secured, he brewed up a pot of the complimentary stuff that was included with the room. He didn't know why he bothered. No matter how fancy the hotel room was, the hotel coffee was almost never up to his demanding standards. Yet, hope sprang eternal in Matt's mind, and so he brewed up a pot.

He almost spat out the foul tasting concoction. He discovered that there was a Starbucks only a block away from the hotel, by Googling it on his phone. Matt really wasn't much of a Starbucks fan, but he felt that their coffee "would do in a pinch" which again, was high praise from someone like Matt. A trip to Starbucks, in fact, often filled him with anxiety. This was because he didn't go frequently enough to ever "learn the lingo" as he would say. He found the fact that he couldn't just order a "medium" or "large" impossibly irritating and all the other Italian names for the coffee were baffling to him.

"I shouldn't have to speak a foreign language just to order a damned cup of Joe!" he would inevitably grumble.

Naomi, who frequently went there, found this quite amusing, especially because the foreign language in question was Italian and she was an Italian American. "You love coffee, but you can't remember a few names for different types of coffee because they're in Italian and you can't remember the difference between large and medium because they're in Italian, yet you've been married to an Italian lady for how many years now?" She would laugh.

"Don't pretend you speak it, cause you don't! And even if you did, it's not like I'm going to learn it by osmosis or something!" he'd invariably reply.

"I may not be fluent in it, but neither are 90% of their other customers, but they seem to get by just fine!" She would invariably point out.

She always found it peculiar that someone who was a trained observer that prided himself on his logical mind and deductive talents, and was such a "people person" had so many hang ups with figuring out what to do at this place. She thought he just had a grudge against them because they had stamped out so many of the local coffee houses that he used to like to go to.

So she was mildly surprised that he saw fit to overcome all his anxieties about Starbucks by going there. *He must be in some serious coffee withdrawals!* She realized.

He had been given a gift card for Starbucks over a year ago as a Christmas gift by someone who obviously didn't know him very well, and had been sitting in his wallet ever since. Before he left, she reminded him that this would be a perfect chance to finally use it.

Of course, he was so anxious about calling the components of his order by their proper names that he still forgot all about using his gift card.

"I must be getting forgetful in my old age!" he told her when he returned to the hotel room, which was a common enough excuse, although he would've been just as likely to do the same thing twenty years prior. Age, he'd found, was as good an excuse as any to cover one's shortcomings.

After sorting out the coffee situation, Matt and Naomi left Autumn and Paul in the room while the three of them headed down to check out the ECPIC convention.

Matt used to attend this convention every year when he first started out as an investigator. he even credited some panels he'd seen there in the past with teaching him some of his favorite tricks of the trade. A few times, he'd been invited to participate in some panels himself, once he'd gotten a bit of fame and notoriety after playing an important role in a case that led to the capture of a serial killer. One year, he'd been asked to lead a workshop for other detectives who might be thinking about adapting their experiences into books since he'd written a few novels that were (very) loosely based on his cases. Naomi had accompanied him on a few of these trips in the past, mostly out of curiosity and because it was something different to do that broke up their typical daily routine.

However, he rarely bothered to go anymore. He felt like he was seen as something of a dinosaur by many of the other PIs. Too many of his fellow private eyes shied away from the traditional image of a PI these days, some of them didn't even like to use the term to describe what they do, and had taken to calling themselves strange things like "legal investigators" or "inquiry agents". Matt, in contrast, was quite the opposite. He leaned and leaned *hard* into the PI stereotype. He was almost always seen wearing a fedora and trench coat, even during the summer months. He peppered his speech with lots of archaic slang words culled from his fascination with pulp fiction. While many of his contemporaries were obsessed with changing the image of a private investigator, Matt was equally consumed by having as much fun as he possibly could playing the more traditional version of the part.

As a result, it made him a somewhat divisive figure in the community. Despite his years of experience and impressive track record, some people complained he was just a ham and gloryhound who was only cosplaying as a private investigator. Matt also knew that there was a bit of resentment towards him because, unlike many other investigators, he didn't come from a law enforcement background before going into business for himself. He wasn't ever a part of that particular club, and he knew some people felt like he hadn't really paid his dues because of it. He didn't need to be around that kind of negativity, so when he became aware of all this ugly chatter about him that was going on behind his back, he stopped attending.

He was really only here this year because the weekend of the convention coincided with the end of the Mystery Smiths' tour, and he thought Kevin could benefit from going to the convention. Maybe his protégée would learn something valuable at one of the panels, like Matt had when he was younger?

They met Kevin down in one of the spacious ballrooms that the convention had taken over. Despite the snowstorm, there was a fairly decent turnout for the convention, which had actually started the previous morning, with many of the attendees driving right before the storm hit.

Kevin was feeling great, in fact he was positively giddy because it was a day before the New Moon, which was basically the opposite of a Full Moon. Kevin, you see, used to be a werewolf. Years earlier, when he was still a teenager, he had run away from home in an effort to ensure that he wouldn't hurt anyone while in wolf form. Matt had been hired to find him, and not only did he locate him, but he ultimately helped find a cure for his condition—sort of. Kevin's moods were still affected to an alarming degree by how near or far he was from the night of the full moon on the calendar. Sometimes this made him a little difficult to be around, especially around people who didn't understand his "condition". As it wasn't his "time of the month" right now, so to speak, he was feeling about as pleasant as he ever did.

Kevin was almost like a surrogate son to Matt. He came into Matt's life when Matt's own son, Joe, was pulling away from him and pursuing his own interests, as was natural for teenagers. So when Joe stopped being very interested in Matt's work and seeing him as some sort of infallible super hero, there, all of the sudden, was Kevin to fill that void.

For his part, Kevin looked up to Matt for his role in saving him from having to spend the rest of his life as a werewolf. It didn't help that his own father wasn't always the most pleasant of people to be around, and since his parents had divorced, he hardly ever saw him anymore. So Kevin kept in contact with Matt and saw him as a more positive role model and father figure than his own dad. Was it really too surprising that Kevin was now trying to follow in Matt's footsteps by becoming a PI?

Kevin was currently looking at a drone that was on display, looking like some sort of miniature mechanical mutant dragonfly. A nearby monitor played video that had been captured by the device and bombastically boasted about its features.

"The Dragonfly 3000 is the latest and greatest in easy to operate smart drone technology!" The video blared confidently as it blasted an orchestral soundtrack worthy of a Hollywood summer blockbuster.

"Hey, Matt, hey Naomi. We should really get one of these things! The picture quality is amazing!"

Matt raised a skeptical eyebrow. "I don't think so, kid. That price tag is a bit hefty." Matt could certainly afford it, but his cheapness, er...I mean "frugality" was legendary. It was almost as if he was on a crusade to prove to the world that even though he was now relatively wealthy, he wasn't going to let it go to his head by making all kinds of outrageous purchases. Thankfully, the salespeople who would normally man this display were out to lunch and were not there to combat Matt's objections.

"Besides, I thought you guys already had a drone?" Naomi added.

Kevin made a face. "You mean that cheap thing that Matt bought from the toy department in Walmart? He crashed it into the big oak tree in the parking lot behind our office two weeks ago!"

"Really? *You* never told me about that!" Naomi laughed as she turned to face Matt with an expectant look on his face, eager to see what excuse he'd come up with to explain this away.

"It um...didn't seem worth mentioning. And I'll have you know that it *wasn't* cheap, it was like $150 bucks! And it still works, too! I can see a bird's eye view of the parking lot if I log into the app on my phone! So we don't need a new one—I'll just have Randy magic it out of the tree when he comes back." Matt probably wasn't aware of how defensive he sounded, or he might've toned it down. Matt took most things at face value and was generally a very serious-minded and earnest person, as he was also oblivious to these quirks of his. He sometimes came across as being somewhat dramatic in casual situations like this. Frequently, he couldn't tell when people were just kidding with him, which was a constant source of amusement to Naomi and some of his other friends.

"Yes, well, like I was saying, this one has a much clearer picture, and it's *easy to fly*, which is an important feature for some of us." Kevin continued, undaunted by Matt's protests.

"If you want it so bad, kid, buy it yourself!"

"You pay me pretty good, Matt, but not quite *that* well!" Kevin replied good humoredly.

"Get your PI license, and you'll get paid a bit more." Matt reminded him, although there wasn't much that Kevin could do about it right now that he wasn't already doing. You needed to have a certain number of years of experience working as an investigator before you could get your PI license, and Kevin still had a few more years to go. However, Matt liked to keep him focused on this goal.

Private Investigators were starting to use drones like the ones they were currently arguing over for surveillance more frequently. In Matt's detective agency, they had their own rather unique ways of conducting surveillance. Years ago, Randy had taught Matt how to astral project, to make his spirit temporarily leave his body. It was a skill that came in handy often in their line of work. Matt hadn't taught this technique to Kevin yet; he wanted the boy to master more down-to-earth methods of surveillance first. Astral projection couldn't meet all their needs, after all. They often had to produce photographic, video and audio evidence for their clients and that's something they couldn't do in astral form. So devices like drones and many other gadgets on display at the convention still definitely had their place in Matt's office - it's just a shame that those drones were so damned expensive and hard to fly! Matt thought.

As they moved around the convention floor, there were plenty of other sneaky spy doohickeys for sale, many of which Matt already owned. There were pens and sunglasses that could record audio and video, and a plethora of devices disguised as ordinary everyday items that also had hidden cameras inside of them. There were even a few firearms on display, all of them pistols despite the tough new gun laws that had recently been put into place within the city in the wake of the tragic Sandy Hook school shooting.

"Hey Matt, when can I start packing some serious heat like this?" Kevin asked excitedly as he pointed to one of the bigger handguns.

"When you're mature enough to not be so excited by the idea, when you realize that carrying the ability to snuff out a life simply by pointing and squeezing a trigger is a burden," he growled at him, sounding a bit more harshly than he meant to. Of course, he couldn't actually stop the kid from getting a gun. He was an adult now, but he *could* prevent him from carrying it while he was at work until he thought he could handle the responsibility.

Matt sighed. He'd been like Kevin once–caught up in the romance of the gun. He'd once seen carrying one as being an essential part of projecting a tough-guy image. Matt used to be very invested in putting out such an image. He supposed that had been partially a result of growing up in the kind of society that we live in, which dictates certain kinds of behaviors, especially violent and aggressive ones, as being masculine. He had always been a fan of noir detective stories and he'd patterned much of his behavior after the heroes of those stories;it had also served as a defense mechanism back when he'd been in High School. If you radiate a certain aura that practically screams "don't fuck with me, or you'll end up hurt really bad," people tend to take the hint, which had been key to his getting through those difficult years relatively unscathed. The problem was that such an image also kept some good people away from him too. He'd held onto that swagger long after it had outlived most of its usefulness. At any rate, Matt had stopped caring about such things years ago and learned how to be more comfortable in his own skin. Sure, he still dressed and talked a bit like a tough, two-fisted film noir detective, but this was due more to the long-established habits of his than it being an accurate reflection of who he really was on the inside.

Matt had found it quite unnecessary to draw his gun on about 90% of his cases as a PI, unlike how things are typically portrayed in fiction. That other 10%? Well, that had to do with the more unusual cases that he sometimes found himself involved in ever since he'd gotten himself mixed up in the secret world of the Guilds. He'd killed people with his gun, as well as quite a few things that couldn't really be called people. It wasn't something he was proud of, although he was pleased to say that on each of these occasions it had been in self-defense, or in defending someone else. These experiences had taught him just how ugly actual violence was, how it scarred your soul.

What a disservice we do to ourselves by constantly glorifying violence and hammering into our young men the idea that they have to be like that to prove their masculinity, he thought sadly. It wasn't just a problem with men either, there also seemed to be this idea that women had to adopt these "male" traits to make it in a man's world. Matt thought the whole idea of declaring certain traits as being inherently "male" or "female" was just so much bullshit. He just wanted people to feel free to be whoever they truly are inside without worrying about if their behavior was perceived as being masculine or feminine enough for society.

He was shaken out of his ruminations by the sound of Kevin's voice.

"I know that killing isn't something to take lightly. I've seen my fair share of death already, if you remember?" Kevin replied, referring to the adventure that had first brought the two of them together, during which they had to fight for survival against an entire army made up of both vampires and werewolves. The whole reason Kevin had run away from home in the first place was because he had believed that he had killed his lover the first time he transformed into a werewolf. The sight of her ruined corpse, still haunted him, would always haunt him. He didn't mind Matt calling him "kid", hell, Matt still called Randy that, and Randy was in his thirties! What he *did* mind was when he treated him like one, which was exactly what he was doing now.

"How could I forget? That little incident still gives me nightmares. I'm sorry if I sounded a little preachy, Kevin. We'll talk about it later, okay?" Matt said more gently, realizing that he'd taken things a bit too far.

Naomi, who had silently been watching the whole exchange, was thinking about how she could certainly attest to the fact that Matt still suffered from nightmares because of that case, even eight years later. How many times had he disturbed her sleep (not an simple task, by the way, sleeping through things was her super power) as he thrashed around in the night? She'd lost count.

Kevin smiled, the distance from the night of the full moon making it hard for him to hold on to his anger. "Sure, it's all good, don't worry about it."

"Well, well well! Do my eyes deceive me? It's been a good few years since I've last seen Matt Spike at this convention!" A familiar, somewhat sultry voice suddenly announced from somewhere nearby.

Matt twisted his head to discover the source of the voice. The form of Sara Berry, a woman who always carried herself with an air of tough elegance, greeted his eyes. He'd once, many years ago, been romantically intertwined with her, having first met her at this very convention back in the early 1990s. The relationship hadn't really gone anywhere, though. Sara had never been very interested in serious relationships and had treated Matt as little more than a "booty call", although he'd wanted something more, which at the time had only annoyed her. She'd been married once, a lifetime ago, and once was enough for her.

He had to admit that she still looked quite good, even after all these years. Matt was approaching his mid-forties now, which meant that Sara, who had always been a bit older than him, had to be pushing fifty years of age by now. Yet she still appeared to be fit, with only a few wrinkles around her eyes and lips, which added a bit of character to her appearance and served to enhance, rather than detract from, her natural beauty. She had long, wavy dirty blonde hair and was dressed in a smart business suit with a somewhat short skirt and high heels. She'd always reminded Naomi a bit of the actress Kathleen Turner when she'd been in her prime.

Sara was a "Hotel Detective" which was a rather antiquated term for a plainclothes detective that was employed by the hotel to keep an eye on security. She was, in fact, the de facto head of security at the Grand Royale Imperial Hotel and had been for many years now. She had begun her career with the NYPD but had been disgusted by the rampant sexism in the department which prevented her from advancing in rank, so she'd quit and accepted the position of Hotel Detective at the Grand Royale and never looked back since.

Matt and Naomi exchanged worried looks. One of the other reasons why Matt had stopped attending ECPIC was because of Sara. Not that he or Naomi were seriously worried about him rekindling anything with his old flame. For Matt, that particular fire had been extinguished long ago. In retrospect, he'd only ever become involved with Sara because he'd considered Naomi to be out of his league back then. It was Naomi that he'd always really wanted. Sara had just been a pleasant distraction.

Naomi had once disliked Sara, not approving of the way that she toyed with Matt's emotions, and yes, she'd been a little jealous of his obsession over her back then, but this was all ancient history. If anything, in the ensuing years Naomi had concluded that it was Sara who should be jealous of her, Naomi had a great family and a great career in academia now whereas Sara seemed to be stuck in a rut, living and working in the same old hotel for decades now. If anything, she pitied the woman, especially since she'd learned what the future had in store for her.

Naomi was the Chief Archivist for the Guilds, and had compiled an exhaustive history of the world using their records, which were far older than anyone else's, which she called the *Magna Historia*

Mundi, or the Great History of the World. She had been quite surprised to discover that Sara was mentioned frequently in the Guild records from World War II and the first few decades following the war. According to what she had read, in just a few years' time, a strange series of events would send Sara back in time where she would go on to play an important part in the history of the Guilds in the 20th Century before disappearing once more under mysterious circumstances. It was hard for her to believe at first, but then she recalled an incident one strange New Year's Eve in '97 when she and Matt had encountered someone who claimed to be a version of Sara from the distant future. She hadn't really believed her at the time either, but in light of what the archives said about Sara, it seemed more likely. She'd shared this discovery with Matt, and they'd agreed that they had to keep this information from Sara, otherwise they risked disturbing their own history and creating a paradox. The simplest way to do this was to avoid her by not attending ECPIC altogether, which wasn't a very big sacrifice since Matt was getting disenchanted with the whole event, anyway.

"Hey, Sara, how're ya doing?" Matt's smile was a little forced. How do you *not* warn someone about what fate has in store for them? How did he keep on winding up in these bizarre situations with these kinds of unusual ethical dilemmas?

"Oh, I'm the same as I ever was. Just counting down the days till I get to retire from this place, then maybe I'll head down to Florida. I've had enough of these New York City winters to last me a lifetime!" She said.

"Retire? When do you plan on doing that? You're too young for that!" Naomi replied, although she knew perfectly well from what she had read that Sara would retire in 2015. She was just making polite conversation.

"Young? Flattery will get you everywhere! Seriously though, I'm thinking of hanging on for maybe another two years. I've been squirreling away all my money from working here for years. I should have enough money saved by then to retire early and live it up down in the sunshine state."

Sara studied Matt and Naomi. The two of them seemed to still somehow be happy with each other even after all these years of marriage, something which seemed inconceivable to Sara. Although she had no desire to ever get married again, she had to admit that sometimes she envied what they had a little bit and regretted letting go of Matt, who had aged pretty well. If anything, he looked healthier than he had back when they had been an item. He used to be a bit too thin and haggard back then; now his face was a lot fuller, almost boyish. The only hint of his age was the slight graying of his hair at his temples and the specks of white in his ever present five o'clock shadow. Naomi, meanwhile, looked as sexy as ever with her long, jet black hair and golden skin; her glasses made her look somewhat bookish, which she supposed was appropriate for a university professor. Sara had no way of knowing that Naomi's vision had been corrected magically years ago and the glasses were just an affectation.

"It looks like the years have been kind to you two." She couldn't help but comment. "And who is this fine looking young man?" She smiled wolfishly as her eyes alighted upon Kevin.

"Whoa, down tigress!" Naomi ordered, recalling well how Sara was the very definition of a "cougar". "He only has eyes for one woman," She added.

"Yeah, but it's a pity she's already spoken for," said Kevin somewhat sadly.

He was referring to Allison, a girl he'd been in love with for years now, but the timing never seemed quite right for the two of them to ever get together as anything more than friends. When one of them was single, the other wasn't. Matt knew Allison from the adventure that had first brought him and Kevin together. Kevin really liked her and felt that she was the sort of girl that was worth waiting around for, but he also didn't like to see the boy endlessly pining over her, just waiting for her current relationship to self-destruct, because that moment might never come. He often told him he just had to accept that possibility, and not try to link his happiness so closely to the idea of being with her like that. He told Kevin that if he was truly her friend, he should just want her to be happy, even if that happiness didn't include her being in a romantic relationship with him.

Matt feared that his advice on the matter was going in one ear and out the other, as Kevin was planning on going to visit Allison while he was in the city. She lived here now, trying to make a living as an actress, like so many people before her with similar dreams.

"Her loss." Sara smiled slyly as she raised an eyebrow.

Matt decided it was well past time to make a few formal introductions.

"Sara, this is Kevin Scott, a *junior* investigator in my agency." He emphasized the word junior hoping she'd back off with her advances. At twenty-three years of age, there was nothing illegal about her and Kevin getting together like that, but since Kevin was the same age as his own son, the idea couldn't help but make his skin crawl a little. Sara was definitely old enough to be Kevin's mother.

"Kevin, this is an old friend of ours, Sara Berry. She's the head of security at this hotel."

Sara reached out her hand, Kevin took it and shook it. "Pleased to meet you Kevin. You can learn a lot from Matt. He's built quite the career for himself. Is this your first convention?"

"Yeah."

"I hope you enjoy it. ECPIC is kinda my baby. It was my idea to have them hold the convention here back in the nineties, and they've been here ever since. You never forget your first ECPIC, eh Matt?"

Matt shifted a little uncomfortably. He'd originally met Sara and they'd had their first *rendezvous* at his first ECPIC convention. Why on earth was she bringing that up? He figured that for whatever reason, she just got a kick out of watching him squirm. It was working.

"Umm, yeah. I thought it would be good for him to experience one." Was all that he could manage to come up with in response.

Sara nodded enthusiastically. "I hope to see more of you guys around this weekend, we've got a lot of catching up to do." And with that, she sauntered off, her hips sashaying from side to side more than a little suggestively.

Naomi watched her disappear into the crowd. "Jesus! She just can't help herself can she? Sometimes I think that woman deserves the fate that's lying in store for her!"

Matt nodded in agreement. "I'm beginning to think this might've been a mistake. She's gonna be hard to avoid, she seems determined to play "catch up" with us."

Kevin overheard these comments. "Huh? What do you mean? What's going to happen to her?" He wondered how they could possibly know anything about her future? And wasn't Matt always talking about how we made our own fates? Then again, Matt and Naomi seemed to know a whole lot about a wide variety of things that they had no business knowing about. *That's how it went once you got yourself mixed up in the world of the Guilds,* he figured.

Naomi's eyes bulged a little as she realized her mistake. "Err...nothing. Forget you ever heard that."

"Just try and steer clear of her, Kev. She means well...I guess. But trust me, kid that woman is nothing but trouble with a capital 'T.'" Matt added.

"But aren't you the one telling me that I should forget about Allison?" Kevin asked, confused.

"He what?" Naomi, ever the hopeless romantic, was pulling for Kevin and Allison to get together someday. She fixed Matt with a somewhat accusatory look.

"I never said that! All I said was that you can't wait around for her forever, you've gotta keep on living your own life. If she's happy with the dude she's with now, you should be happy for her and not be constantly hovering around, waiting for them to break up. You don't want it to be some kind of rebound relationship if you expect it to last. If the time is right, it'll happen, or maybe it'll never happen. Either way, you have to make peace with that. Keep on moving forward, you can't live your life on pause."

Naomi's hard expression softened. She had to admit, this was actually some pretty good advice. Every once in a while, Matt still surprised her.

"Well, I plan on hanging out with Allison after I check out the play she's in later tonight, so I guess I'll just see where the night takes us!"

Kevin said defiantly. Matt and Naomi already knew of his plans, of course. Kevin's distaste for the Mystery Smiths was well known to them all. He wouldn't have been caught dead at that concert.

Matt guessed he couldn't really blame Kevin for his defiant attitude. He recalled that didn't like people trying to tell him what to do with his love life when he was that age, and he supposed that it really *was* none of his business. He just hated to see the kid get hurt. One thing he liked so much about being married was that he didn't really have to worry about all of this crap anymore. He sure didn't miss all the insecurity and self doubt that he'd grappled with when he'd still been single and dating.

That was about all that happened during their first day at the convention that's really worth mentioning. They checked out a few of the panels, and eventually Kevin returned to his room to prepare for his evening with Allison. Matt and Naomi ordered some room service for their family, and started getting everyone ready for the Mystery Smiths concert in a few hours. Paul was bouncing off the walls with enthusiasm over the fact that he'd soon be reunited with his parents.

CHAPTER 3:
A CONCERTED EFFORT

Matt, Naomi, Autumn and Paul all arrived early at the venue where the concert was being held. They'd all been shipped VIP badges and used them to enter the Mystery Smiths' tour bus, which had been christened "the Blunderbus Mark II", the original Blunderbus being the old, beaten up van Penny had used to get the band to their gigs in their early years when they had been called "Lung Collapse". The Blunderbus Mark II was actually a decommissioned Mobile Command Vehicle once used by the UGF, or United Guild Forces, which was the military arm of the Guilds. Randy had used his connections with the Guilds to rescue it from the junkyard. It had come in very handy during their tours, as it was enchanted in such a way that it was much bigger on the inside than the outside, providing the band with plenty of living space and saving them money in hotels.

Matt knocked on the door of the Blunderbus Mark II, rapping out a tune as he did so, as was his habit. The door swung open and the sight of Kiesha Bright greeted him. Technically, she was just one of the band's roadies, and an occasional backup singer. However, Matt and his family knew that she really served a much more important function; she was also Randy's magical apprentice. He had been training her to be a witch for the past two years now. Several years ago, before the band had shifted gears to being more family friendly, Randy had written secret instructions for casting a spell in the lyrics of several songs on one of the band's albums. When the spell was cast, it would send the caster into another dimension and notify Randy that they were trapped there. It was his elaborate plan to find a candidate to be his successor, who would be smart enough for the job. It took a few years before he got any results, and he was beginning to lose faith in the idea when Kiesha became the first and only person to decipher the code and successfully cast the spell. Kiesha was a pretty African American woman. She was twenty-two years old, with ebony skin and long, colorfully braided hair. She beamed at the sight of them, throwing her arms around Matt in a hug.

"Matt! Naomi! Autumn! Paul! Now the whole family is here!" She enthused as she made her way down the line, squeezing each of them with a hug, and saving the biggest hug for Paul.

"Not quite the whole family," Matt observed. "Joe is supposed to meet us here later."

"Did someone say my name?" Joe said, peeking his head out of the door of the Blunderbus Mark II.

Naomi looked up proudly at her son, amazed as always by how much he looked like her late father, Hugo. She hadn't seen Joe since the last New Year's party they'd thrown at their house. This had only been a few weeks ago, but every minute that her boy was away from her and trying to make a living on his own in the big bad city felt like an eternity to her. She worried about him constantly. It was proving to be quite difficult for her to accept that he was a grown man now and she couldn't protect him from everything that was out there.

"You're early!" Naomi said, her breath curling up around head in the frosty air.

"Yeah, well, I got bored. It's good to see you guys. Get in here before you all freeze your asses off!"

With that extraordinarily cordially worded invitation, they all made their way up the narrow few steps that led up into the side of the Blunderbus Mark II. They'd all been inside before, and so none of them were particularly shocked by how spacious it was on the inside anymore. There had been a time when Matt and Naomi had tried to keep their involvement in the strange world of the Guilds a secret from their children, but in time, especially as the kids grew older, it had proved impossible to do so. They were all relieved by how warm and toasty it was inside, indeed a gas powered fireplace dominated one wall. Several members of the Mystery Smiths, the fraternal twins Milo and Valerie, were currently lounging around the fireplace. It would still be over an hour before the opening act was finished, and they had to go on. Once they were inside, Joe did a group hug with his family. They were all quite demonstrative about showing their affection for one another.

"Hey Sensei! The gang's all here!" Kiesha announced rather loudly down a nearby hallway. She always called Randy "Sensei" and he, in turn, called her "Grasshopper".

Randy appeared a few seconds later, his face breaking into a grin as he caught sight of the group. He was a tall man with olive-colored skin and a thick, untidy mop of black hair arranged in a stylish disarray topping a high forehead. He wore a pair of thickly rimmed glasses and a bushy beard with a few premature streaks of gray running through it framed his face. At the sight of him, Paul ran to him. Randy scooped up his son effortlessly in his muscular arms, planting a kiss on his cheek. "I've missed you, kiddo! Have these hooligans been taking good care of you?" He asked as he placed the boy back down on the ground.

He already knew the answer. There was nobody else in the world who he would rather entrust with his son's safety than Matt and Naomi. Besides, he'd frequently checked in on him while on tour by astrally projecting to Matt and Naomi's house. One of the nice things about astral projection was that one could move at "the speed of thought" meaning that as long as you could form a clear picture of a place in your mind, you could quickly travel there at a blinding speed.

"Auntie Naomi and Uncle Matt are the best, although Autumn's kind of a butthead sometimes." Paul informed his father with the unvarnished honesty of a child.

"I love you too, Turnip!" Autumn called out.

"Where's Mom?" Paul asked.

"She's watching the Atmosphere Fishes' performance." Randy explained. The "Atmosphere Fishes" was the band that had been touring with the Mystery Smiths since they had returned to North America. The name of the band was chosen more for its lack of a copyright than for its poetic value or the way it rolled off the tongue.

"Ah, giving Jim a little moral support." Matt noted. Randy nodded in agreement.

Now might be a good time to explain that although Randy and Penny were Paul's parents and partners in the Mystery Smiths, they were no longer a couple, and hadn't been for years. Jim was the lead singer of the Atmosphere Fishes and Penny's current boyfriend. Randy and Penny had a long and complicated relationship; sometimes they were a couple and sometimes they weren't. It used to make Matt's head spin just trying to keep up with what their current status was, however a year or so before Paul was born, the romantic part of their relationship seemed to end for good. Throughout it all, they always somehow managed to maintain a strong friendship and partnership as bandmates. Eventually, Penny felt her biological time clock ticking away. She wanted to experience having and raising a child before she got too old for it and decided that she wanted nobody else but her best friend to be the father. Randy was honored to oblige, and curious to see what a kid that was a combination of the two of them would be like. Even though they technically weren't a couple at that point, Paul was still conceived in the old-fashioned way "Where's the fun in doing it the other way?" Penny had told Matt once, although he rather could've done without knowing that particular detail!

The reason why Randy and Penny weren't a couple had more to do with Randy's peculiarities than with Penny's. Randy liked to say that he couldn't confine his love to just one person. He'd tried over the years to be exclusive with Penny because it was what she needed. She was actually a quite traditional person in some ways, despite her punk rock look. However, Randy's couldn't quite pull it off, it just didn't feel right for him. He had had a variety of partners over the years, even a few men. He was currently in a polygamous relationship with a Valkyrie named Gertrude, whom he often visited in Asgard via astral projection, and Aethera Hoffman, who was half human, half water nymph and *all* pirate. In fact, she was known as the "Queen of the Pirates" as she had inherited the leadership of that particular Guild from her father, the late Brian Hoffman, aka "Captain Skumgutts" who Matt and Naomi had met many years ago.

Matt didn't judge his friend for his unconventional romantic preferences. In fact, the entire idea of Randy being a sexually active person always seemed a little odd to him since he had known him since he was a teenager and would always kind of think of him as a kid because of that. Sometimes it was hard for him to adjust to the idea that Randy was not only an adult now, but a father too. Matt had no problem with other people practicing polyamory. In theory, it seemed fine so long as it wasn't just the men that were allowed to have multiple partners and everyone was being honest about things, he just knew it wasn't for him. Sure, he occasionally found himself being attracted to other women aside from Naomi. It's not like settling down with her had somehow made him immune to the attractiveness of other human beings, but he didn't dwell on such impulses. What good could come of it? He was happy with her, and they were still very much in love. She was still his dream girl, and he was proud to be her husband. Their relationship was a constant source of comfort and security to him that he prized above all other things. Why risk throwing all of that away for something that might not be as good? Why destroy his family and hurt her feelings like that? As a detective, a large percentage of his cases had to do with providing proof of infidelity, and he'd seen all too often how it obliterated people's lives. That kind of ugly drama was the last thing he ever wanted. Even if it was something that he *did* want, Matt doubted he could possibly ever fulfill two people; it was challenging enough trying to be attentive to the needs of one!

He wondered if their work as detectives had been what led Randy to the opposite conclusion, that monogamous relationships were poisoned by jealousy and possessiveness? That the best way to avoid that toxicity was to avoid that kind of exclusivity altogether? Matt thought it seemed like a sure fire ticket for creating lots of jealousy, but Randy claimed that if one was open enough about it, you could avoid all that. Matt doubted that he had the capacity to share his partner with anyone else and really be okay with it, but if others did, then more power to them. He was just happy that his friend had finally found an arrangement that seemed to make him happy.

He was happy for Penny too, who seemed to finally be over Randy and was happy with Jim. Matt hadn't met him yet, but he'd heard all about him when Penny called to check in on Paul, as she frequently did.

"The Atmosphere Fishes are pretty good. Maybe you guys should check them out?" Randy suggested.

Everyone agreed, and Randy asked Kiesha to escort them all backstage, since he still had a few things he had to do to prepare for his own performance. Matt noticed that when he asked Kiesha to take care of that for him he also said, "Oh, and can you take care of that other thing we were talking about too while you're over there?"

"Sure, no prob, Sensei!" She replied.

Matt briefly wondered what "that other thing" was, then dismissed it as probably being something related to putting on their show.

"Alright, everyone, follow me!" Kiesha commanded, and they all trailed behind her, leaving the warm sanctuary of the Blunderbus Mark II and briefly venturing out into the cold before entering the club through a back door. She led them down a bewildering series of dark corridors and into the backstage area until they were close enough to actually see a sliver of the stage through a gap in the curtains. It was a gap that was partially filled with the petite, pixie-like form of Penny.

As soon as he saw her, Paul broke away from the main group and gave her a hug from behind, which, for a moment, quite frankly scared the ever loving shit out of her. In a matter of seconds, her mood shifted completely from a mix of surprise and terror to one of absolute delight. She joyfully returned the embrace once she realized that she wasn't being assaulted by a leprechaun, which was an all too real possibility when one hung around with a wizard. Damn those leprechauns! Those little bastards were real jerks! They'd completely ruined their band's recent tour of Ireland.

"Tiny Dude!" She cried. "You almost gave mommy a heart attack, but I'm glad to see you. I've missed you so much!"

"Me too!" Paul agreed as he held her tighter.

Matt and Naomi were the next to reach her. Matt regarded her as they approached. She was a slender woman with extraordinarily pale skin and freckles. Penny had a sharply pointed nose thaton someone else it might have been an unattractive feature, but somehow it suited her face. She was wearing black lipstick and her trademark heavy eyeliner that always reminded him of a raccoon. Her hair was short, spiky, and dyed two different shades of blue. She was in her early thirties, but she was also one of those people who always looked about ten years younger than she actually was. In addition to being a musical genius, she was also, in her day job, the best damned receptionist Matt had ever had, and his frequent confidant. The Mystery Smiths was a fairly successful band, but not so successful that she didn't have to maintain a day job; Randy's money kept the whole venture afloat. They'd all missed having her around the office this past year. The place was slowly descending into chaos without her.

Penny looked up at Matt, Naomi, and the rest of their family.

"Thanks for taking such good care of him, you two, and making it possible for his crazy parents to go gallivanting around the planet." Penny had resolved that this would be their last world tour. Not only was it expensive to pull off such an ambitious tour, but she saw that it simply wasn't compatible with her idea of motherhood. She wanted Paul to have some semblance of a normal life (whatever that is!) and having your parents disappear for the better part of a year wasn't a good way to provide that. She never would have agreed to the tour, except that she was contractually obligated to do it by her label. It looked like she'd be looking for a new label soon. Hell, maybe she'd even start up her own and just release her music online? One thing was for certain: she felt like she was getting too old to put up with the headache of dealing with the demands of the recording industry anymore.

"Are you kidding? He was a delight! Plus, it gave me an opportunity to master the art of vegetarian cooking." Naomi told her.

"Master it, huh? I think I'm going to have to challenge you to a cook off to test that theory!" Penny countered.

"Gross! Dad, you'll get me some fast food on that night, right?" Autumn asked Matt.

Matt, for once, didn't cave into the pressure from his daughter, whom he was something of a sucker for. "Nah, you need to learn how to expand your horizons. What if you were stuck on an island with a bunch of vegetarians? Would you just let yourself starve to death?"

"Of course not, I'd just eat all the vegetarians!" Autumn answered smartly.

"I see you haven't changed at all!" Penny remarked, approving of Autumn's somewhat morbid answer. Autumn was her little goth punk partner in crime. Autumn very much looked up to Penny and patterned herself after her in various ways, although obviously, she drew the line at emulating the older woman's dietary habits.

They all had to shout to have the conversations I just described, as being so close to the stage at a rock concert is probably one of the worst places one can choose to have a chat. After exchanging a few more pleasantries, Kiesha escorted Paul and Matt and Naomi's family to a section off to the side of the stage that had been reserved for VIPs. There were already a few other people in that section, some of whom Naomi and Matt recognized as being friends and family of the band. Randy's aunt Bernice, who had raised him like a mother, was already there, as were his two older brothers and their families. Penny's parents were there, too. They all made a fuss when they saw Paul, who ate up all the attention from his extended family. They spent the rest of the concert in that section, not counting a few bathroom breaks and the time that Naomi left for a while to buy herself a ridiculously overpriced beer.

Matt had never really bothered to listen to the Atmosphere Fishes before, and he had to say that he wasn't particularly impressed with them. He could see why they were touring with the Mystery Smiths, though. Both bands had a kind of kitschy, goofy, family friendly style. On the surface, they were fairly similar. However, Matt felt that with the Mystery Smiths, they were more genuine. They were just being themselves onstage, performing in a very unselfconscious way. The Atmosphere Fishes were the opposite. He felt they were trying too hard to come across as being strange and quirky; it all seemed forced, like a bad imitation of the Mystery Smiths. The Mystery Smiths had lots of songs that were about seemingly silly things, but there were layers to their lyrics, hidden meanings below the childish veneer that could sometimes be surprisingly profound. They had something to say about the world, about life. They just chose to wrap it in an irreverent and fun package that made it too easy for some to dismiss it all as being just so much stuff and nonsense.

Matt detected no such subtlety and sophistication in the work of the Atmosphere Fishes. It was all just about rocking out and having fun, which was cool and all, but it also left him feeling a bit empty after a few songs. The audience had lots of kids in it though, and they seemed to be loving it though. Maybe he was just being a stick in the mud? An old fuddy duddy who didn't know how to let his thinning hair down anymore and party? It was possible. He tried to stop being so analytical and just be in the moment, to just enjoy himself. He had to admit that they ended their part of the show on a high note, with their popular cover of an old song by They Might Be Giants called "the Guitar". Matt was familiar with the original version of the song, as it was one of Randy's favorites, from one of his favorite bands. Sometimes, the lyrics of some of They Might Be Giants' songs had an eerie way of echoing some events of Matt's life, although this particular one had never fit into that category. He didn't see how it ever could. The lyrics were especially surreal and all over the place, with references to everything from a lion taking a phone call to taking control of a silver spaceship. Randy once told him it wasn't unusual for the universe to speak to us through things like song lyrics.

"You talk about the universe almost like it's a living thing." Matt had said, and Randy had just responded by fixing him with one of his maddeningly enigmatic smiles.

Penny had even joined Jim onstage for this final song, as there was a part of the song that required some female vocals. Jim was a tall, skinny guy with a long mane of wavy, golden hair that stretched down past his shoulders and a carefree smile. They made a cute couple. Matt smiled to himself as he watched them singing together into the same mike, cheek to cheek. They certainly seemed to be in love. Good for her, she deserved it. Didn't everyone? He was surprised when near the end of the song, a short robot came out on the stage and started dancing around, its head was shaped like an old boom box, with the speakers acting as its eyes and the tape deck forming a mouth. Matt had seen this character before on some of the tee shirts worn by the people in the audience. He was the band's mascot, who was called "Hi-Fi". Penny had once told Matt over the phone when she called to check in on Paul that Jim was constantly annoyed because most people nowadays didn't know what "Hi-Fi" meant, and thought his name was "Wi-Fi" as that made more sense to them. It was a cute gimmick, and he was sure it helped them sell lots of merchandise, but he felt sorry for whoever was in the costume. He was certain that they must be sweating their ass off in that outfit.

Finally, the Atmosphere Fishes encore set had ended, and after Kiesha and a few of the other roadies had set up everything, the Mystery Smiths took to the stage. They were in rare form tonight. Despite being exhausted from the long tour, they drew upon some mysterious inner reserve of energy to put on one final, epic show as they tore through their catalog of classics. They were occasionally joined onstage by people dressed up as the villains from their TV show, including, much to Paul's delight, Cownan the Bullbarian. The villains would try to put an end to the show, only to be vanquished by the band. Once again, Matt's heart went out to the people in those hot costumes, one of which he knew was Kiesha, who wore a dizzying number of hats for the band. Matt was pleased to see that both of his kids, who had practically been raised on the Mystery Smiths music, seemed to be having a blast, despite the fact that they were both now "too old" for the demographic that their more recent efforts were aimed at. Naomi, who enjoyed music even more than Matt did, seemed to be having herself a ball. Matt was having a good time too, although he was sometimes distracted by the rumbling of his stomach. He was feeling more than a little hungry, so much so that he was almost wishing for the show to wrap up so he could eat. They served food at this venue, but he was too stingy to pay the inflated prices for the food here, besides he didn't want to spoil his appetite. They all had plans to meet up at a nearby restaurant that Jim happened to own for a private party after the show.

Unbeknownst to Matt and his family, something very strange was about to happen backstage.

Kiesha was struggling out of her "Lady Winnebago" costume (Lady Winnebago being the name of an evil sorceress that she played in one episode of the series) when she noticed Jim walk by her so quickly that he nearly knocked her over, not even pausing to apologize, which was unlike him. Hi-Fi came running after him seconds later, struggling to keep up with his stubby little legs.

"She's back here, waiting for you, sir." She heard Hi-Fi say in his precise, upper crusty sounding British accent, which always reminded her of C-3PO. Kiesha quickly threw off the remaining few bulkier bits of her costume and slipped down the darkened corridor after the pair. The "other thing" that Randy had asked her to take care of was to keep an eye on Jim, whom he didn't completely trust, especially after hearing a few rumors about him recently from some of the other roadies. It certainly appeared that these two were up to something now, and it was up to her to see what it was.

As she crept stealthily down the hall, she could hear muffled voices coming from a room at the end of the hallway, which served as Jim's dressing room. Luckily, the door was still cracked open a little, enough for her to see inside. She felt vaguely guilty spying on them like this, but she trusted her mentor's instincts about people. Plus, Jim had an unusual aura that both she and Randy found impossible to make any sense out of.

As she peered into the room, she saw Jim lounging in a chair. An unusually tall and statuesque woman in a close fitting, silver catsuit and a green cape paced the floor in front of him. She wore a tall skull cap with an oddly shaped antenna sticking out of the top of it.

Aha! Kiesha thought. *The mystery woman herself!*

Several of her fellow roadies had spotted Jim talking to this woman a few times lately, always dressed in the same bizarre outfit. Eventually, the gossip over her identity had reached Randy's ears, prompting him to give Kiesha her current assignment. This was the first time Kiesha had seen the woman for herself, she was beginning to think that she was just a figment of the other's imaginations, or part of an elaborate prank, but here she was, in the flesh right in the other room only a few feet away from her.

Or was she? The woman had absolutely no aura whatsoever. This was impossible. Every living thing had an aura. In fact, even a few non-living things had auras, like certain kinds of machines and other artifacts. But she had nothing at all. She was more like a recording on a TV screen, or a painting than a real person.

She strained her ears to hear what they were talking about, then recalled that she still had her earplugs in, to protect her hearing from the noise of the concert, and quickly pulled them out. No good, she could still barely hear them. What she *could* hear didn't even sound like it was in English, or any other language she had ever heard before. It was a strange, high-pitched sing-song kind of sound. She was about to do a spell to translate it, when right before her startled eyes, the mystery woman blinked out of existence.

One moment she was there, the next there was no trace of her at all.

What the hell is going on here? She wondered frantically. She *definitely* had to go tell Sensei all about this right away.

Before she could make a move, the door was suddenly pushed out, striking her painfully in the face.

"Ouch! Jesus! Fuck! Christ!" he swore with gusto.

"Kiesha! Holy shit, I'm so sorry. I didn't know you were there! Are you okay?" Jim asked, a look of concern covering his face.

Kiesha probed her face with her fingers, then examined them critically. Next, she poked at her teeth with them. "Hmm, no blood, all my teeth seem intact. I guess I'll be alright."

"Well, I'm glad to hear it. Sorry about that again."

"Oh, it's okay. Don't worry about it. Shit happens, y'know?"

Jim's eyes narrowed slightly. "What were you doing back here, anyway? Did Penny send you for me?"

"Oh, uh, no. I was just looking for her and I thought I heard you talking to someone in there, so I thought she might be in there with you, that's all. *Who* were you talking to? I thought I saw some lady in there with you?"

Jim laughed, a little uncomfortably. "A lady? There's nobody else in there, just me and Hi-Fi."

"That's really funny, I could've sworn I saw..."

"Anyway, isn't Penny still on stage? I can hear her from here!" he said, cutting her off abruptly. Kiesha cursed herself internally for coming up with such a lame excuse in the first place to try and explain away her odd behavior.

"Oh yeah, I guess she is...now. She took a little break a couple of minutes ago and I, um...had to ask her something. Well, I guess I'd better go wait for her to come off stage again. Catch ya later!" She said hurriedly as she turned and walked rapidly back towards the stage, trying hard not to run. She could still feel Jim's suspicious eyes boring into her retreating form.

Jim looked down at his diminutive, metallic companion.

"We can't have her getting suspicious and causing any trouble. Not when we're this close to things finally coming to a head. Looks like we're going to need to be a bit more discreet in the future."

"Discreet. Yes, very good, sir. Duly noted." Hi-Fi replied dutifully.

CHAPTER 4:
DINNER AT KIRK'S

Matt pulled into the parking lot of "Kirk's Galactic Grub", a sci-fi themed restaurant owned by Jim, where they had all been invited to attend a dinner party.

It was a pretty remarkable designed structure. The place looked like a cross between a spaceship and a diner. Most of it resembled a traditional, sleek chromed diner from the 1950s, except that it had been jacked up off the ground so that it sat perched on a series of thick pylons that had been modified into faux landing gears. Instead of steps, there was a wide ramp that led up to the entrance, and a pair of large wings were folded up on either side of the building. The wings bristled with imitation laser cannons, while the roof of the building was topped with a big radar dish that reminded Matt of the one on the *Millennium Falcon* from the Star Wars films.

"Wow! I have to hand it to Jim, that *is* one cool looking building." He said as he hunted for a parking spot.

"I'm not sure how much input he really had into the design, but yeah, it *does* look awesome," added Naomi.

"Eh. I've seen better." Autumn said, ever mindful to preserve her reputation for blasé teenaged indifference. Naomi wondered *where* her daughter had "seen better" since she pretty much knew all the places that her daughter had ever visited in her 15 years of life on this planet where she could have possibly seen anything to rival this, but decided not to question it.

"It's like a piece of pop art unto itself!" Joe commented admiringly, being old enough now to not care so much about projecting the same airs as his sister. He'd elected to ride along with the rest of his family to Kirk's. After dinner, he and Autumn would take a subway back to his studio apartment in the Village and spend the rest of the weekend catching up with each other in order to provide Matt and Naomi with some much needed alone time as a couple.

As Matt eased into a parking spot, he noticed that the parking lot had what appeared to be several large piles of snow covered rubble stacked up in some of the corners. It was as if all the debris from whatever building had once stood on this spot hadn't been completely cleared away before Kirk's was built here for some reason. It added to the overall impression that the restaurant really was some kind of spaceship that had just come in for a landing. He wondered if that was why Jim had left these stacks lying around like this. Was it all just for the ambiance?

Matt wondered how Jim could afford to own a place like this. The Atmosphere Fishes were even less of a big name band than the Mystery Smiths, hence having to open for them rather than headlining the tour. He knew that the Mystery Smiths were hardly swimming in money and assumed that the Atmosphere Fishes were in similar financial waters. Maybe Jim had rich business partners that had invested in the restaurant, or perhaps the guy was independently wealthy? Matt told himself that he needed to relax and stop looking for mysteries where there were none. He wasn't here to work; he was here to have a good time for Christsakes!

The family clambered out of the car and back into the brisk February air. Naomi pulled out her cell phone and snapped a few pictures of them all standing in front of the unusual building after shouting directions at them in her efforts to get them all in the shot. Everyone else was just praying for her to hurry and get a picture that would be satisfactory enough to her before they all died of exposure.

"You know who would've absolutely loved this place?" She said as she continued to admire its sleek lines.

"Your Dad." Matt answered as he moved towards the entrance.

Naomi smiled. She and Matt had been together for so long at this point that he could often tell what she was thinking. Sometimes, depending on her mood, this annoyed her, but right now, she found the familiarity comforting.

"Exactamundo." She confirmed. Her father had died many years ago, but he had been a huge science fiction nerd, especially when it came to Star Trek.

Indeed, he'd once written a sci-fi novel called "Your Own Worst Enemy" which had been posthumously published by Matt's publisher after Matt made a few necessary revisions to the manuscript. Her dad had once described the story as "Star Trek on steroids", which was fairly accurate. The plot involved a group of Trek-like space explorers returning home to Earth, only to find the planet under attack by an alien ship. They destroyed the attackers, but only after they've done tremendous damage to the planet below and killed millions. In the wake of this, the Earth abandons its noble ideals and becomes more militant and imperialistic. Earth attacks and conquers the planet that sent the ship that had attacked the Earth, and mistreats the natives. We later find out that the alien ship was actually from the future. The aliens were trying to wipe out their human oppressors *before* they could invade their planet. Their attempts to change their tragic history had only created the very same history they were trying to escape from. Some of the crew members of the original ship that defeated the aliens figure this out. Disgusted by the direction that their civilization has gone in since that incident, they journey to the alien planet to try to stop a group of alien rebels from launching the ship and going back in time to carry out their deadly mission. It wasn't the most uplifting of stories, but she thought there were a few neat ideas in it.

Upon entering the restaurant and identifying themselves, the family was ushered into a private party room in the back. Matt admired the uniforms worn by the members of the restaurant's staff. They were similar to uniforms from Star Trek the Original Series and the more recent Trek movies, but were also *just* different enough to avoid getting the restaurant sued for copyright infringement by CBS or Paramount or whoever the hell it is who owns the rights to Star Trek nowadays. He thought that there was something a little off about the hostess who escorted them into the room. She seemed so stiff, so characterless. She was almost robotic in all her mannerisms.

It must just be a long shift for her and she's feeling burnt out, that's all. I sure hope Jim pays these folks well enough to make it worth it for them. He thought, chastising himself once more for reading too much into things. Why couldn't he just chill out?

Some tables in the party room were occupied already by members of Randy and Penny's family, as well as what Matt assumed must be friends and family of the Atmosphere Fishes. He exchanged a few pleasantries with his friend's families, as it had been so loud at the concert that this had been fairly impossible. From talking to Randy's Aunt Bernice, he learned both bands were still working on packing up everything after the show and would join them a little later on.

In the meantime, Matt amused himself by checking out the plethora of sci-fi memorabilia from different movie and television franchises that the room was decorated with. There were movie posters, autographed photos of various celebrities, and even some props. It was quite an impressive collection, which again, Matt couldn't help but think must've cost a small fortune. Joe joined Matt as he inspected the decor, and they were particularly fascinated by a large display of Star Wars toys secured in a sealed bookcase embedded into one of the walls. Matt had collected many of these toys as a kid, and when Joe entered his life and they started making newer versions of those toys again, he'd bought many of them for the boy. Now, even those "new" toys were old themselves, relics of his son's childhood just as his were of his own. It was so strange how quickly time flew by. They had fun pointing out which ones they had owned and which ones they never could seem to find in stores and hadn't ever seen up close and personal until now.

Naomi was busy posting the picture she'd taken in front of the restaurant and some video she had shot at the concert to her various social media accounts while she sipped from a mixed drink that she'd ordered. Autumn was similarly engrossed in something or other on her phone. Matt looked over his shoulder at the two of them and sighed, wishing that they'd spend a bit more time in the real world for a change. Here they were in this unique place, with people they didn't get to see very often, and they both had their faces buried in their phones. It was a damned shame.

His ruminations were disturbed by the arrival of some newcomers to the party. Kevin was escorted into the room by the same marionette-like hostess that had ushered his family into the room earlier. Much to Matt's delight, he had Allison with him.

Matt hadn't seen Allison in almost eight years, encountering her during the same case where he'd first met Kevin. She looked quite different now; back then she'd had short, platinum blonde hair, but now her hair was quite long and was a particularly reddish shade of auburn. She had put on a fair amount of weight. Matt knew that this was because she had once been a vampire, and spent years unable to eat normal food. Once she was finally able to eat regular human food again, she kind of over indulged in that long-lost pleasure at first, which was what caused the weight gain to begin with. Add to that the idiosyncrasies of her now all too human metabolism and it all added up to a constant struggle to keep the weight off. However, he felt that the extra pounds didn't look unnatural on her and even enhanced her beauty. Unfortunately, that, plus her diminutive stature had hurt her acting ambitions somewhat. Despite her considerable talent, most casting directors were looking for a particular body type for their leading ladies, so she tended to get stuck playing the leading lady's wacky best friend or was given even less significant roles.

"Matt!" Allison squealed and ran over to him. She tried to hug him, but only succeeded in getting her arms around his legs because of the dramatic difference in their heights.

"It's been far too long. Look at you! You're all grown up now!"

"Yeah, it sure took me long enough, huh?" Indeed it had. Allison was technically almost as old as Matt was, having spent sixteen years stuck at the age of fourteen. Thankfully, once the curse of vampirism had been lifted from her, she started aging normally again.

"I was beginning to think you had something against me, never coming to all the parties we've been inviting you to!" Matt and Naomi often hosted big parties at their house for Halloween, Christmas, New Year's Eve, and sometimes the 4th of July. Matt usually invited her through Kevin, but she always seemed to have an excuse for why she couldn't make it.

"I'm sorry. It's nothing personal, really. It's just life, ya know? First, I was always busy with school or family; lately it's been trying to get my acting career going. For what it's worth, I really enjoyed that last book of yours." Allison was a voracious reader, and had always been something of a fan of Matt's literary efforts.

"Well, it's nice to know that *somebody* liked it. I feel like I've been raked over a bunch of hot coals when I read what people have to say about it online." Matt wasn't really as bothered by this as it sounded. He mostly wrote for his own pleasure, and to work out his thoughts on various subjects which had been rattling around in his head for decades. To a large extent, he didn't really care very much what other people made of his writing, but that also didn't mean that he didn't appreciate a kind word of praise or encouragement every now and then, he was only human after all.

"First rule of the internet, Matt - never read the comments!" She reminded him.

"Eh, what can I say? I must be a glutton for punishment!" Matt realized with a flush of embarrassment that he hadn't done the proper introductions and Joe was just hovering around beside them awkwardly. "Geez, where are my manners? Joe, this is Allison, Allison this is my son Joe. He's the one with all the *real* artistic talent in the family."

Joe smiled shyly, a little embarrassed by Matt's endorsement, and shook her hand. Joe was pretty good friends with Kevin, so he'd heard him talk about her often enough. Now he felt that he could see why his friend was so smitten with her; she had a brilliant smile and exuded a bubbly charm, which made her instantly likable.

"Pleased to finally meet you. You guys should come and sit with us at our table." He suggested.

"Yeah, maybe we can order some appetizers or something while we're waiting for the bands to show up." Matt remarked, suddenly remembering how hungry he was. He'd been so distracted by all the knickknacks decorating the restaurant that he'd temporarily forgotten all about his persistently protesting stomach.

Kevin and Allison pulled out the seats closest to Naomi. She was finally awakened from her relentless screen scrolling by the sound of the chairs being pulled out. When she looked up to see Allison, she immediately knew who she was and grinned up at her.

"The famous Allison, at long last!" She said, putting her phone down and extending her hand.

"Well, not so famous, really. I'm still working on that part!" Allison blushed as she took her hand. "You must be the famous Dr. Naomi Waters-Spike, good to finally meet you."

"This is so crazy, I feel like I know you already. Kevin never shuts up about you, and he's shown us all of your movies." Allison had managed to wind up in a few films, but she only had significant parts in a few low budget student films. She had been in a few films that would've been classified as "B-movies" back in the day, but those were typically in roles as an extra that were so brief that Kevin had to pause the movie to point her out. Most movies with a decent budget were filmed in Hollywood or Vancouver these days, so there weren't a heck of a lot of opportunities for this sort of thing in the city. Most of her acting gigs were on the stage.

As she said the part about how Kevin "never shuts up" about Allison, she saw a look of concern roll across his features like a passing storm cloud and realized that she might've inadvertently embarrassed him in front of his lady friend. She sighed at her faux pas. *God, I really am turning into my mother!* She thought ruefully, mindful of the many times her mom, caught up in her own enthusiasm, had done something like that to her. She hated to do that to Kevin. Like Matt, she had come to think of him like an unofficial son. He'd even lived with them for a while when he'd first left his native Connecticut to come work for Matt.

Matt sat down next to her and thankfully saved the situation by providing a timely change of subject.

"So I hear that while we were all at the concert, Kevin was watching you in your latest play. He said something about it having something to do with the 'War of the Worlds,' I hope you didn't get upstaged by all those Martians!" Matt joked.

"She was *great* in it!" Kevin gushed.

Allison waved away the praise. "Oh please! I just had a few bit parts—only four lines of dialogue! Mostly, I just ran around and looked terrified in the crowd scenes."

"Yeah, but I could really *feel* your fear," Kevin stubbornly insisted.

Geez, the kid's really laying it on thick! Matt thought, amused by Kevin's lack of "game" when it came to the business of love.

"Thanks," she said to Kevin, then turned to look at the others. "There weren't really any Martians or little green men or whatever in the play to upstage me."

"Why does everyone always say 'little green men?'" Autumn suddenly chimed in loudly, up until then Matt wasn't sure that she was even aware of the conversation happening around her, she'd been so engrossed in looking at her phone. "If you look at the actual UFO reports, it's usually little *gray* men. How do we know that they're really men, anyway? Maybe the aliens have a different concept of gender?" She noticed everyone was now looking at her and she retreated back to the safety of her cellphone. "Sorry, it's just something that always bothers me when I hear it, that's all." She mumbled as she slowly slid the phone up to cover her face.

"Ladies, and gentlemen, I give you the wonderful randomness of my daughter!" Matt chuckled. "So no Martians, huh? What kind of adaptation of War of the Worlds doesn't even have the aliens in it?" He asked Allison.

"That's just it. It wasn't *really* an adaptation. The story was set against the backdrop of the panic caused by Orson Welles's infamous radio broadcast of the story in the Thirties. It's about a guy who lives with his abusive mother and takes advantage of the chaos caused by the fact that everyone thought the world was ending because of an alien invasion to kill her off."

"So, it was one of those really cheerful, uplifting, feel good kind of stories huh?" Matt joked.

"Actually..." Naomi began. "That's not very historically accurate. There really wasn't all that much of an actual panic."

"Oh, no! Here we go again! She can't help but explain this every time that I watch *Buckaroo Banzai!*" Matt griped. *The Adventures of Buckaroo Banzai Across the 8th Dimension* was a cult science fiction movie from the Eighties that was one of Matt's childhood favorites. The War of the Worlds broadcast was an important plot point in the story. Matt loved that his wife was so intelligent, and was always dropping interesting tidbits of information on him, but being constantly reminded of the historical inaccuracies in many of his favorite things sometimes had a way of sucking all the fun out of them.

Naomi ignored her husband's all too familiar protests and carried on. She was in full professorial lecture mode now, and there was no stopping her once those gears shifted in her head. What good was it to have a PhD if you didn't flaunt it every once in a while? That was her philosophy!

"It's true that the radio station was flooded with calls, and Welles had to apologize the next day, but there isn't much evidence of a real panic in the streets. Most of the people that had tuned in too late to hear the disclaimer at the beginning of the broadcast announcing that it was just a work of fiction simply called the station, or their local police department, to confirm it before flying into a panic. The newspapers exaggerated the panic aspect as a way of trying to discredit radio as a reliable source of news. You see, back then, radio was the only real competition that the papers had, and radio was beginning to steal away some of their ad revenues, and they didn't like it one bit. So, they seized upon this story as an opportunity to blacken the reputation of radio. They blew it out of proportion, and they were obviously pretty successful too. Here we are, in 2013, and people are still making up stories based upon a panic that never really happened. Sometimes I think that ultimately, it really doesn't matter what's true or a lie. Whatever people *believe* happened becomes as powerful as the truth all too often." She concluded a little sadly, taking a sip from her wineglass to punctuate the point.

Sometimes, Naomi wondered if this was what her purpose in life was? To make people appreciate how important the truth really was? The motto of Matt's detective agency was "Truth is our Business". She felt like this statement applied to them equally; they just had different ways of attacking this mission. She was constantly trying to shed light on the truths of the past, whereas Matt was battling to get the present moment to yield up its secrets. Yet, for a pair of people who valued the power of truth so deeply, they also kept their share of secrets from the world, didn't they? Such was the price they paid for being associated with the Guilds.

Autumn looked up from her phone just long enough to roll her eyes at her mom's propensity to show off her knowledge.

"Hmm. I never knew that, fascinating. I'll have to tell everyone else who's working on the play about that!" Allison said.

"Well, accurate or not, I sure thought it was entertaining enough. There is such a thing as dramatic license, you know," Kevin added.

Naomi looked at the way Kevin hung on Allison's every word, and the way Allison looked at him with a peculiar reverence. It was obvious to her that they were in love with one another, she just wished that *they'd* figure this out someday and actually do something about it. Had she and Matt ever really been that young and innocent in their affections? She knew the answer was "yes", but it was hard to believe. Sometimes it all felt so far away.

"So what have you been up to lately, Matt? Any exciting cases I should know about?" Allison asked him.

Matt thought for a moment before answering. "No, not really. Nothing as exciting as the one I was involved in the last time we saw each other. Most of my cases are pretty dull actually, trying to catch people faking workmen's compensation claims and other kinds of insurance fraud, plus the usual cases of people trying to catch a cheating partner in the act, stuff like that."

"That's not quite true. There was that one case...you know? Remember the last time we went out to eat someplace together? That one is kind of interesting." Naomi said.

Matt smacked his forehead melodramatically. "Oh duh! I guess that *was* something! Why don't you tell the story? You do a better job than I do."

"Says the guy who writes books!"

"Hey, you know that's just a hobby that got a little out of control! Besides, you write books too!"

"Yeah, textbooks and histories that nobody will ever read outside of the Guilds, not novels!"

"I'm good with the written word, you're good with the spoken word, that's why *you* need to tell the story!" Matt insisted.

Naomi grudgingly conceded that he was right and decided to just tell them already.

"Okay, so about a month ago, the owners of a local restaurant hired Matt to dig up some dirt on their competitors a few doors down," she started.

"Damn! I never knew the restaurant business was so cutthroat!" Allison broke in, surprised. .

"I know, right?" Naomi agreed.

"It *is* fairly unusual, but in this case, my clients had reasons to suspect that their competitors were up to no good. They'd noticed some strange things about their neighbors, and lots of shady characters hanging around the place at odd hours." Matt explained.

"Hey, I thought *I* was the one telling this story?" Naomi said indignantly, fixing him with her infamous "stare" that typically made those it was directed at shrivel up into a quivering ball of fear. Their years together, however, had rendered Matt largely immune to the deleterious effects of her gaze.

"Just offering the occasional word of clarification, m'dear!"

"Hmm. I'll allow it. Anyways, Matt decided he should start off the investigation by having dinner there."

Matt interrupted her again. "I'd meant to check it out at some point, anyway. Lots of people kept on telling me they had really good food there. There *was* a totally legitimate reason why they were putting their competitors out of business. So this was the perfect excuse to finally go and experience the place."

Naomi cleared her throat loudly and gave Matt another dirty look, but if you looked closely enough, you could also see that she had a playful twinkle in her eye, indicating that she wasn't truly angry with him over his constant "clarifications" to the story.

"So he took me out to eat there on our date night. When we were looking over the menu, I noticed t they had a really expensive wine on the wine list. When I say really expensive, I mean *really, really* expensive! What was it? $1,500? $2,000?" She asked Matt.

"Oh, you mean you're giving me permission to speak now?" He said. This comment earned him a smack on the wrist with her napkin from Naomi.

"It was actually $2,500. If you must know." He revealed with exaggerated reluctance.

"I joked we should get that wine, and when Matt found the wine on the menu, it immediately set his alarm bells ringing."

"Yeah, but sometimes really fancy restaurants have wines that are that expensive. I've been to a few places with outrageously priced drinks like that in Manhattan. I've heard that a lot of restaurants make most of their profits by marking up the wine ridiculously like that. What's so suspicious about that?" Allison skied.

"When were *you* ever in such an expensive restaurant? I didn't think you could afford that kind of thing with what you make acting!" Kevin inquired.

Allison shrugged. "Occasionally, my boyfriend likes to make sure I'm eating something a little more nutritious than ramen noodles."

Kevin did his best not to look upset by this answer, but both Matt and Naomi saw the pained expression that briefly registered on his face. How could he ever hope to compete with a guy that could afford to take her to those kinds of restaurants?

Maybe Allison noticed this too, because she tried to soften the blow with her next statement. "And sometimes I treat myself, too. Don't forget that my adoptive parents are filthy rich because they stole a treasure from an evil vampire a few centuries ago and invested it wisely. Sometimes they kick me a few hundred bucks here and there."

"I don't think I could ever forget *that!*" Kevin replied.

"To answer your question, this wasn't a really expensive restaurant. What was so strange about it was that they didn't have any other wines that were even close to that expensive on the menu. It stuck out like a sore thumb. I started to have a crazy suspicion about it. You see, sometimes money is laundered by purchasing luxury items as a way to get the dirty money into the system. Sometimes, the items purchased only exist on paper. So I decided to order it, just to see what would happen." Matt said, getting the conversation back on track.

"Imagine my surprise! Mr. Cheapo himself ordering a wine that was $2,500 all on a silly hunch! And this guy doesn't even hardly ever drink!" Naomi laughed.

"I am *not* 'Mr. Cheapo.' I prefer to be called 'Mr. Frugality.' Besides, you know that what Randy says about always listening to your gut instincts is 100% valid."

"Whatever, dude! Frugality is just a polite way of saying you're cheap!"

Matt tapped her wineglass with his fingernail, making a sharp ringing sound. "I may not drink, but *you* do! So I figured, what the hell? Either I'll find out something that might help out with my case, or you'll end up with a really nice early Valentine's Day present. Either way, it's a win-win."

"So what happened next?" Joe asked. His parents hadn't told him this particular story yet.

Matt picked up the story again. "It caused quite a stir when I ordered it. The waiter asked us several times if he was sure that we really wanted that wine and tried to suggest others that were more affordable. Then I saw him go talk to some big goons that had come out of some back room. Those guys really kept on staring at me and Naomi, giving us the evil eye. I saw one of them make a phone call while he was checking us out. Eventually, they returned to the back. Then the owner of the place came over to apologize and told us they'd just checked and they were out of that wine and they should've removed it from the menu. He offered us some other expensive stuff at a discount."

"Even at the discount price, it was still about $200!" Naomi laughed.

Matt made a face. "Yeah, and what could I do? I was on the spot, so I still had to buy it so they wouldn't get so suspicious about me."

"It *was* some good wine, thank you dear."

"Hmph! It couldn't have possibly been $200 worth of good!"

"So, was your hunch correct? Were they really laundering money by selling expensive bottles of wine that didn't exist?" Allison wanted to know.

"Yep. When I ordered it, at first they thought that maybe their business associates had sent someone new to do the transaction, then they realized I was just some random person innocently ordering it. I guess they thought that nobody who comes in from off the street that's in their right mind would ever really try to order it. As money laundering schemes went, it was actually pretty inept. After the dinner I started surveillance on the place..."

"Excuse me, *I* was the one who really did all the surveillance!" Kevin said.

"Yeah, well, I couldn't do it myself, could I? They might recognize me since I'd made such a big scene in the restaurant. Besides, it was good for you to get more experience on a long stakeout."

"And I had to dig through their dumpsters looking for evidence! That was nasty! All that old food and rats that were the size of footballs! It's a wonder I didn't get rabies!" continued Kevin.

Matt waved away his protests. "It all goes with the territory in this line of work, kid, so you'd better get used to it if you really want to make this your career. See, Allison, I told you it's not really as glamorous as the movies make it out to be, and this is the perfect example!"

Naomi picked up the story again, privately bemused by how once it had gotten started, Matt had taken over telling it anyway, despite his stubborn insistence on getting her to do it.

"Matt was able to ID some of the characters that were always hanging around the place from photos Kevin took when he was on stakeout as being minor figures linked to organized crime. He also found a few irregularities in their finances from his research online and from the records that Kevin was able to rescue from the trash."

"Records that I had to tape together after they'd been shredded! You have no idea how long that takes!" Kevin grimaced.

"But you *like* doing puzzles!" Matt teased him. It was so nice to have junior investigators on the staff now to do all the dirty, tedious parts of the job that he used to have to do all by himself when he first started out. Rank certainly had its privileges!

"Well, once we had a good amount of evidence gathered together, we contacted our client. We suggested they get in touch with the FBI, since we had enough on the restaurant to suggest that it was a front for the mafia. The FBI shut the place down pretty quickly once they got involved. It's kind of a shame. They really *had* good food at that place. My client couldn't hold a candle to them, but now they get to stay in business serving their mediocre food. They were so grateful that they said we could eat there for free anytime, but I don't really intend to take them up on that offer!"

"I do." Kevin said, turning to Allison. "The food's not really that bad. I should take you there sometime."

"Sure, sounds great." Allison smiled back at him.

Matt made a face at the unpleasant memory of their cuisine. "Each to their own, kid! I wonder what the food is like in this joint? Is that waitress ever coming back?"

"You were too busy 'oohing' and 'ahhing' over all the deeply nerdy decorations in this place to order drinks the last time I saw her, but I'm sure she'll be back soon." Naomi said.

As if in answer to Matt's complaint, the waitress appeared by his side so suddenly that it startled him and he was finally able to order something, in this case a basket of teriyaki wings.

It wasn't too long after that when the members of both bands showed up. There was quite a lot of excited chatter going on amongst them as they walked in. Immediately, Matt could tell that something was up. Before he could ask about it, Randy, Kiesha, Penny, Jim, and Paul all pulled up a chair at their table and Randy spilled the beans.

"Sorry we're so late. Traffic got a little backed up on the way over here because of the UFO. Everyone was pulling over on the side of the road to take some pictures of it with their phones. It was pretty cool. Penny got some video of it, too." He explained breathlessly.

"What?! A UFO!" Autumn, who if you hadn't guessed already, was a little obsessed with the subject, asked excitedly. Like her father, Autumn loved a good mystery, and there are few things as mysterious as UFOs. "For real?"

"For real!" Penny confirmed and leaned over to show her the video she'd shot on her cell phone. Autumn's face lit up as she watched the playback. Matt and Naomi really couldn't see it from where they sat.

Matt whispered to Randy, because of the presence of Jim, "It's not the *Silver Bullet,* is it?" The *Silver Bullet* was a UFO that the Guilds had gotten their hands on many years ago. However, it wasn't from an alien world, but rather from a parallel universe version of the Earth. Most of the people at the table, except Jim, had seen or ridden in the *Silver Bullet* at some point or another over the years.

"I wouldn't be this excited about it if it was. Besides, they're not so clumsy as to let it be seen like this. No, I think this one is an alien for real." He whispered back. It was true that Randy had seen many strange and unusual things in his time, but even he had yet to see a spaceship that was genuinely of extraterrestrial origins, and his excitement was evident.

Penny passed her phone down to Matt and Naomi so they could check it out for themselves. Allison and Kevin gathered around them. The video shows a pair of oddly wobbling silver saucers surrounded by a luminous aura flying out over the water, running parallel to the shore, and then shooting straight up into the sky at a blinding speed. The picture quality was unusually clear and sharp for UFO footage.

"Holy crap, those things look so fake! Like cheap special effects!" Matt couldn't help but remark in a disappointed voice.

"Yeah, weird, isn't it? But it's totally real, we all saw it." Penny said as she reclaimed her phone.

"I dunno. I think you guys are trying to pull our legs. I mean.... we were just talking about the War of the Worlds only a couple of minutes ago! This is too much of a coincidence! C'mon! What are the odds? This has gotta be some kinda prank, right?" A skeptical Matt inquired, hoping to wring a confession from them.

"Oh, it's real enough! I saw it with my own eyes, and I wouldn't use the word 'coincidence' so much as 'synchronicity'. The universe may be trying to tell us something," said Randy mysteriously.

From anybody else, this might have seemed like so much crazy talk, but Matt knew that when it came from a powerful wizard like Randy, it was actually worth taking seriously. He hoped there was nothing to it, though. It had been several years now since the high weirdness that occasionally creeped into his life and tended to turn it upside down had reappeared. It wasn't something he was ever looking forward to experiencing again. He found being unceremoniously thrust into life-or-death situations to be more terrifying than exhilarating. The idea that he might be on the cusp of another such misadventure was almost enough to make him lose his appetite.

"It's real, Uncle Matt! I saw it myself!" Paul replied with the unmistakable earnestness of a small child.

"Okay, *now* you have me convinced. I know what a terrible liar this kid is," he said.

"What's really strange is how much those UFOs look just like the ones that George Adamski supposedly took pictures of in the 50s. Except those pictures were obvious hoaxes." Autumn said.

"George Adamski? Never heard of him." Matt said.

"He's some guy who claimed that he met some 'Space Brothers' from Venus out in the desert who took him, of all people, for a ride in their spaceship. He was a minor celebrity in UFO circles for a few years. Now only crazy people take his claims seriously. The idea of aliens coming from Venus is idiotic anyway. That place can't possibly support any life. But I guess they didn't know that in the 1950's, so it didn't sound as dumb as it does today. You should see his pictures, too! They're just models, anyone can tell that! It's amazing that anyone ever took him seriously to begin with." Autumn told her father.

Throughout this exchange, Naomi had been squirming uncomfortably in her chair. She was proud of her daughter's knowledge on this subject, it showed that she was like her mother, a historian after all, albeit, strictly a historian of weird shit. What was making Naomi so anxious was her battle with herself to resist the impulse to reveal what she knew about this specific subject, which would also mean giving up a few Guild secrets that she was sworn to keep.

"Actually," she started with a whisper, "I found something in the archives about the Adamski case that you might find interesting, but I can't really discuss it right now." She nodded her head toward of Jim.

"Why do you suppose they're here?" Kevin asked, "Maybe they're from the planet Nibiru and they're here now because they missed the deadline to destroy the world a few months ago!"

Naomi rolled her eyes at the mention of Nibiru. According to an author named Zecharia Sitchin, Nibiru was supposedly a hidden planet in our solar system that was the home of a race of aliens called the Anunnaki, who had created the human race. In 2012, a shocking number of people believed that Nibiru was supposed to return and usher in the end of the world. It was, of course, a complete load of horseshit.

"Don't get me started on how flawed Zecharia Sitchin's translations of ancient Sumerian texts are!" said an exasperated Naomi.

"Yeah, please—don't! I have to hear this lecture every time 'Ancient Aliens' comes on the TV!" Matt complained. Naomi playfully hit him with her napkin once more.

"That show is the worst! As if ancient people were incapable of creating or imagining anything without help from aliens! It's insulting to the human spirit!" Naomi exclaimed.

"C'mon Mom, you know you love that guy with the crazy hair!" Autumn teased her, referencing Giorgio A. Tsoukalos, an unusually coiffed fellow who was a frequent commentator on the show.

"The only real mystery in that show is how that man can go out in public with that crazy hair do, let alone appear on TV like that!" Penny laughed.

"Yes! Exactly! Thank you! I'm glad that someone at this table understands my pain!" A grateful Naomi clapped her hand down on the table. Matt wondered if she was already feeling a little tipsy? Their appetizers had yet to arrive, and she had been drinking on an empty stomach.

At that moment, Hi-Fi walked up to Jim, who had been silent, yet attentively observing the entire conversation about UFOs. Matt was mighty confused by Hi-Fi's sudden appearance. Why was that little guy still in that stuffy, confining costume? He would've thought he'd be eager to get out of it.

"Excuse me, sir, but there's a call for you in the back."

"Later, Hi-Fi! Can't you see that I'm busy?" An annoyed Jim told him he hadn't said anything, but it was obvious that he'd been following the conversation closely.

"But sir! It's an urgent call from Kergaali." Hi-Fi told him conspiratorially.

Jim's entire demeanor changed. All the color drained out of his face and he abruptly stood up. A slightly confused Penny looked at him.

"Is something up?" She asked.

"It's my Mom. She's been sick lately, I've gotta take this call, but I'll be back soon." He leaned down and kissed her before he followed Hi-Fi out of the room.

Matt noticed that Randy and Kiesha shared a strange look as Jim walked from the table. Kiesha made a move to get up, but Randy motioned for her to sit down.

"Not yet. Give it a minute." Matt thought he saw Randy mouth to her.

I wonder what that's all about? Matt thought.

Randy seemed to notice Matt staring at him.

"I hear there's been lots of UFO sightings in the city in the past few days, but I didn't really expect to see one myself!" he said.

"Yeah, there have been a few more sightings lately than usual," Autumn confirmed, then she looked at her mother. "What were you going to tell me about Adamski before, Mom?"

"Well, now that Jim's gone, I guess I can tell you. Since everyone here at the table already knows about the Guilds. The ABC did an investigation into his claims and concluded that while his photos were faked and he exaggerated some of the claims in his book, he really did meet aliens from Venus!" The ABC was the rather unimaginative name for the Guilds' intelligence division, they were the real world "Men in Black."

"Get out of town? How is that possible? No life can survive there!" asked Autumn, shocked.

"Here's the twist: they were Venusians from an alternate universe where conditions on Venus were different. They were explorers that were on a tour of the multiverse, trying to map it. The ABC actually made contact with them before they left this reality. Poor old George Adamski didn't have any proof of his experience, so he decided to manufacture his own 'evidence.'" She told her daughter. At this point, Matt noticed that Kiesha suddenly got up and left the table.

"So maybe that's where these ships are from? They're back now for some reason?" Autumn speculated hopefully.

"It could be," Naomi said, taking another sip from her wineglass.

"None of that still answers my original question. What do they want? Why make their ships so visible like that? Do they come in peace?" Kevin asked.

"Of course they do!" Randy said. "That alien invasion stuff you see on TV and movies is all BS. Any of the civilizations that have the ability to meet the huge energy requirements needed to warp the fabric of space/time in order to travel here in a reasonable amount of time are also sophisticated enough to synthesize anything they might need. They can create their own resources, so there's no need to take over other planets to steal them. There's no incentive to invade. It's just so difficult for some of us to imagine a civilization that isn't centered around the ideas of conquest and colonization that we tend to impose these very human impulses on the aliens when we try to conceive of what they might be like."

This was what the Guilds had told Randy about the subject, which was also borne out by Naomi's own research into the matter. The few times that anyone from the Guilds or any governmental organizations had made contact with any aliens, this conclusion had always been held up.

Matt also knew that the aliens considered the Earth to be a potential "Dead End World" - their charming term for a planet where the dominant life form had wiped themselves out before graduating to become a part of the larger galactic community. The aliens had even once offered to help gradually bring us up to their level. Unfortunately, the world leaders at that time had refused their assistance. Accepting the aliens' help would've spelled the end of scarcity, and they couldn't allow that. The relentless competition for scarce resources and the hoarding of said resources was the very foundation of the political class' power. Ever since then, the aliens looked upon our world as a kind of zoo. A big safari park where they could study and observe these poor, foolish creatures before they inevitably rendered themselves extinct, just as so many other civilizations throughout the universe had before them.

Randy wisely refrained from explaining anything about the Dead End World at the table; it probably would've upset the kids and brought the whole mood down. This was supposed to be a party, after all

Matt decided that a change of subject was in order. He addressed Penny.

"We'll be happy to have you back in the office. The place hasn't been the same without you. All those temps that Adecco sends us are crap. They've been driving me and Earl nuts." Adecco was a local temp agency that had been trying to supply them with receptionists to replace Penny while she'd been away on the tour, but of course, nobody could really ever replace Penny. Earl was Earl Rogers, the other senior investigator on Matt's staff. He was a former ABC agent that Matt had first befriended around the same time he met Kevin and Allison.

Penny blushed. "It's time to know what I've been missed. You *do* remember that I'm not coming back for another week, right? I need a little time to recover from the tour and to spend some quality time with my little dude here." She tousled Paul's hair as he said the last part. He didn't seem to mind.

"I remember, don't worry. I guess we can survive another week without you. I was just looking forward to finally being able to get a decent cup of coffee for a change. I haven't had one since you've been gone!"

"Hey!" Naomi protested, kicking him gently under the table. Matt had always led her to believe that *she* made the best coffee, but truth to tell, he preferred how Penny prepared it.

"I mean when I'm at work, *obviously* dear!" he stammered.

"Mmm. Hmm. Sure. A likely story!"

Matt was rescued from the situation he'd landed himself in by the timely arrival of the appetizers. Shortly afterwards, Kiesha returned and scrawled something on a napkin that she passed over to Randy. He quickly scanned what it said and made a face that Matt couldn't quite read. Was he disappointed? Maybe. Matt couldn't quite tell, nor could he make out whatever was written on the napkin.

A few seconds later, Jim reappeared.

"So, is your mother alright? I didn't realize she was sick." Penny inquired as he sat down. It was quite rare for Jim to ever discuss his parents or past in much detail.

"Huh? Oh yeah. Yeah, she's feeling much better now, thanks." He looked across the table at Matt and Naomi.

"So you two must be Naomi and Matt. I've heard a lot about you two. I hope you enjoyed our show." He said. Matt hadn't *really* enjoyed his part of the show very much, but he was prepared to lie about it for the sake of being polite. Thankfully, he didn't have to.

"It was great!" Naomi told Jim. Matt just nodded along. "I really liked that cute little robot that came out and danced at the end."

"What I don't understand is why the midget inside the costume was still running around here in that costume. I would've thought he'd be suffocating in that outfit!" Matt remarked.

"Matt!" A horrified Naomi shot him an ugly look with her "stare".

"What?" He asked, genuinely dumbfounded.

"You're supposed to call them 'little people.' Midget is considered derogatory." Randy explained with a smile, amused at Matt's occasional difficulties keeping up with such social norms.

"Oh shit! I forgot! I have nothing against little people, you all know that! Hell, 'Willow' is one of my favorite movies! I was worried about the person in that costume getting heatstroke or something," said Matt slightly embarrassed.

Jim laughed. "Don't worry about it. There isn't a little person inside. Hi-Fi is a real robot."

Matt almost choked on his chicken wing at this revelation. "Really? He's pretty sophisticated for a robot, isn't he? He must've cost you an arm and a leg!"

Jim just chuckled again. "No, not really. I have a few friends from college that are into robotics and AI who were kind enough to put him together for me."

Naomi had been studying Jim intently since he'd returned to the table. Now that she could get a good, close up look at him, something about him was bothering her.

"Jim, have we ever met before? You seem really familiar, somehow." She asked.

"No, I don't think so."

"Are you sure? You mentioned going to college, I've taught at a few schools in my time. What school did you attend?" She pressed him, wondering if he was a former student, or someone she might've seen around campus.

"Midwestern State University in Texas." He answered.

"That's a little out of my territory. All the schools I've worked at have been in Jersey."

"Yeah, I've never gone to any schools there." He said firmly, ending all debate on the matter.

The main courses arrived. Kirk's had a delicious variety of vegan and vegetarian options, so Penny and Paul had nothing to worry about in that department. This was likely because Jim himself was a vegetarian. Throughout the night, Jim, Penny and Randy floated around from table to table, socializing with family and their bandmates. Matt had noticed, though, that whenever Jim was at their table, he couldn't keep his eyes off of Naomi, and was often found fixing her with an odd, unreadable expression. Penny gave no indication that she noticed. Matt wasn't sure if Naomi had, but it certainly made Matt feel uncomfortable.

Desserts and more drinks followed the main course. At some point during the dinner, Matt found himself looking around his table at the people gathered there. It struck him that most of the people sitting there wouldn't have been there tonight, might not be alive right now, or even exist at all if it wasn't for some of the decisions he'd made in his life. For example, if he hadn't sent Randy undercover to investigate Father Steve's church decades ago, would Randy have ever met Penny? Would the Mystery Smiths exist, or

Paul? He looked at Kevin and Allison as they continued to do their delicate dance of flirtation. Would either of them be alive to enjoy each other's company if he and Randy hadn't become involved in solving the case of Kevin's disappearance?

He remembered feeling something like this many years ago, when his grandmother had passed away when he was in his late teens. Sitting in the funeral home, and watching it fill up with his aunts, uncles, cousins and the children of his oldest cousins, it had occurred to him that none of these people would even exist if his grandmother hadn't taken a liking to his grandfather. An entire room full of people was her legacy at the end of a long life. Now Matt was forty-three years old, and he already had a table full of people who were here as a direct result of his life choices.

It's such an odd thing, isn't it? He thought. *How the decisions we make can affect so many other lives. How these sometimes perfectly casual choices can have consequences that continue to echo down the ages.*

In this moment, he knew that all the challenges he'd faced over the years, all the nightmares that he'd endured, had been absolutely worth it, and that he wouldn't change a thing. As he sat there, just watching the people who mattered the most to him laughing and sharing a meal together, he was overcome with a deep sense of satisfaction with his life thus far that was difficult to put into words, so he didn't even try. He just sat in the moment and let the feeling wash through him.

CHAPTER 5:
THE CASE AGAINST ONE MR. JIM DELEO

As the hour grew later, the party had started to break up. Joe and Autumn left to take a subway back to Joe's place in the Village, and Matt and Naomi had returned to their hotel room. Valentine's Day wasn't until next Thursday, but it was part of their plan for this weekend to celebrate it a little early, while they had the benefit of having some privacy for once.

Even though they owned a large home, it was often hard to get away from the kids long enough for them to find many opportunities for intimacy. Even with Joe all grown up and out of the house, this had still proven somewhat difficult. Autumn was a daddy's girl who, even atf fifteen, was always demanding Matt's attention. On top of that, this past year, they'd also had Paul living with them and small children also required a great deal of looking after. By the time the kids were all in bed, Matt and Naomi typically felt too exhausted from the various trials and tribulations of the day to do anything other than go to sleep. And so it was that their sex life had been lacking of late. Not for any lack of desire on either of their parts, it all had to do with a lack of opportunity and energy when there were opportunities. It was a common enough issue for married couples that still had children in the house. This, then, was the situation that they were hoping to do a little making up for this weekend.

To this end, they had booked a room with a jacuzzi. Naomi started it up and poured two glasses from the bottle of wine she had brought with her from home. It was what remained of her $200 bottle of wine. Technically, it was quite illegal for them to have transported a bottle in their car that had already been opened, but she had figured what the hell? You have to live dangerously every once in a while! Matt didn't drink very often, as he typically eschewed any substances that he felt would impair his reasoning, but on very rare occasions such as this, he made an exception. He joined her in the jacuzzi, and they relaxed as they toasted to each other. Matt loved his daughter dearly, but was it so wrong of him, he wondered, at this moment, to be looking forward to when she was out of the house in a few years so that he could have more times like this with Naomi? Then again, perhaps the fact that occasions such as this were so rare was part of what made them seem so precious?

Who was he kidding? It was strange enough not having Joe in the house anymore and it would be even stranger when Autumn was gone. He'd gotten so used to having kids in the house that it was like he no longer knew any other way of living. How weird would it be when it was just the two of them alone in that enormous house?

Naomi finished off her glass of wine sooner than Matt did and climbed out first. He lingered in the water a bit longer; the drink had hit him harder because he so rarely indulged in such pleasures. So he sat there soaking, pleasantly buzzed, as he studied the details of the ceiling in the old hotel room. At first glance it seemed quite uniform, but the more closely you looked. One could see where cracks had formed and filled in and painted over with paint that didn't quite match the rest of the ceiling. Such trivial things were far more oddly fascinating to him than they normally would be in his current state of mind.

Naomi dangled one of her shapely legs in the bathroom's doorway. The leg was covered in fishnet stockings.

"Perhaps, now that I have slipped into something more comfortable, you wouldn't mind joining me in the boudoir, kind sir?" Her voice called to him from the direction of the disembodied leg.

Matt smiled to himself, reflecting on what a truly fortunate person he was as he turned off the jets and drained the water from the jacuzzi.

"You've just made me an offer I can't refuse!"

"We Italians specialize in that." She replied.

"You said it, I didn't!" he laughed as he finished the last swig of his wine, then rose a bit unsteadily from the tub and stepped out to towel himself off.

No sooner had he finished drying himself when there was a knock at the door.

"Really? Who the fuck could that be at this time of night?" He complained, throwing on a robe as he moved in the direction of the door.

"Whoever it is, if you want some, you'd better tell them we don't want any!" Naomi answered as she posed in the bedroom's door frame and he got a nice view of the new lingerie outfit she'd put on for him.

There was another knock. Which just made Matt even more annoyed.

He peered through the spyhole in the door and was surprised to see Randy pacing back and forth in the hallway.

"It's Randy!" Matt exclaimed. "I guess I'd better see what he wants." He said reluctantly, afraid that it might be some kind of emergency. Maybe something was wrong with Paul?

"No! What are you doing? Don't you open that door!" Naomi hissed from the bedroom doorway.

Matt had already cracked the door open as she said it, just as Randy was about to knock again.

"Just tell him to go away!" Naomi whispered pleadingly.

"Matt! Sorry to disturb you so late, but I really *need* to talk to you," Randy blurted out.

"Are you sure, buddy? Now is, uh...not exactly the best of times." Matt told him, hoping he'd be able to take a hint. He was about to be disappointed.

Randy nodded forcefully. "Yeah, it's pretty important!"

Matt sighed and opened the door wider to allow Randy in. Randy rushed in right past him. Naomi, who was standing nearby, saw him enter. She quickly realized that her current attire wasn't suitable for receiving guests and swiftly backed up, shutting the bedroom door as she moved. A few seconds later, she re-emerged dressed in a robe which matched Matt's, which had been supplied by the hotel.

"What's up, pal? It looks like something's really bugging you." Matt asked as he watched Randy pacing around the room just as he had in the hallway.

"It is! I tried meditating on it, but it didn't help. Then I tried to sleep on it, but I couldn't fall asleep." Randy said, the frustration evident in his voice.

Naomi's initial irritation with Randy's arrival was starting to melt away a little now that she saw how uncharacteristically agitated he was. It was most unlike him. Typically, he was almost annoyingly calm and centered in almost any situation. Her curiosity and concern for him was getting the better of her.

"Why don't you have a seat and tell us all about it?" She asked him.

Randy ceased his pacing and looked at her, then he looked at Matt and for the first time seemed to notice how they were dressed, or barely dressed, might be a more accurate way of putting it.

"Are you sure? I'm not interrupting anything am I?"

"No, nothing at all." Matt said a bit petulantly, resigning himself to the fact that his sexy evening with Naomi was now probably thoroughly ruined. Randy sat himself down in a chair across from the sofa that Matt and Naomi were now seated on.

Randy looked as if he didn't know where to begin. He took in a deep breath and let it out.

"It's Jim. There's something strange about him and I'm not sure what to do about it, or if I even *should* do something about it. I might've done too much already."

"Jim?" Matt asked incredulously. "Don't tell me you're getting jealous or something? I thought you were pretty much over thinking of Penny in that way?"

"It's nothing like that!" Randy answered, a little too quickly, Matt thought.

Randy continued on a little more calmly. "I'll always love Penny. She's my best friend and the mother of my child, but yes, the romantic part of our relationship is over, has been for some time now and I really *am* totally okay with that."

"Uh huh," Matt said a little skeptically. He didn't really buy the idea that Randy didn't still have romantic feelings for Penny. He was fairly certain that if Penny had been accepting of the idea of having to share him with other people, they'd still be together.

"I am! I do want her to find happiness, and I really do genuinely like Jim and I respect him and admire him as a fellow artist. That's exactly why this is so difficult for me. I don't want to spoil her happiness, but at the same time, if I know something, and I do nothing, am I being a bad friend?"

"Know something about what?" Naomi inquired. She was starting to lose her patience with all of this double talk. Part of her just wanted Randy to hurry and get to the point so that she and Matt could pick back up where they had left off before they'd been interrupted. Yet, another part of her was concerned about whatever was distressing her friend enough to bring him to their door at this hour.

"There's been a lot of talk amongst the roadies about him being seen with another woman a lot in the past few days. A mysterious woman dressed in a weird, silvery outfit. Whenever anyone tries to ask him about it, he just denies that she was ever there. I found out about all of this from Kiesha. So I asked her to keep an eye on him, to see if she could find out if there was any truth to all these rumors." Randy explained.

"Aha! So that's what you two have been up to!" Matt exclaimed.

"Hmm. Yeah, I'm not sure that using your apprentice to spy on your ex-girlfriend's new boyfriend looks so good for you. Penny will be *very* pissed off that you did that if she ever finds out. I can't say that I can blame her. This *is* a pretty big invasion of her privacy and Jim's," Naomi said.

"We're Private Eyes, invading people's privacy is pretty much our thing." Matt shrugged.

"Yeah, but this is *Penny* we're talking about here, *our* Penny! She's like family! We don't investigate friends and family members without their permission, do we?" Naomi argued.

Matt had done exactly that with some people his kids had dated, but he wasn't about to tell her that. It was too late, though; his guilty look gave it all away.

"Oh god! Tell me that we don't!" She pleaded.

"Well…sometimes, maybe a little. If you have a certain skill set, it only makes sense to use it to protect the people closest to you, doesn't it?" He said in his most calm and reasonable sounding voice.

He could tell from the stony look on her face that he had failed to convince her, yet he stubbornly pressed on, only to dig his grave a little deeper.

"Look, it's like second nature to us, and there's so much information about people right out there in the open on the internet these days…it's kind of hard *not* to do it."

A highly judgmental "Hmm" was Naomi's only remark.

He knew that she'd probably want to talk about it in more detail with him later. That was a discussion that he was *not* looking forward to. He could see his romantic evening with Naomi becoming ever more distant, like a retreating reflection in a rearview mirror.

He wasn't about to give up quite that easily yet. He had to make her understand things from his perspective. Then inspiration hit him.

"Hey, it's really not that different from when you stalk people we went to high school with on Facebook. Except it's for a far nobler cause."

"I do not 'Facebook stalk' people!" She protested weakly.

Now it was Matt's turn to give her a withering look that said "oh, really?"

"Okay, so maybe I do. Just a little bit. Sometimes my curiosity gets the best of me, okay? So sue me! Nonetheless, I still want to go on the record as saying that we should all do a better job of respecting the privacy of our friends. "She said the last part a little haughtily.

"Duly noted, ma'am." Matt replied and turned to Randy. "Clerk, please make sure her remarks appear on the official record!"

Randy grinned slightly and saluted Matt.

"Don't look so happy, dude! None of this changes the fact that no matter how good your intentions might've been, Penny is totally gonna rip your head off when she finds out about this!" Naomi reminded him.

"Don't you think I don't know that? That it looks like I'm just a jealous ex trying to get some dirt on her man to break them up? But that's not why I'm doing it at all. I'm trying to protect her. And Paul. If Jim is up to no good, I need to find out now, before things get much more serious between the two of them. They've already been talking about moving in together. I need to know that this guy is on the level before I allow my son to be around him all the time. If he's no good for her, Penny needs to know now, before she gets in too deep with him and will be twice as hurt."

"Protect her from what, exactly? Do you think that this mystery woman is a threat? That Jim's cheating on Penny with her?" Matt asked.

"That's what I thought at first. I mean, you have to admit that it sounds pretty suspicious, doesn't it? He's always seen with this woman backstage and then denies it ever happened or that she even exists. Why do that unless you're trying to hide something? We've been on tour, and she's been seen backstage with him at various shows, which means she's been following us around from city to city for a while now. That's some dedication, right? It's got to mean something pretty serious is going on between the two of them, although they've never been spotted kissing or anything like that - yet."

"So there's no proof that this is a romantic relationship? So maybe there's something else going on between them, something more innocent that he wants to keep secret for some reason?" Naomi pointed out.

"That could be. I'm not so sure that I still believe that whatever is going on between them is of an intimate nature, but something tells me it isn't exactly what I'd call innocent, either."

"What makes you say that?" Matt asked.

"It's because of what Kiesha's discovered. Tonight, she finally saw him talking to the mystery woman in his dressing room. They were speaking in a foreign language, so she couldn't understand what they were talking about."

"Why didn't she do a translation spell?" Naomi wondered aloud. She knew of the existence of that spell because when she was compiling the *Magna Historia Mundi* she often had to work with texts written in forgotten languages and had to get Randy to cast this kind of spell to decipher them.

"She didn't have time. By the time she thought of it, they'd already finished their conversation. What's *really* weird is what happened next—Kiesha swears she saw the mystery woman disappear when Jim was done talking to her."

"Disappear? Like as in a teleportation spell?" Matt asked. From his past associations with various witches and wizards, he knew of this kind of spell, which was one of the most commonly used ones.

"No, this was different. If magic had been used, she would've felt it. But that's not all that's strange about it. This woman, she had no aura." Randy revealed. He almost told them about how Jim also had an unusual aura, but thought better of it. Sometimes artistic people and people who were "old souls" had peculiar auras, so there might not really be much of anything to it other than that.

"But that's impossible!" Naomi gasped. Although Matt and Naomi were not magic users, both of them had learned how to astral project many years ago, and in that state, they can see auras too. From that experience, they both knew that all living things gave off an aura. Indeed, oddly, some non-living things gave off a faint one as well as they possess a rudimentary form of spirit as well.

"It isn't as if she was some kind of recording, or transmitted image. That's the only possible explanation that I can think of," Randy said.

"That would mean that she's what? Some kind of hologram?" Matt suggested.

Randy nodded. "That's what I was thinking. Although it would have to be a *very* sophisticated kind of one. Everyone who's seen her says that it looks as if she's right there in the room with him, and looks as real as anyone else."

"So her disappearance could be explained away as simply as someone just turning off the hologram." Naomi concluded.

"Or breaking off the transmission." Matt added.

"It does make the most sense, doesn't it?" Randy agreed.

"But what doesn't make sense is how would Jim get his hands on that kind of fancy hologram tech? For that matter, where did he get Hi-Fi from? Or the money for that restaurant?" Matt said.

"He already explained where he got Hi-Fi from." Naomi reminded him.

"And you bought that story? I keep up on the current state of technologies like robotics that are usually featured in sci-fi stories because that kinda stuff interests me. Believe me, a robot that can jump around and dance as smoothly as Hi-Fi does, and that has such a sophisticated AI is almost impossible to create with our current level of technology. Something like that would probably cost millions to develop! Ditto, for some of the things he has on display in his restaurant, he has original props from TV shows and movies that are almost priceless." Matt knew how expensive some of these things were, he'd looked into acquiring some of them for his own humble collection, but in the end he couldn't justify spending so much money on something so useless.

Naomi shrugged dismissively. "His AI doesn't seem all that much more highly developed than the Siri on my phone from what I saw. And maybe those props are just copies?"

"I suppose it's possible that those are prop replicas, but the placards on them claim otherwise." Matt allowed. "But I'm telling you that robot is way too smart and interactive. It's as bad as the robot that Rocky gave to Pauly for his birthday in Rocky IV. It was way beyond the technology of the Eighties, and this is the same thing!"

"The disappearing possible hologram mystery woman thing isn't even the weirdest part." Randy continued.

"You mean there's more?" Naomi asked.

"Yeah, he talked to her again tonight..." Randy started.

"At dinner, right? When he said he had a call from his sick mother?" Matt interrupted him.

"Yes, precisely. So I had Kiesha follow him again. He's got an apartment in the back of Kirk's. She snuck in there and found him talking to that woman again. This time, she was able to do a translation spell. Unfortunately, she still had a hard time figuring out what they were saying because they were talking so low, and she was in the hallway. She did make out a few snippets of conversation, but it didn't make much sense. The woman wanted him to meet her tomorrow around noon on top of a building at this address." Randy pulled the crumpled napkin Kiesha had written on at Kirk's from a pocket.

"Ah, so that's what that was all about. I saw her give you that napkin." Matt revealed.

"Yeah, she memorized the address. Luckily, the mystery lady repeated it several times while Jim wrote it down for himself. I looked it up, it's only a few blocks from this hotel, closer to the UN building. But what's really crazy is what it sounds like she wants him to do on top of that building..."

"Make sweet love to her?" Matt asked.

Everyone looked at him. Naomi realized that Matt really *couldn't* hold his liquor.

"Hey, that would be pretty crazy, considering how cold it is outside this weekend!" he said lamely.

Randy continued without acknowledging Matt's odd outburst.

"Kiesha could barely make it out, but she heard the phrase 'flight path' and it sounded to her like the mystery lady wanted Jim to shoot something down." Randy said darkly.

"What?! This sounds like some terrorist stuff!" said a shocked Naomi. "Is she sure that's really what she heard?"

Randy shifted in his seat uncomfortably. "No, it was so difficult for her to hear that she can't be, and that's the problem. That's why I've come to you guys for advice. If what she thinks she overheard is really what they were talking about, then I can't ignore it, I've got to do something about it. But the only way I can be sure is to spy on Jim myself. I was thinking of following him to that address astrally tomorrow."

"You should definitely do it!" Matt urged.

"Should I? Like Naomi was saying earlier, I feel bad about even snooping around as much as I have already, of violating Jim's privacy like this. I haven't even tried to research anything about him online, all I've done is ask Kiesha to follow him and report back to me. I've tried to resist doing a proper investigation into him. But if I start using astral projection to follow him around...I feel like that's crossing a line."

"But we do it all the time in our investigations, what's the difference here?" Matt pressed him.

"The difference is that you're *hired* to investigate those people! Nobody is hiring Randy to investigate Jim. He's taking it upon himself to do this. While I'm not so sure that she'll think he's trying to break them up for his own purposes, since they have been broken up for a while now, I *do* think that Penny might look upon the whole thing as if he's patronizing her. You know, thinking that she can't take care of herself without needing Randy to come charging into the rescue all the time like some kind of knight in shining armor?" Naomi clarified.

"I'm so afraid of screwing up my relationship with Penny!" Randy said in a pained voice. Naomi didn't think she'd ever seen him look so vulnerable ever before.

Randy exhaled loudly. "Yet, at the same time, there is something legitimately bizarre going on here. I can't just ignore it. He's conspiring with someone to shoot something out of the sky over the city! Even if it turns out to be something far less dire, I still feel like I need to know what's going on. Is it safe for Penny and Paul to be around someone who's always sneaking off to talk to a hologram lady in a foreign language and feel the need to lie about it? What is it he's trying to hide?"

"In my book, you've already crossed the line, pal. You did the minute you asked Kiesha to tail him. In for a penny, in for a pound - no pun intended! You might as well see it through to the end. I think Penny will forgive you if he turns out to be a creep that's up to no good. God knows she's forgiven you for much worse over the years. Have you tried asking her about any of this? Has she noticed anything off about Jim herself?" Matt asked gently, only just now fully appreciating how very distressed over all of this Randy truly was.

Matt's heart went out to him. Not only did he know Randy valued his relationship with Penny in and of itself, but because he had a child to co-parent with her, and they were in a band together, it was extra important for him to maintain a strong friendship with her. Their lives were hopelessly intertwined. A nasty falling out between the two of them would completely derail his life.

"No, not that I can think of. If she has noticed anything, she might be too blinded by love to pay much attention to it," Randy said miserably.

"Matt's right." Naomi said.

"Excuse me, what did you just say?" Matt asked.

"Matt's right." Naomi repeated.

"Ah, music to my ears. Say it one more time so I can savor this rare moment!" Matt smiled. Closing his eyes in anticipation.

Naomi just shook her head and carried on.

"Maybe we're all underestimating Penny. Sure, she's got a bit of a temper, but if you find out something about Jim that she should really know, I think in the end, after she's given you the riot act about how she's a grown ass woman who's entitled to make her own decisions about her partners and make her own mistakes, she'll understand and forgive you. She'll figure out that what you did ultimately came from a good place, even if it is a little naïve of you to think that you can and should protect her from heartbreak. It's all in how you break it to her. Hopefully, this whole thing will turn out to be nothing but a big misunderstanding, in which case, you should probably just keep all of this to yourself."

"Soooo, now you're saying that I should go spy on Jim tomorrow?" Randy asked her.

"I can't believe I'm saying this, but yes. If what Kiesha heard is right, that can't be ignored. Either way, you're going to drive yourself nuts until you get to the bottom of it." Naomi told him.

Randy looked thoughtful for a moment, then turned to face Matt. "And what do you think?"

"What are your famous instincts telling you?" Matt turned the question around on him. Randy was always telling other people to trust their instincts, and he typically did a good job of practicing what he preached. Matt was wondering if part of his current turmoil came from him letting his emotions interfere with what his gut was telling him.

"That I need to find out what's going on." He said with resignation.

"Then follow through on that feeling," Matt told him.

Randy stood up. "You're right, I just wish it didn't feel so wrong at the same time that it feels like it's what I have to do. Thanks for letting me barge in here and bend your ear so late at night. I'm gonna see if I can finally get some rest."

"Goodnight. You know we're always there for you, right? No matter what, partner." Matt told him, forcing an encouraging smile.

"I do. And I appreciate it, really."

"Keep us posted on whatever you find out, Randy, and please, be careful." Naomi said and gave him a little hug as she opened the door for him. Randy could tell that she was now thoroughly intrigued by the oddness of what Randy had reported to them. She wanted answers as much as he *needed* them.

As soon as he was out the door, Matt and Naomi looked at each other with wide eyes and shook their heads.

"First those UFOs and now this! The weirdness is back again, isn't it? In full force!" Matt bemoaned. When the weirdness came back, it usually meant that he'd be spending his time in the near future both killing people and trying to avoid being killed himself. Neither was something he particularly enjoyed. Was a nice, quiet, uneventful life too much to ask for? Naomi knew how much Matt was bothered by the idea that his life was about to become hopelessly complicated and squeezed his shoulder in sympathy.

"You don't think the two things could be related, do you?" she asked thoughtfully as she sat down beside him again.

Matt blinked in confusion. "Huh? What do you mean?"

"I mean, the guy has access to a high-tech robot, possibly also an advanced hologram projector of some kind and he owns a restaurant that looks like a spaceship. You figure it out!"

"Are you trying to say that Jim is an alien?" Matt laughed.

"Sure, maybe. Or he's in contact with them. Working with them."

Matt laughed harder.

"Don't laugh!" She slapped his leg lightly. "You know it's possible! You know that aliens are real." She argued.

Just because aliens really existed, it didn't mean that they were behind this any more than they were behind building the pyramids, as far as Matt was concerned. There were plenty of other, more rational explanations that needed to be explored first before jumping to the most outlandish conclusion. Yes, their friends had just seen some UFOs earlier that very night, but it could all just be a coincidence. Correlation did *not* equal causation.

"Sure, that'll be his legal defense if he shoots down a plane or something tomorrow - the aliens made me do it!"

"Let's hope that Kiesha misheard him, or perhaps hasn't quite mastered her translation spells yet. If Adamski's Venusian Space Brothers really have returned to this reality, they're nothing to worry about. Basically, they're a bunch of Space Hippies. I can't imagine them inciting anyone to do something violent. So I don't know *what* to make of that." She confessed, a worried expression on her face.

"Yeah, well, I don't know what to make out of *any* of it. It's obvious that Jim is a big sci-fi nerd, and for whatever reason, he seems to have a lot of money to throw around. Is it really so unreasonable to assume that a guy with that much dough and those kinds of obsessions wouldn't spend it on robots and holograms that are on the cutting edge of technology? Maybe we're all just letting our imaginations run wild? What if we're making a mountain out of a molehill?"

Naomi studied her husband. She knew him too well to buy any of this. She could tell when he was trying to convince himself of something that he didn't really believe. In this instance, probably to calm his nerves over the notion that the weirdness was about to disrupt their lives far more thoroughly than Randy had just done to their evening. It was time for her to call him out on it.

"*You* were the one who kept on insisting earlier that Hi-Fi was too advanced to be a product of our science, and now you're trying to rationalize him away as just being on the "cutting edge". I think Randy isn't the only one around here who's having trouble listening to what his gut is trying to tell him. Besides, even if you're right about that, it still doesn't answer the question of who the mystery woman is and why he's keeping her a secret from everyone."

"Yeah, well, I just hope that whatever is really going on here, it doesn't end up tearing Randy and Penny apart. And if it does, I don't want to have to pick sides. I love 'em both too much for that, ya know?" Matt said sadly. She could see that the thought that this could destroy the informal family they'd formed with their longtime friends was eating at him. These people had been a constant in their lives for decades now. The possibility that one or both of them might not be around anymore like they always had been was unimaginable. It had been bad enough trying to get through the past year without them. There had been other times over the years when Penny and Randy had been feuding, but these periods never usually lasted for very long, and they rarely tried to draw Matt and Naomi into it. The fear that things might somehow be different this time had clearly been bothering Randy, and now his anxiety had spread to Matt.

"I know. Believe me, I feel the same way about them. But they've been on the outs with each other plenty of times before and they always bounce back. I believe they'll do it again. Especially now that they have Paul to think of. I wouldn't worry about it too much." She yawned and glanced at a clock on the microwave oven hanging above the oven in the kitchen attached to the room they were in. "Geez, it's really damned late! C'mon let's turn in, we've got a busy day of conventioning ahead of us tomorrow."

She got up from the sofa they'd been sharing and headed back towards the bedroom. Matt trailed behind her.

"Any chance we can pick up where we left off before we were so rudely interrupted?" He asked hopefully, one eyebrow raised.

Naomi looked at him and tilted her head slightly, a somewhat melancholy look in her eyes.

"I'm sorry, but all of this stuff with Randy and Jim and Penny...it's kind of a buzzkill. I'm just not in the mood anymore. Don't worry, hon, we've still got tomorrow." She gave him a light kiss as she turned away.

Matt thought about it for a second. If he was going to be completely honest with himself, then he had to admit that really wasn't in the mood anymore either. At this point, he was far more tired than he was horny. Such was life in your forties. "That's alright. I feel about the same way too right now." He said as he headed for the bathroom to brush his teeth.

***

The next morning, Naomi awoke to the sound of the steady clackity clack of a computer keyboard from the next room.

She threw her robe back on and followed the sound into the next room. There she found Matt typing away on his laptop.

"Couldn't sleep, huh?"

"Au contraire, mon frère! I slept like a baby...for about 5 hours, *then* I couldn't sleep." Matt said, indulging in his occasionally annoying habit of being more precise than necessary with his explanations.

She massaged his shoulders. "What're you working on? Another novel? I thought you said that you felt like you'd run out of things to say about the world after that last one?"

"I did. And I still feel that way, I'm taking a break from all of that for the foreseeable future. At least until I can find some inspiration." He told her. It was true. He'd been feeling burned out by his writing career lately, which was really just a hobby that had kind of gotten out of control.

"So what's all this, then?"

"I'm doing a little research on our new friend Jim."

"I *knew* it! Couldn't resist, could you?"

"You know me when it comes to a mystery."

She sat down next to him at the table where he was working.

"So, you finally caught the bug, huh? What've you found out? Did you prove that he's an alien yet?" She said teasingly.

"Not quite, but I'm starting to think that maybe it's not the stupidest idea I've ever heard after all."

"Gee, thanks! Why the sudden change of heart?"

Matt blew out his breath. "Where to begin? I started my research by checking out his band's official website. They have little bios for all of the Atmosphere Fishes posted on there. His bio claims that he's from someplace called "Oxnard, NJ." Does that sound familiar?"

"Never heard of it." Naomi said. They were both from Jersey, but even after a lifetime of living there, it wasn't so unusual for them to still discover towns they'd never heard of before. For such a relatively tiny state, New Jersey had an insane number of towns, villages and townships. Every few miles, it seemed like you were crossing over into another one.

"That's because it doesn't exist! There *is* a real town named Oxnard, but it's in California, not NJ." Matt revealed with a touch of pride.

"I wonder why he'd lie about something like that? It seems like such an easy thing to disprove."

"Good question. I don't know. The best I could come up with is that maybe it helps avoid those awkward situations that you run into when you meet someone new who's from the same town or area where you grew up? You know how it is, they start asking you if you know some of the same families they do, or are familiar with some places around from there? If you don't seem to be familiar with the place, they might get suspicious about you. Well, that can't ever happen if you come from a made up place. Anyhow, that's just the tip of the iceberg. It gets even weirder. I found out that he's using the social security number of someone who died over twenty years ago."

"Hold up for a sec! You got his social security number? *How* did you do that?"

She knew that Matt had gotten pretty good at researching things online in the past decade, but this still seemed like something that was beyond him. He'd never really been a big computer enthusiast, and in the past he'd depended more on Penny to do this kind of thing for him. His online research skills had improved more lately because it was something that had become a necessity for him to master if he was going to continue to stay competitive as a detective in a world where most records were now digitized. Also, with the rise of social media platforms, it was so much easier to gather a great deal of information on people quickly. He'd be a fool not to learn how to use such a thing to his advantage, and he was no fool.

Matt smiled at her mysteriously with his lopsided grin. "I have my ways, dear, I have my ways."

Not all of which are always completely legal. He thought to himself. In this case, he'd hired someone to hack the information for him. Matt didn't mind spending money on this. His cheapness was confined to himself, not the people he cared about. If getting this information would help protect Penny, it was well worth it to him. He had connections within the Guilds who probably could've gotten this information for him for free, but he didn't like owing them too many favors. He never wanted to risk becoming too dependent on them to solve his problems for him.

The hacker was a former client who he'd helped out of a tight spot a few years ago. He'd made a point of keeping in touch with her because he knew that the same computer skills that had landed her in trouble in the first place might prove useful to him someday. Getting the social security number that Jim was currently using had unlocked boatloads of information on him that would normally be closed off to Matt. Information that had only served to deepen the mystery of who Jim might really be. He couldn't wait to share it with Naomi.

"Using a dead person's social is a common form of identity theft." He informed her. "Anyhow, his finances are *very* interesting. Most of his money is stashed in offshore accounts and as far as I can tell, there are boatloads of it. The guy is just shy of being a billionaire. His band hardly makes any money; in fact it's kind of a money pit. The restaurant really does do pretty good business though, but not enough to make him as rich as he is of course. If he's working for aliens, they're paying him well!"

Naomi buried her head in her hands and remained like that for a few moments, trying to digest all this new data before she looked up again and spoke. "So basically, we know nothing about who Jim really is. We don't know where he really grew up, or even what his real name is. And it's safe to assume that poor Penny isn't aware of any of this. Consorting with holographic ladies seems to be the least of his sins. He said something at dinner about going to school at MSU. Did you find anything to back that up?"

"Nope, they have no record of him ever attending classes there. In fact, there's no actual record of him I can find on the internet to indicate that he's ever actually been anywhere or done anything prior to ten years ago. That's why I said that the idea that he's from outer space might not be so silly after all. He might as well have dropped out of the sky for all the evidence that I can find of his past prior to a certain date."

"A fake identity and a fortune stashed in secret bank accounts. It sure sounds like he's mixed up in something sketchy. But if you're trying to hide your past, why do something as high profile as being the front man of a rock band? That seems pretty idiotic," Naomi said.

"Agreed. Unless he's employing the old 'hiding in plain sight' trick."

"I wasn't kidding when I said he looked familiar last night. I could've sworn he was in one of my classes, back when I worked at Rutgers."

"Well, that was over ten years ago now. So if you're right about that, it would be proof of him being around from earlier than anything I've been able to churn up. Remember how defensive he got when you mentioned that? He shut down that conversation pretty quickly. Then he just kept on staring at you the rest of the night. I thought I might have to deck him!"

"It's so cute when you get jealous." Naomi laughed. "You noticed that too, huh?"

"Pretty hard not to! He was really brazen about it, doing it right in front of Penny."

"I didn't get the feeling that he was checking me out in quite *that* kind of way." Naomi thought about the odd look in Jim's eye from last night. Where had she seen that look before? Then she recalled her mother dragging her to church after her father's death. She'd seen that same look on the faces of some of the churchgoers, the ones who were the real true believers amongst the congregation.

"He was looking at me with...reverence."

"Oh, well, I can totally understand that." Matt smiled at her.

"Keep saying sweet stuff like that about me and there might just be some more lingerie in your future tonight. Hopefully without any further interruptions from Randy this time!"

The mention of this name reminded Matt that he needed to call him. "I wonder if Randy is up yet? I should probably share what I've uncovered with him."

"I'm sure he is. It's shocking how few hours of sleep that guy functions on." Naomi remarked. Indeed, it was true, Randy was infamous for pulling all-nighters reading books or playing video games. Even when he appeared to be sleeping, he often wasn't, but rather was in a kind of trance and was off doing things in his astral body.

"Truth!" Matt agreed, as he reached for his phone to dial Randy's number.

CHAPTER 6:
THEY WALK AMONG US

Randy hung up his phone and put it back in his pocket after he thanked Matt for getting the information on Jim that, up until now, he'd been afraid to gather himself. The information Matt had just given him on Jim had helped to reaffirm his constantly wavering faith in the idea that he was right to investigate Jim.

He tried to make sense of what Matt had told him as he sipped from a mug of herbal tea and stared absently out the window of the *Blunderbus Mark II*, which was currently parked at one end of a large retail store parking lot. The *Blunderbus Mark II* was his home, not just when the band was on tour, but in general. When it wasn't being used for a tour, he usually had it parked on some land he'd purchased a few miles from Matt and Naomi's house, just out of range of the magic spell cancelling effects of the Orb of Sinister which they guarded.

He split his custody of Paul with Penny through an informal, friendly, non legally binding agreement. Typically, he had Paul on the weekends, and Penny had him during the week at her house in New Brunswick. In reality, though, he usually saw Paul almost every day since his life and Penny's were so interconnected. They both worked at Matt's detective agency, in addition to that, he was often over her house to help compose new music and work on other business related to the Mystery Smiths. This weekend, since they were all in the city, Penny had taken Paul to go spend some time with her parents who lived in Manhattan. Later on, at some point tomorrow, they'd all return to NJ together in the Blunderbus. Randy was glad that his son had a relationship with at least one set of his grandparents. He didn't foresee the boy ever having one with his own parents, from whom he was estranged, although if Paul ever decided he wanted to get to know them, he wouldn't stand in his way.

"Speak of the devil!" Randy exclaimed as he spied an older looking woman working her way across the asphalt wasteland of the parking lot making a beeline for the *Blunderbus Mark II*.

He knew she wasn't really quite as old as she appeared to be. Her prematurely haggard appearance was mostly due to the terrible things she'd done to her body over the years. He thought he'd seen her in the audience during the concert last night, but he hadn't been certain. After all it had been many, many years since he'd last seen her. It was part of the reason he'd been so agitated last night and unable to sleep. It wasn't just the situation with Penny and Jim that had been weighing so heavily on him lately. He hadn't wanted to share this part of his angst with Matt and Naomi. It was too private to be shared with anyone, even them. How ironic was it she should show up now, just as he was thinking about Paul spending time with his grandparents? His life seemed to be hopelessly riddled with such synchronicities. Such was the way of things once you embraced the path of being a magic user.

He decided he couldn't just stand around her pontificating; he had to get rid of her. Send her packing in such a way that hopefully she'd never dare to trouble him again. He set his tea down on a nearby table and set off towards the entrance to the RV with a heavy, determined stride.

Suddenly, there was a nervous knock from the door.

"I've got it, Sensei!" Kiesha, who was also still living in the RV, announced. She'd been sitting in front of the fireplace reading a book when the knocking had started.

"No! Don't let her in!" Randy shouted as he emerged from the corridor and entered the room.

But it was too late, Kiesha had already cracked the door open to reveal an anxious looking woman who was bundled up against the cruel winds of February in a knit cap, long dark coat and a colorful scarf and matching mittens. The woman caught sight of Randy as he stepped up beside his apprentice, his face twisted into a disapproving grimace.

"Randy! Please, let me in. I just want to tell you that I saw your concert last night, and I wanted to let you know how proud I am of you, and to apologize." The woman pleaded desperately.

"No amount of apologies will ever make up for what you've done! How did you find me here? Did Bernice tell you? One of my brothers?" Randy bellowed back at her. All of them had been pressuring him to talk to this woman lately, but he wasn't having any of it.

"No, my sister doesn't know anything about this. Please don't be upset with her. Your brothers had nothing to do with it, either. If you must know, I hired a private eye to find you!"

"You what?" Randy laughed bitterly at the incredible irony of that. Synchronicities piled upon synchronicities! He prodded himself on being able to tell when someone was tailing him, but he'd been so preoccupied with this business with Penny and Jim that he figured his mind just hadn't been in the game.

"Please, can we just talk? For a little while?" The woman begged him.

"No. It's too late for us," Randy said gravely. He began muttering strange words and gesticulating with his hands. Kiesha's eyes widened as she realized what he was doing and she looked at him questioningly.

The woman who had been standing on the steps to the *Blunderbus Mark II* disappeared completely.

"Whoa! Where did you send that lady?" Kiesha asked. She couldn't believe that he'd just done a spell like that in public. It was an unusually reckless thing for him to do. It was exactly the kind of thing that he would've yelled at her for doing.

"Someplace appropriate for someone like her." Randy told her there was a certain finality in his tone.

The woman re-materialized atop a stinking, filthy pile of trash. She blinked in disbelief as she looked around her. How did she wind up here? Was she losing her mind? She looked around in astonishment, trying to get her bearings. She appeared to be on a garage scow in the middle of the East River. She had no way of knowing that Randy had walked past this same boat last night on his way to see Matt and Naomi. It had still been tethered to a pier then.

She did not know how she had ended up here, or how she was going to get off of this boat. She sank down and began bawling.

Maybe this is where I belong after all? For all the things I've done...and didn't do. She thought sadly.

"Who was that lady, Sensei?" Kiesha asked Randy as she closed the door.

"The woman who gave birth to me," Randy answered.

"Hold up! You mean that was your mom?" She couldn't believe it. Randy never talked about his parents -ever. And she had never expected to see either of them. It was a sore spot and something that you just didn't bring up in conversation with him if you knew what was best for you. She wondered where he'd sent her off to.

"No, like I said, she was just the woman who gave birth to me. A mother actually cares for her child. That woman is no mother." He hissed.

The obvious anger and pain in his voice shocked Kiesha. It was a side of her normally maddeningly calm and Zen-like sensei she'd never seen before. She definitely preferred the calm, cool version of Randy to this unfamiliar, dark-side iteration.

Randy took a deep breath and seemed to realize that he might've scared Kiesha. She was looking at him in a way he'd never seen her look at him before, and he didn't like it. In fact, it kind of broke his heart a little. The last thing he ever wanted was for her to fear him.

"I'm sorry you had to see all of that. Don't worry about that woman. She's quite safe. I didn't hurt her. I wouldn't do that, even if she deserves it."

He took another deep breath and put on a wide smile. The sudden change in his demeanor, as if nothing had just happened, was more frightening to Kiesha than his manner was from a few moments earlier.

"Are you doing anything later on today? Around two?" He asked lightly, in the same casual tone that someone would employ when making small talk at work.

"No. Why? Are you going to go see what Jim is up to?"

"Precisely! And I could use a little company when I do, if you don't mind?"

She shrugged. "You're the boss, boss. Besides, I'd like to know what's really going on too."

And I might have to keep you out of trouble, with the crazy way you've been acting lately! She thought.

As two o'clock approached, Randy and Kiesha sat cross-legged across from each other on large cushions that were sitting on the floor in Randy's bedroom. They both went into the trance that allowed them to astral project with practiced ease. In their astral bodies they were like living ghosts, tethered to their physical bodies only by a slender, golden umbilicus. Randy paused for a moment to glance at a paper print out from Google Maps of the location of the address that Jim was supposed to be going to relative to the position of the parking lot where the *Blunderbus Mark II* was currently parked. Even though he'd grown up in the city, he wasn't all too familiar with this area, having grown up in Brooklyn. Having committed the path to the building to memory, he nodded to Kiesha, who hovered patiently beside her body and they both rose through the ceiling of the RV and out into the cold winter air, which thankfully, neither he of them could actually feel in their present state. Soon they were flying high above the skyscrapers of Manhattan. Randy, still in the same cross-legged position his physical body was in, while Kiesha was flying in a pose like Superman, one arm thrust forwards the hand balled up into a fist.

No matter how often she did this (which was quite often, her first lessons in magic all coming astrally before she could move halfway across the country to be close enough for in person instruction) she never got used to it. Kiesha reveled in the heady freedom of flight, of being free from the weight of her physicality. It was almost enough to make her forget for a moment about her concern for Randy and the erratic way in which he'd been behaving lately. She just hoped that whatever they were about to discover regarding Jim wouldn't make it any worse.

Kiesha had never imagined her life would be like this. She'd been a huge fan of the Mystery Smiths, having grown up on their music. She also always had a strong interest in the occult, having lived in a haunted house as a child. When she got the crazy idea that there were secret instructions to perform a magical ritual embedded in the lyrics of one of their albums, she went ahead and performed the ritual on a lark, never expecting it to yield actual results.

The next thing she knew, she was trapped in some sort of strange, psychedelic alternative dimension, which was frankly, kind of terrifying until Randy showed up to save her from it. Now here she was, working for the band she'd idolized and learning how to do amazing things that she never would've even dreamed possible directly from one of the most important members of the band. However, truth be told, Randy had never been her favorite member of the Mystery Smiths, that honor belongs to Penny, who she'd looked up to as a kind of role model. She loved to tease Randy about the fact that he hadn't been her favorite before they met, although of course they had quite a strong mentor/student relationship nowadays.

To be honest, while the occult and paranormal had always intrigued her, and she reveled in her new abilities, a great deal of her motivation in seeking to become a magic user was purely mercenary.

Once she was no longer an apprentice and was a full member of the Temple of the Old Gods, she would be paid a generous monthly stipend. She'd seen the good Randy had done for his family with this money, and she hoped to do the same for her own. Her mother had worked several jobs at once to raise her and her siblings, and she hoped to repay her for it. The first thing she'd do was buy her a nice new house in a better neighborhood. It was dreams like that that kept her so motivated to master Randy's lessons.

"That's it down there." Randy told her as he began lowering himself towards the rooftop, Kiesha followed his lead.

She looked around herself at the vacant rooftop. They were alone up there, aside from a few pigeons. "Looks like we're early." She observed.

"Or he's late. Are you sure you heard that address correctly?"

"I told you, she repeated it to him a few times while he wrote it down. It's about the only thing she said to him that I am sure I got right."

They waited a few minutes in silence until they both saw the doorknob on the door to the roof begin to glow, as if it was red hot.

"Look at that!" Kiesha exclaimed.

A second later, the smoking doorknob clattered to the ground, and the door was thrown open. The pigeons on the rooftop all took flight at the sudden noise. Jim stepped out onto the roof, carrying a large guitar case in one hand. He was quickly stuffing something back into a jacket pocket with the other. He paused for a moment, cautiously checking his surroundings before stepping further out and closing the door behind him.

He moved to one corner of the rooftop and pulled a small, oval device from his pants pocket, pressed down on it and tossed it into the air. It hovered there for a second before the form of an extremely tall woman dressed in a tight fitting silvery outfit with a regal green cape formed over it. She wore a strange skullcap which made the top of her head seem somewhat elongated. It was topped by an ornate kind of antenna. A few stray fronds of jet black hair poked out of the head covering.

As soon as she saw Jim, she addressed him in that strange, sing-song language unlike anything Randy had ever heard before, and Jim spoke back to her.

"That's the same lady I saw yesterday." Kiesha confirmed.

"Aha! I knew it! So she *is* a hologram!" Randy said excitedly, then he made a disapproving face. "That cape is a bit much, though."

"That whole ensemble is a bit much!" Kiesha laughed, happy to see that her mentor seemed to be back to his usual jovial self —at least for the moment. "Also, that's the same exact thing she was wearing yesterday. Does she have just the one outfit, or a closet full of identical clothes?"

"Hmm. We'll have to ask her if I ever get a chance to talk to her. That reminds me, it's time to decipher all that gibberish they're saying. We could be missing something important."

Randy closed his eyes and chanted the words to a language translation spell. It was difficult to cast because of the building's proximity to the hotel where Matt and Naomi were currently holding the Orb of Sinister. Ordinarily, it would be impossible to cast a spell this close to the Orb, however Randy and Kiesha were currently occupying a different layer of reality that sat above our own like a window. Long ago, Randy had worked out that he could still perform a few basic spells like this one when he was within range of the Orb's effects while he was in this dimension. However, doing so required a great deal more concentration and focus than it normally would, as some of the vast power of the Orb bled through even into this layer of reality.

As soon as the spell was completed, he and Kiesha could hear English words in place of the bird song like words that had been filling the air earlier.

"Hurry!" the mystery woman with the questionable fashion sense urged Jim. "The ships will be here soon! We might never get another opportunity like this. If you can destroy Drogalla's command ship, it'll throw their entire plans for the invasion into chaos."

Jim snapped open his guitar case and pulled out a long, tubular object that reminded Randy of some sort of futuristic bazooka. He set it down on the ground and pulled out another object from the case, which proved to be a tripod. He swiftly connected the "bazooka" to the tripod and adjusted the height of it so that it came up to his waist by the time he was done fiddling with it.

"I know, I know. Don't worry, I'm as determined as you are to protect the people of this planet from this attack. Stop worrying so much, I've got this."

"Holy crap, Sensei! They're talking about an alien invasion, aren't they?" An astonished Kiesha asked.

Randy stroked his astral beard thoughtfully. "It sure sounds like it!"

"I would feel *much* more confident about our chances of success if you had agreed to use your ship for this attack, as I had originally suggested! From what you've told me, your ship far outclasses anything that they have. With the weapons systems you're carrying aboard it, you could probably take out the entire escort squadron too before they ever knew what hit them." The strange woman argued.

"No way! I've already told you a million times, I'm not using my ship. It's bad enough that I'm doing this. Do you know how many regulations I'm violating here? If I ever get caught, I'll be in big trouble with my own people. I'm supposed to be sworn to only observe the people of this world, not interfere in their development like this."

"You would leave them to their fate, like all the others? To be ground beneath the heel of their conquerors? Even your precious Penny?" she asked scornfully.

"Of course not! I'm here now, aren't I? I'm trying my best to stop all of this, but I'm also trying not to get caught in the process. By the invaders or my own people!" Jim shot back in annoyance.

"Omigod! My people? Is Jim an alien too?" Kiesha whispered to Randy, who had wandered over to the weapon and was checking it out curiously.

"Wait! Why am I whispering they can't hear us!" Kiesha said as she chuckled a little self-consciously.

"They way he's talking, it seems like he is." Randy said absently, still studying the weapon. He was surprised that he wasn't more surprised by this revelation, but it certainly answered a lot of questions. He knew from what Matt had told him this morning that this had been Naomi's theory. She'd certainly be pleased to know she was, as usual, right. Although he didn't wager, she'd be too happy to learn that the whole planet was about to be invaded. But by who? Why? It didn't make any sense! It flew in the face of everything he'd ever been taught about aliens. More importantly, what, if anything, was he going to do about it? What *could* he possibly do about it?

"You might have to accept that there may come a time when you cannot continue to have it both ways. Not if you are truly committed to keeping this world safe." The mystery woman told Jim gravely.

Jim attached a scope to the weapon on the tripod, and peered down into it.

"I don't see anything yet. What direction are they supposed to be approaching from again?" He asked.

The woman rattled off a series of coordinates to Jim which, even with the magic of the translation spell, sounded like so much nonsensical technobabble to Randy and Kiesha. Jim made some adjustments to the scope and looked into it once more.

"Ah! There, I think I can just see them coming in over the ocean. I don't have a lock on them yet. They're still too far away." He told her.

"Truly, your technology is amazing! To be able to even spot them from so far away while they're still shrouded. I was right to contact you. With such wonderful weapons on our side, we might just have a chance!" The strange woman said with an almost fanatical gleam of enthusiasm in her eyes, which Randy noted were remarkably cat-like.

"I don't see anything." Kiesha complained. "So I guess they're supposed to be shooting down a spaceship that belongs to someone called Dragula?" She speculated, trying to make sense of the conversation they'd overheard.

"It sounded more like 'Drogalla' to me. 'Dragula' is a Rob Zombie song." Randy corrected her.

"Oh." Kiesha said, still straining to look up for any sign of a ship.

"That lady did say it was 'shrouded'. I take that to mean that they're using some kind of cloaking device. However, that shouldn't matter to us. Once they get closer, we'll probably be able to see them. In these astral forms, we can see all kinds of energies that aren't visible to the naked eye." Randy told her.

"C'mon, just a little closer..." Jim said as he continued to look through the weapon's sights.

"Hey, Sensei! I think I can see something now." Kiesha said, pointing skyward.

Randy looked to where she pointed and he could see a few fuzzy halos of energy far in the distance. He guessed it was the power given off by the approaching ships.

"I've got them now!" Jim grinned as he tightened his finger around the trigger of his strange weapon.

Inside the shining silvery interior of the lead spaceship, an alarmed crew member noticed a flashing indicator on their control panel.

"Leader! Something down there has locked weapons on us!"

"What? Impossible! The humans don't have anything capable of such a thing! Unless... the Baandergi are behind this? Evasive maneuvers - NOW!" The Leader shouted.

The ship swiftly tilted to one side and dove sharply, the other ships escorting it following suit. They all just managed to avoid a sizzling blast of energy from below.

"Damn! Missed 'em!" Jim swore as he adjusted the angle of his weapon and looked down the sight again.

"I've got a target on the source of the attack! Returning fire now!" The same crewmate that had first detected the attack declared excitedly.

"No! You'll jeopardize the entire mission!" The Leader commanded, but it was too late. An invisible beam of energy danced forth from the underside of the equally invisible flying saucer and lanced towards the city below...

Randy and Kiesha saw it first. An elongated bolt of energy appeared, slamming into the top of the building next to the one that they were standing on. Blowing away the topmost floors and causing one side of the building to crumble away as debris rained down onto the street below.

"They're firing back! We must get out of here *now!*" The mystery woman next to Jim screamed.

"Oh really? Ya think!"

Jim fired off one more shot, which also missed before he pulled the weapon off the tripod and hoisted it up onto his shoulder. He reached into the image of the mystery woman and grabbed the hovering holographic projector, turning it off and slipping it into a jacket pocket.

Randy and Kiesha saw another blast of energy from the lead ship heading straight for them.

"Look out!" Kiesha shouted, completely out of instinct, forgetting that only Randy could hear her.

Jim ran to the edge of the rooftop just as it began to disintegrate beneath his feet and jumped off into the air.

All around Randy and Kiesha, the rooftop fractured and burned away. They could barely see one another through all the dust and smoke. They both flew upwards, away from the destruction. Once clear of the dust cloud, they could see Jim landing on the ground below, unharmed.

That jump would've killed any normal human being, good thing for Jim he's some kind of an alien! Randy noted as he lowered himself down towards the alleyway that Jim was in. Kiesha trailed after him.

They watched as Jim blasted away a manhole cover with his weapon, then slipped down the hole. Randy looked over at her and shrugged.

"Shall we?"

"I'm just glad we won't be able to smell what it's like down there!" Kiesha commented as she sank right through the ground, not bothering to go through the same hole that Jim had just disappeared down. Randy, for once, followed her lead.

They both found themselves in some kind of service tunnel beneath the street rather than an actual sewer. Jim was leaning against a wall. He removed the hologram projector from his pocket and tossed it up into the air. The mystery woman reappeared; she glared at him hopelessly.

"We've failed!" She complained.

"Have we really, Kergaali? We at least goaded them into showing their hostile intentions." Jim suggested, trying to turn lemons into lemonade.

"No, we've failed. They were invisible, and so was the discharge of their weapons. The humans won't be able to connect these events to them."

Jim opened his mouth as if he was about to argue the point, then his eyes widened and he ran down the tunnel as fast as his legs would carry him. The mystery woman followed after him.

Randy and Kiesha looked up to see what had prompted such a reaction and saw that the street above them was beginning to collapse, sizable chunks of it breaking off and plummeting down. One of the pieces passed right through Kiesha, who flinched out of habit.

"Let's catch up with them!" Randy told her as he zoomed down the tunnel until he was hovering right behind the running forms. Jim and the mystery woman ran down a branching side tunnel, the path of destruction following right along behind them.

"How are they tracking me?" Jim wondered plaintively

"Your weapon! It must be the power signature from your weapon! Turn it off, quickly!!" The mystery lady told him urgently.

"Oh, duh! Of course! I'm a fool for not seeing it earlier!" Jim said as he thumbed the switch on the weapon.

Immediately, the destruction happening over their heads came to a screeching halt. Randy and Kiesha looked at each other.

"Well, that seems to have done the trick!" Randy observed, glancing over his shoulder at the collapsed tunnel behind them.

Inside the main saucer, the trigger-happy crewmate frowned. "I've lost my lock on them!"

The Leader stalked forward and flung the crewmate's seat around so they were facing each other.

"Cosfreele! Why didn't you obey my command and continue to fire? Get up! You're relieved of duty!" The Leader's eyes flashed angrily.

"But Leader! They had to be neutralized! They were threatening this ship..." Cosfreele stammered.

"No excuses! Get out of my sight before I forget myself and do something we'll both regret. Return to your quarters or I'll have you confined to the brig!"

Cosfreele gulped and rose from the station, head hung low in shame.

"Get me someone to take over this station!" The Leader barked to the room as Cosfreele exited the bridge.

On the view screen, they could all see the carnage below. A building gone, the one next to it partially destroyed. The alleyway between the buildings and part of the street was a smoldering crater.

If the humans figure out that we were behind all this destruction, they'll never believe that our intentions are peaceful. The Leader thought gloomily.

The other members of the bridge crew looked to the Leader expectantly.

"Leader Drogalla, the other ships in the squadron are hailing us. They're wondering if we should proceed to the United Nations building as planned." The Communications Officer announced.

Drogalla sighed. "No, order them back to the forward base for now. We'll try again later. I want one ship to remain behind. Tell them to beam down a security team to scan for Baandergi agents in this area. If they find them, they should deal with them *discreetly*. I don't want anymore fiascos like this."

"Deal with them, Leader? What does that mean, exactly?" The confused Communications Officer asked.

"Capture them if possible. If not, they are authorized to kill them. So long as it is done without attracting undue attention from these Earthlings, I don't particularly care." Drogalla clarified.

"Kill them? But Leader! What about the law? We do *not* kill our own people! If we kill any of the Baandergi wouldn't it be seen as an act of war?" Another crewmate asked in astonishment.

"Don't you quote the law at me! We are forbidden to kill our own, yet we are all committed to the idea of facilitating others to do it for us? What's the difference? It's a mere technicality! Yes, it could be seen as an act of war—but only if they can prove that we're behind it. That's why I'm asking for discretion. Besides, we've deluded ourselves. We're already at war with the Baandergi, albeit a cold war. If it heats up now, that's not our fault, is it? Just remember who started shooting first!"

"I thought the entire point of this mission was to save our people without compromising *who* we are. This latest course of action makes me feel uneasy." Drogalla's second in command, Goymaalt said. Drogalla laid a reassuring hand on Goymaalt's shoulder.

"I know, I'm not happy about it either. But perhaps we were naïve to ever think that we could go to war and *not* be changed by it? Such is the burden I have accepted to carry for our people. Don't worry yourself. I shall make sure that we never forget that we are the Children of Pfoff and conduct ourselves accordingly."

Noble words, but what will it mean to be the Children of Pfoff when this is finally over? Goymaalt thought doubtfully.

"We might have other problems, too. Cosfreele's actions were rash, yet they might have saved us all. How did the ones who fired on us know we would be flying this way today, at this time?" Drogalla asked.

"Do you mean..." Goymaalt started.

"Yes, there are probably spies within our ranks. From now on, we must be very careful what information we share with our subordinates."

Down in the tunnels, the mystery woman held up a hand to her ear for a moment, then lowered it and looked at Jim.

"I've just received word from one of my accomplices amongst the Saawgauth. It appears that this incident has caused them to temporarily alter their plans. They're leaving for now, but they might be back later on today, once they've swept the area to make sure it's secure from future attacks by our agents. I suggest that you get out of here as quickly as possible. The ground team's scans might pick up the non-human tech in this transmitter, so long as you keep it active. Get back to your ship and I'll be back in touch as soon as I can." She told him in a no nonsense, somewhat imperious way, as if she was not used to having to debate her decisions with anyone.

"What'll we do when they try again? If I can't even turn on my weapons without them immediately detecting them and firing on their source? It sounds like we're pretty screwed here!"

"You'll be, 'screwed' as you so colorfully put it if you continue to speak with me for much longer while they have people out scanning the area for anything unusual! You might have to finally accept that we have to make use of your ship. With the advanced shrouding technology built into it, we could destroy them before they knew what hit them."

"I think you overestimate the capabilities of my ship." Jim griped, but even as he said it, he knew he was making a weak argument.

"Am I? Our scans have failed to detect it so far."

"Yeah, but you knew that there were other Galactic Federation ships active on Earth, or you wouldn't have bothered to send out that message asking for our help."

The woman laughed for the first time that Randy and Kiesha had ever heard. Somehow, it seemed a little unnatural and forced coming from her.

"Oh please! Even the humans know that there are Federation ships here, although most of them don't know that's what they're called. Honestly, some of your colleagues don't do a very good job of hiding their presence here. All those UFO reports that the human authorities are so intent on ignoring!"

"True, too many of my fellow researchers have a bit too much fun messing with the humans' minds. Alright, I'll *think* about using my ship. We'll talk about it later, you know how to reach me. Be careful."

"And *you* should be careful heading back to the surface. They already have people on the ground searching for you."

With that, Jim shoved his hand into the midsection of the woman and deactivated the hovering holographic emitter, replacing it in his pocket.

"I'll never get used to that! It always looks like he puts his hand right through her!" Kiesha said.

"Yeah, I know! Freaky isn't it?" Randy agreed as he watched Jim wander off down the tunnel, hunting for a manhole to the surface.

"What'll we do now, Sensei? If aliens are about to attack the Earth, we've gotta tell someone!" Kiesha said gravely.

"Yes, I've been thinking about that, too. The Guilds are the only ones who would take any of this seriously, and they're also the only ones who can probably really do much to stop them. I'd like to know a little bit more about what's going on here before I take this to the Inner Council, though. I'm going to confront Jim, tell him what I know, and see if I can get him to give us more details about these new enemies." Randy said as he began to float up out of the tunnel and back to the street level. Kiesha followed up after him.

As they flew up into the sky, they could see the extent of the damage caused by the alien ship.

Kiesha whistled through her teeth. "Whew! They really did a number on this part of town, didn't they? Do you think they killed many people?"

Randy looked around. He didn't see any ghosts around. Well, no more ghosts than usual, that is. "I hope not. Fortunately, it looks like these were mostly office buildings that were closed for the weekend. If this had happened on a weekday..."

She caught his meaning and gulped. "Do you really think we can beat them? With just one ship, they did all of this." She gestured towards the devastation surrounding them as emergency services began arriving on the scene with their discordant chorus of blaring sirens and flashing lights.

"We don't have much choice, do we? We have to succeed. We took on a Titan once and managed to win. Don't lose hope, we'll find a way. We always do." He frowned suddenly as he thought of something.

"Honestly, it might be a little selfish on my part, but right now I'm a bit more worried about how I'm going to break all of this to Penny!"

"Oh shit! I totally forgot about that! What *are* you gonna tell her, Sensei?"

"I have no idea at all! How do you tell your best friend and baby momma that her new boyfriend is an alien? I'm still not sure that any good can come of it. If she's happy, why does it matter? It sounds like part of why he's trying to stop the invasion is for her, so that proves that he sincerely cares for her. I was only worried about the idea that he didn't, or was mixed up in something bad. Human or not, he seems to be a decent guy - someone who's trying to save us all. What right do I have to do anything that might spoil their happiness?"

"It sounds like you're trying to weasel your way out of it. Personally, I know that if I'd sure want to know if I was dating an alien!" She told him.

"I don't know. I need to talk to Naomi and Matt and bring them up to speed on things. They usually know what's best." With that, he flew off back toward the *Blunderbus Mark II*. Kiesha cast one more worried glance down at the minor cataclysm below her before she followed him, praying that it wasn't a harbinger of things to come.

***

Matt and Naomi were attending one of the last panels of the convention, which was winding down. It being a Sunday, there were only a few events scheduled before the official close of the convention. They were both seated near the back of the conference room where the panel was taking place. Neither one of them was really paying much attention to the speakers at this panel. Naomi, not being a detective, had quickly grown bored with the subject of the panel and taken to scrolling on her phone. Matt, on the other

103

hand, had met up with Kevin and they both sat next to each other while Matt pressed him about how the night had ended with Allison after they all left Kirk's.

"I can't believe that you didn't try to put the moves on her! I'm telling you, kid, she's still got feelings for you. It's obvious." Matt whispered to him.

"Put the moves on her?" Kevin said incredulously in a low voice. "What does that even mean? Was I supposed to just grab her and kiss her or something like they do in the old movies? C'mon! This is the 21st Century! I respected her boundaries. That's what you're *supposed* to do. Besides, she's already got a boyfriend, remember? The one who can afford to take her out to nice, expensive restaurants?"

"She was just trying to make you jealous by telling you about him, can't you see that? If you ask me, she's just playing hard to get. Some women are like that, they like a little drama, they want you to have to fight for them—and Allison is nothing if not dramatic!" Matt whispered back.

Kevin shook his head. He usually respected Matt's opinions, but in this case, he felt like his romantic advice was as dated and cliched as the way he dressed. "I don't regret how the evening ended. I can't deny that I still dream about maybe being with her someday, but I also accept the fact that may never happen. Either way, I still really enjoy just being with her, okay? We had a nice time together last night as friends and that's good enough for me. I just enjoy having her around in my life - in any capacity."

"Yeah, keep on telling yourself that, kid," Matt said, obviously unconvinced, as he crossed his arms over his chest. Matt understood the value of a good platonic relationship with a member of the opposite sex, but his skepticism in this instance came from the idea that in this case he didn't think such a state of affairs would ever really satisfy Kevin because his feelings for Allison were so intense.

Naomi had been so engrossed in her phone that she hadn't really heard any of this conversation, otherwise, she would've definitely had a few things to say on the matter. She doubted that at Kevin's age, Matt would've followed the advice he'd just given him, at least based on how he and she had interacted when their relationship was platonic. She broke from her glazed eyed screen scrolling long enough to whisper a "Wow!" In response to something she just saw on her phone.

"What is it?" Matt asked her.

"There was a big explosion today, only a few blocks away from here!" She told him.

"That's terrible! Were any people killed? It's not terrorists, is it?" Matt asked, a slight edge to his voice. He recalled all too well the 9-11 attacks and the effect it had on the city and the countryl. He couldn't stand the misguided wars and wave of Islamophobia it had launched. Matt long feared another terrorist attack on that scale and how the nation might react to such an event, how it might further erode our commitment to our stated values as a people.

"No, they think an old Con-Ed gas line might've exploded. It sounds like they're unsure about the number of casualties. They're still busy sifting through the rubble, this just happened only maybe a half hour ago." She informed them, then her face suddenly creased with worry. "I'd better text the kids to make sure they're okay."

Matt didn't see why Joe and Autumn would've been in the area, but he understood the need to make sure. If she didn't check, the worry would constantly eat away at her.

After a few tense seconds, she grinned with relief as she got her answer. "Oh, thank goodness! They haven't even left Joe's apartment yet today."

"I wonder why we didn't hear the explosion?" Kevin wondered, having overheard all of this.

"We must not have been close enough." Naomi offered.

Matt's phone started ringing. Some of the other people in the room looked at him in annoyance for forgetting to put it on "silent". He mumbled some apologies as he fished it out. Naomi hated this particular ringtone, because it was one of those melodramatic musical flourishes that made it sound like something magical had just happened. Whenever she heard it she expected to see that big pink bubble that Glinda the Good Witch from the *Wizard of Oz* likes to tool around in descending from the sky, only to be perpetually disappointed that it's something as run of the mill and nonmagical to the 21rst century mind as a text message— and not even one form Glenda at that! Matt studied the screen.

"Randy just texted me. He found out some things. He wants to meet us up in our room to go over it with us," Matt told Naomi. *It might not be a text from a witch, but at least this time it's from a wizard.* Naomi smiled to herself.

"Found out what things?" Kevin asked.

"Don't worry about it. It doesn't concern you." Matt said a little coldly.

"When does he want to meet up?" Naomi wanted to know.

"ASAP. He's already on his way over."

"Sounds good to me, this panel is boring as shit. Let's get outta here." Naomi started to get up.

Matt followed suit. He patted Kevin on the shoulder as he got up. "Enjoy the rest of this boring as shit panel. I'll see you next Wednesday at the office if we don't run into each other again today." Matt and Naomi were planning on spending one more day in the city tomorrow so they could hang out with Joe and show Autumn some sights of the city. Then Matt planned to spend Tuesday relaxing at home before returning to work.

"See ya later, you guys." Kevin smiled as they left the conference room. Naomi gave him a little wave on her way out.

As they walked towards the elevators, Matt noticed a group of about four of five extremely tall women exiting the elevator. They stood out not only because of their height, but the fact that they were all wearing sunglasses indoors, poorly fitting baseball caps and clothes that were generally mismatched or somehow inappropriate. For example, one of them was wearing "Daisy Duke" style shorts when it was still quite snowy outside.

Naomi saw them too. "Wow, their momma sure dresses them weird!" She commented conspiratorially as she leaned in towards Matt.

"You hang around long enough in this city and you get to see all sorts!" he replied as he stepped into the now empty elevator.

As soon as they were back up in their room, Matt turned on the TV and switched it over to the local news. Not surprisingly, there was lots of live coverage of the carnage.

"Will ya look at that! That whole building and a good chunk of the street are just gone!" Matt exclaimed.

"That other building is pretty badly torn up too!" Naomi observed.

There was a knock at the door. Matt checked the spy hole and saw Randy standing out in the hallway. He opened the door and let him in.

"That was fast!" he said, then noticed that Randy didn't look so good. He seemed nauseous.

"Are you okay, pal? You seem a little green around the gills."

"I teleported over here. It didn't agree very well with my lunch, I'm afraid."

Matt nodded knowingly, having been whisked away by a teleportation spell enough times in the past to know that it could sometimes do a number on your stomach, especially if you'd just eaten something that was hot and spicy.

"Maybe you should sit down before you blow chunks all over our room?" Naomi suggested.

"I'll be okay." Randy said, but he did as she suggested, anyway. He noticed what was on the TV.

"I see you're already familiar with the damage our alien friends have done today. Have they confirmed any casualties yet?"

"So far, it sounds like only a few people who were unfortunate enough to be walking nearby when the explosion happened were injured by falling debris. Luckily, the offices in those buildings were closed today. What do you mean by 'alien friends?'" Naomi asked.

"Kiesha and I were there when it all went down, in our astral forms. That was no gas line explosion. UFOs caused it! You were right about Jim, Naomi. He's not from this world."

"Ha! And I'm not even a detective!" She said triumphantly. "In your face, Matt!"

Matt stuck his tongue out at her in response. "It wasn't *that* hard to figure out, I just didn't wanna say it first because it sounded so crazy." He muttered under his breath.

"Uh, huh, sure." Naomi smiled at him.

Matt turned to Randy. "Are you saying that Jim caused all of this?" He asked.

"Well, in a way, not directly..." Randy started, noting their confused expressions, then sighing. "Okay, let me start from the beginning..." he said, before he proceeded to tell them everything that he and Kiesha had just witnessed. But you just read about that, so let's skip that bit, okay

After explaining everything, Randy took a deep breath and looked at his friends.

"But the main reason I rushed over here was because I still don't know if I should tell Penny about any of this."

Naomi wasted no time in letting her opinion be known. "Heck yeah, she might wanna know that she's dating an alien! What if he's in disguise or something and he's really all gross and has tentacles or something?"

"I dunno," Matt said slyly. "Some girls might be into all those tentacles!"

Naomi shook her head. "Nasty! You've been watching too much of all the wrong kinds of anime!"

"I resemble that comment!" Matt replied sarcastically.

"C'mon you two, focus! This is serious!" Randy complained.

"You're right, I'm sorry, man. You have to admit, it *is* a pretty strange situation. It's hard not to find the fun in it."

"Easy for you to say, you don't have to figure out how to break it to her. I'm still not even sure that I should." Randy said sadly.

"Naomi's right though. Maybe not about the tentacles, but she has a point that Penny has a right to know the truth."

"Even when ignorance is bliss?" Randy asked forlornly. "I guess you two are right, though. The way things are escalating, the truth will probably come out soon, anyway. I guess it's better that she finds it out now, when we can break it to her gently, than later on when it might be too much of a shock.”

“Hey, maybe she won’t even care? It sounds like Jim’s a good guy alien. Trying to stop an invasion and all that, a real heroic type. By the way, the bigger problem seems to be what we’re going to do about this invasion. Those aliens did a good amount of damage today. It sounds like they might be pretty tough to beat. Have you thought about contacting the UGF about this?” Matt was referring to the United Guild Forces—the military arm of the Guilds.

“Of course. First, I’d like to confront Jim about it though, and get his cooperation. We’ll need to know everything he knows about the threat before we try to take it on.”

“Yeah, I guess that makes sense.” Matt said.

“What I’d really like to know is who these aliens are and why they’re invading? All the information we’ve ever had on the aliens that can actually make it here from their home worlds indicates that they’re all peaceful.” Naomi wondered aloud.

“The same thing has been bothering me. Unfortunately, all I could see of the ships was the energy pattern that surrounds them, so I can’t be sure that they’re the same ones I saw last night. From the way Jim’s mystery ally was talking, I inferred that these aliens aren’t part of the Galactic Federation like all the known aliens that have been studying the Earth are, and their technology is also a bit more primitive than that of the Federation. I’m assuming that this mystery lady, Kergaali, is what he called her—is one of the invaders, part of a group of traitors to their cause that’s been trying to get the Federation to stop this invasion. Unfortunately, it sounds like Jim is the only one that’s willing to do anything about it, because of his love for Penny. It all makes me feel twice as bad about doing anything that might wreck their relationship. He’s willing to risk everything in order to save her, to save us all. I’m just afraid she won’t look past the secrets he’s kept from her long enough to see that. You both know how strongly she feels about being lied to.”

This was true. Penny had faced her fair share of betrayals in her life. When she was younger, she felt abandoned by her self-absorbed Yuppie parents who’d given up their old hippie ideals, seduced by the glorification of greed that was prevalent in the 1980s and early 90s. She'd found some degree of solace in a religious cult, only to discover that the leader of that group was hopelessly corrupt and decadent. And to his great shame, Randy had also contributed to this cycle of her being betrayed by the people and institutions she put her trust in. He'd been cheating on her with a Valkyrie he'd met while astrally projecting when she thought he was just sleeping. Eventually, Randy confessed it to her. Randy had been young and foolish then, just discovering who he was and what he truly wanted out of life, but he'd always hated himself a little for how he'd hurt her with that affair. She eventually forgave him, and they even got back together after that, but she'd had problems trusting her partners in many of her relationships since then. As a result of all of this, she had zero tolerance for being lied to. He knew that what he'd done to her had made that tendency even worse than it already had been. Would she really be able to look past Jim's deceptions, no matter how noble his intentions might be or how deep his feelings for her might run? How many betrayals of her trust could she overlook? Not to mention how she might feel about the fact that Randy felt compelled to spy on her boyfriend to begin with.

"We sure do, she'll freak out for sure—at first. But after she's had some time to digest everything, she might come back around. She eventually learned to trust you again. Maybe she'll give Jim another chance too?" Naomi said.

"I sure hope so," Randy said.

"So, how *do* you plan to tell Penny about this?" Matt asked.

Randy looked over at the time on the microwave in the oven. "Penny and Paul will be back at the *Blunderbus* soon. I was thinking I could tell her that I want to see her and Jim together to discuss some band business with them, like a new collaboration or something. Then maybe I can talk to Jim privately first to see if I can convince him to come clean with her. She really should hear the truth from him directly. I'd better get going. Thanks again for the advice, you two." He said as he got up to leave.

"Good luck with everything, and keep us posted, okay? Let us know if there's anything else we can do to help out." Matt said.

"I will, later guys."

As soon as Randy was gone, Matt turned to Naomi, a worried look in his eyes.

"Do you really think we're gonna get through this one? You saw how much destruction these aliens have caused and they haven't even begun the invasion yet! Maybe we should go get the kids, take them both back home to Jersey with us and barricade ourselves inside the house?" He said as if on the verge of a panic.

"I'd be lying if I said I wasn't worried too, but I also know from my studies of Guild history just how much raw power the Guilds have at their command, and the kinds of massive threats that they've overcome in the past. Having the Guild magic users on our side gives us a huge advantage. Believe me, this planet is hardly defenseless. I don't think we should change any of our immediate plans just yet. Let's just try to go on with life as normal for now. I think Randy and the Guilds have got this one. I have confidence in them." Naomi tried to reassure him.

"How do we know the aliens don't have wizards, too? Space wizards! You know, like the Dark Lords of the Sith or something?" Matt said.

Naomi considered it for a moment. "I guess we don't. There's not a whole lot that any of the aliens have ever voluntarily told us about themselves. They seem to be primarily dependent on technology, but also kind of spiritually advanced too. As to the question of if that spiritual wisdom has ever led them to discover the same magical secrets that our own magic users possess...I don't know. It is a possibility, I suppose. I do know that I don't intend to give in to despair so soon. I've got faith in our friends. I don't intend to let this ruin my weekend!"

"Hmph! And people say that I'm the stubborn one!" Matt observed dryly. "You're over here all like 'I'm not about to let a little thing like an alien invasion mess up my good time!'"

"Hey, if these are our last moments together before the shit really hits the fan, then I intend to make the most of them, to savor every minute while we still can. It sure beats driving myself crazy with fear. "

"I'll admit that sounds a lot more appealing. But I can't help but feel so... powerless. It's frustrating."

"Try not to dwell on it, dear. Let's go down to the bar and get a few cocktails. We still have tonight. I'm not gonna let any damned extra-terrestrials take that away from us!"

"Yeah, under the circumstances, I think that for once I could use something to drink that's a little stronger than my coffee!"

She raised an eyebrow at him enticingly. "C'mon down to the bar with me, Mr. Spike, and I'll do my best to make you forget all about little green men and focus on little tan Italian ladies instead."

"Umm...excuse me, but I think you mean diminutive gray, non-gender specific alien beings." He said in his best imitation of his daughter's somewhat nasal voice, mocking her in that loving way that only a parent can.

Naomi laughed and rose from the sofa. "I miss her too. Now let's get those drinks! We'll get smashed and have a night of unbridled passion before the world burns down."

Matt couldn't argue with that logic.

CHAPTER 7:
LOVE WILL TEAR US APART, AGAIN

When Randy returned to the *Blunderbus Mark II*, Penny and Paul were already there, as he had predicted. He'd taken a taxi to the RV. On the way over, he had called both Penny and Jim to get them to agree to meeting with him right away. Jim had sounded reluctant, but Randy had assured him not only that this was important, but that it wouldn't take up too much of his time to hear out his proposal, and that it was something that he could only go over with him in person. Kiesha was only all too happy to spend some time babysitting Paul, whom she found to be a fascinating amalgamation of her two favorite people. So it was that Randy and Penny piled into the taxi that Randy had left waiting outside the *Blunderbus Mark II*, its meter running while he waited for her to get ready to go. On the ride over to Kirk's Galactic Grub, Penny had tried to pester him with questions, but Randy had stubbornly insisted to her that this was something that he didn't want to discuss until everyone was together. She finally gave up.

"You're in a weird mood today." She sulked as the taxi rode past rows of cars that had yet to be liberated from their snowy prisons by their owners. Randy didn't respond. He felt like he was on the way to a funeral. In a way, maybe he was. This could end up becoming a funeral for Penny and Jim's relationship, or maybe even his own relationship with her. He still wasn't sure that he was making the right call here, but everyone he'd asked seemed to think this was the right course of action.

As they arrived at Kirk's, they went around to the back of the building, where there was a separate entrance to Jim's apartment. Randy had been here once, almost a year ago, when he'd met with Jim and his band to help plan the tour. After buzzing the doorbell, the door whooshed open like the doors in a sci-fi show. The last time he'd been there, Randy had attributed this to Jim's well-known obsession with all things science fiction, but of course, now he knew better. Hi-Fi was standing at the threshold, waiting for them.

"Greetings Master Randy, Mistress Penny. It's great to see you again! Master Jim has been waiting for you. If you'll follow me, please?" The robot suggested.

"Lead on, MacDuff!" Penny told him.

"Who the hell is MacDuff, anyway?" Randy asked.

"Beats the hell out of me," Penny replied.

Hi-Fi led them into Jim's living room, which was filled with as many knick-knacks and collectibles as his restaurant, plus mementos from his recording career, like gold records and tour posters. Jim was sitting in a recliner when they walked in. He put down a book he'd been reading on a side table and sprang to his feet as he saw them. He'd changed clothes since Randy had last seen him maybe an hour or two ago. This wasn't all that surprising since his previous outfit had been ruined by all the dust from the street collapsing above him.

"Hey, baby!" he smiled as he kissed Penny and wrapped his arms around her waist. Then he looked at Randy. "So, what's this all about? Some new idea you had for a collaboration that was so great it couldn't wait until tomorrow?"

"Something like that. Do you think I could see you in private for a minute first, though?" Randy asked.

Jim looked a little confused, Penny looked even more surprised by this suggestion than Jim did. "Sure, let's talk in the bedroom." Randy followed him into the room and closed the door behind him.

"What's up, man?" Jim asked.

Randy thought he should just go for broke and be as blunt as possible. "I was wondering when you were planning on telling Penny that you're really an alien."

Jim laughed, but Randy detected a bit of a nervous edge to his laughter.

"She's already seen how I play the guitar, she knows I'm a resident of planet Funk!"

"I'm serious, Jim. I saw everything that happened earlier today. I saw you shoot at those spaceships, and I saw how they responded— how they kept on shooting until you turned off your gun and they couldn't track you anymore!"

Jim couldn't conceal his surprise. He looked up towards the ceiling as if looking for divine inspiration and sucked in a deep breath before he finally spoke.

"How could you possibly know any of that?"

"Because I don't just play a wizard on TV, I'm a real one! I'm sure you Galactic Federation types have probably heard of the Guilds? Well, I'm with one of them. I followed you to that rooftop today in astral form."

Jim thought about this for a second. He had indeed heard of the Guilds; they had tried several times to open up diplomatic relations with the Federation, claiming to be the true rulers of this planet, but the Federation refused to recognize them as such. He also knew that magic was real. Several of the major races of the galaxy had their own magical traditions, however, it was something that his own people never had much of an affinity for.

"I had no idea that you were a wizard!" Jim said with obvious surprise in his voice. "I've always been curious about how human magic users compare to some of the other ones in the galaxy." If Randy's offer to help thwart the invasion was serious, Jim hoped he might be a valuable ally in the upcoming struggle.

"I'm shocked that you didn't suspect anything when you hung out with us inside the *Blunderbus.* The fact that it's bigger on the inside is kind of a dead giveaway."

"You said it was an illusion, that it was all done with mirrors. I had no reason to doubt you."

"I can't believe that you really believed that!" Randy said. *So much for superior alien intellects!* He thought.

"Hey, you can do some pretty amazing shit with mirrors," Jim replied, but something else was bothering him. "Why were you spying on me to begin with? Did your Guild ask you to do it?"

"No, I heard stories about you being seen talking to the same strange woman several times while we were on tour. I was afraid that maybe you were messing around behind Penny's back, so I decided to investigate. I just didn't want to see Penny get hurt."

"Well, there's nothing like that going on between me and Kergaali. Kergaali is a very courageous individual that's risking everything to save this planet from the invaders. I decided to help with that effort even though it'll land me in a heap of trouble if word ever gets out. I'm doing it because I've grown to love this planet, and its people, Penny most of all."

"I believe you, and I want to do anything I can do to help with that. I think you should tell Penny the truth though, she really, really can't stand being lied to. If she realizes you've been keeping a secret this big from her, she might never forgive you. You've gotta come clean with her now, before things get any more serious between you two. The truth is going to come out sooner or later." Randy argued.

"I wish I didn't have to keep things from her either, to share my true self with her, but it's more complicated than you think."

"Why? Penny is a pretty open-minded person. I think she'll still accept you, especially once she understands what you're risking to protect this planet."

Jim sighed. "I suppose I'll have to show you."

Jim closed his eyes, and a strange glow began to surround him. Jim looked a lot like the singer Jon Bon Jovi when he was in his prime. Now, right before Randy's astonished eyes, his features swiftly melted away until his face was perfectly smooth, then just as quickly, new ones came bubbling up to the surface to replace them. Now instead of Jon Bon Jovi, he looked more like Ron Perlman in that old TV show from the Eighties, "Beauty and the Beast", which is to say that now he looked like a kind of human/lion hybrid. If my references here are too dated for younger readers and you have no idea who Jon Bon Jovi is, or what Ron Perlman's character looked like in "Beauty and the Beast", go Google it right now. I'll wait. Okay, now imagine Jon morphing into Ron in all that beast makeup, and it was sort of like that. Future people who may be reading this after Google is a relic of the past, go use your future person search engine. Heck, you might even have to use your future search engine to find out what Google was. Go do that too if you must. Okay, are we all on the same page now? Good! Now let's move on.

"You think she can still love me when I look like this? This is my true form," Jim asked as the glowing subsided.

"How did you do that?" Randy asked, astonished by the transformation

"This body is made up of countless bio mechanical nanomachines that can be reconfigured to assume a variety of forms. My real body is still on my home world, controlled remotely. The Federation has a network of hidden hyperspace relays that carry the signals across the light years. It's kind of like that movie 'Avatar.'" Jim chuckled a little at his reference to a human sci-fi movie. "If you haven't noticed, I've become kind of obsessed with studying how you humans perceive the idea of aliens and interplanetary travel. It's quite fascinating to see what things you people get right and what you get wrong."

Randy nodded. That much was obvious from any visit to Kirk's. He also wasn't terribly surprised that Jim's "body" was a remotely controlled avatar. It certainly explained his strange aura. The Guilds had long suspected that most aliens didn't come here in their own bodies. In many cases, their bodies were so incompatible with our environment that such a thing would be impossible without an environment suit.

"I think you look pretty darned cool, actually! It's not like you've got slimy tentacles or anything. Hey, if she could stand being with a guy who looks like I do for so long, I don't think she'll have a problem with your appearance. She's not shallow like that." Randy smiled at him.

"Thanks, man. You're not going to tell her, are you? You'll let me handle it, right?"

"Of course, as long as you promise that you won't put it off for too long and that you really will tell her soon. She has a right to know what she's getting herself into by being with you, especially with all the danger that you put yourself in today."

"Don't worry, I will. And I plan on doing my best to keep her away from that danger, although it might be hard to do. I'm afraid that we might all be in great danger soon."

"Okay, it's agreed then. I won't say anything—for now. Luckily, I really *do* have an idea for a collaboration between our two bands that I can show you, so she won't get too suspicious about why I called us all together." Randy said, waves of relief washing off of him as he said the words. He dug a flash drive from his pocket that held a recording on it of a rough version of the song he'd come up with and held it up for Jim to see.

"Cool. But that's the least of problems. We should discuss what help you might have to offer in stopping this invasion."

Randy nodded enthusiastically. "Definitely! I think if you spoke before the Inner Council of the..."

At that precise moment, Penny opened up the door, and she playfully poked her he'd inside the room.

"You boys have been in here for a while now. What devilish plot against me are you cooking up?" Her eyes widened as she caught sight of Jim's current appearance.

"Penny!" Jim and Randy said in unison at the sudden intrusion.

"Wow! That's one cool costume! Is this the surprise? Are you gonna wear that in a video you're planning or something?" She asked as she walked fully into the room. She walked up to Jim and stroked some of the fur on his exposed arms. Then she yanked on a strand, pulling out a hair.

"Ow!" Jim yelled reflexively.

"It looks pretty good, but maybe this costume is a little cheaply made. That hair came out way too easily." She said studying the hair she'd just pulled out.

"Cheaply made?" Jim said indignantly. "This is no costume! That's my real hair!" Jim complained.

Penny laughed. Randy and Jim just stared at her. "I'm not kidding Penny, this is what I really look like!" Jim insisted. "Penny, I'm really an alien from another planet, here on a secret mission." He confessed.

She laughed even harder.

"Jim, are you really sure you wanna do this right now? Like this?" Randy asked warningly.

"What's the alternative? More lies? The cat is out of the bag now— literally!"

"I dunno, I have a bad feeling about this..."

Penny punched Randy in the arm. "You guys are so crazy!" She turned to Jim. "Alright, you got me! Good prank! You can take the mask off now!" She yanked on Jim's snout. A look of annoyance with a dash of confusion crossed her face when it didn't pull away from his face as she expected it to.

"Aaargh! Stop that!" Jim batted her hand off of his nose and rubbed it.

Penny's eyes narrowed. She whirled around to look at Randy. "Holyyy shit! He's not kidding, is he?"

Randy looked down. "I'm afraid not."

She laughed again, but there was no happiness in that laugh. "Of course you're an alien! First, I'm dating a wizard, and now an alien! It's just my luck, isn't it?"

Penny suddenly felt like the room was spinning around her; she sank onto the bed. "What the hell is really going on here?"

"I, uh, heard some strange stuff about Jim. Stuff the roadies were talking about that Kiesha shared with me, so I decided to check it out..." Randy began hesitantly.

"And you what? Took it upon yourself to bring us all together here so you could expose him? Why?"

"I thought you deserved to know the truth."

She stared at Jim. The intensity of her gaze burning a hole into his soul. "And when were you planning on telling me any of this? Or weren't you?"

Now Jim looked down.

"It shouldn't matter, should it? I'm the same person on the inside!"

"You're not answering my question!" Penny now got up from the bed and got right up in Jim's face until they were almost nose to nose.

"If Randy hadn't found out your little secret, when were you planning on telling me? Before or after we got a place together?"

Jim wore a pained expression on his face. "If he hadn't found out... I don't know that I would have. I just don't see how it matters..."

"It *matters* that you've been lying to me all along about who you really are! You know how much trouble I have trusting people, letting them get close! You knew all of that and you still chose to get close to me when you had a secret that you never planned to reveal!" She was shouting at him now.

"I'm sorry, Penny, truly I am. I never meant to hurt you." He said quietly.

"Well, it's too late for that! Too late for us!" she screamed. "God! Why is my life so crazy? Other people don't have these kinds of problems! This is so fucking ridiculous!"

"Penny," Randy started and placed a hand on her shoulder. It was meant to be a comforting gesture. She looked down at his hand venomously, like it was made of something foul. She brushed it off and turned around to face him.

"You! Why couldn't you just let me be happy, even if it was a lie? What's this really about? Are you trying to punish me because I wouldn't agree to be a part of your little harem?"

"Harem! It's not a harem! A harem is a very patriarchal, male dominated idea. It's not like that at all! Everyone in our polyamorous group is free to have other partners, and they do. It doesn't revolve around me." He was insulted that she was suddenly judging his lifestyle like this.

"I didn't want other partners! I never did! I just wanted you! Why couldn't I just have you? Why was I never enough for you?" She said sadly.

In the past, it had seemed like Penny had been okay with the idea of being in an open relationship with Randy, then had later pushed him for more exclusivity. The truth was that she'd never *truly* been okay with sharing him with others and had only ever half heartedly pursued other relationships for herself when they'd been together. It had been something that she just felt she had to put up with, and pretend to go along with as the price to pay to be with him.

Randy couldn't believe she was reopening these old wounds. it had been years since they'd had this same argument and he'd believed that they'd finally put this all behind them. Was it really all that surprising that she'd jump to these kinds of conclusions about his true motivations? He supposed he'd brought it upon himself. This reaction was exactly what he'd been so afraid of when he decided to investigate Jim.

"You know why," Randy said, with an uncharacteristically dark edge to his voice.

Penny rolled her eyes. She hoped she didn't have to listen to him go on and on again about how he "had too much love to give" or some other such bullshit. In her view, it was quite the opposite. It wasn't that he had too much love to give away so much as it was that he *needed* more love than any one person could ever possibly supply him with. For all of his endless navel gazing, she felt like she still understood him better than he'd ever understood himself. The worst part of it was that she really couldn't blame him. His own parents had been hopelessly addicted to some pretty hard drugs. They'd abandoned him at a ridiculously young age, and it had been up to his aunt and older brothers to pick up the slack and raise him. It was a deep wound that he'd never really properly dealt with and it had continued to fester over the years, eating away at him.

Penny had been neglected by her parents too, which had led her to rebel against them, looking for any other family that would have her. She'd gotten mixed up in a cult as a result. Then the cult imploded after its leader disappeared, making music became her outlet instead. Her devotion to her music, and the support of Matt, Naomi and especially Randy helped to heal her, and in time, when she was ready, she repaired the rift with her parents.

But Randy was different. The neglect he had suffered had been criminal—literally. It was abuse. He still had no relationship with his parents at all, even though they were both clean now and had been for years. For all his pretty hippie talk of love, compassion and forgiveness, what they had done to him was the one thing he could *never* forgive. At his core, despite all his pretensions of being so spiritually advanced, he would always be a broken little boy who had been discarded by the people who were supposed to love and care for him the most. He was always looking for someone to fill in that hole in his heart, but no matter how many adoring fans he had, or romantic partners, she didn't think that *anything* would really ever fill that gap.

She had dared to believe that having Paul in his life had started to heal some of those wounds. Indeed, his painful childhood abandonment issues drove him to make sure that history doesn't repeat itself, making him into an excellent father. But now, based on his current behavior, she wasn't so sure anymore that fatherhood had really healed him the way she'd wanted to believe that it had. They seemed to right back to square one all of the sudden. He obviously still couldn't stand the idea of her moving on and being with anyone else, while she was supposed to do what? Happily put up with him having as many other partners as he wanted? It didn't make any sense! He wanted to have his cake and eat it too, but she wasn't just a damned piece of cake to be had.

"We've been over this a thousand times already. It's just not the way I'm hardwired, okay? If I have feelings for someone else, I can't just ignore that and shut it down. I can't be something that I'm not, no matter how much I sometimes wish that I could be for you, and it's not fair of you to expect me to."

"And it's not fair for you to expect me to be something I'm not for you either!"

"But I don't! Not anymore. This is all ancient history, Penny! I've moved on too, I really have! That's not what any of this is about this time. I don't want you back like that! I treasure the kind of relationship we have these days, and I really *want* you to find happiness with someone else. It's not why I looked into Jim. Like I said, I heard some weird rumors about him, and I felt like I had to check it out. That was all there ever was to it! I felt like it was my duty as your friend. I was only trying to protect you, to protect our son."

"Don't you dare bring him into this! This has nothing to do with him!"

"But it does! It has everything to do with him! The sort of people you allow into your life will be in his life too, and I have to make sure that they're safe. I care about you both, I just want to make sure you're going to be okay."

"How very noble of you! How heroic! But it's not up to you to decide who's safe enough for me to fall in love with. I'm not a damned child! You don't have any right to make those decisions for me!"

"Of course not. That's not what I was trying to do. I just thought that you had a right to know the truth about Jim.

"Even if that truth hurts?" She barked out a bitter little laugh.

"I finally found someone who seems to really feel like I'm enough for him and you have to spoil it all by showing me he's not even an actual human being? That he's been lying to me this entire time! You know how I feel about lies!"

"All the more reason for you to know the truth. So you're not living a lie," Randy told her.

"But I was happy, damn you! Happy! Why can't you understand that? And you've taken that away from me! You had no right! No right!"

She furiously pounded Randy on the chest with both fists. Repeatedly.

"No right! No right!" She mumbled, her heavy eye makeup running down her face, morphing into a kind of war paint bourne of anguish.

He just let her do it, making no move to stop her or defend himself. Now that he saw just how deeply he'd hurt her, a little pummeling from her was far less than what he thought he probably deserved. After a while, she gave up, bored and frustrated with the futility of it all. She threw herself into a nearby chair, becoming a miserable, sobbing heap.

"I'm sorry." Randy muttered, rooted to the spot. Warm, salty tears were rolling down his cheeks, too. "So sorry."

Jim had been watching this entire argument in a kind of stunned silence. He now moved towards Penny hesitantly, awkwardly laying one shaggy paw on her shoulder.

"We can still be happy, Penny. We can still be together if you still want me. My feelings for you were always real and they still are. I still love you and want to be there for you— always. Nothing has really changed..."

This seemed to startle Penny from her stupor. She uncurled herself out of the ball she'd huddled into and glared at him angrily.

"Nothing has changed? Nothing has changed? Are you fucking kidding me? Wake the fuck up, you idiot! Everything has changed!

You—you're not even a person, you'd some kind of fucking...*lion thing*! I don't even know who you are! Nothing you ever told me about your past was true! I mean, we are *literally* from two different worlds! You still have the audacity to think that you can still make this work somehow? I loved you, but that was never really you, was it? I don't know who you are and I guess I never did. The man I thought I was in love with was just a dream, someone who never even existed."

She laughed her hoarse, hollow, broken glass laugh once again.

"I was even thinking that maybe we could have children together someday. Did you know that? Is that even possible now? And if it is, what am I supposed to do? Give birth to a litter of goddamned kittens? This isn't what I signed up for!"

Jim looked truly hurt, stung by her words.

"But you *do* know me. You know my heart. I may not be from your planet, or your species, but none of that should matter. I am a sentient being with the same feelings, the same hopes, dreams, and needs as any human being. On the inside, we *are* the same and my feelings for you were never a lie. Please, you *must* believe me."

"I don't have to do a damned thing, Lion-O!" Penny shot back.

"I can always change back to my other form if you have a problem with this one..."

"It's not just about how you look! Sure, it's a little...unsettling, but ultimately, it's not what the actual issue is here. You should know that I'm not that shallow. It's the fact that you didn't trust me with the truth. That it took an overprotective ex to pry it out of you."

"Penny, I'm sorry. I wanted to tell you the truth, really I did. So many times! It hasn't been easy, having an entire dimension of my being that I couldn't share with you. But how and when is a good time to tell your girlfriend that you're an alien? You know how crazy that sounds! How do you even begin to explain that to someone in a world where most people don't even believe that such things are possible?"

"Oh, I dunno. Maybe tell them before you start sleeping together? You could've given me space cooties! And *definitely* tell them before you start talking about moving in together! Don't give me any more of your bullshit, Jim, or whatever your name really is! The truth is that this mysterious mission of yours was more important to you than I was. You had to maintain your cover for the success of your mission, didn't you?"

Jim closed his eyes. "Yes." He admitted in a low voice.

"But it truly is an important mission. Or at least it is now. You don't understand."

"Then please, enlighten us poor, primitive Earthlings. What is it about your mission that is more important than being honest with the woman you claim to be in love with? I'm curious. I'd *really* like to know!" She folded her arms and looked at him expectantly.

"Originally, they sent me here as a cultural observer. To go undercover and learn as much as I could about human culture by living and working among you. That's why I started a band, to learn about human music and recreation. But then, one day, I picked up a signal that changed everything. A signal pleading for help. You see, there's an invasion heading your way and I'm trying to stop it. I'm trying to save you all!"

Penny laughed her joyless laugh.

"Oh boy! What a lucky girl I am! I'm just surrounded by heroes tonight aren't I?" She pointed to Randy, who was still standing where he had been, hanging his head in shame.

"This one wants to save me from lying boyfriends, and the other one wants to save the whole planet! Neither one really respects me enough to give me what I need!"

"I'm serious! Your planet is in dreadful danger. The aliens who want to invade your world are not all of one mind. There are some who disagree with the invasion plans. One of these dissident aliens sent out a distress call, trying to reach the other aliens who are here on Earth on missions similar to mine, studying you, asking for their help in stopping the coming attack. They all ignored it. We're sworn not to interfere in such things, only to observe. But I couldn't just ignore such a warning. I care too much about this planet, about *you*, Penny, to let anything terrible happen to you. Ever since then, I've been working with this sympathizer within their ranks to stop the invasion."

So many emotions had been dancing around inside Penny's head that she was barely listening anymore. She was beyond really caring about anything Jim had to say at this point. She was numb to the whole situation. Yet she goaded him on a bit more, mostly out of a perverse sense of curiosity about what kind of bullshit he'd pull out of his ass next to try and win her back over.

"I thought you extraterrestrial types were supposed to be so far above us humans that there was no need to invade planets. You can just make whatever you need, you don't have to take it from anyone else. At least that's what Mr. Wizard over there has been telling me for years." She motioned towards Randy again.

"That is true of the worlds that belong to my group, the Galactic Federation. However, there are more backwards planets out there that can't yet create everything that they need. The resource that these particular invaders crave the most is one that's quite hard to create, even for us. They need *land,* they need a home. Their world is dying and they've decided that taking yours is the most convenient thing for them to do."

"And where do these invaders come from, exactly?"

"Venus."

This time, when Penny laughed, it was a rich, genuine laugh.

"You must think I'm an idiot! Everyone knows Venus is a hot hellhole of a planet! No life can survive there!"

"That's true of Venus now. But it wasn't always so. Venus was quite pleasant and habitable for billions of years, up until about 750 million years ago. These invaders come from the past, from roughly 700 million years ago. They've built a sort of tunnel through time to reach this era."

Penny had to give him points for originality, but she immediately saw a glaring problem with his claim. She decided to keep on talking about this subject. It was distracting her from her pain. It was much easier to talk about stupid hypothetical alien invasions than it was to talk about her feelings right now.

"Okay, so aliens from ancient Venus want to escape a world that is turning into a shithole. I can sort of buy that, I guess. But why not invade Earth in their own time period? There weren't any people around to fight back 700 million years ago. Shit, I don't even think that there were dinosaurs to worry about being eaten up by."

"Earth was not very hospitable at that time. It was a barren, frozen world, like one big ball of ice. Their scientists predicted though, that in the future it would be more like Venus was in its heyday, so they have traveled forward to this time."

She wasn't buying it. "And again, why this time period? Why not go to medieval times, or better yet, a time when there are no people around at all to oppose them?"

"From what I understand, they've had trouble finding an era where they can establish a stable time tunnel. For whatever reason, there's something about this time period that makes it easier for them to do so."

"My, how convenient!" she said skeptically.

"It's all true, Penny. They plan to land at the United Nations building later today, claiming to come in peace. Their plan is to send ships to every nation on the planet to distribute a device that's a kind of...super factory that can synthesize anything as a gesture of goodwill, supposedly to end hunger and need for mankind. But it's a Trojan horse. Once their ships are in place, they'll attack simultaneously. The factory devices they were giving to humanity will churn out more ships to help with the invasion until all resistance is crushed. That's why there have been so many sightings of UFOs lately. They're trying to get people used to the idea that they're here. To normalize it. They were supposed to begin their plan earlier today, but I attacked their ships before they could reach the UN and they had to reschedule."

"He's telling the truth this time." Randy dared to try speaking to her again. "I saw him shoot at the UFOs when I was tailing him. I also saw them fire back. That explosion that happened today wasn't because of a gas leak like the news reports are saying. The UFOs did that when they were trying to zap Jim."

Penny let this new information sink in without saying anything. This was all a bit too much to process all at once. She was still furious with Randy, but despite everything, she still trusted him. They had too much history together for her not to. If he said this was true, then it probably was. Jim mistook her pensive silence for more disbelief.

"If you still don't believe me, then stick around for a while longer. The Venusian who I've been working with, Kergaali, is on the way here right now to meet me so we can plan our next move."

"In person this time? Not another hologram?" Randy asked him.

"Yes, in the flesh this time," Jim affirmed.

"I'd like to meet her. I have many influential friends in the Guilds, and I'm sure I can convince them to help you fight this invasion if she can meet with them."

"We'll take any help we can get, we're gonna need it," Jim said gratefully.

And that's the real reason why you're here, isn't it, Randy? Trying to save the world again and my broken heart is just some of the collateral damage. Penny thought bitterly.

Then she felt a pang of guilt at this bitterness. If the world really was in danger, then so was she and, more importantly, so was Paul. Maybe she should be grateful that Jim and Randy were trying to do something about it? Yes, they'd both done her dirty today. Jim with his lies and Randy with his unwarranted interference in her personal life, but maybe it was also a little selfish for her to cling to her anger so closely when much larger things were at stake? And dammit if she wasn't beginning to believe that Randy really had done what he did out of a genuine concern for her rather than out of jealousy over her relationship with Jim.

Ex relationship with Jim, that is. She thought. She couldn't see things ever continuing with Jim, even if he was some kind of good guy alien defying orders to save the human race. He'd still lied to her constantly, and she still felt well, for lack of a better word, *alienated* from him now. Like she'd never really known him. She was too busy mourning the loss of the man she thought had existed to care much about learning to love whatever the thing that he really was. It was all too weird, even for her. Randy might be into dating Valkyries and human/water Nymph hybrids, but she didn't think it was *too* demanding of her to expect that her romantic partners at least be completely human. That didn't make her racist, did it? Or a speciesist? *Was speciesism even a thing?* She wondered.

The doorbell buzzed. It made the same sound as the one in George Jetson's apartment.

"That's probably her now!" Jim said. They all moved to the living room, even Penny, whose curiosity over all of this strangeness was overriding her grief.

"Exterior scans indicate it is indeed Mistress Kergaali. Allow me, sir!" Hi-Fi said as he moved forward to open the door.

The door slid aside and revealed an extraordinarily tall woman dressed in loose fitting sweatpants. She wore a NY Yankees baseball cap on her head, which seemed to sit on her head oddly, like it needed to be pulled down a little further and was just hovering unnaturally. Brightly colored, oversized gag sunglasses concealed her eyes. She also wore a NY Mets jacket that was adorned with buttons for the Knicks and the Jets, plus an "I Love NY" button. Under the jacket, it looked like she was wearing a dress shirt and a tie. She wore wingtip shoes that definitely clashed with her sweatpants. Randy was reminded of a similar outfit from the movie "Coming to America", whose wearer was as oblivious to how ridiculous he looked as Kergaali seemed to be.

"Mistress Kergaali! How wonderful it is to see you! Please enter!" Hi-Fi invited her. She appeared to catch sight of Jim, Randy, and Penny all standing behind the robot.

Apparently, she had seen Jim in his true form before in the past, because she didn't even question a six-foot-tall lion-man wearing jeans and a t-shirt. She was more disturbed by the fact that Randy and Penny were there.

"You have...guests?" She asked incredulously.

"It's okay, Kergaali. They know all about the invasion, and they want to help us."

Kergaali shrugged as she appraised the two seemingly normal humans standing beside Jim. "What is that charming expression that they have on this planet? Beggars cannot select things?" She asked as she stepped inside.

CHAPTER 8:
A CORNUCOPIA OF DOOM

Once Kergaali was inside Jim's apartment, Randy and Penny had a better opportunity to study her. Her skin tone appeared to be Caucasian at first, but upon closer inspection, it had an odd orange cast to it. Her skin also had a very oily appearance, as a thin layer of Vaseline coated it entirely. She removed her ridiculous looking sunglasses and her hat and they noted other features that made her seem slightly less human. Her eyes were more like those of a cat than Jim's were, which was interesting considering that everything else about Jim was cat-like at the moment. Jim's eyes had, in fact, remained stubbornly like those of a human. When she removed her hat, they saw that there was a rubbery, flexible antenna protruding from the top of her head that was quite intricate looking. This was obviously why her hat had fit so poorly on her head. As she opened her mouth to speak, they also saw that her teeth were like tiny needles.

"Who are these...people?" She asked Jim haltingly.

As she did so, Penny giggled a little. She bumped Randy with her elbow and whispered to him. "She sounds just like Bjork when she talks! It's so cute!" You might have to Google "Bjork" too, kids. All my references are getting as old as Matt's typically are! It's so difficult to write something timeless, isn't it? Possibly impossible.

Randy was pleased to see that Penny was talking to him again and joking around, almost as if nothing had just happened between them. Maybe this meant that she was starting to forgive him? He could only hope. She had a point, though. When this newcomer spoke English, she sounded uncannily like the beloved Icelandic pop star. The translation spell he'd cast earlier had concealed this fact as he still heard her speaking in her native tongue, but the spell put the meaning behind her words directly into his mind.

"You're right." He whispered back with a smile.

"This is Randy, he's a wizard who is going to use his magic to help us." Jim told her.

"Wiz-ard?" She said, testing the unfamiliar word out on her tongue, then a light of recognition appeared in her eyes. "Ah yes, I recall you mentioning Randy. The father of your mate's pup, yes?"

Randy could also see that the translation spell did a better job of translating her words than she did herself.

"Pup? We call them kids, lady! And I'm nobody's mate, not at the moment." Penny bristled.

"My apologies. Now it occurs to me that the correct term is 'girlfriend' is it not? What a strange concept. And you are?"

"Penny. The girlfriend, or rather the *former* girlfriend herself!" Penny answered and looked over at Jim pointedly. He looked away.

Kergaali tittered a little laugh. It sounded disturbingly like chirping. "*This* is the human you are so obsessed with? It's so, so...*small!*"

"I might be small, but at least I know how to dress myself!" Penny shot back.

"Are these garments not appropriate? I asked the Duplo-Ray to provide me with typical human attire based upon a random sampling from intercepted transmissions. I even asked it to give me geographically specific details. Are these not the insignias of your beloved local athletic competition groups?" She asked, pointing to the Mets and Knicks logos on her clothes.

"Yes, but you may have overdone it—just a bit." Jim smiled, clearly amused.

"What's a Duplo-Ray?" Randy asked.

"What we use to make things. Even I was made by a Duplo-Ray." Kergaali said somewhat unhelpfully. Her explanation was as clear as mud.

"It's kind of like the replicators they have on Star Trek. It rearranges matter to make other things. Remember how I said they had a super factory machine that they planned to give to mankind? Supposedly with the intention of ending world hunger and need? Well, that's their Duplo-Ray. It's like a replicator, only on a massive, industrial scale. Except instead of churning out food as promised, it's going to create a fleet of drone ships that will attack the Earth." Jim clarified.

"Duplo-Ray! What a dorky name!" Penny sniggered.

"What's wrong with it? It's a ray that duplicates things. It seems a very sensible name to me." Kergaali said, sounding somewhat offended.

"Beware of Venusians bearing gifts." Randy said, raising an eyebrow.

"Quite! It's a virtual Cornucopia of Doom! Shit! That's a good title for a song, I should write that one down!" Penny added.

Randy had more questions for the spacewoman. "You said earlier that the idea of a girlfriend seemed odd. Don't you have such things on Venus?"

"Not really. Our people reproduce asexually. Once we reach the age of maturation, we produce two copies of ourselves. We no longer have any need for such couplings. We are familiar, of course, with such concepts, though. It's how most of our animals reproduce. Even the animals we were created from once did it that way," Kergaali informed them.

"Created?" Penny echoed questioningly.

"Yes, my people were created as servants by what we call the First Generation. They were masters of what you would call genetic engineering, their whole technology was based on creating living things to do the work that most species use machines to do. The First Generation vaguely resembles your 'squid' animals, only much larger. They created us from predatory animals they found in the equatorial jungles that resemble your 'lemur' creatures, accelerating our evolution and eventually eliminating the males."

"No men! After what I've been through today, I'm starting to think that might be my kinda planet!" Penny remarked snarkily. Both Randy and Jim shifted uncomfortably at the comment.

"Yes, Pfoff is indeed a truly wonderful planet. The males were no longer needed once we were re-engineered to reproduce asexually. We maintain what you would consider being an outwardly 'female' configuration because it is necessary for us to be able to give birth to live young and nurture them when they crawl from the pouch. However, we do not truly have a sense of 'gender' as you people do.

We simply are what we are. Gender seems a very peculiar idea to us."

Randy's head felt like it would burst. He had so many questions! She mentioned a "pouch," were these people also a kind of marsupial? He wondered what other biological differences lurked under the skin, despite their superficial similarities to humans.

"What happened to this First Generation? You mentioned them in the past tense." Randy asked.

Despite the urgency of the reason behind her visit, the intellect that Randy displayed with his questions pleased Kergaali. She didn't mind talking to him. Penny was another matter, though. She was small and weak looking. She reminded Kergaali of a deformed, seriously mutated child from her world. Such children were put down before they could pass on their genetic contamination. It was considered a mercy. It was extremely distressing for Kergaali to see a fully grown version of such a thing. Why were such abominable things allowed to exist on this planet? And how could a superior being like Jim feel such a strong attachment to a pathetic creature like that? It boggled her mind.

"We were their slaves. They used us to do everything, and became completely dependent upon us. In time, we realized this gave us a kind of power over them. Without us, they were virtually helpless. We rose up and destroyed them." She said matter-of-factly.

Randy was flabbergasted. "What? You mean you committed genocide?" He could understand hating your oppressors, your enslavers, but even so, this seemed pretty extreme.

"Geno-cide? What is that?" She asked in confusion.

"They don't have a word for that in their language." Jim explained quickly, then he turned to Kergaali. "It means to completely destroy a people." He told her hurriedly.

"Oh. No, there are some who still exist, living within our oceans. Aboriginal tribes that never developed a sophisticated technology were not considered a threat and so were allowed to live. They live on in other ways as well. Our language comes from their language, and other aspects of our culture come from them. We consider ourselves to be just a later generation of the same continuum of life that they arose from. Unfortunately, we lost much of their knowledge of genetics in the War and we were forced to develop machines."

Randy was relieved that she wasn't from a race of space Nazis, it made liking her a lot easier. Despite her earlier joke about Venus being her kind of planet, something about the coldness of Kergaali's words and some of the other things she'd revealed about her world disturbed Penny.

"No men, no couples, no sex? Venus sure is an inappropriately named planet!" She complained.

"We call our planet Pfoff, and call ourselves the Children of Pfoff. What do you mean by that comment?" Kergaali asked.

"I mean that Venus is named after the Goddess of Love. But your world seems kind of...cold. Is there no love on Pfoff?"

"No love?" Kergaali said angrily. "Of course there's love! Life is meaningless without love! There's lots of love! Love of community, of country. Love of children, and our friends and colleagues. Love of work and duty! We also have pets that we are quite...attached to." She made a peculiar sound like a bird call and a long, fuzzy creature protruded from out of the collar of her jacket, poking its upper body out. It looked a bit like a small, slender sloth. She cooed at it and it made a soft, burbling sound in response and rubbed its head against hers.

"This is my pet bipit, Zaa. He goes wherever I go." She explained. "Don't worry, he won't bite!" Randy touched Zaa's soft fur and stroked it. He was quite soft and pleasant to the touch. The bipit was indescribably cute, so I will not attempt to describe its cuteness, as that is obviously futile. It was exactly the sort of adorable little beast that invariably winds up science fiction movies as a thinly veiled marketing ploy to sell toys, you know, like Ewoks or Porgs.

Penny thought he was pretty cute too, but there was no way she was about to touch that thing. Where the heck had she been keeping it, anyway?

"I would argue that our love is more pure, because any primitive, animalistic urge to reproduce does not taint it." She continued to argue.

"You might not *need* to couple up biologically, but don't you people ever...you know? Mess around anyway because it just *feels* good? Like sensually?" Penny asked. It seemed inconceivable to her that they wouldn't have discovered that skin to skin contact can be incredibly pleasant. Surely, these people still had nerve endings? Certain needs that couldn't be fulfilled by mere pets?

Kergaali's face blanched in embarrassment. "There are...some who indulge in such...*deviant* behavior. It is not considered proper, and we discourage such things."

"Great, even the aliens are homophobic! And I thought you guys were supposed to be so superior!" Penny complained.

Randy, who considered himself to be pansexual, was also rather disappointed by this attitude. Up until that moment, he'd found their new friend to be rather enchanting. He'd even become a little smitten with her. She was quite attractive, if you looked past her outlandish outfit. He was too diplomatic to say anything about how she'd just offended him, though. He needed her help if they were going to learn more about this invasion and figure out a way to stop it.

"Enough of these questions! I did not come here to be interrogated!" Kergaali said impatiently, sensing the sudden disapproval in the room.

Randy was annoyed that his line of questioning had been cut off so abruptly. He still had a million more questions for her. Was it even proper for him to still refer to her as being a her? He wondered. See? He still had lots of questions! Like, for example, what she had meant when she said she'd been created by a Duplo-Ray when she had also said that her people basically gave birth to a pair of clones of themselves. Wasn't that a contradiction? He didn't see how both statements could be true.

"Of course. You said you had news for me?" Jim asked.

"Yes, there have been important developments. But first, do you have any refreshments? It has been a few cycles since I last had any consumables, and I am supposed to be on my dinner hour aboard the mothership instead of being here."

"How rude of me! Hi-Fi! Initiate Waitress Program!" Jim commanded the robot, who was always standing a few feet away from him in case he should be needed.

"As you command, Master Jim! One waitress coming right up!" he said in his overly cheerful way. A small compartment opened up in his body and a small hovering holographic emitter flew out. A second later, one of the waitresses from the restaurant appeared.

"May I take your order?" She asked.

"That's one of the waitresses from last night!" Penny said in a surprised voice.

"Yup. They're all holograms. Much cheaper than hiring real staff. And much better at keeping my secrets too," Jim said in a slightly smug voice, obviously enamored with his own cleverness.

"Display the special menu." Jim ordered.

The waitress opened one of the menus she carried under her arm and held it up before Kergaali's face.

She quickly scanned the contents. "You have Nostroga? But that's cuisine from Pfoff! How is that possible?"

"Long ago, the Federation sent observers like myself to study your world too." He told her.

"Hmph! And they left us to our fates, left us to die, just as they are willing to let these humans die? I see that nothing much has changed in the Federation over the millennia." She noted testily. Jim couldn't really blame her for feeling that way.

"Regardless, they were at least able to preserve many of the details of your culture in our databases. I reconstructed a recipe for Nostroga from those ancient records. I thought you might enjoy it."

"Enjoy it? It's my favorite! I'll have the Nostroga, please. And a Coca Cola. I have long wanted to try one of those." She told the waitress.

Jim ordered something they'd never heard of, then he turned to face the only two humans in the room. "Do you guys want anything too?" Jim asked them.

Randy and Penny both placed an order. To their mutual surprise, no sooner had they given their orders than they appeared in front of them, on a silver dining cart that materialized out of thin air.

"What? How? Is this another hologram? How am I supposed to eat a hologram?" She picked up her plate from the cart. It *felt* solid enough. "And if it's real, how is it ready so quickly?"

Jim chuckled. "The food is real enough. I just had it teleported here from the 'kitchen' of the restaurant, which is really just a kind of replicator."

"Duplo-Ray!" Kergaali corrected him.

"If you insist, yes, we can call it a 'Duplo-Ray,' although I feel idiotic saying that. Penny is right. It *is* a dorky name. The general principle behind such technology is the same regardless, so for all intents and purposes, it is the same thing. In the restaurant, we create intentional delays when making the food so we don't arouse suspicion. In this case, there was no need for such theatrics. Now let's all sit down and eat. I'm pretty hungry too," Jim said as he took his plate and led them to a corner of his apartment that held a table and a few chairs. As he sat down, he looked at Hi-Fi.

"End Waitress Program!" he ordered. The waitress winked out of existence and her emitter flew back into Hi-Fi's chest. "I get creeped out when she watches me while I eat," He explained unnecessarily.

They all began eating. Penny looked over at Kergaali's plate of "Nostroga". It looked like a kind of salad. She fed a bit to Zaa every so often, who nibbled on it appreciatively and made adorable sounds

"Delicious! As they say on this world, 'Just like mother used to make!'" Kergaali said, smiling more genuinely than either Randy or Penny had ever seen her do before

"Is that a vegetarian dish?" Penny asked.

"Do you think I'd actually eat flesh? All of my people are what you would call 'vegetarian' as—are most civilized races. We may have been evolved from predators, but we abandoned such barbaric practices long ago!" She sounded mildly offended at the suggestion that she could ever be anything *but* a vegetarian.

"Do you hear that Randy? All the civilized races are vegetarians! I always told you so!" she teased him as he took a bite from a steak.

"Yeah, well, you know who was also a vegetarian? Hitler!" he countered.

Penny rolled her eyes. *Not this old chestnut again!* She thought. Bringing up the fact that Hitler was a vegetarian was a common technique people used to mock vegetarianism. As if the fact that one very evil man was one of them somehow invalidated the entire concept.

"Ha! I invoke Godwin's Law! You just lost this argument, sucker!" Penny laughed. It was nice to hear her laughing again after how upset she'd been less than an hour earlier. It was almost as if nothing had happened between them. Such was the power of their friendship that they couldn't help but fall back into their old, familiar patterns of behavior, even when a part of her still kind of wanted to rip Randy's head off. By the way, in case you didn't know, "Godwin's Law" states that "as an online discussion grows longer, the probability of a comparison involving Nazis or Hitler becomes more likely." When that happens, it usually means the discussion has come to an end.

"And that only applies to online conversations, so I *don't* concede defeat. Making you a vegetarian doesn't automatically confer sainthood upon someone. You can be a vegetarian and still be an awful person—like Hitler." Randy pressed her, undaunted.

"Who is this Hitler?" A befuddled Kergaali asked.

"One of the worst villains in our history. You want to know more about our concept of genocide? Well, just look him up and you'll learn a lot about that subject! He tried to destroy my own people," Randy explained.

"If Naomi was here, she'd tell you that as far as historical villains go, technically Stalin was worse. He killed more people." Penny rebutted.

"Nah. If she was here, she'd tell you that Chairman Mao was actually the worst. He killed more people than both of them." Randy said with a bit of triumph in his voice.

"Wow! I didn't know that! Is that true?" Penny asked. Randy nodded.

Kergaali shook her head. "How savage! How can you discuss the slaughter of millions so casually, over a meal? I can't believe that you people kill each other like that. On Pfoff, it is forbidden for us to kill another Child of Pfoff. It has not happened since we defeated the First Generation in the War. It is one of our highest laws."

"It's not exactly legal here either, but that doesn't stop us from doing it. Do you mean to say that there is no war or murder on your planet at all?" Penny replied.

"No wars since that first one where we won our freedom. That's why it's called *the* War. There has only ever been one. Sometimes there are murders, but it is very, very rare; the shame is too great." Kergaali said.

"And yet, your people are planning to invade the Earth? How do they plan to do that without killing?" Randy demanded.

"That's...different. You are not Children of Pfoff. The same rules don't apply. Some of my people, the ones behind the invasion, see you humans as being little better than dumb animals."

"But your people are vegetarians. That implies that you value the lives of animals." Penny said.

"We do, but you must understand that our world is suffering from a massive ecological disaster. It is on an irreversible path. Someday it will be uninhabitable. In this time period, this has already come to pass, as you well know. Some of our people, the nation that is called the Saawgauth—they see invading your planet as the only way for our people to survive. And they will stop at nothing to ensure that we do."

"What is the environmental disaster that ruined your world? How did it start?" Penny was particularly curious about this. She had always fancied herself to be something of an eco-warrior, always championing green causes. Fortunately, Kergaali seemed to be feeling more talkative again now that she had a little Nostroga in her belly—or wherever her species kept their stomachs.

"It was part of the legacy that we inherited from the First Generation. They powered their civilization with energy from natural gasses. They forced us to mine it on their behalf. One day, we hit an unbelievably vast pocket of it, too much to ever completely capture or contain. It poured into the atmosphere and slowly heated the planet. This event also triggered massive volcanic eruptions around the world, which continued on into my era and only made the problem worse. The First Generation had no idea what to do about it. They didn't fully appreciate the danger or think about the long-term consequences. They only cared about the moment. Once we finally took control from them, it was too late. We thought we could fix it with our Duplo-Rays, use them to convert the gasses into something less harmful, but there's simply too much of it. The Duplo-Rays have their own large energy requirements and there isn't enough power on the planet to fuel a Duplo-Ray big enough to solve the problem. We have most of the largest ones working around the clock to mitigate the problem, but all they can do is buy us time. Time to escape. It's a very long process, but eventually our world will become as you know it in this era. The volcanoes will someday resurface the entire planet, leaving no trace that our people had ever even been there. Even if this disaster hadn't happened, our world is simply too close to the Sun, which continues to expand. Pfoff becoming uninhabitable was always unavoidable, the disaster just sped up the process dramatically. In this time period, the only life that still exists there are a few microbes, stubbornly clinging to existence in the upper atmosphere." There was an unmistakable sadness in her tone as she explained all of this.

"Why travel through time to Earth? There are probably countless hospitable planets in space that don't have any intelligent life on them. If your people are so inclined to peace, why not go to one of those worlds?" Randy asked.

"That is precisely what the other 12 major nations of Pfoff plan to do. They have been busy constructing a massive fleet of space arks to take us away from Pfoff. But our space travel technology is not like that of the Federation. We cannot warp space. It will take us a thousand years to reach Armenclius, the world we plan to colonize. It's a very risky undertaking. The trip is fraught with dangers. The Saawgauth believe that going to distant Armenclius is a fool's errand. They say that instead we should take the Earth. They claim that when they sent their first probes into this future time, they detected no sign of life or industry on Armenclius in this era. They took that to mean that our fleet will never reach it and we will be destroyed on the long journey there. Yet they refuse to give the rest of the nations proof of these extraordinary claims. Doing so would mean sharing the secrets of their time travel technology with them, so they can independently confirm these findings, and that is something they are not willing to do."

Randy was surprised that the Venusians didn't have warp drive technology, yet at least some of them had developed time travel. He would've thought that warp drive would be easier to invent than time travel, but what did he know?

"It sounds like you don't believe what these Saawgauth discovered yourself." Penny observed.

"I don't. And even if I did, it doesn't mean that our people really went extinct. If we didn't reach Armenclius we could have found a safe haven on another world."

"But wasn't that all millions of years ago from our perspective? Wouldn't the Federation know what became of your people?" Randy asked.

"If they do, he won't tell me!" Kergaali said in frustration.

"I'm forbidden from revealing anything about the future of your people to you that you can't work out for yourselves. I've broken plenty of rules for you so far, but that's one which I won't *ever* break!" Jim said firmly.

"So you really don't have one united government? It's just one country that's planning to attack us?" This surprised Randy, but perhaps it was also good news. One country would surely be easier to defeat than an entire planet?

Jim laughed. "That's one of the funny things that you humans always get wrong about us aliens in all your science fiction stories! You always think that we have one big planetary government, but oftentimes we have lots of factions and countries on our planets, just like you do. The difference is that we're a little better at living in harmony and appreciating our differences than you humans tend to be."

"What about you? Aren't you one of these...soggy goths? Why are you so willing to help us?" Penny wanted to know. Kergaali didn't strike her as being very altruistic. In fact, she appeared to be rather aloof and arrogant. It seemed like she thought of humans as disgusting primitives herself.

"Saawgauth. Not 'soggy goths.' No, if you must know, I come from a nation called the Baandergi. Some of us have become concerned by the actions of the Saawgauth and decided to take action to stop them. We've infiltrated their ranks and are trying to stop this invasion, but we don't have the full backing of our government. They don't want to divert too many resources away from the work of constructing a fleet to carry us to Armenclius." She paused and took a drink from her can of Coke.

Penny thought her answer told her nothing that she really wanted to know. Nothing personal about why *she* in particular wanted to fight this fight, why she was risking her life to save the Earth, nothing but a list of dry facts.

"When we detected the presence of more advanced aliens on this planet, of the Federation, we thought we could enlist their help, but so far, only Jim has answered the call to action. It seems that the Federation wrote your planet off long ago as being a lost cause, whose destruction was inevitable. I can see why. On my planet, by the time we realized it, it was already too late for us to reverse the damage to our environment, which is slowly dooming it. But for you humans, it isn't too late and yet you do *nothing* to try and reverse this outcome! Sometimes I almost think I can see why the Saawgauth think you don't deserve this world." The contempt was apparent in her voice.

Jim could see from the shocked looks on Randy and Penny's faces that Kergaali's opinions weren't making her very popular and changed the subject.

"What is this news that you have for me about their next move? Why did you insist on coming here in person for the first time, despite the risk to yourself?" He asked her suddenly.

"They plan on landing at the United Nations again tonight. In about an hour from now. You *must* use your ship to intercept them. We have no other options. I can help guide you to them so you can intercept them as they emerge from their forward base. It's imperative that they don't reach the UN and put their plan into motion. We might not get another chance to eliminate Drogalla like this!" she pleaded with more passion in her voice than either Randy or Penny had yet to hear from her before.

Jim sighed heavily. He was so reluctant to use his ship in battle because it also served as a hyperspace relay that allowed him to control this body from millions of light years away. If it was seriously damaged or destroyed, the body he was using on earth would become a lifeless heap, and the feedback could possibly even kill his real body back on his home world. But what else could he do? He closed his eyes and stayed like that for a long, pregnant moment before snapping them open and speaking again. "Very well. We can use my ship. I guess we really have no other choice right now. Hi- Fi! Close the restaurant once the last customer has left. If they're not out in a half hour, force them out. Begin making preparations for flight, and set up the decoy hologram."

Hi-Fi saluted. "Yes, sir, very good sir!" And he marched off like the good little tin soldier that he was.

"You've made the correct decision, Jim, and on behalf of the Baandergi, I thank you," Kergaali told him and placed her hand on his paw tenderly for a moment before withdrawing it.

Penny was surprised to discover that a pang of jealousy rose within her at the gesture, even though she now knew that Kergaali was supposedly devoid of romantic feelings for Jim—or for anyone else, apparently. It would seem that Penny still had strong feelings for Jim, despite everything. In fact, the more she learned about his determination to try and save them, she couldn't help but admire him more than she had before, just in a different way.

Perhaps as impossibly weird as all of this was, it wasn't too late for them after all? She could see now that he was right, in a way. He *was* the same person she had grown to love. All the best parts of him, his essence, were still there, just wrapped up in a decidedly odd new package. She was still quite mad at him, though. For not trusting her with his true self, for thinking so little of her he felt like had to hide, especially in light of what she had told him about her own past. But had he really been so wrong? It was a hell of a secret to share with someone, and her initial reaction had been so bad that it had proven his point for him.

She was so confused right now, everything was happening so fast. She didn't know what she really wanted anymore. Part of her still wanted Jim and part of her wasn't so sure she could ever fully adjust to the weirdness of all of this. She wasn't like Randy, who seemed to go out of his way to court the bizarre. Although she had genuinely appreciated unconventional things, at the end of the day, when all was said and done, Penny just wanted a normal life for herself and Paul. She'd have a lot to think about when this was over with—if they were all still alive. She just knew that she was beginning to regret some of the harsh things she'd said and done earlier to both Jim and Randy, while at the same time, a part of her still felt perfectly justified in how she had reacted. Jim's keeping secrets from her and Randy's interfering with her love life like he had was *not* cool, even if their intentions had been benevolent.

Something else was also bugging her right now though. "Why do you have to clear the restaurant?" Penny asked Jim.

"The restaurant *is* my ship. A hologram on the outside makes it look like an old diner with ship parts welded onto it. But the ship parts are what's real, the diner isn't. Even the interior is just a bunch of hard light holograms projected over the ship's cargo hold. This was just a vacant lot when I landed it here. My replicator..."

"Duplo-Ray!" Kergaali shouted.

"My *Duplo-Ray* can create cash if I want it to. I created enough to buy the lot and pay for the permits to operate this place as a restaurant. It's all part of my cover. Not all of my money comes from the Duplo-Ray. Hi-Fi is actually a mobile interface for my ship's computer. I created him in the form of a cutesy robot because it cracks me up how in so many sci-fi stories the hero has some kind of cute robot companion to help him out. He's actually far more powerful than any computer on the planet. So much of your world's money is virtual, just a mental construct that you all go along with for some reason, nothing more than numbers in a computer file. It's child's play to create the illusion of wealth for oneself if you can get into the right systems and manipulate them convincingly. With Hi-Fi's help, I was able to do that."

"Ha! I had a feeling that the restaurant was really a spaceship. At least I did once I knew that Jim was really an alien." Penny told Randy.

"Yeah, I had my suspicions about that too," Randy told her, then he looked Jim in the eye. "Jim, I've been wondering about how these replicators of yours work..."

"Duplo-Ray!" Kergaali repeated, doggedly keeping up her routine.

Randy ignored her, by now, all too predictable outburst. "Like, where does the matter come from that you make the food from?"

"Oh. It's um...recycled waste products mostly." Jim admitted reluctantly.

Penny spat out her food and pushed her plate away

"I think I've lost my appetite. You don't mean like...poop do you?"

"That's exactly what I mean. Biological waste products, wastewater all of it goes into storage tanks and are recycled as raw materials that the repli...Duplo-Ray uses to construct new meals, or anything else I ask it to make for me. It's not as gross as it sounds."

"Yes! It is most efficient!" Kergaali said with enthusiasm as she finished off her food with gusto.

"I think I'm gonna be sick." Penny frowned, not buying it.

"Jim and Kergaali, do you think we could fly this ship to Guild Headquarters once you've dealt with the Venusian ships? I believe if you presented your case to the Inner Council, they'd help fight off this invasion. They have their own military, with technology that's more advanced than what the rest of the planet currently has, not to mention lots of magic users." Randy asked.

"Yeah, that's a good idea—if we survive!" Jim agreed.

Jim looked at Penny. "You'd better go back to the *Blunderbus*. I don't want to put you in any danger and we're about to fly off into battle. I really do care about you, Penny, whether you believe it or not."

"I know." Penny said gently. Now it was her turn to put a hand on his paw. It felt kind of nice.

"But I'm not going anywhere. I want to see this thing through to the end. It's my planet, you know? I want to make sure it's safe."

Kergaali nodded approvingly. Perhaps this Penny creature wasn't so worthless after all?

Randy had quite a different reaction. "Penny! What about Paul? If something happens to both of us, he'll be an orphan. What do you really think you can do to help?"

"I don't know! But I know that I'm sick of always sitting on the sidelines when something like this happens, having to hear about it after the fact!"

"Something like this happened before?" Kergaali asked in surprise.

"Sister, you'd be surprised!" Penny quipped.

"Randy, look. I remember Naomi telling me about that first adventure you all went on. Matt had wanted to send everyone back home then, too, for the same reasons. But Naomi wouldn't hear of it. She wanted to do something... anything to make sure that the world would be safe for her son to grow up in, and thank God that she did! I want to do the same thing! I don't know how I can help exactly, but I'm sure I can do *something*. Naomi was just a regular person back then too, but she could still help save the world. Why can't I? I know I can't just go home now, twiddle my thumbs, and pretend that everything is normal when I know that it's not. I won't be able to live with myself if I don't do something to help save my planet, to make sure that our son will have a future! If you don't want me on this ship, you're gonna have to throw me off!"

I could just teleport you out of here. Randy thought, but he had no real intentions of doing so. She was mad enough at him as it was.

Randy sighed. He knew how impossible it was to talk Penny out of something once she made up her mind about it.

"Okay then, welcome to the team." He said, hoping that he wasn't making the biggest mistake of his life. When Paul was born, he swore that he'd never abandon him like his own parents had, and now he was about to fly off into a situation where Paul might lose not just him, but his mother, too.

Randy would just have to make sure that didn't happen—no matter what the costs.

Hi-Fi came running back into the room. "Master Jim! All the customers are gone and the preparations for the flight are complete!" The robot seemed positively giddy at the prospect of taking off.

"Good job, man!" Jim said and put up his hand for Hi-Fi to give him a high five.

Kergaali checked a device on her wrist. "Excellent. We should get moving. They'll be leaving their hidden base soon."

"Alright everyone, follow me to the cockpit. Let's get this party started!" Jim said. They followed him through a side door that led into the restaurant, only now the restaurant was gone. In its place was a mostly empty space save for the posters and display cases filled with the various science fiction collectibles that decorated Kirk's.

"All those things weren't just holograms?" Randy asked.

"Nope! They're all authentic. I've been collecting this stuff for years. I really am obsessed with how you humans perceive us extraterrestrials. I'm thinking of writing a research paper about it, maybe even a book."

He led them into a cockpit where the kitchen of the restaurant used to be. Hi-Fi plugged himself into a slot next to Jim's chair. All the others found a seat behind him, with Kergaali sitting closest to him. He placed a thin crown on his head and flicked a few switches on the control panel before him.

"Hi-Fi, activate decoy hologram and engage stealth mode." He commanded.

"Done and done, Master Jim!" he cried out positively joyfully. Was it just Randy's imagination, or was the robot getting more and more cheerful after each new task he was given? It was getting annoying.

"Alright. Lift us off. Kergaali, where are we headed?"

If you had been standing out in the parking lot of Kirk's Galactic Grub, you wouldn't have seen anything, as a hologram shimmered into place at the same moment that the restaurant disappeared. You might have felt a wave of unusually warm air wash over you as the now invisible ship took to the skies. The hologram it left behind switched to a "hard light" hologram as it hovered over it, so that anyone who came up to the "building" wouldn't walk through the illusion.

"Fly out towards the ocean for now, I'll direct you to the forward base once we're over the water." Kergaali suggested.

"Okay everybody! Put on your seatbelts. That's right, unlike Star Trek, we actually have seat belts! No being tossed around the bridge on *my* ship!" he proclaimed proudly.

"Well, here goes nothing!" Penny said as the ship accelerated out over the city, and they rushed towards the ocean at an alarming speed. She hoped that none of the others could hear the nervousness in her voice that she felt as her stomach started churning. Did she have her acid reflux pills on her? Penny often got a bad case of GERD when she got too stressed, and so far today has been nothing if not stressful. She tried to dismiss such thoughts and calm herself using some of the techniques Randy had taught her. Penny didn't know what the future held for any of them, but one thing was for certain, it sure would be interesting to find out!

CHAPTER 9:
SPEED IS THE KEY

As Jim's ship roared out over the open ocean, Kergaali looked at the device strapped to her wrist and read out a complicated sounding string of letters and numbers to Hi-Fi.

Coordinates. Penny realized.

"Correcting course!" Hi-Fi shouted it out as if he was having an orgasm.

The ship veered off in one direction and, a few seconds later, it came to a rest, hovering over a churning stretch of turbulent sea. The sun was just beginning to set on the horizon.

"I don't see anything. What are we waiting for?" She asked.

"The Saawgauth have a mothership that they're using as a forward base of operations parked on the seabed right below us. It's where I've been stationed since I infiltrated their organization."

Penny gazed through the forward viewport in the cockpit at the sea below her. It was hard to imagine that lurking beneath such a normal-looking scene was some kind of giant alien spaceship.

"Their ships can go underwater too?" She asked incredulously.

"It's not such an unfamiliar environment from outer space in many ways." Randy told her, seemingly unfazed by these revelations. "There is a long history of sightings of USOs— Unidentified Submersible Objects here on Earth. Aliens love to hide their stuff in our oceans." He informed her.

"Really? Well, that's news to me!" Penny remarked. She wasn't really into all the paranormal stuff that Randy was interested in, so this wasn't that unusual for her to be unaware of this.

They hung in the sky there for some time, waiting for the ships to emerge from the waters below.

Randy looked over at Penny a little nervously. She caught a glimpse of this from the corner of her eye.

"What is it?" She whispered to him.

"I was just wondering...are we cool? We're about to go into a dangerous situation here. We could die, and well...I don't wanna die knowing that you're still angry with me. I want us to be cool with each other if the end comes sooner than we'd like."

He seemed quite vulnerable, as he said it. A part of her just wanted to give him the world's biggest hug and let him know everything was going to be okay when she saw him looking so miserable and uncertain. To tell him that, of course, they were cool, that they always would be cool. How could they not be? After all that they had been through together and shared in the past? Another part of her hated herself for feeling like it was her job to comfort him like that, especially after what he'd just done. She felt weak for not being able to hold on to her anger at him. Yet didn't the true weakness lie in continuing to take refuge in her anger? Of being unable to venture beyond it? What did continuing to be mad at him actually gain for her, aside from a feeling of righteousness in the justification for her feelings? Yet if she forgave him, she had everything to gain: she would get to keep one of the best friendships and creative partnerships in her life. Of course, she also felt pressured to make it work because this was the father of her son, and he was a good father, too. She didn't want to deprive Paul of a relationship he had a right to just because she was pissed off at his dad.

She looked into his deep, questioning, brown eyes and saw the pain there. *Fuck! Why am I always such a sucker for him? Why can I never say no to those damned eyes?*

"I don't want to die being angry at you, either." She shocked herself as she said the words, startled by the truth of them. She sighed. "I know what you did you did because you were genuinely concerned about me, and about Paul. I know it came from a good place. The way you went about doing it might've been a little weird and fucked up, but what else should I expect? Everything you do is a little weird and fucked up!"

They both shared a brief laugh at that last line.

"Maybe the way I reacted to it was kinda fucked up too, though. Although you have to admit, it's a hell of a lot to lay on a person all at once! Some things I said might've been a bit more...*harsh* than intended, and I know they're not true. I don't *really* think that you were trying to break us up so you could get me back. I don't know why I said that, it…just came out. Sometimes when I'm pissed off, I say crazy shit. Who doesn't? But yeah, if anything should happen to us, I do want you to know that I love you and I always will. Maybe not love in *that* particular way anymore, you know what I mean, but love nonetheless."

She reached out and gave his hand a brief squeeze, and let it linger there for a while before finally releasing it. She really felt a little better now about everything.

"Thanks, Pen. I love you too, and I'm really sorry…" He began, his eyes welling up, just like hers were.

She waved her hand. "No! Enough. Enough of the mushy stuff already! Let's not concentrate on dying, okay? I'd much rather focus on living! Our son needs us alive, remember?"

Randy nodded gratefully.

Kergaali studied the humans. Such strange creatures! Such complicated relationships! She'd never understand them. Focusing on something as irrelevant as interpersonal relationships at a time such as this? Did they not understand what was at stake?

Jim, for his part, wondered if Penny was also having second thoughts about some of the things she'd said to him earlier, too? Could he dare to hope that he'd get an apology, too? That she'd take him back, now that she'd had more time to think about things? He resolved that he'd just have to earn back her love by showing her how much he was prepared to risk for her, and for her planet. Earth girls liked heroic types, right? Well, he could play that role if he had to. He'd played many roles in his time; it was what he was good at doing.

There was even more waiting. The minutes grinded on.

"How long are we gonna have to wait here like this? How do we know we didn't already miss them?" Penny asked in frustration. She was starting to get bored. He had to chuckle a little at that realization: here she was, sitting in a real, bona fide spaceship with a pair of aliens waiting to attack some flying saucers that were supposed to come out of a giant spaceship hidden under the ocean, and she was bored! It was ludicrous, but it was true. The whole situation was ludicrous. She pulled out her phone to find something to amuse herself with, only to see that she had no bars of service this far out from the shore. Typical.

Well, at least watching the sunset and the moonrise over the ocean had been nice, she thought. This far from the shore, it wasn't as cloudy as it had been today back in the city, so such celestial events had looked spectacular.

Kergaali consulted the device on her wrist once more. "We are not too late, we are early. Don't worry, you shall not have much longer to wait. My sources below inform me they are currently preparing the ships for launch."

"Why wait for the ships to come out? If we're hovering above their mothership, can't we just blast it and destroy the whole thing?" Randy asked.

At first, Penny was a little taken aback that he'd suggested such a bloodthirsty course of action. However, she also knew that he often liked to go through all the possibilities in a given situation, as a kind of intellectual exercise, including the ones he didn't like. Then again, this was war now, she supposed. They might have to get a little ruthless in order to come out on top, and Randy was enough of a realist to understand that.

"Yes! This is an excellent idea, Randy!" Kergaali said, her cat-like eyes glittering with newfound excitement. "Can you make it happen, Jim?" she asked as she stroked Zaa, who now sat curled up in her lap. At this moment, she reminded Penny uncomfortably of a villain from a James Bond movie.

"Don't you have allies that are still down there on that ship? The ones that've been feeding you information?" Penny asked her, a little horrified that she seemed so willing to sacrifice her comrades like that.

"Yes, but they knew the risks when they joined." Kergaali said coldly. "It would be a small price to pay for such a victory."

"It's an enormous ship, and it's pretty far down below the ocean's surface. I'm not sure that even my weapons are powerful enough to take it out like that," Jim said, as he consulted scans of the ship that were projected in the air in front of him.

"Why do you even have weapons on your ship if your mission is so peaceful, Jim? Hell! Is Jim even your real name?" Penny asked. It suddenly occurred to her she now felt like she knew more about Kergaali and her people than she did about who Jim really was and where he came from.

"Because sometimes we run into space pirates from more primitive systems. And for the record, my name really is James." He answered.

"Really? James! Not some weird, exotic sounding, hard to pronounce word like Kergaali?" As she said it, Penny realized she'd put her foot in her mouth.

"Errr, Sorry, Kergaali. No offense."

"None taken. I don't like my name either. It means 'sweeper of the floors' in the Old Tongue. We were once such a disgustingly servile race."

"Is it so hard to believe that your people would be the only ones in the entire universe to come up with the combination of sounds that form the name James, and use it as a personal name? In fact, there's a planet where the name Maurice is so popular that it can be quite confusing to visit. It feels like everyone is named Maurice there!" Jim asked.

"I guess it could be one of those monkeys with a typewriter coming up with Shakespeare kinds of things." Penny said

"Right, exactly. Except in my world, the diminutive form of my name is 'Ames', not Jim. I've never understood how you people ever got 'Jim' out of 'James!'"

"Me neither. Would you prefer to be called Ames, then?" Penny asked.

"Nah, I've been on this planet since '92 and I've gone by Jim for most of that time. At this point, being called anything else would feel weird." He told her.

Penny was surprised that Jim had been on Earth for that long. She was what? Eleven years old? Or maybe twelve in 1992? How old *was* Jim really? She assumed he had to have been at least an adult when he was sent out on a mission like this all by himself. She decided she didn't want to know what the age gap between them might be, Penny had a feeling that it would only piss her off all over again.

At that very moment, far below the waves, Drogalla, Leader of the Saawgauth prepared to board the lead saucer. Goymaalt, ever the loyal second in command, was already waiting at the bottom of the ramp.

"Goymaalt! I want you to remain behind this time, assume command of the mothership in my absence. "Drogalla ordered as they approached one another.

"But Leader, I want to be by your side for this important phase of the mission!"

"I know, and believe me, I want you by my side. However, there may yet be danger. Should our ships be ambushed again, I don't want our entire high command to be destroyed all at once."

Especially since we don't know who we can trust and who we can't. Drogalla thought. Perhaps the next person in the chain of command after Goymaalt was the traitor? It was possible. They couldn't give the enemy the opportunity to take control of the entire operation like that.

"But our ground teams didn't find anything, the danger is minimal." Goymaalt continued to argue, clearly upset at the idea of being left behind.

"No, the danger is *unknown*. And it isn't completely true that they found nothing. There were some anomalous energy readings detected inside that one hotel..."

"Which did not match the signatures of any known form of weapon, so we decided they constituted no threat! Please, let me accompany you on this flight."

Drogalla sighed and then smiled. The Leader laid a hand on Goymaalt's shoulder and looked into the eyes of the one whom they held most dear.

"Please, don't make this any more difficult than it already is. I need you here, it's where you can do the most good. Besides, it's bad enough that I'm exposing myself to this risk, but if anything were to ever happen to you..."

Goymaalt swallowed hard, choked up with emotion. "I understand. Please, come back to me."

"I intend to, my dearest, I intend to!" Drogalla promised, and looked around quickly first to ensure that they were alone before planting a passionate kiss on Goymaalt's lips.

The Saawgauth didn't have the same taboos against forming physically intimate relationships with each other that the Baandergi did. Despite this, it was still considered bad form for the leader to make such an open display of affection while on duty.

How Drogalla had wanted to linger there forever, with lips pressed against delicious lips, but duty, as ever called.

Inside the cockpit of Jim's ship, the atmosphere was now quite tense. Hi-Fi had just announced that his sensors had detected five ships leaving the mothership which were currently on a fast approach towards the surface. They were due to appear above the frothy seas any moment now.

Just then, the first saucer broke the surface and wobbled into the skies ahead of them, quickly followed by the others. Randy got a good enough look at them to determine that they were indeed the "Adamski" style ships they'd seen last night on the way over to Kirk's. He now knew that Adamski's Venusians were quite different from Kergaali's people. The most glaring difference being that they had two sexes and gender identities, so he found it interesting that their technology, at least superficially, appeared so similar. He wondered what other differences and similarities there were between the Venusians of that parallel universe and those of his own?

Jim's ship, invisible to the saucers, gave chase. As they approached them, they could see that they were flying together in a tight formation, with two ships in each corner around a central ship that was double the size of the others. Then the ships shimmered out of view. They'd just engaged their "shroud" as Kergaali put it.

It caught Penny by surprise. "Where did they go?"

"Nowhere. They're still in front of us. They're just using their primitive cloaking technology. Don't worry, it's no problem for a ship like this to keep track of them. I know exactly where each one of them is." Jim bragged, obviously proud of what his ship was capable of.

Penny could just make out the famous NYC skyline coming into view on the horizon again. The lights of the city twinkled softly.

"What are you waiting for, then? They're almost to the city!" Penny didn't relish the idea of these ships crashing into the crowded streets of one of the biggest cities on the planet.

"I know, I know, they're just so darned fast!" he complained.

"Master Jim, I have acquired a weapons lock on the entire formation!" Hi-Fi cried ecstatically. His joy was so palpable that it was disturbing.

"Then fire all weapons at them, full spread!" Jim shouted.

The ship's particle beams blazed forth, striking all five saucers simultaneously. Everyone inside the cockpit could immediately tell that they'd hit their targets because, as the ships were struck, they briefly became visible before disappearing once more.

"Direct hit, sir! OH! *VERY* good, sir!" Hi-Fi gushed.

It definitely sounded like maybe the robot was touching himself inappropriately as he said it. It made everyone in the cockpit feel a little dirty. Except for Jim, who thought it was hilarious, and Kergaali, who seemed to have little concept of such things.

"Hmm. Their shields aren't quite as rudimentary as I'd assumed," Jim mumbled, disappointed that he hadn't destroyed the ships with his first attack. "Hi-Fi, divert power from all non-essential systems and fire another full spread round the second you get another weapons lock!" he commanded.

"Targets acquired! FIRING NOW, SIR!" Hi-Fi replied with an enthusiasm that made Randy wince in pain.

This time, though, as the beams of energy arced from Jim's guns, several of the saucers swiftly returned fire. They must've targeted their weapons at the source of the beams. Their weapons struck his ship before they eventually exploded themselves, peppering the sea with their flaming silver debris.

Jim's ship rocked violently. The blows fiercely jerked Penny forward, but remained securely fastened to her seat.

"Ha, ha! See? What'd I tell you? Seatbelts! Indispensable in a battle! If we'd been on the bridge of the starship *Enterprise,* half of you guys would've been tossed to the other side of the room by that blast! You'd all have concussions and stuff! Hot damn! My ship *rocks!*"

He seemed to be having entirely too much fun.

"Don't celebrate yet, the big ship is still intact!" Randy pointed to the viewscreen ahead of them. They could all see the largest saucer still flying ahead of them, trailing smoke behind it as it traced an erratic path through the sky. Its cloaking device must've been destroyed by the last attack

"That's Drogalla's ship! She must not reach the UN building or all is lost! Destroy it! Destroy it now!" Kergaali hissed.

"I'd hardly call that ship 'intact!' Jim told Randy, sounding a little insulted. "Maybe I should give them a call? Give 'em a chance to surrender first? It seems like the civilized thing to do, now that we've clearly got the upper hand. Having the enemy leader as a prisoner would make for one hell of a bargaining chip!" Jim mused.

"No! Stick to the plan! These people are fanatics—they will never surrender. Destroy them now while you still can!" Kergaali pressed him.

"Okay, okay! Hi-Fi, you heard Kergaali. Target the remaining ship and give it all you've got!" Jim ordered.

"Giving it...ALL...I...HAVE, SIR!!" Hi-Fi replied in his strange way. Penny covered her face with one hand in embarrassment. That *definitely* sounded dirty. The robot must've really meant it though, because the lights inside the ship briefly blinked out as multiple beams of energy sizzled forth to vaporize the remaining ship. Jim's ship flew right on through the cloud of dust that was all that remained of the enemy ship.

"Woo-Hoo! Yeah, baby! *That's* how you do it!" Jim cried triumphantly as he punched the air.

Kergaali laughed her strange, alien laugh as she stroked Zaa.

Penny, however, just frowned as she watched the sparkling bits of dust that were once been a flying saucer falling around them.

"What's wrong, Penny? We just won that battle!" Randy asked, sensing her mood.

"I don't know. I was just thinking about how there were real people in those ships we just shot down. And now they're dead. Celebrating their deaths seems kind of...obscene in a way," said Penny.

She wondered if Luke Skywalker ever felt this way after blowing away a TIE fighter? Did he ever think about the other pilot? Sure, the bad guys in those stories were serving an evil order, seeking to bring darkness to their galaxy, but they were also somebody's baby. Somewhere there was someone who cared for them, someone whose world just got a little darker. Darker by the hand of the hero of the story, the one who's supposed to be serving the light. Was it possible, she wondered, to ever serve the light without also bringing a little darkness too? Was something "good" so long as it caused less pain, per capita, in the grand scheme of things? Who knew what the correct balance was? Who tallied up the scores? Was anyone really out there keeping track? Such questions had always bothered her. The line between "good" and "evil" often seemed so arbitrary to her. Just a matter of perspective. Her dad would probably say something like "Can't make an omelet without breaking a few eggs." If he knew what she was thinking right now, but such sentiments had never really satisfied her. It must be nice to live in such a black and white world, but she just couldn't see things that way. Allowing oneself to fall into the trap of thinking so simplistically seemed to be the one truly "wrong" thing in her opinion.

Randy was about to agree, but before he could say anything, Kergaali interrupted him.

"It was necessary. I wouldn't mourn their deaths. Those people are plotting geno-cide against you." The alien said, the new word still sounding uncomfortable on her tongue.

"*What*? You didn't mention that before!" Randy said, shocked by this latest revelation.

"What did you people think they were going to do with you once they had this planet under their control?"

"I don't know, enslave us or something?" Penny said.

Kergaali did her odd little laugh once again. "We have the Duplo-Ray to make anything we need. We have little use for slaves for farming or manufacturing. We have machines to help us with the menial tasks. Besides, we were once slaves ourselves, so it is one of our highest laws that we must never enslave another. We consider it to be more merciful to kill someone than to reduce them to slavery! Far better to die free, with your dignity intact, than to live as a slave!"

"What twisted logic!" Randy was astounded by this attitude. To him, so long as there was still life, there was still the hope for freedom, that things would get better. What hope was there in death?

"Yes. Drogalla was a true monster, You should rejoice in her demise. She considered your people to be little better than vermin that are infesting this world and destroying it. You should celebrate her passing, but unfortunately, her followers still remain. They are fanatics, and will carry on what she's started. They'll be in confusion for a while, but this will only buy us a little time before they try to pick up where they left off with their plans. Remember that they still have that underwater mothership, and a larger base on the dark side of the moon where their Time Tunnel is located. Your planet will remain in immediate danger until both of those targets are eliminated."

Randy considered her words. "That's why our next move should be to go to Guild Headquarters. We can get the UGF's help with attacking them. How fast can you get this ship to the South Pacific, Jim?"

"Are you kidding me? I can get us there in just a few minutes, just point the way, Randy!"

Randy pulled his Guild Communicator from a jacket pocket. He called ahead and explained some of the situation to his girlfriend, Aethra. From anyone else, getting a call that your boyfriend was currently sitting inside of a spaceship with two aliens and a robot who wanted to come and visit to discuss thwarting an invasion of the Earth might be surprising. But by now, Aethra was used to such ridiculousness from Randy. She promised that she'd call an emergency meeting of the Inner Council when they arrived. He also got map coordinates to the secret island that served as Guild Headquarters for Jim to feed into Hi-Fi.

"New course laid in, sir! Now proceeding on course!!" Hi-Fi shouted as if he'd just won the Publisher's Clearing House Sweepstakes.

"What's wrong with him? Is he supposed to be that happy?" Randy asked.

"Oh, shit! I forgot that I had his emotions set on 'relentlessly cheerful.' It cracks me up, but I realize it can get annoying for other people. Hi-Fi! Assume baseline emotional responses!" Jim commanded.

"Assuming baseline emotional responses now, sir," Hi-Fi said in a markedly calmer tone.

"You can just literally mess with his emotions like that? That doesn't seem very nice!" Penny opined.

Jim laughed. "Hi-Fi doesn't have any genuine emotions. His 'feelings' are just part of the interface program, it's strictly an emulation. He's not truly alive. We're forbidden from creating sentient machines to serve us. There are several civilizations within the Federation that are made of sentient machines, or have evolved into machines. It's immoral to deliberately create such beings just to be your servants, so we don't."

"Oh. I guess that's okay, then." Penny said, feeling a little foolish.

"It's sweet of you though, to show such concern for him. If he had been sentient, you would have been quite right to do so," Jim added, sensing her embarrassment.

Kergaali just shook her head, unable to comprehend feeling such misplaced sentimentality over a mere machine.

Such weakness will be the undoing of these Earth creatures! She thought bitterly.

And with that, Jim's spaceship, the restaurant formerly known as Kirk's Galactic Grub, was once more roaring out back over the ocean.

***

Sydney Yu hated work. Or at least, she had until she started working for Sara. Now her job was slightly more...tolerable. There were so many things she disliked about working, like all the vapid, empty small talk: "Some weather we're having, huh?" Or "So, how was your weekend?" People loved to say shit like that, but she'd learned long ago that despite this nervous need to say something to you, most of them didn't really care and were ultimately afraid to ever make anything close to an actual human connection with you. Inevitably, there will be a muted expression of horror that will cross the face of the average coworker if you dare to tell them how your weekend *really* was, or that you kinda like the shitty weather outside because it matches your mood. People can't handle honesty from strangers, especially people who they don't think of as strangers because they see them every day. But the truth of the matter is that they're *still* strangers despite that, strangers because these people understand nothing about who you really are, where you've been, what you've seen, or what makes you tick. And if they did, most of them would likely run away in terror.

Work had been a lonely affair for her. There had been a time when some of the people she worked with seemed to have an interest in her beyond that superficial politeness needed to function together as something resembling a team, a time when she thought she could have friends at work. But time and time again, such people had betrayed her. It seems that no matter how small and relatively unimportant of an environment you're working in, there is a certain hierarchy and pecking order. Even in a job as seemingly lacking in all prestige as a fast food restaurant or a convenience store, there are people who will sell you out in a minute so they can climb higher up that hierarchy to become queen of the 7-11 or whatever. She knew everyone wasn't quite that bad and cutthroat, but it was just safer to assume that they were. She gave up on making anything resembling real friends at work long ago. Better to stick to your old friends you met outside of work who had nothing to personally gain by spilling your secrets in order to suck up to the boss.

Life, to her, was often a very frustrating experience. You could cry about it or you could laugh about it. She preferred to laugh about it. She fancied herself to be something of an aspiring comedian. Sydney had started working in the hotel bussing tables in the hotel's restaurant. She didn't have the capacity to put on the kind of bubbly false face that would ever earn her tips as a waitress. She was too real for that. It took every ounce of her effort to hide her interior pain enough to get through each day. To cram herself into the mask of normalcy. She'd also learned long ago that she couldn't be herself at work. She was just too weird for most people, too sardonic. Her caustic observations on life which worked (kinda) on the comedy stage just alienated people at work. They couldn't handle the truth she spat out. So she kept her head down, and tried not to be noticed, counting down the minutes before she could tear off the confining mask and breathe freely again.

How many years of your life did the typical person spend at work? What percentage was squandered playing at being some distorted, highly self edited version of yourself? What truly terrified Sydney was the idea that she might spend so much time in that role that she'd completely forget how to be herself. That her "professional" personality would become her default setting, the one she could never turn off. Or even more frightening: it would happen so gradually that she wouldn't even know it had already happened to her.

The only way to avoid this fate seemed to be to cling to her unprofessionalism like it was a life raft in a tempestuous sea. She would be only just professional enough to remain employed.

One good thing about that stupid job in the restaurant, though, was that it allowed her to watch people and gave her plenty of material. She'd gotten in trouble more than once for writing this material down when the busybodies at work thought she should be doing something else. She had always been getting into trouble for her slacker ways. It was no secret that she had a terrible work ethic, but this was only because she felt like her job had a terrible *worker* ethic. In other words, management was screwing over the workers, so she delighted in screwing them back by not busting her ass for the crumbs from their table. She'd tried to master the subtle art of just working well enough not to get fired, and of looking like she was working when she wasn't actually. Unfortunately, she hadn't really mastered this. She wasn't nearly as good at it as she liked to think she was, and sometimes her lack of anything resembling actual dedication got noticed.

That's how she met Sara, the Hotel Detective. Someone had been stealing money from the restaurant, and of course, because of her crappy attitude, suspicion had naturally fallen onto her. Sara had gone undercover to find the truth, masquerading as a customer in the restaurant, she'd offered to buy Sydney a drink when her shift ended, and Sydney, not being able to turn down a free drink, had accepted, although she found it a little odd that this older lady wanted to have drinks with her. Was the lady trying to pick her up? Sydney didn't have a gay bone in her body, but what could it hurt to humor the lady? A free drink was a free drink, it didn't obligate her to do anything with her. So she accepted. Sydney would later discover that although Sara was bisexual, she had never been even slightly interested in her in that way. For one thing, Sydney was far too young for Sara and for another, she wasn't her "type." Even though Sydney had no attraction to Sara, it had still disappointed her to discover that she wasn't her type. Her vanity didn't like to be reminded that she wasn't anybody's type.

Sara had plied her tongue loose with alcohol, which had been her plan. Sydney had confessed all her slacker tricks to her, all the ways she enjoyed "screwing over the man" while at work, but none of them included actually stealing money. There were some lines she wouldn't cross, no matter how exploited she felt her labor was. Sara had been greatly amused by Sydney's terrible attitude. Mainly because Sara herself felt very exploited by the hotel, too. She'd worked there for decades and had been treated very well by the family that owned the place, but when they died and their spoiled trust fund brats inherited the business, they had no intentions of trying to run it. So they'd sold it to some faceless corporate chain that didn't seem to know what to do with the property. The new management had let Sara keep her job, but they'd also cut deeply into her benefits to save money, delaying Sara's long awaited retirement plans for the next several years. She hated them for it. The last thing she was going to do was rat out a slacker of a worker like Sydney. Indeed, Sara herself had adopted some of the same tricks that Sydney employed, just doing her job well enough to keep it, but never going above and beyond. The old owners had deserved that kind of loyalty, but not these corporate stooges that were jogging the place into the ground. So Sara had written a glowing evaluation of Sydney into her report, allowing her to keep her job—at least for a little while.

Sara would eventually discover that the real thief was the Hotel's Night Auditor, whose job was to reconcile the receipts from the restaurant with the cash and credit card transactions. He'd been pocketing some of the cash and blaming the irregularities on the restaurant staff. Sara would often hang out with Sydney after that, getting a drink or two at the end of her shift became their nightly ritual. When it seemed like Sydney's poor work habits had finally driven her manager to the brink of firing her, Sara had her transferred to her department in security. Was it charity? Maybe. Sydney knew that Sara genuinely appreciated her sense of humor and she enjoyed having her around because she made her laugh. She also knew that keeping an employee as worthless as she was on the company payroll was part of Sara's own secret way of getting even with the hotel.

In either way, it had backfired. Sydney actually kind of did a good job now that she was in security. That's because she didn't think of herself as an employee of the hotel so much as she thought of herself as an employee of Sara, someone who she actually admired and felt loyalty for. So she tried to do a good job, not for corporate, but for Sara, because what she did reflected on her. She had finally found one real friend at work who she wasn't afraid to trust, who had her back, so she tried to have Sara's back. She felt like someone had finally seen her and appreciated her for herself. Sydney was eternally grateful to Sara for her role in keeping her employed. As much as she hated working in the restaurant, she still needed that job to pay her share of the rent with her six other roommates. She didn't have many options. She could either continue to work until her comedy act took off or try to shack up with one of the sugar daddies that were always hitting on her at the hotel, but she had too much self-respect for that. She liked her independence. Sara had let her keep both her self respect and independence by not ratting her out to corporate, then later hiring her into her own department. She'd never forget that.

So that's why even though she had just thought of a killer joke and desperately wanted to write it down before she forgot it, she instead lifted up her walkie talkie and reported the strange woman in the silver suit who was currently wandering around the lobby waving a long, wand-like device around.

In the security office, Sara lifted the walkie talkie to her ear. "Hey boss, look at the cameras in the lobby. Check out the crazy refugee from a B-Movie dressed in silver latex that's waving a dildo around in the lobby!" Sydney said.

"Jasper, bring up the video from the lobby." Sara told the young man next to her. Most of the hotel employees believed Jasper was actually the head of security for the hotel. It was deliberate deception that Sara encouraged because it allowed her to go undercover when employees were suspected of wrongdoing. In actuality, she just used Jasper to do all the boring paperwork she didn't feel like doing. Technically, he was her second in command, but she liked to think of Sydney as her true protégé. The kid had surprised her. She had mainly hired her because she knew keeping her around drove the assholes who ran the restaurant and upper management crazy, but she was actually turning into a decent security guard. The same skills that made her able to so sharply observe the absurdities of life also allowed her to quickly identify potential threats in the hotel.

Sara studied the screen. "I don't know what that is, and thank God it doesn't look like any kind of weapon, but it's no dildo. Seriously, you think that *everything* looks like a dildo. You have issues, girl."

"Guilty as charged! Hey, I'm a very lonely person, so sue me! What about that outfit, though? Kinda kinky, right? I thought that the pornography convention wasn't until next month." Sydney quipped back.

"It isn't." Sara confirmed.

"So, do you want me to throw her out? I think she's making some of the other guests a little uncomfortable."

"No, just hang back and monitor her for now. Call for backup if she does anything too crazy, *don't* try to eject her yourself."

One bad thing about having Sydney on security, Sara had learned, was that she tended to get a little drunk with power. She had an unfortunate tendency to want to use her taser at the first sign of resistance. Perhaps the girl was too inherently misanthropic to be completely trusted with such a device? The last thing they needed were any lawsuits—at least not until Sara's retirement was finalized. A new idea occurred to Sara when she recalled Sydney calling the intruder a refugee from a B-Movie.

"Is anybody filming her?" She asked. They'd had trouble in the past with guerilla film makers trying to film scenes inside the hotel without getting a permit. She couldn't blame them. The stately old hotel made an excellent location for a movie, and had indeed been featured in a few over the years, but there were proper channels one had to go through first to obtain permission. Maybe her weird outfit was a costume for a movie?

"Not that I can tell." Sydney replied over the crackle of the radio

"Okay, well, like I said, just keep watching her for now and keep me updated." Sara ordered. The hotel policy was to treat everyone who was inside like a guest until they got too out of hand. The management hated bad press and word of mouth almost as much as they hated lawsuits. This lady might have a room for all they knew and was just a little kooky. Maybe she was off her meds? She saw no reason to create a scene by confronting her. She hadn't really done anything threatening—yet.

"Roger that." Sydney said. She watched the weird lady pull up one of her green gloves and look at some kind of computer looking thingy that was strapped to her wrist. Then the lady marched off towards the elevators, hesitated for a moment, looked at her wrist once more, then moved towards the stairwell instead. Sydney stepped forward to follow before she lost sight of her.

Drogalla climbed the stairs, occasionally consulting the flashing sensor wand held gripped in one hand. Yes, they were definitely getting closer now. Soon, the Leader would be at the source of the bizarre energy readings. It had to be some sort of secret Baandergi base, cleverly hidden within one of these hotel rooms.

Drogalla wasn't sure where the Baandergi had gotten the technology they'd just used to destroy the Saawgauth saucers, but they'd pioneered time travel technology, so it wasn't very difficult to believe that they also had weapons beyond anything the other Children of Pfoff possessed. These strange energy readings had to be more of their work. Perhaps both of the attacks today had been directed from here? Drogalla intended to make certain that no further attacks would be coordinated from this location. That's why when a crewmate had used the last of the ship's power to teleport the Leader (over Drogalla's objections) into the city right before the command saucer was destroyed, Drogalla had immediately headed for this hotel. Its location was in the report made by the scanning team that had been sent down earlier, and a copy of said report was stored in the Leader's wrist computer. Drogalla was too far away from the mothership to be teleported back there, and couldn't risk summoning another saucer to retrieve them. Not while this Baandergi base was still in operation. Otherwise, it was likely to suffer the same fate as the other ships.

Drogalla's sensor wand showed that this was now the correct floor. The leader opened the door and exited the stairwell to move down the hall.

Sydney had crept up the steps after the weird lady as quietly as she could. Luckily, she'd been so engrossed in looking at her flashing dildo-thingy that she hadn't noticed her. Now Sydney watched through the glass set in the stairwell door as the lady wandered down the hall.

"Boss, that lady is out on the fifth floor now. She's stopped in front of one of the rooms. She's just standing there staring at the door. It's a little creepy." She reported.

"Which room?" Sara asked.

Sydney squinted and pressed her face against the glass. "Hard to tell from here. 508, I think."

"Jasper, give me the cameras on the fifth floor." Sara ordered.

The monitor screen was split into 4 different views. In one of them, she could see the bizarre woman. *Yeah, that's room 508, alright. Matt Spike's room! It figures...* Sara thought. Yes, she'd been a little nosy and looked up what room her old flame was staying in. She was annoyed over how little she'd seen of him or Naomi during their stay, almost as if they were avoiding her. She knew they were booked for at least another day, and she was hoping to drop in at some point to catch up with them before they headed back to Jersey.

Back in the control room, Sara's eyes widened. On the screen, she saw the woman pull something from a large pouch on her belt. Something that sure looked like a gun of some sort.

"Boss! She's got a—" Sydney shouted through her walkie talkie.

"I see it!" Sara yelled back. "Stay where you are. Wait for me! I'm coming right up!"

She ran for the door.

"What do you want me to do?" Jasper asked in a panicky voice.

"Keep an eye on those screens! If things get too crazy, call the cops!" Sara ordered as the door slammed shut behind her. She was hoping she could still de-escalate this situation without having to call in the local boys in blue.

"Great! Perfect! She tells me to call the police if things get too crazy without defining what constitutes 'too crazy!'" He complained to the empty room.

All he could do was look on with mounting anxiety as the lady on the screen kicked in the door to room 508....

CHAPTER 10:
THE OMEGA SEED

Anne Moore stood on the landing pad, staring up at the sky. A warm breeze stirred her long, honey blonde hair ever so slightly. Beside her stood her top aide, Oliver Johns, whom she'd "inherited" from her predecessor, Bronson McDowell. He looked as if he was about to burst with excitement at the news that an alien ship from the Galactic Federation was actually coming here to Guild HQ. Although he was a much older man, this wasn't readily apparent. He certainly had the energy of a man half his age, as he hopped around from one foot to another like a little boy about to get a new toy to play with. For as long as she'd known him (which was quite a long time), he'd been fairly obsessed with the idea of aliens. He had an almost childish hope that the aliens would do something someday to save us from ourselves.

Anne wished she had his optimism, she really did. But she was far too much of a hard-nosed realist to feel anything but trepidation about the upcoming meeting. Anne was the kind of person who didn't expect anyone to do anything for her—ever. No, if you wanted to see something happen you had to *make* it happen for yourself. She certainly didn't expect a bunch of space aliens who had done nothing other than act aloof and superior, who had repeatedly rejected their many attempts to make diplomatic overtures to them to suddenly come blazing to their rescue.

Especially when another gang of them was apparently the source of the threat itself. In her time with the Guilds, Anne had seen her fair share of crazy things: headless floating Frost Giants, Angels, Demons, Gods and even Santa fucking Claus! Not to mention vampires and werewolves. And now this...alien invaders! She sighed. She supposed it was inevitable. Why did it have to happen on her watch, though? She'd only just recently replaced her "uncle" Bronson as the Chairperson of the Inner Council of the International conference of Guilds and Director of the ABC after spending years as his heir apparent. She'd barely had a chance to start putting this place in *her* kind of order, and now she had to deal with this, her first major crisis as the leader of the Guilds.

Anne liked Randy well enough, even considered him a friend. The same was true of Matt and Naomi, that whole crew. She regularly attended the undeniably awesome parties they threw at their house every year to commemorate certain holidays. It was one of the few times when the normally very tightly wound Anne allowed herself to let her hair down a little and have some fun. But she also had to admit that the group had an irritating knack for landing themselves in major trouble, trouble that the Guilds often had to dig them out of. Her uncle Bronson hadn't seemed to have ever minded doing so.

But she was not her uncle Bronson.

To her other side was her friend, Aethra Hoffman, the Queen of the Pirates. Or more accurately, the "Supreme Matriarch of the Ancient Order of Mariners" as her official title read. Aethra was excited too, but for entirely different reasons. Randy was her boyfriend, and the two only got to see each other in person a few times a year. Their lives were each too hectic to allow them to spend much time together. It might seem like an unfulfilling arrangement, but Anne knew that they actually spent a great deal of time with each other through astral projection, which allowed people's spirits to travel great distances in a relatively short period. Aethra was currently sitting in a device that was kind of like a rolling fish tank. She was half human and half water nymph, so she had to spend several hours out of each day immersed in water to keep her strength and vigor. Aethra was accompanied by her own aide, a man called One Eyed Willie. The name always cracked up Anne. She was originally from the UK, where such a term was a euphemism for a certain part of the male anatomy. However, as far as she could tell, he was blissfully unaware of this and used the name earnestly. His name really was William, and he really had one eye.

Aethra also wore an eyepatch, but Anne knew this was an affectation. She had a perfectly good eye hidden underneath it. Not only did her eyepatch make her seem more "piratey" but it served a practical purpose as well. There was a series of hidden lenses built into it that gave her a range of vision to rival that of Superman. Not only did she have his X-Ray vision, but infrared vision and yes, also the equivalent of the Man of Steel's "heat vision" which allowed her to shoot lasers from it. Because she was currently in her water tank on wheels, she was dressed in a bikini rather than her typically somewhat stereotypical pirate gear. Only her ever present tricorn hat and eyepatch hinted at her buccaneering inclinations. She was an attractive woman, if you could get past the unnatural, light blue hue of her skin and the three gills that flapped rhythmically on each side of her neck while she was immersed in her tank. Oh, and her hands, which had a delicate, transparent webbing up to the first knuckle of each finger.

"I think I can see them!" Aethra cried out happily.

Anne looked in the direction that her friend was pointing in, and thought she could barely make out a gleaming, silvery shape headed their way.

Here comes trouble. Anne thought glumly.

Inside the cockpit of Jim's ship, Penny could see the outline of the island that housed Guild Headquarters now that they were past the perimeter of the enchantment that concealed it from passing air and sea travelers. At Randy's suggestion, as a gesture of good faith, Jim had deactivated the ship's cloaking device.

Now both parties could see each other plainly.

This wasn't the first time Penny had ever seen the island, although it was her first time visiting it "in the flesh," so to speak. The last time she'd been here, she'd been a teenager, back when Randy was just an apprentice wizard. His order, the Temple of the Old Gods, had perfected a method of astral projection, which was quick and easy for anyone to master. He'd taught her how to do it back when they had first started dating. It was his way of showing off to impress her, and it had worked, although she'd already been impressed enough with him before she ever knew that he could do any magic. Those had been happy days, they had traveled the world in astral form, seen all the sights: Big Ben, the Eiffel Tower, the Pyramids of Egypt *and* Mexico, the jungles of the Amazon and even Mt. Everest (which was surprisingly spooky on account of all the ghosts they ran into there). The world had been their oyster, their playground.

Inevitably, the super secret base of the Guilds had ended up as a destination on their first world tour. It had turned out to be an unwise choice to visit. There were always several magic users on the island representing the interest of the Temple of the Old Gods, and they could see Randy and Penny's astral bodies. It was only a matter of time before they were spotted by a witch and captured by a spell. Randy's mentor, the witch Wendy Sommardahl, was *not* amused, to say the least, by Randy bringing a civilian to the island. If Randy hadn't had been such an unusually talented pupil, she probably would've dismissed him from the order for such shenanigans. She smiled at the memory.

It would be quite interesting, she thought, to experience the place in her physical body, and after so many years. When she had last been there, much of Guild HQ had still been under construction after an attack destroyed the original base a few months prior. Now she could see the angular, decidedly modern edifice of Guild HQ thrusting itself out of the canopy of thick jungle surrounding it. As they approached a circular landing pad that jutted from the top floor of the building, she could make out several tiny figures waiting for them on the tarmac. She wondered which of their friends in the Guilds had come out to meet them? She wouldn't have much longer to wait to find out. The ship swiftly came to a landing. Its boarding ramp lowered, and Randy, Jim, Hi-Fi, and Penny emerged from inside. Kergaali and Zaa were the last ones to come out.

Penny took a moment to look up behind her and study Jim's ship as it truly was: it was made of a smooth, seamless gleaming silver (what was it with aliens and their obsession with making everything silver?). The wings that had been attached to the outside of the restaurant remained, albeit now in a different, downward position, but that's where the similarities to Kirk's ended. The ship had a much longer and more slender design than the pill shape of the diner. If Penny had been more than just a casual Star Trek viewer, she might've realized that it shared a certain resemblance to a Klingon Bird of Prey.

Oliver smiled at the sight of Jim. "Oh! I've never seen one of those types before!" he whispered excitedly. He had read through the

ABC's files on all the known types of alien races that had visited the Earth—*several* times, but he'd never heard of one of these lion-looking things.

"Randy!" Aethra shouted, rolling forwards and standing up out of her tank to wrap her arms around him in a soggy embrace. They shared a brief kiss.

"I've missed you too." He smiled back at her. She looked over at Penny and frowned slightly, trying to hide her displeasure and failing.

"Penny." She said.

"Aethra." Penny replied.

They knew each other from when Aethra was able to take time off from doing whatever it was that a Pirate Queen does a few times out of each year to vacation with Randy. There was always an awkward energy between the two of them, though. A tension that neither of them seemed prepared to acknowledge or discuss. Randy loved her though, and so did Paul, who thought of her as a second mom, and that was good enough for Penny.

"Good to see you again, Randy, Penny." Anne said as she walked up to meet them. She knew Penny from Matt and Naomi's parties. She now looked to the others, and found herself somewhat appalled at the mismatched way that Kergaali was dressed. "This must be Jim and Ker Gauly? I hope I said that right!" She said sheepishly, hoping that she hadn't just caused a fresh interplanetary incident with her possible mispronunciation.

"Close enough." Kergaali shrugged. "Now please, there is much to discuss and our time may be short. Take me to your leader!"

Everyone on the tarmac laughed.

"I can't believe she really said it!" Jim said, literally roaring with laughter.

"It was bound to happen sooner or later!" Randy said, wiping a tear from his eye.

"We probably should've started a betting pool for it!" Penny added.

Kergaali looked at them all in confusion. "I don't understand. I wasn't trying to make a joke. We are here because of a very serious matter!"

"Yes, of course you are," said Anne, who was normally so grim and serious, yet still couldn't help but grin over her saying the infamous line. "You're looking at her. I am in command here. Anne Moore at your service!" She held out a hand and Kergaali grasped it, giving it a brief, perfunctory shake, having already familiarized herself with the importance of such gestures on this world

"You? Yes, in my world one with your regal bearing would be, but I thought your males typically dominated this world?" Kergaali replied, still a little confused.

"It is, but not always. There have been a few changes around here lately. We like to think that in the Guilds we're getting to be a little more ahead of the curve than the rest of our planet is." Anne told her.

"It is so odd, this distinction you people insist on making among yourselves based upon something as arbitrary as genitalia! And using it as a basis for what roles you will take on in your society, for how you must behave! It's baffling! Such differences do not exist on Pfoff outside of our animals." Kergaali couldn't help but comment.

This reminded Anne of something Aethra had mentioned when briefing her on Randy's call. "Yes, I have been informed that your people have no personal concept of gender. I've been wondering what kinds of pronouns you would prefer us to refer to you by?" She asked, not wishing to offend her visitor. Randy had been wondering the same thing but kept on forgetting to bring it up.

"Pronouns?" Kergaali could speak English quite well, but she wasn't so familiar with it as to know the intricacies of our grammatical terminology.

"You know... words like he, she, they?" Anne prompted.

"These ideas are meaningless to us. They are not part of our identity. I am still Kergaali whether you call me a 'he' or a 'she.' I suspect that such questions have more to do with your own comfort level than my own! Since I am biologically what you would call a woman, it's probably easier for you to think of me as such. So, if it makes you more comfortable to call me a 'she' or a 'her' then you may, it makes no difference to me." She replied, a little impatiently. *Why were these humans so obsessed with these ridiculous notions?*

"I meant no offense. It's just that such things sometimes mean a great deal to us." Anne replied, surprised by her attitude. She knew, of course, that there were plenty of humans right here on earth who probably didn't identify with one gender more than the other, but she didn't personally know any of them. She suspected that many of them would likely view this differently than Kergaali did, anyway. This was all quite new to her.

"No offense was taken." Kergaali assured her.

"Well then, let's move inside, shall we? The Inner Council is already convened and, as you say, there's much to discuss," Anne said as she led the way towards a door. As the group followed her inside and down the broad, marble hallways, the sight of Aethra caught Kergaali's attention, who she seemed to only just now notice. She stared at her intently for a few moments.

"See something you like, honey?" Aethra asked sarcastically.

"Forgive me. I was just...not aware that there was so much *variation* amongst you humans. You are a human, aren't you?"

"Well, I'm not another space alien, if that's what you're asking! My dad was a human and my mom was a water nymph. My sisters and I are all hybrids. Half human, half water nymph. It's not so unusual in our Order, many pirates have at least a little water nymph in them."

"Water nymph? What is that? I have not yet come across this term in my studies of your planet. I thought humans were the only intelligent life in this world. Do you mean to tell me there are others?" She seemed upset by this possibility for some reason.

"Water nymphs are creatures of the Aether, but sometimes they manifest here on this plane of existence. The pirates enjoy the favor of the god Poseidon and sometimes he sends his nymphs here to aid them." Randy explained, or rather tried to. In this instance, his explanation just baffled her further.

"God? What is that? This is the second time you've used that word now."

"Gods are powerful beings that many people believe are the creators of life in this world. In reality, *we* created *them*, dreamed them into existence. They dwell in another level of reality made up of our mental energy that we call the Aether. They feed off of our worship and sometimes do favors for us in exchange. Aethra's people, the pirates, are some of the only ones left who still worship Poseidon, and he takes good care of them as a result." Randy tried to clarify.

The fact that Aethra's people were Poseidon worshippers always amused Penny a little. She loved Randy's Aunt Bernice, the one who had raised him, she'd always treated Penny well, but she also knew that on a certain level, Bernice had been a little uncomfortable with the idea of Randy dating Penny back when they were a couple. Even though Bernice wasn't particularly traditional, there was always a part of her that wanted to see Randy end up with a "nice Jewish girl". When Bernice heard about Aethra, and heard her last name, she assumed she was Jewish like her family was. It was true that Aethra's father's ancestors had been at until they joined up with the pirates. Randy had done little to dissuade his aunt of this notion, and he'd never introduced her to Aethra, although he had ways of making her look more human via his magic. He didn't have the heart to break it to Bernice that the nice Jewish girl she'd always wanted him to fall in love with was really a Poseidon worshiping Pirate Queen! Or, for that matter, that he was also in a relationship with a Valkyrie who lived in Valhalla. The less that Bernice knew about Randy's unconventional love life, the better. Bernice was something of a bohemian herself, but there were probably quite a few limits as to what someone of her generation could understand and accept.

Kergaali considered Randy's words before speaking. "Ah, I think I understand now. Amongst the primitive tribes of the First Generation, there are those who feel the need to worship a fictional being they think is their creator. My people are above such superstitions. We know exactly who our true creators are, and our science has shown us how they came into existence."

As she said this, Randy wondered what those gods of the First Generation Venusians must've been like. He figured their imaginations would've called them forth into existence in the Aether, too. Randy had heard of strange beings that had been encountered by the first magic users to explore the astral plane. They claimed to be the gods of a race that had died out long ago. With no worshippers, they had dwindled away until they were barely more than shadows. Strange phantom creatures that were so utterly alien and inhuman that they were completely terrifying, even in their weakened form. Most of those who looked upon them were instantly driven to madness. Randy now speculated if these entities had been the twisted remnants of the alien gods of Venus?

"Aethra is your name?" Kergaali asked the Pirate Queen.

"Yeah, don't wear it out!" She smiled at her.

"Are you named after this 'Aether' place then?"

"No, although I can see why you'd think so. I'm named for one of Poseidon's daughters." She informed her.

Kergaali fell silent again. Troubled by this strange idea of another world where the things we imagined took on a life of their own and could even interfere with things in this world. If such a thing really exists, why had their scientists not discovered it yet? It was unbelievable! Yet these people all seemed to believe it was true and the blue woman in the water tank was even a descendant of such creatures, if she was to be believed.

Anne ushered them into the chambers of the Inner Council. It was a large, circular chamber carved out of dark stone. Seats ringed the chamber, stacked above each other in two rows. In the center was a raised podium that a single bright light shone upon. As they entered the chamber, Aethra and One Eyed Willie veered off to take their normal position within the room. As they did so, an older black woman with long dreadlocks, dressed in a flowing floral gown, rushed past them and threw her arms around Randy in an embrace.

Kergaali rolled her eyes at this sight. Another one? How many of these Earth females were obsessed with this Randy fellow? She supposed that he *did* have a certain soft spoken charm—for a human, but his popularity with the women of this world seemed excessive.

"Randy! It's so nice to see you again. I just wish it was under happier circumstances." The woman said.

"Me too." He replied, "it's been too long." He meant it. Randy hadn't seen much of her this past year, what with being on tour with the Mystery Smiths.

Randy noticed Kergaali's puzzled stare and decided that an introduction was in order. "This is Kergaali, the Venusian who's trying to help save our planet. Kergaali, this is April Sommardahl. She represents my order of magic users, the Temple of the Old Gods here on the Inner Council. Her wife Wendy was my mentor—the one who taught me everything there is to know about magic. We're all practically family."

Kergaali blushed a little, feeling foolish that she had mistaken April for yet another one of Randy's past or present sexual partners when their relationship was of a completely different nature.This planet was so confusing! As she studied them, it was now apparent to her that April was more of a maternal figure to him. She took the woman's hand and shook it.

"Pleased to meet you, April." She said.

"Likewise." April said. "Hopefully we'll have a chance to talk later on. I've never met a real alien before."

"Lookin' good, laddie!" A rough voice called, and a gnarled, calloused hand shook Randy by the shoulder. The hand belonged to Prospero, a wizard that now worked as April's top aide.

"Prospero! It's good to see you again." Randy smiled.

"Aye, well, someone's gotta keep this lass out of trouble, don't they?" He said, jerking a thumb toward April

She raised her eyebrows. "Excuse me? I think it's more like the other way around! Anyway, we'd better go take our seats. It looks like Anne is pretty eager to get this meeting started."

Anne indicated that Jim, Randy, Penny and Kergaali should all sit down in the folding chairs that Oliver had hastily set up behind the podium for them. Hi-Fi stood next to Jim. She then took her place at the podium, picked up a gavel, and hammered it down loudly.

"I hereby call this emergency session of the Inner Council of the International conference of Guilds to order." She announced authoritatively. Back during Bronson McDowell's time in this position, the Chairperson would've worn a powdered wig and a ceremonial gown like the judge in a British court, but Anne had been all too happy to put an end to such antiquated traditions upon ascending to this position. It was time to bring the Guilds, kicking and screaming if need be, into the 21st Century.

"I have asked you all here today to address a grave new threat to the planet that I have only recently been made aware of. Here to explain it is Kergaali, a native of the planet Venus." She motioned for her to join her at the podium.

Kergaali then went on to explain everything she's already explained so I won't bore you with that part of the speech. She explained it all with no sign of nervousness at having to address such an unfamiliar audience, as if she was used to giving such presentations. There was a great deal of excitement in the chamber, as you might imagine, when she described the Venusians' intention to wipe out humanity. Anne, in particular, also seemed particularly shocked by this. Apparently, this was something that Randy had neglected to mention when he called Aethra earlier on. For Anne, it was a total game changer. The stakes in this conflict had just become much higher than she had ever dared to imagine.

"Why do they want to destroy us? Why can't they just share the planet with us?" Ernesto Peregrine, the representative for the Highwaymen, asked. "Surely, we could find someplace on Earth for your people? The Guilds own several uncharted islands scattered around the globe that might be suitable. Why can't we find a peaceful solution?" He pleaded.

"There are several reasons. Firstly, our population is relatively small compared to yours. And remarkably stable. Our people all live for a genetically predetermined number of years, and we reproduce at a predictable, steady rate. This is why the Saawgauth must rely on a fleet of drone ships created by their Duplo-Rays to affect their conquest. There are simply not enough of them to do it on their own. In contrast, your human population continues to constantly grow out of control, while your life expectancy rises as well, straining this planet's ability to provide for you. They believe that because you outnumber us so heavily, this will inevitably lead to a situation in which you will dominate us. We would constantly find ourselves outvoted and overruled. Our needs second to those of humanity. Such a state of affairs is made doubly unacceptable because they believe you are poor stewards of this world. If you continue to be left in charge of it, you will inevitably make it uninhabitable for all life. We would become second-class citizens of this world, forced to sit idly by while it suffers the same fate as Pfoff. Thirdly, they fear cultural contamination, that some of our people will adopt your peculiar human ideas about gender identity and intimate relationships and therefore threaten the stability of our own society. For all these reasons, they see any attempt to peacefully cohabitate with you to be highly undesirable at best, at worst impossible." Kergaali explained with her cool, clinical detachment.

"How do they plan to wipe us out?" Another representative, this one from one of the Houses of Assassins, asked.

"Neutron missiles, fired by the drone ships that the Duplo-Rays will create. It will leave your buildings and infrastructure intact for our own use, but wipe your population out. They had considered creating a biological weapon, but their knowledge of human physiology wasn't up to the task of crafting a pathogen they believed would be virulent enough." She answered in the same bored, unemotional tone.

There was a stunned silence for some time.

"And what about the Galactic Federation? Do they intend to just allow this to happen?" Aethra asked.

Anne motioned to Jim. "Perhaps you'd like to take this question, Jim? Thank you for your testimony, Kergaali, it was most...*informative*." She told her. Kergaali inclined her head and returned to her seat.

Jim walked up to the podium a little nervously. This looked like a tough crowd compared to the friendly audiences they were used to.

"Well, in a word, yes. The Federation policy in such a situation is not to interfere. They view this strictly as a dispute between two primitive planets, neither of which are Federation members. They have no jurisdiction over it. If it looks as if the human race might face imminent extinction, they could take a random group of humans to one of our worlds to live in a sanctuary to preserve the species. I'm afraid that's about the most assistance you can expect from them, aside from whatever help I can provide."

Jim knew that in fact, some of his fellow Federation scientists had been abducting humans to extract genetic samples for years now in order to make a kind of "backup copy" of the human race, but he wasn't about to reveal *that* to the Guilds.

A shiver ran down Anne's spine at the notion. The remnants of the human race reduced to living out their lives in some kind of an alien nature preserve? Nothing but zoo animals for a bunch of arrogant aliens to study? Better to die free than live under such humiliating circumstances! If you even really could call that living! Although, she thought chillingly, how sure could she really be that this hadn't already happened to mankind before? Could she really be sure that we weren't already living in this kind of menagerie? She tried to dismiss such disturbing notions from her mind and focus on the matter at hand.

"Thank you, Jim," Anne said as she took the podium once more

"In light of these recent revelations, and in view of the presence of an immediate threat to our very existence, I move that we vote to take the extraordinary step of using the Omega Seed against this menace." She said gravely, seeming to age twenty years as she spoke the words.

There was an immediate gaggle of raised voices echoing around the room as soon as the words escaped her mouth.

Sitting beside her, Penny heard Randy gasp at Anne's words.

"Hey, what the fuck is an 'Omega Seed?' She whispered to him.

"A terrible magical weapon. Anne had it created when she first came to power, to serve as Earth's ultimate defense. It completely destroys everything it's been specifically primed to target everywhere on the entire planet, all at once. It reduces its targets to atoms in seconds." He said with horror.

"It's far too much power for anyone to be trusted with. I suppose she just can't wait to play with her new toy." He muttered disgustedly. He was greatly disappointed that his friend would even bring up the idea of deploying this weapon before all other alternatives had been exhausted. As far as he was concerned, the

Omega Seed should always be a last resort, if it should even be used at all.

Kergaali, seated nearby, listened to their exchange with great interest.

"What does 'priming' this Omega Seed entail?" She asked Randy.

"Introducing a small piece of whatever you wish to see destroyed to the seed. Like, for example, if you wanted to kill all the rats on Earth in an instant, you would just have to 'feed' a rat's hair, or a nail clipping from one to the seed." He told her.

Kergaali whistled appreciatively. She had never dreamed that the humans had such powerful weapons. These Guilds were formidable indeed, privy to many secrets of the universe that her own people, with their superior grasp of science had somehow missed. She was pleased that she had connected with them and could enlist them to join her in her cause.

April shot to her feet. "I object! In the strongest terms possible!" She said firmly. "With the Omega Seed, you could potentially destroy all of the Venusians! The Temple of the Old Gods will not be party to such an atrocity!"

"Relax. Nobody is proposing that we do such a thing. I thought we could prime the Seed to only destroy their ships. We can acquire a sample from one of the saucers that Jim shot down over the ocean." Anne replied calmly.

"My ship's computer automatically recorded the coordinates where the wreckage went down. The details should be in my robot Hi-Fi's databanks. I'd be happy to share it with you," Jim told her loudly enough for everyone in the room to hear.

"Excellent. Our local ABC field operatives could recover a piece of one of those ships and bring it here. Once it's introduced to the seed, and it's activated, it will wipe out any ships that are similar enough to it wherever they may be on the planet.

"It could work. However, it may be unnecessary to waste your time recovering the pieces of those saucers from the ocean bottom. We flew through a cloud of debris from the last ship we destroyed. There are likely still small particles of it clinging to Jim's ship. It may be enough to prime your Omega device." Kergaali told Anne.

"Excellent. I can call my contacts at the UN, warn them not to accept any gifts from the Venusians should they try to land there again. In the meantime, we could prime the Omega Seed and use it to destroy their ships." Anne told the council.

"If I may make another suggestion?" Kergaali asked. "If your United Nations does not grant permission to give your people the Duplo-Ray, they will still try to deploy the ships containing the Duplo-Rays to each of your nations. They merely wanted permission because our military technology is only about 50 years ahead of your own. There is some fear amongst the Saawgauth that even with their ability to shroud their ships, that your people will figure out a way to detect them and overwhelm them with your superior numbers before they can get into position and produce enough drone ships to exterminate humanity. I believe that the most efficient thing for you to do would be to destroy the ships containing their Duplo-Rays at their source. Those ships are currently still on Pfoff, at the other end of the Time Tunnel on the Saawgauth moonbase. Jim's ship could reach that base quickly. If you can get the Omega Seed through the Time Tunnel, you could eliminate all those ships before they ever get to Earth. It would be such a spectacular show of force that it would likely force them to abandon their plans for invading this world."

"Really? They'll just give up that easily?" Anne said, not being able to hide the skepticism in her voice

"I believe so. Our people are not natural warriors." Kergaali replied.

Anne looked pensive. She was obviously thinking about it all very carefully.

Penny was too. She definitely thought that it made the most sense to make sure that the ships that carried these giant Duplo-Rays were the ones that the Omega Seed destroyed. They were the real threat. She wasn't sure she shared Randy and April's misgivings about using the seed, so long as it was only used to destroy the saucers. Penny supposed that any Venusians unfortunate enough to be inside one of these ships when it was used would be killed, too. She wasn't particularly happy about that, but if it's what had to be done to save humanity, she supposed she could live with it.

Again, Penny was struck with how casual Kergaali seemed at the prospect that people who she worked with aboard those ships may be killed in the process. Come to think of it, were the ships of her own people, the Baandergi, so different from those of the Saawgauth that they might not be affected too? If Kergaali had thought of such things or been bothered by them in the slightest, she gave no sign of it. Did she really love and respect human life so much that she was this comfortable at the idea of helping to facilitate bringing so much death to her own people? If anything, Penny felt that she sometimes displayed a thinly veiled revulsion for most things human.The space woman definitely had an irritating superiority complex. She still wasn't sure she fully understood her motivation for helping them. Perhaps she just felt that the fact that some of her people were willing to exterminate another group of sentient beings was too much of a dishonor for her race to bear?

She looked over at Jim. At least she felt like she knew why he was in this fight. No matter what the validity of his self professed love for Penny may or may not be, there was little doubt that he *did* genuinely love many aspects of human culture, particularly our music and science fiction, which was a virtual obsession.

"This is a good plan, and I believe we can pull it off. *If* the council will approve the use of the Omega Seed, that is." Anne said pointedly. She turned to face the representatives of the most powerful of the various secret societies that had been allowed into the Guilds over the millennia. She leaned forward towards the microphone that snaked out of the podium until her lips were almost touching it. "Let's put it to a vote, shall we? Will you authorize the use of the Omega Seed for the destruction of the Saawgauth fleet? I strongly recommend that we do. It may be our only hope."

There was a flurry of mumbling from the assembled representatives and their aides. Each of them pressed a button before them that registered a vote of "aye" or a "nay". The results were instantly tabulated on a computer screen set into Anne's podium as soon as all the votes were registered. It was unanimous. Even April, despite her earlier objections, had voted in favor of the plan in the end. Anne looked down at the results with a grim sort of satisfaction.

"The ayes have it. Thank you. I swear to you all that you will not regret this decision. I will do everything in my power to ensure that the awesome power you have entrusted me with this day is used correctly to protect the Earth and its people from these invaders. To this end, I command that the Omega Seed be brought forth from the vault and prepared to be primed. Let's also gather a crew of technicians out to Jim's ship to see if we can find enough particles of that ship for our purposes."

"I can help with that, M'am." Hi-Fi said. "I can scan the surface of the ship for traces of materials matching those of the saucers I scanned earlier."

"Sounds good." Anne told the strange looking little robot.

"Okay, I hereby call this emergency session of the Inner Council of the International conference of Guilds to a close. We will keep you apprised of any further significant developments as they arise." She brought the gavel crashing down decisively.

Anne looked at Oliver, who was hovering nearby her. "Contact our people at the UN and let them know what's going on."

"Very good, M'am." He said and hurried out.

She turned her back on the representatives as they filed out of the chamber, and looked squarely at Penny, Randy, Jim, Kergaali, and Hi-Fi.

"How soon can you reach the Moon, Jim?" She asked him.

"Should only take about two hours, tops."

"Great. Kergaali, have you ever been to this moon base? Do you know what kind of defenses it has? I'm wondering what sized strike force we'll need to fight our way to this Time Tunnel?"

"I have been there. We all arrived in this time period through the Time Tunnel located there. It's a small time operation, it exists only to maintain a stable connection to the Time Tunnel on Pfoff. Security is very minimal since they never had reason to expect an attack. It's on the dark side of your moon and so is invisible from Earth. Even if you humans did know it was there, they knew how difficult it would be for you to reach it, let alone attack it. Jim's ship, however, will breach its defenses with ease. Only a very small team will be necessary. Most of their forces in this era are in that mothership under the sea." The alien told her.

"Excellent. I plan to personally lead the attack. We'll need Jim to fly the ship, Kergaali to guide us, and Randy to kick some ass with his magic."

Randy interrupted her. "I'm still not so sure that I approve of the use of the Omega Seed. I don't think I really want to be a part of this."

"I could really use your help. You're one of our most powerful wizards. And if you have a better plan, I'd love to hear it." Anne said.

Randy exhaled slowly. "I don't." He grimaced as if he'd just tasted something unpleasant. "I suppose I can be a part of your team; if nothing else, I can make sure that the seed is used responsibly."

"Thanks." Anne replied, feeling a little irritated by his reluctance and lack of confidence in her intentions.

I might bring a few assassins with me. I'm thinking of probably Smoke and Wisp," Anne said.

Randy nodded at the wisdom of this decision. Smoke and Wisp were some of the most skilled assassins, a brother and sister team that hailed from the House of the Slow Blade. They often functioned as Anne's loyal bodyguards.

"What about me?" Penny asked, feeling a bit left out.

"No offense Penny, but you might be safer waiting for things out here at HQ." Anne told her.

"No way! I've already been over this with Randy and the rest of them—I intend to see this through to the end!" Penny answered, infuriated at the thought of someone trying to cut her out of the action all over again, even if she had little appetite for real violence.

"Okay. Maybe you can just stay with the ship then?" Anne suggested. Like Randy before her, she also knew how difficult it was to talk Penny down from an idea once she'd made up her mind.

"Maybe. We'll see." Penny answered.

"I want in too!" Aethra said as she rolled over to the group.

"No. I have other plans for you. We still have that mothership in the Atlantic to deal with. If we send the Omega Seed through the Time

Tunnel, it'll only destroy the enemy ships on Venus, the ones back here on Earth will be out of range, in terms of both time and space. I was planning on using our orbital laser to fry it..." Anne began.

"Wait, you've got an orbital laser?" Penny asked in surprise.

"Who doesn't?" Anne shrugged. "Anyway, I was thinking that if that's not enough to take it out, you could also lead a fleet of your ships there? Maybe drop some depth charges on the thing as a backup measure?"

"I don't see why I have to personally lead my ships there. I was hoping I could take this opportunity to spend a little time with my Randy." She pouted.

"This is a serious mission, not some kind of date!" Anne complained. Then she said a bit more softly. "I'd really feel far more secure knowing that it's *you* leading those ships instead of one of your subordinates."

"Oh, alright! So long as I get him afterwards." She said, winking at him with her one visible eye.

Randy blushed.

"Whatever. I don't care what you two get up to after this mission is completed successfully. In fact, I really, really *don't* want to know what you get up to!" Anne replied.

It was at that moment that she looked over at Kergaali and did something a little curious. She reached out and touched the antenna coming out of her head, feeling it down to near its base, where it sprouted from her head. As she did so, she jerked her hand away, tearing out a thin strand of the alien's hair in the process.

"Ouch! What are you doing?" Kergaali complained.

"Sorry. My ring got caught in your hair when I was checking out your antenna, I guess. I let my curiosity get the best of me. Outwardly, you appear very human, aside from that antenna coming out of your head. I wasn't sure if it was really a part of your body, or an attachment. What is its purpose?"

"It...it prevents us from doing certain things. A kind of failsafe that was put there by our creators. I don't wish to discuss it," she said.

Everyone thought this was an odd answer, but it was obvious from her tone that it would be a bad idea to press the matter any further. The way she explained it, Randy assumed it might be an anatomical holdover from her people's days as slaves. That might also explain her reluctance to talk about it. He couldn't imagine what it must be like to have a part of your body that was a constant reminder of such a painful history.

From there on, things moved quickly. As promised, Hi-Fi helped Anne's technicians locate enough residue from the vaporized saucer from off of the hull of Jim's ship for their purposes. The Omega Seed was then quickly primed in a brief and secret magical ritual, then placed in a combination locked steel briefcase that was given to Anne. The dreaded device was only about the size of a hand grenade, so it easily fit inside. Anne was going to bring a small arsenal of weapons with her, but Jim assured her that this would be unnecessary as his ship's replicator could create a range of formidable handheld weapons suitable for their assault. He also recommended they replicate a few armored space suits to wear in case the battle caused a breach in the walls of the moon base.

Once everything was in order, Jim prepared the ship for takeoff. Smoke and Wisp joined them aboard the ship. Smoke was a tall man wearing a black, tight-fitting outfit and a hood. Bandoliers of pouches criss-crossed his chest. He had a pair of weapons holstered at his hips, while a pair of swords were sheathed on his back. Wisp, as her name implied, was a thin, yet powerful looking woman dressed in an outfit similar to Smoke's, but in dark brown. Neither of them ever removed their hoods or spoke very much. April and Prospero arrived to see them off and wish them all luck, but Aethra wasn't with them, much to Randy's confusion. Penny sensed his disappointment.

"She's probably busy with her own preparations to lead her fleet against that mothership." She told him comfortingly.

"Yeah, I guess so." He said glumly as they walked up the ramp and into the ship.

A moment later, the small ship carrying the Earth's last, best hope for survival was blasting off into the upper atmosphere, bound for the moon.

CHAPTER 11:
O RANDY, WHERE ART THOU?

"**W**hat the hell was *that*?" Matt exclaimed.

Inside the safety of their hotel room, Matt and Naomi had been soaking in the Jacuzzi again, finishing off some of the drinks they'd brought up from the bar. They were doing their damnedest to try and *not* think about alien invasions or worry about what was going on with Randy and Penny. For the most part, they were succeeding admirably. Things were just about to get rather sexy between them again.

That is, until they both heard a loud bang from the front door. Within moments of hearing the sound, Naomi was up.

"Could be trouble!" She whispered.

She stepped out of the tub and slipped on her robe without bothering to dry off. She always wore a chain around her neck which held a ring on it. Not just any ring, a very special ring given to her by Randy's mentor, the witch Wendy Sommardahl, and later supercharged by a goddess. With practiced ease, she undid the clasp on the chain so that she could put the ring on her finger. The second she did so, an impenetrable, transparent, glowing bubble of green energy surrounded her. Matt stood up and groped for his own robe.

"Hey! Wait for me!" he cried, but it was too late—she was already out the door of the bathroom.

The moment that Drogalla kicked in the door to the suspected Baandergi base, the Leader had squatted down near the closest available cover, in this case the kitchen counter, and raised a pistol. A few seconds later, a sopping wet earth woman came running into the room, an unusual green bubble surrounding her. A personal force field supplied by the Baandergi, perhaps?

So, they have humans working with them? Drogalla thought. Were they buying their loyalty by sharing their technology with them?

"Surrender, traitor! Lead me to your Baandergi partners and I will spare you!" Drogalla said, training the pistol upon the woman. Even the best portable force fields could only withstand a few shots at this range before it would need to recharge, and the woman didn't appear to be armed. Drogalla was confident of victory in this encounter.

"Yeah, it's trouble alright!" Naomi called out loudly.

Matt peeked his head around the corner and saw what the situation was. Within moments, the *Vermillion Avenger*, his trusty flying sword, was whizzing out from where it had been hovering under their bed and sailing through the air. With one motion that was entirely too swift for the eye to follow, it sliced off the barrel of Drogalla's pistol. Before the alien could utter the Venusian equivalent of "dafuq?" The sword had swung around and clocked the Leader out cold with its oversized pommel. Drogalla collapsed in a heap on the floor. Matt crossed the room and tried to close the door, but it wouldn't stay all the way because of the broken lock. He quickly abandoned the effort and stepped back over to where Drogalla lay

"C'mon! Help me drag her into the bedroom," Matt said.

"This is one of those aliens, isn't it? Could this be Randy's mystery lady?" Naomi asked as she took one of her arms.

"Looks like it. I wonder what the hell she's doing here, in our room? Did you happen to bring those handcuffs with you?" He asked.

"Yeah, I was saving them for later...for, you know, our sexy fun times?" Naomi confessed.

"Well, it looks like we need 'em right now, for an entirely different reason unfortunately." Matt replied bitterly. He couldn't believe their romantic night had been interrupted yet again!

When Drogalla regained consciousness moments later, they found it quite difficult to move either arm. A glance upwards revealed that they were handcuffed to a bedpost. The handcuffs, curiously enough, were covered in a bright red, fuzzy material for some unfathomable reason.

"Don't even think about breaking those cuffs, lady! Or you'll get the business end of my sword this time. I saw what you did to our door, so I know you're strong enough to snap those bonds if you really want to." Matt told her.

Drogalla could see that he meant it. The strange sword floated over the Leader's body, angled down towards their chest. Looking around the room some more, Drogalla could see that the woman was there too; the bubble of energy still surrounded her, but now she was armed with a sword too. A sword with an unearthly flame dancing off of its surface. The tip of the sword protruded from the bubble, breaking its surface. She held a pistol in the other hand. A pistol that was pointed straight at her.

Before Drogalla could say a word, there was the sound of footsteps coming from another room. Naomi glanced through the gap in the bedroom door and frowned. "Shit! It's Sara!" she whispered.

Matt sighed.

"Keep an eye on the Queen of Mars here. I'll go talk to Sara. If our guest acts up, use the *Avenger* on her," he whispered back and hurried forward.

Naomi grimaced at his instructions. She had no intention of following them. *I'm trying to get out of the murder game, thank you very much!* If she got free, she'd just knock her out with the massive sword like Matt had done.

Sara had collected another one of her security guards, a burly Samoan fellow they called Buster on her way up to room 508. The door wouldn't close properly any longer and hung halfway open. She and Buster took up opposite positions on either side of the door, and she cautiously peered inside. The room beyond looked empty, but looks could be deceiving. Sara glanced at the broken lock on the door and sighed at the property damage. At least there had been no sound of gunfire—yet. She ordered Sydney to hang back in the hallway as she and Buster burst into the room. Buster was armed with his Taser and Sara was a bit more heavily equipped with her .38 revolver. The room really was empty, but she could hear voices coming from the direction of the bedroom. She carefully moved forwards into the hallway, silently motioning Buster to stay back. She saw Sydney nervously clutching her own taser and looking in through the doorway.

Sara could barely see inside the bedroom, through the half-closed door, but it looked like the woman who'd kicked in the door was now handcuffed to the bedpost! At least she *thought* those were handcuffs. They were covered in red fur for some strange reason.

What the hell is going on here? Sara wondered. Then she had to catch herself against the wall, as she almost slipped on a small puddle of water that was on the floor. Her shoe made a loud squeaking noise as it skidded. She swore under her breath

Just then, Matt appeared, coming out of the bedroom, dressed in only a bathrobe. She damn near shot him.

"Sara!" he exclaimed.

"Spike, do you mind telling me what's going on around here?" she growled as she lowered her gun.

"Sure, it's a little...um, it's embarrassing really." He laughed nervously.

Matt placed a hand on Sara's shoulder, leading her away from the bedroom. "Well, ya see, me and Naomi have been married for a long time now and we have to do certain *things* from time to time to, uh, keep things fresh. Soooo...we invited a friend over to join in a little role-playing situation, if you know what I mean?"

Sara nodded. Her own brief marriage had soured after scarcely a year and a half. She'd promised herself she'd never make that mistake again. She could only imagine the lengths people who'd been married for as long as Matt and Naomi had been must have to go to "keep it fresh" as he'd put it. Sara had to admit that she was a bit surprised though, she'd never imagined that they were this kinky. She was also even a little hurt that she hadn't been included. She still found Matt a bit attractive, and Naomi very attractive.

"Well your 'friend' busted down the door! You're gonna have to pay for that lock, you know!"

"I'm sorry about that. She gets a little... over enthusiastic. She really gets into her role! Just add it to our bill. We're good for it."

"*Over enthusiastic*? She must be strong as an ox to have done that!"

"She works out. She's a very fit woman!" Matt added hastily.

"You can sure say that again!" Sara said in disbelief, then she remembered something else. "I thought I saw her with a gun on the security cameras. Please tell me that wasn't real either."

"It was just a toy. Role-playing, remember?" he assured her.

"Are we okay here, boss?" Buster asked as she and Matt emerged from the hallway.

Sara thought about it for a moment. Matt's story was a little weird, but she supposed it checked out. "I suppose so. Send someone from maintenance up here to repair that lock." She ordered. Buster pulled out his walkie talkie to make it so.

She looked at Matt again, a stern look on her face. "Tell your friend to calm it down a little in the future, okay? I could have you all thrown out for this, you know? If it was anyone else but you…"

"I'll make sure she curbs her enthusiasm. I really appreciate it, Sara. Sorry if we gave you a big scare. Oh, and I'd appreciate it if you'd keep this under your hat, okay?"

"Don't worry, your secrets are safe with me." She smirked playfully at him as she followed Buster out the door. "Oh, be sure to enjoy yourself in there—so long as you don't disturb the other guests with too much noise. And keep that bedroom door closed—I don't want you freaking out my maintenance man!"

"Thanks again, Sara. You're a real lifesaver!" Matt gave her a little salute as she walked out.

"You owe me one, Spike—and someday I might decide to collect on it!" she said, pointing at him and waving a finger.

"Aww man! I didn't even get to taze anyone!" Matt thought he heard a female voice complaining as the footsteps of Sara and her team faded away down the corridor. The voice, of course, had been Sydney's.

Matt tried to close the door, forgetting that it wouldn't catch shut, and used the chain to keep it mostly closed, then he hurried back into the bedroom.

"She's gone!" he announced breathlessly.

"Thank goodness! How'd you get rid of her so quickly? What'd you tell her?" Naomi asked.

"Believe me, you *don't* want to know!" he smiled.

***

Elsewhere, half a world away at Guild Headquarters, Prospero was about to drown his sorrows in a bottle of gin at the bar in the commissary. He studied the clear fluid in his glass mournfully. He was worried about Anne's chances for success. Prospero thought the fate of the planet was hanging from the thinnest of threads.

Ah well, it's been a good run. I've had a longer life than most. He thought glumly. In fact, Prospero was so old that nobody, including himself, knew exactly how many centuries he'd been alive for, his oldest memories were gone—there simply wasn't enough room left in his head to contain them.

"Well, nuthin' else for it!" he said to no one in particular as he raised his glass and downed the entire contents in one go. He smacked his lips as he brought the glass, slamming down onto the mahogany of the bar.

"Imperious Caesar, dead and turn'd to clay, might stop a hole to keep the wind away. O, that that earth, which kept the world in awe, should patch a wall to expel the winter's flaw!" he said, quoting Shakespeare, as he was fond of doing, and poured himself another glass.

"Prospero! I need to talk to you!" A familiar voice called out to him. He craned his neck around to see who was trying to get his attention.

"Oh, it's you." He said disappointedly as he recognized Carlos, one of his fellow wizards who was stationed here at Guild HQ, moving across the room towards him. Carlos was in charge of all the magic users that were enlisted in the UGF. As such, he often worked closely with Anne. They'd had their share of disagreements over the years, the worst one involving the creation of the Omega Seed. Carlos was one of the wizards who helped to create the weapon, a weapon that Prospero felt should've never been born.

This conviction was made doubly strong by the fact that the weapon would've never been possible to invent if it hadn't been for Prospero himself. Years ago, he'd once served Mortus Locke, one of the worst dark sorcerers of all time. When Prospero eventually betrayed Locke, he stole several his spell books as he made his getaway. Upon joining the Temple of the Old Gods, he turned over these volumes of lost, forbidden knowledge to them. It was the information in those books that made something as terrible as the Omega Seed possible. It was one of reasons he was currently trying to drink himself into oblivion. He couldn't help but feel responsible for the existence of the seed, and he never thought he'd see the day when it would actually be used. Sure, it might end up saving the Earth, but not before it killed lots of aliens. Truth to tell, he wasn't too terribly worried about those aliens, they were trying to wipe out mankind, after all. What he was more concerned about was the precedent that using it would set. He feared that the powers that be would point at the way it was successfully used on this occasion and start using it more frequently, to solve every little problem they encountered. It was like using a jackhammer when all you needed was a chisel.

Carlos took a seat next to him and eyed his bottle of gin judgmentally. "Jesus, Prospero! Tell me you're not planning on drinking that whole bottle by yourself!"

"Yer welcome, help me, lad. Contrary to popular opinion, not all Scots are stingy. I could use a drinking buddy right now."

"As...tempting as that offer may be, I'm afraid I'll have to decline. Something important has come up and I don't know what to do about it."

Prospero downed another glass in one gulp and faced Carlos. "Now you've got my interest! Go on."

"You know how my son is the one who primes the Omega Seed, right?" Carlos asked. Prospero nodded sagely, although this was actually news to him.

"Well, he just told me something rather...disturbing. At the last minute, Anne switched out the substance that they were using to prime it. She took away the vial containing the particles they gathered off of that spaceship and had them prime it with a single strand of hair instead."

If he hadn't already gulped down his last drink, Prospero surely would've spat it out at these words. "What?? A hair? *Whose* hair?"

"That's what my son asked her. She just told him something like 'don't worry, I guarantee it isn't human.'"

"And the boy went ahead and primed it, anyway? Doesn't he understand? The Omega Seed won't just destroy the person whose hair it came from, but anyone else who is remotely similar!" This was precisely what April had feared when Anne first proposed using it.

"What could he do? Disobey a direct order from the Chairperson herself? She would've just found someone else to do it and he would've landed himself in a heap of trouble. Besides, I've known Anne since she first joined up. She's a close friend of the family. We all trust her."

"But at least he wouldn't be the one with all that blood on his hands!" Prospero cried in horror.

"I'm just glad he didn't waste any time in coming to tell me about it. All those arguments we used to have about the Omega Seed *did* eventually get me thinking. I realize you were right, we should've never created it. At the time, I just looked at it as a challenge. I wanted to see if we could really craft a magic item that powerful. I didn't really think about the implications of such power. And I trusted Anne not to abuse it, but now..." Carlos trailed off, his voice thick with regrets.

"I'm glad you've finally seen the light of reason, but it's a little too late, isn't it?" Prospero complained.

"Maybe not. They haven't been gone that long. Didn't Randy go with her? If we could get a message to him, maybe he could take the seed from her?" Carlos suggested, lowering his voice.

"Most would probably consider it treason."

"Isn't a little treason warranted under the circumstances?"

"Aye. That it may be. But it might not be so easy, she brought those two assassins with her—Smoke and Wisp, her personal bodyguards. Now I suppose we know *why* she insisted on dragging them with her. Bah! Bronson McDowell never needed any bloody bodyguards! First Wendy retires, who, by the way, would've never let any of her magic users cooperate with the creation of something like the Omega Seed, then Bronson retires too and this whole Guild thing starts to go to hell!"

Carlos had to agree. Wendy Sommardahl, April's wife, the witch who was Randy's mentor and the former leader of the Temple of the Old Gods, would've never allowed the Omega Seed to come into existence. Unfortunately, she had retired several years ago to a humble home in New Hope, Pennsylvania, so she could raise her daughter Celine in a more normal environment. April had stayed on to represent the Temple on the Inner council and now divided her time between Guild HQ and PA.

Prospero lifted his hand to reach for the bottle and pour another glass. Carlos shot out his arm and caught it.

"Don't. Let's at least *try* to do something. I don't know that I can live with myself if we don't. Let's go explain all of this to April and see if we can reach Randy on his communicator. It might not be too late after all."

Prospero looked down and made a face. "Alright. It's worth a shot. Let's track down April." He took the bottle with him as he hopped down from his barstool.

A few minutes later, Prospero and Carlos were standing in April's apartment, having just explained everything to her. She paced around the room for some time, clearly troubled by the news. She had known Anne for years and had always been quite fond of her.

"This is so unlike her!" she finally declared in disbelief.

"Is it though?" Prospero challenged her. "She's changed. All the power we've given her has gone to her head. Only you've been blinded to it by your friendship with her."

"I think I'm guilty of the same mistake," Carlos admitted sadly.

"I can't believe she just stood up there and lied to us all! Why didn't she just stick to the plan she told us? It was a good plan! Why does she want to wipe them all out?" She finally said, unable to fathom the betrayal.

"Never mind that. What are we going to do about it?" Prospero asked.

"I know one thing—we can't just stand by and let her destroy an entire race of people, even if some of them are willing to do the same thing to us, it sounds like the vast majority of them are just trying to escape their planet and colonize some other world. That Kergaali person's people are risking themselves to try and help us, they don't deserve to all be wiped out like that, hell does anyone? I guess we can try what Carlos suggested. Wisp and Smoke are tough, but they're no match for a wizard as powerful as Randy."

"Is it fair for us to ask him to do that? This is a dangerous path we're headed down." Prospero warned.

"I don't see that we have much choice. Ultimately, the decision is his own, but Anne did lie to the entire Inner Council, and we can prove it. I'll ask Randy to place her under arrest. We can begin impeachment proceedings against her when they get back. I can't imagine that the others will continue to support her when they realize how she's misled us."

"The Venusians are still a threat, though. If we will not use the Omega Seed against them, how will we defeat them?" Carlos asked.

"I've been thinking about that, too. Maybe Jim could use his ship to destroy the Time Tunnel itself? It would cut them off from all their saucers. If they should make a new Time Tunnel and try to attack the Earth again, we can re-prime the seed to destroy their ships, like in the original plan. The important thing is that we reach Randy on a private channel right away!"

She lifted her Guild communicator from its charging cradle and dialed Randy's number. There was no answer.

"Well fuck! They must already be out of range," she announced angrily.

"Maybe someone in the control room can boost the signal for us?" Carlos suggested. Guild headquarters had a global communications control room that was used to coordinate UGF operations.

"Good idea. Alright, let's move!" April said as she dove for the door. The others struggled to keep up as they followed her down the maze of corridors to the control room, her dress swirling around her legs as she moved with the determined speed of a woman half her age

As she entered the room full of technicians, she spotted Oliver and made her way over to him. He was busy monitoring the pirate fleet that was headed to the location of the mothership under the Atlantic.

"Ollie, can I borrow one of your people for a minute? I need to send an important message out to someone, but I'm having trouble reaching them on my communicator. Do you have anyone you could spare?" she asked as she reached him.

"Huh? Oh, uh yes, sure." He pointed to a bored looking young woman a few seats to his left.

"Millicent can help, can't you?" He raised his voice slightly as he said it and looked at the woman. She pulled off some headphones she'd been wearing and looked at him questioningly.

"What?" she asked. "Were you trying to tell me something?"

"Yes, I need you to assist April with whatever she needs." Oliver commanded.

Millicent gave him a thumbs up as April, Prospero, and Carlos surrounded the computer console she'd been working at.

"I hope we're not interrupting anything too important?" April asked diplomatically.

"Nah, boring stuff, really. I'm just monitoring government intelligence agency chatter in the NYC area, trying to see what they might know about the recent UFO activity that we don't already know. As usual, they know jack. What can I do for you?"

"I need you to see if you can reach a certain Guild communicator for me that's out of range right now."

"Out of range? But the whole planet is in range of our communicators!" Millicent balked.

"Exactly my problem. This communicator is on the ship that's bound for the moon right now."

Millicent whistled.

"You want me to call someone on the spaceship for you? But Director Moore wanted us to maintain radio silence until the mission was completed!" Millicent protested.

"Don't call us, we'll call you, eh? That sounds like her!" Prospero noted sourly.

"She was concerned that the aliens might pick up our communications. She didn't want to tip them off." She replied defensively.

"Oliver ordered you to give us whatever help you can, and when Anne is gone he's in charge," April reminded her, "Please try to make that call."

"Alright, but it won't be easy. They went into stealth mode right after takeoff, so we have no idea where they are right now. I'll have to divert a few resources temporarily to give you the boost we'll need."

April gave her the code to reach Randy's communicator. Millicent's slender fingers danced over her keyboard with blinding speed as she made her attempt. She was starting to have fun. Despite her earlier misgivings about breaking communications silence, she became completely caught up in the challenge of solving the problem. She waited a few minutes, eagerly checking for any results, then hit her desk in frustration.

"It's no good! I'm not getting any response. They're probably moving too darned fast for the signal to reach them, or they're already on the dark side of the moon."

April chewed her lower lip. "Thanks for trying." She turned to her companions. "Anyone have any ideas of what to do now?

"I suppose we'll have to try astral projection." Prospero said. They all knew that Randy, as a wizard, would be able to see and hear them in their astral forms, but nobody else in the spaceship would.

"It might be too late by the time we find them that way!" Carlos complained. It was certainly possible for someone to travel to the moon in their astral body, and to even do so relatively quickly. However, finding one small, cloaked spaceship traveling between the Earth and the moon would be a tall order because there was such a vast distance between the two heavenly bodies.

"Agreed. It's too much of a long shot. Even if I got all of the magic users here at Guild HQ to assist in the search, we probably couldn't find them soon enough that way," April said. "There's nothing else for it. I'm going to have to tell Oliver what's going on and see if he'll let us use the *Silver Bullet.* We could fly out far enough into space that our communicators will be in range again.

The *Silver Bullet* was the name of a captured UFO that had belonged to the Guilds for years now. They'd spent years studying it, trying to build more ships like it, but with no success.

"Are ye daft, woman! This is treason, remember? Now you want to involve the top aide to the very person we're plotting against?" Prospero whispered in her ear.

"That's just a chance we'll have to take. The way I see it, Anne is the one who committed treason against all of us when she lied to the Council. And she's betraying our basic principles by plotting to commit genocide. Oliver is a man of honor, of principles. He might see it that way, too. I'm not going to just give up!" She told him in no uncertain terms.

She knew that if they didn't reach Randy in time, not only would an entire race of sentient beings be destroyed, but it would be even harder to remove Anne from power. And, as much as it hurt to admit it to herself, she was now sure that Anne *absolutely* had to be replaced. She feared that if Anne was allowed to go ahead with her deadly mission, most people on the Inner Council would see her as a hero who'd just saved humanity. They'd never vote to impeach her.

There were certain spells that they could use to prove that Carlos' son was telling the truth about what Anne did if she tried to deny what she'd done, but would enough people care? Or would they see it all as a trick that the Temple was trying to pull to get rid of Anne and seize power for themselves? Many years ago, the Temple of the Old Gods had tried to do exactly that. She knew that despite all the good work that she and Wendy had done to repair their reputation, there were still many on the Inner Council that didn't trust them as a result. If they didn't handle this right, it could split the Guilds between magic users and non-magic users.

That was something she had to avoid—at all costs.

Carlos had been thinking hard about their problem. He grabbed April's arm as she walked off towards where Oliver was standing. "Wait! We don't need to risk involving Oliver. You're both forgetting that I'm a high-ranking officer in the UGF - I can just commandeer the *Silver Bullet* and a pilot for it too. I can even make sure everyone keeps quiet about it by telling them our mission is highly classified."

"Hmm. Not a bad idea. Okay. Let's give it a shot." April said approvingly.

A few minutes later, April, Carlos, and Prospero were striding through a large hangar on the edge of the headquarters building where the *Silver Bullet* was kept. Carlos used his security clearance to get them inside. They walked past the gleaming flying saucer, which had a variety of wires running from its surface to various machines stationed around it at regular intervals. Technicians hurried to and fro between these terminals like a colony of busy worker bees.

Carlos walked up to one of the technicians. "Excuse me, but we need to see the CO. Do you know where he is?" The technician pointed upwards. Carlos followed the direction of his finger and smiled. "Thank you."

Carlos led them up a flight of steel steps and into an office overlooking the hangar. Inside was a bored looking, middle-aged man dressed in a nondescript pair of gray fatigues. He had been looking at something on the laptop computer on his desk, but he quickly closed it up as he heard them enter the room, a somewhat embarrassed look on his face.

"I wasn't expecting any visitors! What brings you here today, Colonel Conception?" he asked, calling Carlos by his military rank. He was surprised to see that he also had a high-ranking diplomat like April Sommardahl with him, and some old man who was carrying around a half empty bottle of Gin for some odd reason.

"Hello, Albert. I'm afraid that we need to take control of the *Silver Bullet*. We've just been given orders for a new top-secret mission. We're also going to need someone who knows how to fly it." Carlos told him.

"What? But we're in the middle of some very important tests right now! Why wasn't I informed about this?" The man complained.

"You're being informed of it now. This mission is of a very sensitive nature, the fewer people that know about it the better. That's why I'm telling you in person. I'm sorry about your tests, but *we're* in the middle of an alien invasion and the *Silver Bullet* is one of the only lines of defense that we've got against the enemy ships. We need it - now."

Albert looked unconvinced. He reached for a phone on his desk. "I'm going to just check with Deputy Director Johns then, if you don't mind, and verify all of this."

April and Carlos exchanged worried looks as Albert picked up the receiver. Prospero started chanting the words of a spell and waving his hands around wildly. But not just any spell, it was a forbidden spell he'd learned from one of Mortus Locke's spell books.

As he finished the words of the incantation, he spoke to Albert in a gruff, authoritative tone. "Put down that phone! You will order the *Silver Bullet* ready for immediate flight and give us the pilot we asked for! You will also order everyone in this hangar not to speak of this and send them all home for the evening. Then you will return home and tomorrow you will forget that any of this ever happened! Now do it!"

"I obey, my master." Albert said in a dull, lifeless tone as he put the phone down. He picked up a microphone that was also on the desk. "Attention everyone, this is General Spooner. Prepare the *Silver Bullet* for flight. Once the ship is ready, you are all dismissed from duty for the rest of the evening and are not to speak of this to anyone. Major Thompson, report to my office right away." He put the microphone down and just stood there listlessly, like some kind of a zombie.

April shot Prospero a withering look. "That spell is highly illegal!"

"This entire enterprise is 'highly illegal,' Lass! In for a penny, in for a pound!"

She sighed. He was right, but she was also worried about where all of this was ultimately taking them. Bad enough that they were stealing the *Silver Bullet*, but now they were using mind control spells on people? How many more crimes could they find righteous sounding justifications for committing? Were they now traveling down the same road that had led Anne to believe that something as severe as genocide was necessary?

It only took a few minutes for the technicians to remove all the wires and sensor pads from the outside of the ship. Soon, they were all strapped into the bright, white interior of the *Silver Bullet,* Major Thompson, a young Asian man who looked like he was barely out of his teens at the controls. The ship lifted off of the ground, went into stealth mode and April worked a spell that created a mirror image illusion of it - the magical equivalent of Jim's hologram, before the ship shot off into the darkening sky at a blinding speed. Its stealth mode effectively masking it from the Guild's detection as the island disappeared behind it.

"Where are we headed to, Ma'm?" He asked April, whom Carlos had informed him was in command of this mission.

"Take us to the dark side of the moon." She ordered, wondering if she was making the worst mistake of her life.

CHAPTER 12:
DESTINATION: MOON

Now that he finally had a minute to do so, Matt regarded their prisoner. She appeared to be a good-looking young black woman with high, aristocratic cheekbones. Her pupils were more like those of a cat than those of a human, but this wasn't immediately obvious. She was dressed from head to toe in a tight-fitting, silver outfit with occasional red accents. She wore a ridiculous looking skull cap with some goggles built into it resting upon her forehead. A pair of golden, stylized wings on either side of her head, topping it all off was an elaborate antenna.

"I'm gonna call Randy and see if he has any idea why she's here." He said as he moved towards his phone, which was charging on the nightstand.

"Don't bother, I've already tried. There's no answer. I also tried calling Penny too, to see if she knew where he was, I got the same result. Same thing when I called his Guild communicator. Crazy idea: we could just try asking her—she seems to speak English." Naomi informed him.

"Really? He always has that communicator on him!" Matt said, his voice choked with concern. They couldn't reach either of them? He hoped his friends were okay. He whirled on Drogalla angrily. The *Vermilion Avenger* inched forwards menacingly until its tip was hovering mere inches from her face.

"Okay lady, time to spill the beans! Why did you barge in here and start pointing a gun at my wife?"

"Lady? Beans? What nonsense are you speaking?" Drogalla replied.

Naomi stepped forward. "Never mind. My husband has a colorful way with words sometimes. What he means to say is why did you attack us?"

"You attacked us first! Shot down my saucers! Are you not working with the Baandergi to coordinate these attacks?"

"Now you're the one talking nonsense! We didn't attack anyone! And what's a band derby?" Matt asked.

"Don't play stupid with me, human! There's no other explanation for the strange energy readings coming from this room! The Baandergi obviously supplied you with the strange weapons you now threaten me with, as well as that personal force field! Your people are not capable of creating such things!" Drogalla said defiantly.

"Holy crap! Matt, I think she thinks our weapons came from aliens." Naomi said, in a dawning realization.

He nodded in agreement. "And those energy readings she's talking about are probably coming from the Orb in our safe."

"Lady, you've got us all wrong. Our weapons, and that thing giving off the energy you've been picking up, are all from magic items, not alien technology."

"Well, technically, the *Vermilion Avenger* isn't a magic item. It's made of exotic materials of an extraterrestrial origin that have certain specialized properties. Even though it's made of extraterrestrial materials, it wasn't given to us by aliens, though." Naomi added.

"Thanks a bunch, professor! You're gonna confuse her with all those unnecessary details! 'Our big sword is made of alien stuff, but aliens didn't give it to us, we swear!' Yeah, that's really helpful!"

"I guess that *is* a little confusing." She admitted.

"Oh gee, ya think?" Matt said sarcastically.

Drogalla was beginning to get a headache from listening to these two idiots.

"You must think me a fool! Magic! That's just one of your bizarre human superstitions. It's not real! Most of your own people wouldn't even believe such an outrageous tale!"

"I know! I've been living it for years now and I can barely believe it myself sometimes!" Matt confessed.

"But it *is* true!" Naomi insisted.

Drogalla wasn't buying it. "You humans are fools to work with the Baandergi! How can you betray your own people for a few trinkets?

Did you believe their false promises that they'd spare you, or are you just unaware that they plan to exterminate all humankind?"

That got Matt and Naomi's attention. They glanced at each other in worry.

"Wipe out mankind? I thought this was an invasion, not genocide!" Naomi exclaimed.

"Hold on a second here! Are you trying to tell us that you're not with the aliens that are trying to invade this planet? You're on the other side?" Matt demanded.

"I wonder if she's from the same group Jim was working with? What was that one alien's name? Kerplunk? Kerfuffle?" Naomi pondered aloud.

"Nah, it sounded more like Ker Goalie, I think."

"Are you fools trying to say Kergaali?" The Leader asked in exasperation.

Matt snapped his fingers. "That's it! Do you know her? Is she a friend of yours?"

"Hardly! She's a monster! The leader of the fanatical faction trying to take over this world."

"Great! That's the one Jim was helping out! Is she tricking him into helping him to destroy the wrong bunch of aliens?" Matt wondered.

"I don't know, but we need to figure it out, and fast! Randy was going to get the Guilds to help her out, remember?" Naomi said.

"Maybe we're getting too ahead of ourselves here. Let's back this up a little and start from the beginning. Lady, who are you and what are you doing on my planet?"

"I am no 'lady' despite my outward appearance. I am Drogalla, Leader of the Saawgauth Nation of Pfoff, the world you would call 'Venus' in your tongue. I am here on a mission of mercy, to give your people the means to defend yourselves against invaders from a rogue nation of my own world, the Baandergi. "

"Mission of mercy! You have a funny way of going about it, kicking in people's doors and ruining their sexy fun times!" Matt said skeptically.

"I've already explained that I thought you were Baandergi agents who assisted with destroying my ships! I'm still not entirely convinced that you're not!"

The mention of Venus had piqued Naomi's interest.

"Why would the people of Venus want to invade this planet? And why in this universe? Why not invade your own version of Earth?" She assumed these Venusians were the same as Adamski's, knowing that our Venus is devoid of life.

"Universe? I'm not from another universe, but from your ancient past. Our planet is dying. Most of our nations are cooperating with creating a fleet to escape to a distant world, except for the Baandergi. They've always been an odd nation, traditionalists, isolationists, fiercely independent. As usual, they decided to tackle our planet's greatest problem in their own unique way. They came forward in time to this era, when your planet would be more hospitable. But they have no intention of trying to share this planet with you. They want to destroy you all. They're building a fleet of drone ships armed with neutron missiles to kill you. That's why I'm here. Our laws forbid us from fighting them directly, but they don't prevent us from giving you the means to fight them off yourselves. I was on my way to your United Nations to explain all of this and give you our Duplo-Ray technology so you could build a fleet capable of fighting off their drones. But then my ships were intercepted for the second time today and destroyed! One of my subordinates managed to teleport me to safety just before my ship exploded."

Something about the sadness in Drogalla's voice as those last words were spoken moved Naomi.

"I believe her. And if she's telling the truth, we've got to reach Randy and stop him before he makes a terrible mistake," she told Matt.

"I know one way we can tell if she's being truthful. Randy has a spell that can compel someone to speak nothing but the truth for 24 hours," Matt said.

"Oh! Like in the movie *Liar Liar*?" Naomi said. "How is it that I didn't know there was really a spell like that?" She really loved that movie.

"That's where he got the idea from when he created that spell," Matt confirmed. "Believe me, it comes in handy in our line of work. He has a way of casting it where people don't even know it's been put on them."

"There's only one problem—we can't get a hold of Randy right now."

"Ah, but we can try to reach Kiesha. I'll bet he's taught her that spell. And if we can't reach her, we can get Wendy to come to the city. She can probably re-create the spell," Matt said.

"But we can't have someone do a spell in here, the Orb will cancel it out." Naomi reminded him.

"No problem. One of us will just have to drive it out of range long enough to cast the spell."

Drogalla was silent, listening to all of this. This strange couple was definitely acting as if magic was something real. The Leader decided they must be insane. There was no reason to put on such an elaborate show for Drogalla's benefit. It was just like the Baandergi, to take advantage of the mentally deranged for their own purposes.

Naomi called Kiesha. It turned out that she did indeed know how to do the spell in question and agreed to come over right away to cast it. It was soon decided that Naomi would be the one to take the Orb out of range. She grabbed some clothes and went off to the bathroom to get changed first, while Matt monitored their prisoner. When she returned to the bedroom, they switched places so Matt could get dressed.

"Good luck, and don't do anything with the sexy alien tied to the bed that I wouldn't do." Naomi said, giving Matt a kiss on the cheek as she took the keys to the car.

"Hardy, har, har, har." Matt replied. "What're you gonna do while I handle the interrogation?"

"I figured I'll drop in on my mom over in Brooklyn. Her place should be just out of range."

"Say hi to your mother for me! I'll call you when it's safe to come back. Oh!" he exclaimed suddenly and dug something out of his wallet. He handed it to her.

She smirked at the card in her hand. "You still haven't used this Starbucks gift card? Isn't it like 2 years old by now?"

"It keeps slipping my mind, okay? Pick me up some coffee on your way back. I'm gonna need it—I have a feeling this is gonna be a long night."

When Kiesha showed up, she was surprised to see someone replacing the lock on the door to Matt and Naomi's room. Naomi hadn't explained very much to her over the phone. Matt, for his part, was surprised to see that she had brought Paul with her.

"Hiya, kid!" he said cheerfully, but then he took Kiesha to one side and whispered to her. "You didn't say you were bringing the boy!"

"I'm babysitting him for Randy and Penny while they're off doing whatever it is that they're doing with Jim. I couldn't just leave him by himself. Why? Is it a problem that he's here?"

"Well, I currently have a woman handcuffed to the bed in the next room, and I sort of prefer that he doesn't have such an image burned into his young, impressionable mind," Matt whispered back.

"Don't worry, I'll just find some kid appropriate shows on the TV and tell him to keep out of the bedroom. You know how easy going he is."

This seemed to placate Matt, and after Kiesha put on some SpongeBob, Matt led her into the bedroom.

"Nice handcuffs you have there," Kiesha smiled, while Matt's face became almost as red as the fuzz on the handcuffs.

"That's not the same alien that we saw earlier, but her style of clothing is just as questionable." She commented after laying her eyes upon the Leader's outfit.

"This is Leader Drocula of the Sogmoth Nation of Venus." Matt attempted to explain.

"That's Drogalla of the Saawgauth Nation!" The leader testily corrected him.

"Oh, yeah. Sorry. I can never get these weird alien names right. That's why I could never finish those Lord of the Rings books, all those crazy impossible to pronounce names! I could never keep the characters straight until I saw the movies."

"Drogalla!" Kiesha exclaimed. "That's the same alien that Jim was trying to kill earlier."

"It looks like he made another attempt, and they were a bit more successful this time. They destroyed Drogalla's ships, and she barely escaped. Then she came here to harass us, because she picked up an energy reading from the Orb and thought it was some kinda alien tech. She thinks we have something to do with the attack on her ships."

"And you obviously do! You just admitted that you know someone who attacked us earlier!" Drogalla said defiantly.

Matt ignored the outburst. "Anyhow, according to Drogalla, she's one of the good guys, er—girls. Jim has been fooled into attacking the wrong bunch of aliens. So I need you to put that truth spell on her so we can be sure who to trust."

"Why bother? I watched her ships blow up a few buildings today. She's gotta be the real villain, trying to trick us into helping her."

"Naomi thinks otherwise, and I've got a few doubts myself."

Kiesha nodded. She recalled that Randy had planned to convince the Guilds to help Jim, so she knew how important this was. She chanted the words of the spell, and as she did so, a golden glow surrounded Drogalla, and the Leader felt a peculiar tingling sensation.

"How is it that you are doing this to me?" Drogalla demanded.

"I already explained, it's magic!" Matt told her. "Now, I need you to repeat that same story you told us earlier, you know? The one about how you came here to help the human race?" Drogalla, compelled by the threat of the almost comically large sword hovering uncomfortably nearby, soon did as instructed.

Kiesha looked visibly upset by the time Drogalla was done speaking. "Shit! She's totally telling the truth!"

"Oh man! Try to call Randy again. I'll let Naomi know that it's okay to bring the Orb back." Matt told her, typing out a quick text to his wife to return to the hotel.

"Umm, if she's on the side of the human race, don't you think you oughta uncuff her from the bed first?" Kiesha suggested.

"Oh, yeah, good idea!" Matt agreed, with a thought. He made the *Vermilion Avenger* fly away from Drogalla and he had it hover over his shoulder instead. He moved towards the bedpost to remove the cuffs.

Drogalla snapped them in two effortlessly. "Don't bother, human!" The leader sat upright and glared at Matt.

"Hey! You owe me a pair of fuzzy handcuffs!"

"And you owe me an apology! I came here from millions of years in the past to save your race and *this* is the kind of treatment I get?"

"Uh, sorry. But you did bust in here waving a gun around. You can't blame us for taking certain...precautions."

"I suppose so," Drogalla said, a faint smile appearing on the face of the leader. "I guess you aren't working directly with the Baandergi after all, and your friends have only been tricked into doing so. I also surmise that there really is something to this 'magic' of yours, as difficult as it is for me to understand how it could possibly work. I still feel a definite effect from the 'spell' which has been cast upon me."

Matt realized that this was the closest he was going to get to an apology from the alien.

"I can't get in touch with any of them. Randy, Penny or Jim." Keisha told Matt from across the room.

"Not too surprising. We tried earlier, I was just hoping that something had changed since then. Okay, let's try calling the Guilds directly. For all we know, they might've already gone to them." He took out his own Guild communicator from his coat pocket.

He tried calling Anne first. Then, after having no luck reaching her, he called April next, as she was the most high-ranking person in the Guilds that he was friends with who hadn't retired yet. He had better luck contacting her. Seeing that the call was from Matt, she picked up the line over the protests of Carlos, who wanted her to maintain radio silence.

They quickly compared notes. Matt was horrified to learn that Anne was already on her way to attack a base on the moon with a device capable of killing all the Venusians. April was equally horrified to discover that the base that the Guilds were about to attack didn't even belong to the right group of aliens.

"This is a real clusterfuck, isn't it?" Matt sighed. "What are we gonna do about it?"

"It's the clusterfuckiest, alright." April agreed. "Does this Drogalla person know how to reach the moon base? I mean, it's their base, isn't it? Maybe they could guide us there?" April asked.

"Yeah, probably. But how are we gonna get there in time?"

"I'm in the *Silver Bullet* right now. We, err...borrowed it to fly out to where we could try to call Randy on Jim's ship." She had thus far decided to spare Matt any of the details of how they'd stolen the ship. She especially didn't want to reveal this in case Major Thompson overheard. She wanted to avoid the need for any further mind control spells, if possible.

"We haven't gotten very far yet. We'll head over to pick you up right away. Meet us on top of the roof of the hotel with your new alien friend," April said.

Matt couldn't believe that he'd almost forgotten all about the *Silver Bullet*. "Okay, it's a plan, we'll meet you there!" Matt said as he hung up.

By this time, Naomi had returned. Matt filled her and Drogalla in on everything he'd just learned. Naomi certified the clusterfuckiness of the situation. He also had to explain to Drogalla what the Guilds were first; it was a concept that the leader found to be quite peculiar.

"I see that your people and ours are not so different, only in all the worst ways. Just as the Baandergi seek to destroy you to preserve their way of life, so too do your people when presented with the same dilemma." The Leader said with a mixture of anger and sadness.

Matt opened his mouth reflexively to defend humanity, to justify its right to life, but realized that he simply couldn't find the words to do so in this instance.

"I must contact my mothership, to warn them of the coming attack on the moon base," Drogalla said, removing what Matt assumed was a communications device from a belt pouch. Drogalla's attempts to reach the ship soon proved to be futile.

"There's no answer. I'm not surprised, though," the Leader frowned. "The mothership was monitoring my flight. Goymaalt, my second in command, would've seen how our saucers were intercepted mere moments after leaving the ship, and destroyed with such ease. Goymaalt would've realized that the enemy knew the location of the mothership, and that it was also in danger of coming under attack by a force with superior weapons. Under such circumstances, Goymaalt would've moved the ship, probably falling back to reinforce the moon base since it is logical to assume that it would also become a target. My ship is probably out of communications range now, just like the one your friends are on."

"It looks like we'll both have a few calls to make when we get closer to the moon." Matt said as he took a sip from the coffee Naomi had brought back for him.

"We? So you're planning on going along too? I thought you'd had enough of the weirdness." Naomi asked Matt, taken aback by his sudden shift in attitude.

"Yeah, but I'm also sick of feeling helpless while our planet comes under attack. Sick of trying to pretend that everything's okay when I know that we're all in danger. I want to do whatever I can to help out, to help Randy and Penny. I may be a little older, but I've still got plenty of fight left in me."

Naomi stood on her tiptoes and gave him a kiss. "That's the spirit! I'm coming too, for all the same reasons. Besides, I always wanted to be the first mom on the moon."

"I'm afraid that you're too late for that. All of my people are mothers, and both the Saawgauth and Baandergi have moon bases, so you see there are already plenty of moms on the moon." Drogalla said

"Well, I'll still be the first *human* mom on the moon—provided that we beat Penny in landing on it." Naomi said, undeterred.

"April's on the *Silver Bullet* too, and she's a mom," Matt reminded her.

Naomi threw her hands up in the air in exasperation. "Why is everyone so determined to rain on my parade?" The curious verbal expression drew an equally curious facial expression from Drogalla, who was perplexed as to its meaning.

"Did you just say that *all* your people are mothers? Don't you have any men in your forces?" Matt asked in confusion.

"Men? We have no males. They are no longer necessary for our procreation." Drogalla explained.

"Huh! An entire planet full of women, imagine that! I guess that women *really* are from Venus, or at least some of them." Matt laughed, referencing an infamous book from the 1990s called "Men are from Mars and Women are from Venus" which furthered the popular fallacy that there are certain inherent differences between men and women that go beyond the physiological ones.

Naomi wrinkled her nose in distaste at the mention of the book. "Ugh. That book was a hot mess."

"Yeah, it was," Matt agreed, finishing off his coffee.

"We don't have women either. Females, but not women. Your concept of 'womanhood' is an intriguing, yet alien one to us. I do not like being referred to as a 'lady,' simply call me Drogalla." Drogalla clarified.

"Oh, sorry, I didn't know." Naomi said. She'd had a few non-binary gendered students over the years, and had always been careful to use the correct pronouns for them. It only seemed decent to do so.

"I'm sorry too," Matt said, feeling slightly embarrassed as he realized that he'd already called Drogalla a lady a bunch of times.

"I can see that I'm going to have a lot of interesting questions for you on our trip to the moon!" Matt said as he broke out the case that he kept the *Vermilion Avenger* in when he needed to transport it, and snapped it open on the bed. He mentally commanded the sword to float into it.

"You'd better put your angel sword in here too if you're really planning on tagging along." Matt told Naomi.

"Good idea." She agreed as she placed it inside. There was plenty of room in the capacious case for both weapons.

Matt, Naomi, and Drogalla left the bedroom and emerged into the hotel suite's living room. Kiesha and Paul were still there, watching

TV together. Paul was a little surprised by the sight of the tall, statuesque Drogalla.

"Who's the lady in the tin foil clothes?" He asked.

"A friend, and don't call her a lady," Matt answered. Then he looked over at Kiesha. "We're off to save the world again. You and Paul are welcome to stay here while we're away. Order some room service for yourselves and just have them add it to my tab."

"Thanks, this place sure is a lot nicer to hang out in than the *Blunderbus.*" She answered.

"Also, we're gonna need you to act as the Guardian of the Orb while we're gone." Naomi added.

"What? How can I defend it? I can't use any of my magic while I'm around it!"

"Hmm. Good point. Here, take this," Matt said, as he pulled his .45 from its hidden holster under his jacket and carefully handed it to her.

Kiesha took it and held it like it was a dead fish.

"What the hell am I supposed to do with this? I don't know how to use one of these things!"

"It's not that complicated—just point it and squeeze the trigger, like how they do it in the movies." Naomi said as she swung the now repaired door open.

"It'll be a piece of cake. Nobody's tried to take that Orb from us since '97. It's the easiest job in the world, just don't let the kid play with it. See ya later!" Matt said as he followed Naomi and Drogalla out the door, shutting it before Kiesha could protest any further.

They took the stairs to the roof. The air was particularly chilly up there, but fortunately they didn't have very long to wait before they saw a bright, white doorway shaped opening appear in the otherwise empty sky slightly above them. A silver ramp appeared beneath the opening, its edge hovering a foot or so from the surface of the roof. Prospero stuck his head out of the doorway, his long, wild gray hair was blown around by the winter winds, making him look even more crazed than usual.

"Welcome aboard!" he called down to them far more merrily than the circumstances warranted. He was obviously a little intoxicated.

They all scrambled up the ramp and took their seats inside. Moments later, the *Silver Bullet* was once more shooting off towards the cold expanse of outer space, leaving the bright lights of the city far behind.

CHAPTER 13:
I'LL MEET YOU ON THE DARK SIDE OF THE MOON

Penny had been sitting behind Smoke and Wisp for the entire trip through space and hadn't yet heard a peep out of either of them. Somehow, they seemed more alien to her than either of the actual aliens on the ship. She decided she'd finally had enough of this unbearably awkward silence.

She leaned forward and tapped them both on the shoulders. They slowly turned their heads to gaze in her direction, their eyes empty and vacuous looking.

"So, you two are assassins, huh? I've never met actual assassins before. Have you whacked anyone interesting lately?"

They stared at her blankly for a moment, then turned back around wordlessly.

"Geez, just trying to make some conversation. Deadly and humorless, what a combination!" She complained under her breath.

Randy had been watching this exchange with some amusement.

"They're in a kind of trance right now that they go into before a battle. They also take a type of drug that deadens their emotions. It makes all the killing a little easier for them to cope with psychologically, allegedly. Under other circumstances, they're actually quite lively." He explained to her.

"It's certainly comforting to know that the trained killers are usually the life of the party." She quipped.

"Hopefully, there won't be much killing," Jim said. "I've issued everyone nonlethal weapons from my replicator. They'll knock the Venusians out, but won't kill 'em."

"Now that *is* comforting to know!" Penny said approvingly.

"A little killing, however, will be unavoidable." Kergaali replied flatly.

"How so?" Penny asked.

"The base has a few gun emplacements surrounding it. I recommend that we destroy those before landing. It's best to neutralize any defensive capability this base possesses while we're here. The chaos that such an attack will create should also make it easier for us to slip inside.”

“A sound strategy. I'm surprised that someone from such an otherwise peaceful race was able to come up with it.” Anne commented.

“It’s only logical, and our peoples are not really so different in many respects. When pushed to the limit, we are both quite capable of doing whatever we need to do to survive.” Kergaali said.

“Indeed.” Anne said gravely.

“Approaching Luna now!” Hi-Fi announced from where he was plugged in up in front, the slightest hint of his former over enthusiasm in his voice.

Penny gasped as the moon filled the viewscreen. She’d seen the moon almost every night of her life, but she’d never seen it quite like this. To think, she’d only ever seen views like this in grainy films taken from the Apollo missions from over 40 years earlier. When she watched those images, she never imagined that she’d actually be here in person someday.

She craned her head to get a better look as the ship skimmed the surface, flying over pearlescent craters and vast expanses of endless grayness.

So desolate, yet serenely beautiful. Penny thought as she gazed out upon it. It reminded her of when the Mystery Smith’s tour had brought them to the sands of the southwestern United States, only it was far less colorful. However, the more she looked at it, the more she could make out a variety of subtle shades in the silvery lunar landscape.

If Randy was as moved as Penny was by this up close view of the moon, he didn’t show it. After a rather emotional start to the day, he’d finally reverted to his default “cool as a cucumber” emotional state. In actuality, Randy wasn’t particularly impressed by the lunar surface. He’d already explored it in his astral body years earlier and by now this was all old hat to him.

“Coming around to the dark side now.” Hi-Fi announced.

“Luke, if you only knew the power of the Dark Side!” Randy intoned, doing a surprisingly good impression of Darth Vader. Penny and Jim both giggled like little kids at this. Even Anne cracked a smile.

"Sorry, couldn't resist." Randy said.

"Man, I'd be disappointed in you if you didn't crack that joke," Jim told him

Kergaali began reciting a list of coordinates from off of her wrist computer to Hi-Fi, and they could all feel the ship suddenly lurch to the side as it made a sudden course correction.

"Okay everyone, you'd better suit up and grab your weapons. We'll be coming up on the base soon." Jim said.

All of them got up and started donning the space suits that Jim had given them earlier.

"I still don't like the idea of you coming with us," Anne told Penny.

"Yeah, but you can't order me not to come. I'm not in the Guilds!"

"It's your funeral." Anne replied. She wasn't just worried about Penny's safety, but the idea that her presence would prove too much of a distraction for Randy and Jim, who might be too focused on protecting her to be of much use.

"She'll be okay. I'm gonna give her an extra layer of protection," Jim said as he struggled into his suit.

"What do you mean?" Penny asked.

"You'll see; it's a surprise." He smiled at her enigmatically, savoring her confusion.

"You'd better fit me for one of those suits, too." A voice said as the door to the cockpit slid open.

Randy couldn't believe his eyes. Aethra was standing there, framed in the doorway, now dressed in her traditional pirate garb.

"Aethra! What are you doing here?" he exclaimed, equal parts happy and annoyed to see her.

"Yeah, what *are* you doing here? I specifically ordered you to lead your fleet against the mothership!" Anne said angrily

"Don't have a cow, Anne. The fleet is in good hands, I put my best man in charge of it. You should be happy to see me, your chances of success just improved by about 50%!"

"Humble as ever!" Anne smiled despite herself, shaking her head. Well, at least she had been just given another capable warrior for her mission—and one who wouldn't be unduly distracted by Penny being there.

"C'mon you old pirate! My replicator needs to take your measurements for a spacesuit. I'll show you the way." Jim said, leading her from the cockpit.

"Wow, she must really love you to stowaway with us like that," Penny remarked.

Randy shrugged. "Yeah, but mostly I think she just doesn't want to miss a good fight.

Penny thought about what an odd couple they made: the peaceful, undisturbed Randy and his fierce, scrappy Pirate Queen. She guessed it was a textbook example of opposites attracting.

Jim and Aethra soon returned to the cockpit and Jim returned to his seat, while Aethra stood between Randy and Penny, she leaned down and gave Randy a kiss. Kergaali rolled her eyes, clearly disturbed by any kind of show of physical affection.

"We're in range of their destructo-ray guns now." The Venusian informed them, looking at the wrist computer that was now attached to the outside of her spacesuit.

"*Destructo-ray* guns?" Penny sniggered at the name.

"Yes. They're ray guns that destroy things. It's a very sensible name. I fail to find any humor in it." Kergaali said indignantly.

"I see them. Hi-Fi, lock on with all weapons." Jim said. Penny could see them too—large, double-barreled cannons, which vaguely resembled World War II anti-aircraft cannons. There were at least four of them she could see, radiating out from the central dome of the Baandergi moon base like the ends of a pinwheel. They were connected to the rest of the base by what looked like partially buried tunnels.

"Affirmative, Master Jim!" Hi-Fi replied. As soon as he said it, Penny saw six beams of energy arcing out from their ship and striking the gun emplacements. She realized that there must've been two other guns on the opposite side of the dome, which she couldn't see.

The firing ceased, but the guns were still there. They suddenly came alive, swinging around wildly in circles and firing rapidly, lighting up the sky with blasts of red energy. One of these random shots hit the ship, and it shook violently. Aethra pitched forward, but Randy shot out an arm that stopped her forward momentum, giving her a chance to get a grip on Randy and Penny's seats and steady herself.

"The guns are shielded! We're gonna have to make a few more passes before we can take 'em out. Hang on tight everybody! Aethra, for god's sake find a seat and strap yourself in already!" Jim shouted, having seen what had just happened to her in the rear-view mirror from a car (complete with fuzzy dice dangling down from it) that he had attached to the viewscreen in front of him in a fit of whimsy one day. Did I mention that Jim also had one of those little statues of a dancing Hawaiian lady in a hula skirt on the "dashboard" of his spaceship that jiggled its hips suggestively every time the ship moved? No? Well, he had one of those, too. That Jim had a real love of Earth kitsch.

Aethra did as she was told, finding a seat next to Anne. The ship made another pass at the moon base's defenses, deftly dodging all the beams of energy that were filling the sky overhead.

"These are the 'minimal defenses' that you were talking about?" Anne complained to Kergaali.

"I was referring to the security arrangements inside the base." Kergaali said curtly.

Jim fired all his guns at once again and studied a holographic readout that was projected in front of him. "Yes! Almost there! The shields are down, one more pass oughta do it, then those cannons will be nothing but hot space slag!"

"Huzzah!" Hi-Fi exclaimed, the present circumstances having triggered his jubilation subroutines.

Suddenly, the ship was struck from behind and they all saw the lunar surface rushing up towards them at an alarming speed. At the last moment, the ship finally pulled back up

"What the fuck was that?" Jim cried. "That came from *behind* us!"

"A large ship matching the profile of the Venusian mothership is indeed approaching rapidly from the rear, sir," Hi-Fi reported.

They all watched as an array of red energy beams zapped out over the sky in front of them, coming from somewhere behind them.

"Damn! What are they doing here? Now we're caught between them and the guns from that base!" Jim fretted.

"At least they can't get a lock on us," Randy, ever the optimist, said

"Yeah, except for when we open fire! And with all this random shooting, we're bound to take a few more hits. That mothership packs a real wallop!" Jim explained.

"But this ship is superior, right? It can take it, can't it?" Penny asked nervously.

"Uh, yeah, sure. This ship is centuries ahead of what they've got!" Jim said, but his tone betrayed his lack of confidence. He knew that even people armed with weapons as primitive as spears or bows and arrows could eventually overwhelm something as tough as a tank if they swarmed it with enough warriors. Right now, he felt like the tank in that scenario

As if Jim's fears were part of a self-fulfilling prophecy, the ship shook violently again, as it was struck once more.

"This is getting old! Hi-Fi, turn off the ship's cloak and plot a course that will take us closer to those guns!" Jim commanded.

"What? Are you nuts?" Anne shouted

"If that mothership wants a piece of us, they're gonna have to follow us straight into a barrage from their own cannons!" Jim explained.

"Deactivating cloak now, sir!"

Jim's ship shimmered into visibility as it wove a dizzying path through the sky, narrowly avoiding countless red bolts of energy from below. The mothership gave immediate chase, and as Jim had hoped, because it was a much larger and slower ship, it could not avoid being peppered by dozens of shots from the base's cannons. Its shields flickered rapidly under the onslaught. At the same time, Jim fired another volley from his own ship at the cannons. Six explosions flared up below them simultaneously.

"Booyah, baby! Hi-Fi, re-engage cloak and target all weapons on the mothership. Maximum power!" Jim shouted triumphantly. Jim's ship flipped over and made a run straight towards the mothership. The lights in the cockpit dimmed as all the ship's weapons blasted out at the gigantic ship, over and over again as it grew bigger and bigger in the viewscreen. Jim's ship then pulled up and continued firing on the ship as it flew over it. As Jim's ship passed the end of the mothership, it swung back around to attack again, but everyone aboard could see that there was no point to it, the mothership was listing to one side, gasses venting out into the thin lunar atmosphere from a variety of hull breaches. After a few moments of hanging there like that, it suddenly came crashing down to the ground.

Penny heard shouts of celebration break out from everyone else in the cockpit. Even Wisp and Smoke stirred from their stupor long enough to show their appreciation. Once again, even though she now knew the terrible fate that the Baandergi were planning for humanity, Penny just couldn't quite bring herself to take such delight in other people's demise. At best, she felt relief that she and her companions had survived the encounter unscathed

"Nice flying, Jim." Anne smiled.

"Hey, give me a chance and I can probably win this war for you," Jim boasted, so swept up in the adrenaline rush of battle that he seemed to be freed of any of his previous misgivings about breaking his oath of nonintervention.

"Okay, don't get too cocky now!" Anne admonished him

"Hi-Fi, find us a nice, deep crater nearby and take us down."

"Affirmative, Master Jim."

"So Randy, do you think you could teleport us inside the base with your magic?" Anne asked.

Randy screwed up his face in an expression of distaste. "I don't know. There's nine of us, it's a lot of people for me to teleport all at once, and you know how doing back-to-back teleportation spells makes me sick. Plus, if their guns were shielded, the rest of the base might be too. I can't teleport through magic based force fields. I assume that the same thing is true of technology-based ones too."

"The rest of the base is still shielded." Jim confirmed. "But the shields are down where those gun turrets were, and they're connected to the rest of the base by tunnels. My ship can teleport us in at one of those points. Our attack caused most of those tunnels to collapse, but my scans found an intact one. We can enter through there. Make sure you've got your environment suits powered on. There's no air in those tunnels because of the damage we caused."

"Sounds good to me," Anne said.

"How do we turn these suits on?" Aethra asked.

Jim pointed to a blue button on the control box on the front of the suit. Immediately, his head was engulfed by a transparent bubble of a tough, but surprisingly flexible material that appeared from out of his tall collar. Everyone else followed his lead.

Hi-Fi unplugged himself from the front of the ship and walked over to Jim. "Now, sir?" He asked, pointing to Penny.

"Yes, initiate symbiosis mode," Jim ordered. In the blink of an eye, Hi-Fi seemed to melt down into a pool of silvery material, the pool spread out on the floor, moving towards Penny. She instinctively started to back up.

"Don't panic, I know it looks like he's about to go all *Terminator 2* on your ass, but I promise it's safe," Jim tried to reassure her.

The silver pool that was Hi-Fi now spread over Penny's space suit until it was completely covering everything but the transparent bubble holding her head.

Good evening, Mistress Penny. She heard Hi-Fi's voice inside her head.

Whoa! How am I hearing you? She thought.

At this proximity, I can form a neurological link with you. Feel free to use my body as an extra layer of protection, or as a weapon. My body will reshape itself to form whatever you can imagine—within reason. For example, try thinking of a hammer.

As soon as he said the words, she saw the edge of her hand form into a perfect hammer, like the kind one would use when building something.

Good! But I think you can do better than that. Imagine a hammer so big you could knock out a few people just by swinging it.

The small hammer at the end of her hand immediately changed into a long handled mallet that was as thick as a small child.

"Noice!" Penny exclaimed.

She immediately pictured a long blade in her mind, and the other hand transformed into one.

I wouldn't recommend that, mistress. You could too easily puncture one of our companions' space suits.

As he said it, she allowed her hand to return to normal.

There's something else which you may find useful. Hi-Fi said.

Tiny rockets appeared in the soles of Penny's feet and she found herself hovering several inches off of the ground.

We can fly too? Bitchin'!

Indeed, mistress, it is most bitchin'.

"How do you like it?" Jim, who had been watching her try out all the features with pride, asked her as she lowered herself back down onto the ground.

"I love it! Thanks!"

"It's nothing, I could never let something happen to my Penny!" he replied.

"I'm not 'your Penny' anymore." She told him. Although she had to admit that she was warming up to this new version of Jim, even if he looked like a reject from a Meow Mix commercial.

"Of course, my bad," Jim said sheepishly.

Please don't be too hard on the Master, he really is quite fond of you.

Stay out of it, Hi-Fi!

Staying out of it, Mistress

"Alright, if everyone has their weapons ready and their suits on, let's get moving. Hi-Fi, beam us into those tunnels!" Jim ordered.

"Energizing transporter now, sir!" Hi-Fi responded Apparently, being bonded with Penny didn't interfere with also being interfaced with the ship. He was one hell of a universal remote control.

The next instant, they all found themselves inside what looked like the bottom of one of the gun turrets. Thick bulkheads had closed over the damaged guns overhead, sealing off the area from the hard vacuum of space. Penny immediately felt lighter and soon realized that she could do one of those "moon jumps" like the astronauts.

"No artificial gravity, huh?" She commented.

"We must've knocked it out in this section of the base when we destroyed the gun above us," Jim guessed

Just then, something bumped into the dome over Penny's head. She turned her head to see what it was and screamed.

What had bumped into her was the desiccated-looking corpse of a Venusian. The face was hollow and sunken, and where eyes should have been were only two black, empty eye sockets. Purple spheres poured out of these holes and splattered up against Penny's arm, sending a spray of smaller spheres radiating out from the impact point.

Blood! That's blood! She thought with dawning horror.

Correct, Mistress. Hi-Fi verified unnecessarily.

"Killed by the feedback from the Destructo-Ray blowing up. A particularly unpleasant way to die," Kergaali said as she pushed the body away and it went spiraling backwards. As she said the words, Penny was reminded of one of those peculiar phrases that old people were so fond of repeating: "she looks like the cat who ate the canary," it was one of her grandmother's favorites. Yes, right now, that's exactly how the alien looked.

Jim unclipped a device from his spacesuit belt and he'd it up to the door. A second later, it whooshed open, revealing the tunnel ahead. "Let's go." They all followed him forwards. As they did so, the gravity returned to something closer to Earth-normal. Penny missed the sensation of lightness she'd felt in the other room.

"Smoke, Wisp, take point." Anne ordered. At her command, the two assassins snaked forward to the front of the group.

"Multiple life forms detected moving towards us." Hi-Fi warned.

As he said it, a group of about four Venusians appeared around the bend of the tunnel, all dressed in spacesuits. They appeared to be a mix of medical personnel and repair people. They were all carrying cases of equipment with them. The one in the lead's eyes bulged almost comically as they rounded the corner and saw the group of intruders. They all turned to run back the way they'd come.

"Light 'em up!" Anne commanded.

Smoke and Wisp wasted no time zapping them, handling the unfamiliar weapons Jim had given them as if they'd been born to use them. Anne also hit one of them with the pistol that Jim had given her. She wasn't able to carry a larger weapon (much to her chagrin) because she had to lug around the briefcase holding the Omega Seed.

Each of the Venusians went down with a startled cry, except for one who was a little faster than the others.

"Intruders in the west tunnel! I repeat intruders in the west tunnel. We have been breached!" The Venusian said frantically into a communications device in one hand before being blasted in the back by Wisp.

"So much for the element of surprise." Anne observed testily. The spacesuits that Jim had supplied them with instantly translated the strange, singsong language of the Venusians into English.

"It was bound to happen sooner or later." Aethra shrugged as a klaxon started blaring and the surrounding lights changed to a reddish hue.

Penny looked down at the crumpled bodies at her feet as she picked her way through them. Jim caught the expression of distaste on her face.

"They'll be okay. Like I said earlier, they're just stunned. They'll be out for a few hours, but are otherwise fine." He told her.

Anne overheard this and couldn't help but shake her head. What was Penny doing here if she had no stomach for what had to be done? This was war, not a bloody PTA meeting! People died. Anne didn't like that, but she also didn't waste her time whining about it. She really wished that Jim had made her stay on the ship. Under normal circumstances, Anne liked Penny, but she was a civilian with no combat training or experience that they all had to babysit, which made her a constant liability to the success of this mission.

Kergaali indicated a door off to the side; it was marked in an alien script as leading into the main base. Jim once again opened it with his device.

"Keep heading straight ahead and we'll soon reach the Time Tunnel, it's at the center of the base." Kergaali told them.

They didn't get very far before they were met by a group of about six Venusians that were decked out in some kind of futuristic armor.

They wore what looked like motorcycle helmets over their heads and had angular metallic wing-like protrusions coming out of the backs.

"Shit! I wasn't expecting Daft Punk!" joked Penny.

"Shock troopers! I didn't know any of them were stationed here!" Kergaali exclaimed.

The Shock Troopers took to the air, floating up towards the ceiling and immediately opened fire on the group. Everyone fell back to around the corner they'd just rounded. Smoke and Wisp occasionally poked their heads out and fired a few shots at the Shock Troops, then quickly ducked back around the corner. One of Wisp's shots struck them, but seemed to have no effect on the trooper.

"Our weapons are useless against that armor!" She griped.

"No, they aren't, turn them up to maximum!" Jim shouted, demonstrating how to do so by twisting a knob on his rifle. Everyone else imitated his movement.

"We can't keep her pinned down like this! Randy, give us a shield!" Anne ordered him

"I was thinking the same thing!" he smiled conspiratorially.

Randy quickly uttered an incantation that caused a wide, transparent shield made of glowing green energy to appear in front of them, which was almost as wide as the corridor itself.

"Everyone, get behind this and follow me!" he shouted as he moved forward, the shield moving ahead of him he fired the rifle Jim had given him over the top of the shield, trying to keep his head down at the same time. The others all followed suit.

The troopers had an annoying habit of using their ability to fly to zip around the confined space like angry insects. Randy had to move the shield around constantly by gesturing with one hand so it would still block their shots as they tried to fire over his shield. He started chanting a new spell, one which would make it impossible for his team's weapons to miss their targets. He cursed himself for not thinking about doing it sooner. Their guns were all suffused with a golden glow for a moment as the spell took effect.

Thanks to Randy's spell, they quickly picked off the armored troopers, the blue beams of their shots twisting into improbable angles as they changed direction to hit their targets.

As the fifth Shock Trooper fell, the remaining one decided to take a rather rash course of action, seeing it as being the only way to stop the invaders. The Venusian removed a grenade that was magnetically attached to its armor, pulled the clip, and tossed it over Randy's shield too quickly for him to block.

"Scatter!" Randy barely had enough time to shout before the device exploded. The blast instantly blew Smoke and Wisp, who were the closest to the explosion, to pieces. Pieces which were immediately sucked out of the base and out into the freezing vacuum through a hole in the wall that had been opened up by the explosion.

I didn't even get to see them do any really impressive ninja assassin shit! Penny thought, shocked by the absurdity and callousness of this thought.

The others had survived the explosion, thanks to the fact that as Randy had run from the grenade, he had also brought his shield with him. It had blocked the worst of the explosion for everyone on the right side of it, but their space suits were all now shredded in various places, except for Penny's which had been protected by the silvery coating that was Hi-Fi, and the fact that he had generated a force field over her right before the explosion struck.

Penny looked on in despair as the others were being sucked towards the hole in the wall, as were the prone shapes of the unconscious Shock Troopers they'd just fought against. She watched as one, then another of the Shock Troopers tumbled through the jagged aperture. Randy's shield remained immobile, hovering a few inches off the floor in the same position it had been in right before the grenade went off. The shield, as the product of a spell, seemed immune to the laws of physics, subject only to the whims of the wizard who had cast it into existence

The members of her team then slammed up against Randy's energy shield, being held there like bugs on a windshield. Everyone except for her, that is.

Why aren't I being sucked away? Penny wondered.

I took the liberty of anchoring us in place, Mistress. Hi-Fi answered in her head. She looked down and saw that her feet had transformed into claws that had dug themselves into the floor.

Oh, cool! Thanks, man! She thought to him.

Don't mention it, Mistress. I am programmed for self preservation, which under the present circumstances, automatically entails your preservation as well.

New inspiration struck Penny. She willed her arms to extend out unnaturally long, like tentacles, then she grabbed everyone who had been held fast up against the energy shield. She pulled them back to where she stood, her arms wrapped around them like thick cables. Ordinarily she wouldn't have been strong enough to do this; it was Hi-Fi's strong, pliable body that made it all possible.

"Randy, plug the hole with your shield!" She told him.

With a wave of his hand, he sent the shield up against the opening, and it conformed to fit its shape, sealing it perfectly. As the pressure in the corridor slowly returned to normal, Penny released them all, and they stood on their own feet again

"Look! The bulkhead is closing! We'll never make it in time!" Aethra shouted as she pointed straight ahead. They all caught a glimpse of the retreating shape of the remaining Shock Trooper, the same one who had thrown the grenade. The trooper flew through a gap in a rapidly closing series of bulkhead doors that were now sliding into position to seal off that section of the base.

"Oh yes we will, everyone link hands—now!" Randy ordered. Randy recited a quick teleportation spell, teleportation being no issue now that he was under the base's force fields.

They all felt a stomach churning sensation deep in their intestines, and caught the briefest of glimpses of a bright, multicolored dimension that magic users called *the Place Between Places*. The next instant, they reappeared in front of the Shock Trooper, who was, appropriately enough, quite shocked by this. The trooper got over its surprise and raised its weapon, but Penny turned her hand into a large hammer like she had in Jim's ship, swung it widely and knocked her into the wall. The trooper continued to hover in the air, but its limbs hung limply by its side.

"Nice work, Penny!" Anne enthused. Maybe bringing her along wasn't such a bad idea after all?

"Thanks! It's too bad about Smoke and Wisp, though."

"There's nothing you could've done to save them. It all happened too fast." Anne reassured her.

"Our suits are totally trashed!" Aethra said, taking stock of what was left of the group.

"They'll seal up again, they're self repairing, but it's gonna take a few minutes, they're pretty badly shredded." Jim told them.

"And I lost my gun!" Aethra continued.

"So did I, but you've still got the laser in your eyepatch," Randy told her. "The important thing is that Anne didn't lose the Omega Seed."

"I can't! This briefcase is handcuffed to my wrist!" Anne showed them, holding up her arm.

"C'mon, let's get going. They must be desperate to stop us if they're willing to blow holes in their own walls! We're not that far from the control room for the Time Tunnel, follow me!" Kergaali said.

They all ran down the halls occasionally coming across a surprised looking member of the base's crew. They typically just ran away, but either Anne or Kergaali, both of whom still had their weapons, would always zap them just to be safe.

As they approached the central part of the base, Penny noticed that the roof was getting higher until it transitioned into a large transparent dome through which she could see the stars. The hallway was also getting broader. Up ahead, she could see a large open area ahead of them that was surrounded by a glass barrier. Inside that area was a massive mechanical archway, wide enough to fit a mothership through. There was some sort of spiraling vortex inside the arch. The glass wall was broken up by a pair of wide double doors, and arrayed in front of the door was another squad of Shock Troopers, at least ten of them this time. They were all pointing their peculiar alien rifles at them, with rectangular barrels that crackled with some unknown energy.

"Great! More of these jokers!" Randy grumbled, creating a new energy shield as he saw them.

Aethra wasted no time blasting at them with the hidden laser in her eyepatch, instantly zeroing in on a vulnerable spot between the helmet and the breastplate, taking the heads off of the ones she struck.

Damn, Aethra! Penny thought as she saw the awful lethality of her attack. She thought she might be able to neutralize the threat in a slightly more humane way. Penny flew over the shield, much to Randy and Jim's alarm.

"Penny! Where are you going?" Randy cried out, but she ignored him. She got hit a few times, but thankfully, Hi-Fi detected the incoming shots and put up a force field just in time. Penny transformed both hands into massive mallets, flew into the middle of the squad of Shock Troopers, then spun around wildly, striking the troopers and tossing them around the room with each fresh blow.

In a matter of seconds, all the resistance in their path had been eliminated. The ground was littered with groaning or motionless troopers, as well as a few headless ones. Penny landed and her companions surged forth to join her.

"Maybe I should've recruited you years ago? You've got a pretty powerful imagination for battle!" Anne commended her again.

Penny glowed with pride. She has to admit that this was a bit of a rush. Then she spotted one of the Shock Trooper's severed heads near her foot and sobered up a little.

It's all fun and games until someone loses a head. She thought grimly.

I believe the correct phrase is "loses an eye", Mistress. Hi-Fi corrected her.

Nobody asked you, Hi-Fi!

"Yes, the little one is proving her worth." Kergaali admitted in a surprised tone. "We've got to get this door open, this is the control room for the Time Tunnel. In its present state, only messages can pass through it, but if you can get me inside, I can open it up wide enough for you to throw the Omega Seed through."

"Say no more!" Jim replied as he once more made use of the device he'd been using to open all the sealed doors they'd encountered. Just as before, the door started to slide open. As the group entered the room, they could see a few technicians were inside huddled together in one corner of the room.

"Please! Don't hurt us!" One of them shrieked. It felt strange to Penny to suddenly be the object of such fear.

Kergaali raised an eyebrow. "I honestly don't know if this hurts or not, but it won't kill you —supposedly." She said as she fired her rifle at the technician that had spoken. The alien fell to the ground, and the others screamed and scattered in different directions, Anne and Kergaali went to work on them, taking them down with precision thanks to the lingering effects of Randy's "can't miss" spell from a few minutes earlier.

"Was that really necessary?" Penny asked Kergaali.

"All that whimpering would've been an unwelcome distraction. We don't need them, I can operate these controls." She said coldly. "Jim, make sure that door is triple sealed. I don't want any visitors."

"On it!" he said, waving his device over the door until two more layers of steel slid in place over the original door.

Ahead of them they could see the Time Tunnel itself. Kergaali allowed herself a brief smile of triumph as her hands raced over the control panel before her. The Time Tunnel soon changed from displaying a swirling vortex, instead they could now see what looked like an airfield, rows of silvery saucers arranged in neat rows stretching out towards the horizon on the other side.

"There is your target, Miss Moore: 384,000 kilometers away from here and almost 800 million years in your past, and you can reach it simply by passing through that door..." She announced, pointing to a door on the opposite side of the room from where they'd entered.

Anne tapped a code into her handcuffs, and they released themselves from her wrist. Next, she snapped open her briefcase and removed the Omega Seed. It was tiny, not much bigger than a baseball. It was a wonder that such a harmless-looking thing could ever be so deadly. The seed was black as night, but glowing red veins encircled it at irregular intervals. As she lifted it, her entire arm tingled with the unfathomable, malevolent power held inside. She could feel it pulsating like a living thing. All she had to do was utter one word to activate it, a word chosen for its irony: Love. Yet she dared not activate it until it was on the other side of the tunnel. As far as any of them knew, the range of the weapon was limited to just one planet.

Anne steeled herself for what she had to do next. She didn't look forward to it. A childish part of her that still couldn't help but believe a little in fire and brimstone felt like she was about to damn herself forever by what she was about to do. She tried to push such doubts from her mind, she knew all too well that things didn't really work like that. No, this was the only way to make sure that the Earth would remain safe, that these people wouldn't try again someday.

It was what her Uncle Bronson would do.

Wasn't it?

CHAPTER 14:
GENOCIDE IS BAD, M'KAY?

It had been an uneventful trip from the Earth to the moon aboard the *Silver Bullet*. Uneventful, except that this was the first time in space for everyone aboard, save for Drogalla and Major Thompson.

Matt looked down on the Earth as they left orbit and was reminded of a sentiment that had been expressed by some of the astronauts: the idea that if everyone could just have the experience of seeing the planet like this, as an oasis of life hanging in the emptiness of space that they'd all realize how fragile life is and how abstract ideas like national borders are and work together to protect the planet. He couldn't help but agree, the sight of the planet from this vantage point was oddly moving.

How weird is it to think that everyone I've ever known and every place I've ever been is all down there? He thought.

Naomi must've been having similar thoughts. She gave his hand a squeeze and smiled as they looked at the planet together, and he thought he saw a tear in one of her eyes.

The trip through the space between our world and its natural satellite was not quite as moving. They took the opportunity to pepper their alien guest with various questions. They learned about how the Venusians had been created by the First Generation and rebelled against them. They also learned that the Baandergi were quite secretive about their technological innovations. Nobody had believed that they had figured out time travel. It took a group of Saawgauth spies to verify it and eventually steal the secret for themselves.

Even though they had eventually learned for themselves that the Baandergi were telling the truth about not finding any signs of Venusian life on the planet they were planning to colonize, they didn't abandon their plans to build a fleet of ships to take them there. They theorized that they might have decided to colonize a different planet while on their long trip through space. Or eventually abandoned their new world for yet another one? Or perhaps they'd evolved beyond the need for physical bodies? There were dozens of possibilities, and the information that their probes could collect on such distant worlds was quite limited. They didn't believe that this information meant that they were extinct in the future. It certainly didn't justify invading an already inhabited planet and destroying its people. So they sent Drogalla on this mission to help the humans.

Matt studied the antenna atop Drogalla's head. Drogalla noticed his staring eyes and sighed.

"Is there something I can help you with?" The leader asked.

"Huh? Oh, sorry. I was just wondering...that thing on top of your head, is it part of your hat, or part of your body? It looks kind of...fleshy."

"It is something unique to the Third Generation of our people. It is how the Second Generation syncs up with us. It also prevents us from doing certain things which are forbidden, such as using the Duplo-Ray to create a Fourth Generation." She answered him. All of this was about as clear as mud to everyone in the ship.

"Duplo-ray? What the heck is that? Does it shoot out those toddler LEGOs?" Matt joked.

"LEGOs? I am unfamiliar with this human word. What is it?" The baffled leader inquired.

Naomi smiled. "It's not important, Matt is just being Matt again. But I'd love to hear about this Duplo-Ray of yours. I believe you mentioned it once before. Isn't that the device you were going to give us so we could create a fleet of our own ships to fight the Baandergi drone saucers? Is it something that duplicates things?"

"Yes, precisely. It was first discovered about a decade ago in my timeline. It has created quite an upheaval in our society. We can create a perfect copy of anything. The only limit is the power required to operate the machine and the size of the machine itself. We have industrial scale ones capable of creating entire fleets of spaceships in a short amount of time. We were planning to give one of these large Duplo-Rays to each nation on your planet, so that you could defend yourselves from the Baandergi."

"Hmm! Doin' something like that would create quite an upheaval in our society as well!" Prospero chimed in.

"That has been a concern of ours. That's why we wanted to distribute them equally to all your nations, so that it would prevent an imbalance of military power in your world once the Baandergi had been defeated. We also hoped that the Duplo-Ray would assist you with rebuilding in the wake of the invasion, and even someday advance your society beyond your primitive competition for resources."

"Unfortunately, a lot of powerful people have a vested interest in perpetuating that primitive competition for resources—their fortunes depend on it." April said bitterly. *Including quite a few people in the Guilds.* She almost added, but thought better of it.

"But surely they would see that such pursuits are unsustainable, are precisely what has led your planet to the brink of ecological collapse, and do what is best for the greater good—would they not?" Drogalla reasoned.

"If only!" Matt said.

"It is that kind of greed and lack of long-term planning which has led Kergaali to conclude that you humans are no better than animals, unfit to dictate the fate of your planet." Drogalla said sadly. "Kergaali doesn't believe that any truly intelligent race would so willfully pursue its own inevitable destruction. It is how Kergaali justifies the atrocity of the Baandergi plan to commit against you to their citizens, and anyone else who will listen. Unfortunately, it would seem this propaganda has swayed some of my own people to conspire against me." The leader said, recalling the spies who must've been feeding Kergaali information on the location of the mothership and the flight paths their saucers would take to reach the UN building.

Naomi felt like they were getting off topic. She still didn't understand all of Drogalla's earlier talk about different generations, although she had an inkling of what the leader had been implying.

"Drogalla, were you trying to tell us earlier that you were created by a Duplo-Ray too?" She asked.

"Why yes, of course. When the Duplo-Ray first became widely available, our people abused it. They created copies of themselves to do their jobs for them, then those copies made copies of themselves to avoid the same work, and so on."

"Geez! It's like that silly movie with Michael Keaton, what was it called?" Matt commented.

"Multiplicity," Naomi answered, she had an excellent memory for comedies. "Go on, Drogalla."

"It became quite confusing, as you can imagine. So we created a law that was adopted by all the thirteen nations of Pfoff, even the Baandergi. Each Venusian of the Second Generation was allowed to create one copy of themselves, a Third Generation, if you will. We Third Generation Venusians are fitted with a control chip in our brains that prevents us from creating further duplicates. We also have these antennas that allow us to be deactivated if, for some reason, we go rogue, as well as to synchronize our memories with the Second Generation if they wish to swap places with us."

"Swap places?" Carlos asked.

"Yes, most of the Second Generation engage in comfortable lives of leisure while we of the Third Generation do their old jobs. Oh, occasionally they might get bored with their games or art projects and swap places with us, in which case they can gain access to all our memories so they will understand what's been going on while they were away, but such incidents are rare. For the most part, we of the Third Generation run the planet and do all the work." There was an odd pride in the alien's tone as the leader concluded the explanation.

"My god, you're all slaves!" April said in horror.

"Slaves! Never! What a repugnant idea! Our people abhor the idea. We *were* slaves once, under the rule of the First Generation, but that was ages ago." The passion in Drogalla's voice indicated that they had clearly struck a nerve by likening their situation to slavery.

"I fail to see what the difference is! All these Second Generation people do is sit around on their asses painting pictures and playing games while your people are busy building a fleet of giant ships to go colonize another world? Sounds like slavery to me!" Matt said.

"How can I possibly be a slave to myself? I am Drogalla and Drogalla is me. I have all of the Leader's memories up until the point when I was created, and we last synchronized. I recall what it was like to raise Drogalla's children. I love them just the same way, we are one and the same. I take great pride in my work, that I am working to save my people - and yours. I am happy to know that back at home there is a version of myself which is able to explore its full potential because it is free of the burden of having to do the tedious daily activities that must be done to maintain our society's existence."

Naomi shook her head in disbelief. She wondered if the 'control chip' in Drogalla's head also forced her to think a certain way. "But don't you see? You're not the same person! You've had your own set of unique experiences that make you different. That's like saying that identical twins are the same person. How long has it been since you last synchronized with the original Drogalla?"

"Shortly after I was created, roughly the equivalent of seven of your Earth years. But I don't understand how that's relevant." The Leader said defensively.

"Seven years! Seven years of experiences that the other Drogalla hasn't had! Of relationships the other you haven't formed! Don't you see how that makes you special?" Naomi pressed her.

Drogalla recalled Goymaalt, and the love they had found for one another as they worked together on this project to save the Earthlings. This *was* something "unique" to this version of Drogalla.

"Perhaps, but this is a very odd new notion to me. I don't wish to discuss it further. Besides, we are approaching my base, I will need to go up front to guide your pilot." Drogalla said dismissively, unbuckling from the seat and moving forwards to go talk to Major Thompson.

The others all looked at one other in exasperation, each of them unable to quite believe everything they'd just heard from the alien.

On the screen before them that displayed the view outside of the ship, they could see a large base built into a crater. The central part was like a large dome which was transparent in the middle, and there were other parts radiating out from it like a wheel. Those parts that were far from the central dome were in ruins. They all heard Drogalla gasp as a large saucer that must've been the size of a football field (why do people always measure the size of things in football fields?) jutted from the surface, half buried in the lunar soil, which, by the way, is called "regolith" in case you're ever on Jeopardy! And it should happen to come up (if so, I expect a share of your winnings).

"Goymaalt was on that ship," Drogalla sobbed.

"Who is that?" April asked gently.

"My...partner." Drogalla replied. April understood what the alien meant by Drogalla's reaction.

"Well, maybe Goymaalt survived? There are still plenty of lights on inside that ship. Try to look on the bright side." She said, the irony of asking someone to look on the bright side while literally being on the dark side was lost to her at the moment.

"Yes, this is true, I must not lose hope, even though I fear that we're probably too late. Obviously, your friends have already been here. I can't believe how much damage they've done. These Federation ships must be very advanced."

"Their technology is centuries ahead of anything either of our planets has" Carlos confirmed.

"We've gotta be close enough to call them by now. I'm gonna give it a shot." Matt said as he pulled out his Guild communicator and pulled up Randy's number.

Inside the control room to the Time Tunnel, Randy was shocked to feel his Guild communicator start buzzing on the belt that it was clipped to. Penny looked at him incredulously.

Anne was about to head out the door into the large chamber that held the Time Tunnel, with the Omega Seed, but she stopped in her tracks, distracted by this latest development.

"You're getting a call? Here on the moon?" She asked.

Randy unclipped it and flipped it open. "It's from Matt!" he told them as he pressed the button to answer it.

"Matt, is that really you?" He asked tentatively.

"Randy! Kergaali has tricked you guys into attacking the wrong bunch of aliens! Call off your attack right away! Don't use the Omega Seed!" Matt's excited voice told him.

"What? Are you sure? How do you know *you're* not being tricked? And how are you even able to call me here?"

"We're on the *Silver Bullet* headed your way now. And yes, I'm sure! We had Kiesha do a truth spell on Drogalla, our new alien buddy, to make sure they weren't pulling our leg!"

"Drogalla!" Randy exclaimed, recognizing the name.

Hi-Fi had been listening to all of this with his much more sensitive hearing. He immediately directed a force field around Kergaali, trapping her.

"Hi-Fi! What is the meaning of this? Release me immediately!" Kergaali demanded.

"I'm afraid I can't do that, Kergaali." Hi-Fi responded.

"Oh no! Hi-Fi's gone all HAL 9000 on us! What's up with you, buddy?" Jim asked.

HAL 9000? The killer computer from 2001: A Space Odyssey? You're not going evil on me, are you Hi-Fi? Penny asked him in her head. She was in something of a panic, as she didn't particularly fancy the idea of being symbiotically linked to an evil robot!

I am only doing what's necessary, Mistress. There is no need for alarm. Kergaali is a threat according to your friend Matt, and as he is the husband of the Naomi, I believe he can be trusted.

The Naomi? Penny asked. *That was an odd way of referring to her!*

Forget that I mentioned that. I am not authorized to speak about that topic any further.

"It's all right, Jim. She's been lying to us this whole time," Randy told them, drawing shocked expressions from everyone else. Randy wasn't too surprised, though. He'd had a bad feeling about her all along.

"There's one more thing, pal. Anne is also...using...Seed to...all the...don't let...gotta stop...arrest..." Matt said his voice became increasingly staticky until the call dropped completely.

"Matt? Matt, are you there? Matt!" Randy asked, but it was no good, he was gone.

Inside the *Silver Bullet,* Matt tried frantically to call Randy again, with no success. "Damn! I lost him! I don't know if he heard me warn him about Anne!"

"It must be interference from us being so close to the Time Tunnel. It can distort communications that aren't tuned to the right frequency range. It's extremely fortunate that we were able to reach them at all." Drogalla told them.

"I only hope that he's able to stop her, I gotta keep trying to call..." Matt replied.

Back in the moon base, Jim had a few questions for his former ally. "What exactly have you been lying to us about?" He demanded.

Kergaali smiled at him. "I suppose there's no point in keeping up this charade any longer, is there? Very well! Let it be known that I am actually the Supreme Leader of the Baandergi, and it is we, not the Saawgauth, who intend to take over the Earth! The Saawgauth came here to stop us, but with your help, we've just crippled their mission!"

"I...I don't understand..." Jim struggled with this new information. He'd trusted Kergaali, been willing to risk so much because of what she'd told him.

"It's simple. We were concerned about the success of our mission. Worried that the humans would be able to destroy too many of our drone saucers with their jet fighters. You've seen how weak the shields are on our ships, how primitive our shrouding technology is compared to yours. Much of our military technology is only about 50 to a hundred years ahead of what the humans have, and they have the numerical advantage. The AI in our drones is limited in sophistication, a poor substitute for a living pilot. We became even more alarmed when our spies discovered that the Saawgauth planned to give you the means to create ships that were the equals of our own! So, for all those reasons, when I detected the presence of other non-humans on this planet, I decided to make contact. It was obvious that these aliens were more sophisticated than we were. If I could get close enough to one of their ships, scan it, then I could use the Duplo-Ray to create an invasion fleet that would be invincible! So I posed as someone trying to stop the invasion, to get their sympathy. They all ignored me, all of them except for you, Jim. Noble Jim! So eager to play the hero! Tired of just watching all these ridiculous science fiction dramas that the humans distract themselves with, you wanted to live one out! How easy you were to manipulate!"

"How could you?" Jim said in disbelief.

"How could I not? At first my people cooperated with all the others in their stupid plan to evacuate our planet, but at the same time we were also conducting experiments on time travel. When we first succeeded in penetrating the future, we had the probe we sent through the Time Tunnel look for signs of higher life on Armenclius, the world we were relocating to—it found none! It meant our plan was doomed to failure, that we'd never reach that world, that we didn't exist in this future. Before that first unstable Time Tunnel collapsed, our probe also told us that the Earth was now far more hospitable than it was in our own time. So we decided we had to concentrate all our efforts on creating a stable Time Tunnel and colonizing this future Earth. The other nations didn't believe us, they refused to help us! Eventually, they stole our Time Tunnel technology once we had perfected it, but even then, they refused to aid us, refused to see the truth—that this was the only hope our people had for survival!"

"I trusted you..." Jim said, his anger rising. He thought of all the ships he'd shot down, the gun emplacements he'd destroyed, all the people he'd killed because he believed what Kergaali was telling him.

"Yes, but not enough to bring me to your ship. I had hoped that when I suggested that you shoot down Drogalla's saucer, you'd bring me to the ship, so I could acquire the scans of it I needed to duplicate it, but you insisted on shooting it down without your ship. So I had one of my agents hidden among Drogalla's crew scan for your weapon and do a convincing job of trying to kill you once it was found, barely missing you. I hoped this would convince you that the only way to stop Drogalla was to use your ship and it worked! You let me on your ship, and I got the scans I need! My bipit, Zaa has a scanner hidden inside him, we now have all the information we need to copy your ship!" She boasted, as she did so, Zaa rose slowly out of the large collar of her space suit and nuzzled up against her.

He's been in her spacesuit all this time? I thought she left him aboard the ship! Seriously, where DOES she keep him down there? Penny wondered.

It's actually quite fascinating! The bipits are cousins of the original creatures that the Venusians were hyper evolved from by the First Generation. As such, due to their biological similarities, they can form a symbiotic link not dissimilar to the one we currently enjoy. Kergaali likely keeps her bipit inside her...

Never mind! Eww! I really DON'T want to know!

Very well, Mistress, as you prefer.

Kergaali wasn't quite done boasting yet. "Never in my wildest dreams did I imagine that you would not only unwittingly provide me with the scans, but go on to defeat my enemies for me! I had no idea that these humans had such wondrous things as the Omega Seed! It's a pity you found me out before you could use it to destroy those ships containing the Duplo-Rays that the Saawgauth were planning to give you so you could create ships that could match our drones, but either way you've done considerable damage to their operations here. It was all worth it!" She actually did a full on evil villain laugh then.

Anne had been watching all of this with increasing fury, a fury which she could contain no longer.

"Oh yeah? You think you're *sooo* clever, don't you? Manipulating all of us like some kind of puppet master? Well, the joke is on you, Kergaali! I'm still going to use the Omega Seed—only it's not going to destroy those ships out there, it's going to wipe out your whole stinking race! I had it primed with a hair I took from you earlier!"

"What? Anne, you can't be serious! That's genocide!" Randy cried.

"So? They tried to genocide us first! We might've caught the ringleader, but it doesn't matter! Someone else will just replace her, someone just as bad. Don't you see? This is the only way to save the Earth for good. These people won't quit, they won't ever stop. They'll keep on coming at us because they believe that their very survival depends on the success of this invasion. They've got nothing to lose and everything to gain! We can't win against that kind of desperation unless we get a little ruthless ourselves!"

"A little ruthless? This is completely ruthless! There has to be a better way! There's no point in winning if we lose our humanity in the process!" Randy continued to argue. "That's no real victory!"

"Wake up! You can have the luxury of moralizing about it all you want once this is over with! There won't even be any of us left to question the ethics of this unless I do what I have to do now in order to win! Besides, Venus is already a dead world. It has been for ages. How do we know that this isn't why it's that way? That I was always meant to do this? That I'm not just fulfilling some kind of destiny? Why are you so concerned about people that are already nothing but dust? That was dust long before any of us were even born?"

"I can't accept that! This isn't who we are!" Randy shouted.

"Isn't who we are?" Anne laughed now, too. It turns out that Kergaali wasn't the only one who was good at doing a villain laugh in that room that day. "Get real! Tell that to the Neanderthals! Mankind is built on a foundation of the skulls of our rivals. It's who we've *always* been! It's how we got to be where we are in the first place!"

"Well it's not who I *want* to be. It's not who we *have* to be. There has to be a better way, and I'll be *damned* if I'm not going to find it!" Randy shouted back defiantly.

"Randy, may I remind you that I'm your superior officer and any action you take against me could be seen as treason. Now I intend to walk through this door, throw this seed through the Time Tunnel, and activate it..."

"Superior? You're not superior to me in any way! And I'd be a traitor to everything I believe in if I don't stop you. I know what it's like to come from a people that someone else decided didn't deserve to live!" he shouted at her.

"I really didn't want to do this, but..." Anne said, pulling out her pistol and aiming it at Aethra, who unfortunately happened to be the one standing closest to her. "Make a move to stop me and your girlfriend gets it!"

"Holy shit? Really, Anne?" Penny exclaimed.

Aethra sighed, then she just calmly turned her head and blasted Anne's pistol with her laser eyepatch, which was incapable of missing. "Randy, now!" She shouted.

Randy said a few magic words and Anne was immediately propelled backwards by an unseen force into the very door she had been so eager to pass through. Her body struck the door with such ferocity that she was knocked senseless.

"Yeah! Don't mess with the Jewish Bear!" Penny enthused, that being one of her many nicknames for Randy ever since they'd seen the movie *Inglorious Bastards*.

Aethra moved forwards and scooped up the Omega Seed, which had fallen to the floor when Anne had been thrown backwards. She swiftly put it back in its case, snapping it shut. She even closed the handcuff over her wrist for good measure.

Kergaali, who'd been watching all of this, clapped slowly. "Well done, Randy! I almost admired her. At least she understood what's really at stake in this situation and was willing to do what it took to succeed. Perhaps when this is all over, I'll allow a few of you to live on in some kind of nature preserve, like we did with the First Generation. You are a curious species."

Randy was worried by her words. She didn't sound like someone who was defeated.

"What are you up to?" He asked, his hands crackling with magical energy.

"Only this…" Kergaali said as she twisted a dial on a box attached to her belt.

Suddenly, there was a blinding flash of light. Hi-Fi made a high-pitched sound that reverberated both in Penny's ears and inside her mind. She screamed too.

Then everything went dark.

CHAPTER 15:
PLANS FROM OUTER SPACE

Penny slowly opened her eyes. She felt like she had a hangover that had a hangover. A face slowly came into focus. It belonged to Naomi. *How the heck did she get here?* She wondered, and was disappointed not to hear Hi-Fi's voice immediately, providing some sort of insight into the matter. It was like becoming too dependent on your iPhone's Siri, only to find out that it had somehow been deleted.

"She's finally coming around." Naomi said to some other blurry shape nearby.

The nebulous shape swirled into that of Randy, a concerned look on his face. "How're you feeling?"

"Ugh. Like someone dropped a truck on me. What happened?" She tried to sit up, but it felt like her arms were made of rubber and she sank back down. As her vision cleared some more, she could now see that she was in some kind of bed that was oddly contoured to fit the shape of her body. Jim, Matt, and Aethra stood nearby.

"As far as we can figure, Kergaali triggered some sort of device that overloaded Hi-Fi's force field. Since you were linked to him, it did a real number on you, too. The energy pulse was so strong it even knocked out all the power in the base for a minute. Then she was gone. Must've teleported out while the shields were down."

"Teleported out? To where?" She asked.

"Probably to her own moon base. Drogalla says it's actually not that far from here. How're ya doin'? You really had us worried for a minute!" Matt said.

"I'll live, I suppose. How did you guys even get here?"

"We came here in the *Silver Bullet*, with April. We landed right before all the lights went out," Naomi explained. "I'm glad you're okay, even if I'm a little miffed that you beat me to being the first woman on the moon."

"Thanks, April's here too? Where *are* all the others? Omigod! I just remembered! Where's Anne? Is Hi-Fi gonna be okay? I was really getting attached to him—no pun intended."

"Chill out. The Venusians put Anne in a cell. Everyone else is with Drogalla, trying to figure out what our next move is." Matt said.

"And Hi-Fi will be fine, he just needs a little time to... reconstitute. I've got him right here," Jim said, lifting up a bucket and tilting it slightly so she could see that it held a silvery liquid.

"Hmm. Even their buckets look all futuristic." Penny commented, feeling more like her old self. "What do you mean they're figuring out our next move?"

"This isn't over yet. Kergaali escaped with the scans to Jim's ship, remember? According to Drogalla's sources, they have one of those industrial scale Duplo-Rays at the Baandergi base. They can start churning out a fleet of ships just like Jim's with that information." Randy told her.

"They won't even need a whole fleet. Just a few ships like mine would probably be enough to overwhelm your planet's defenses." Jim added sadly, "And it's all my fault! I can't believe I was so stupid to have believed in her!"

Some of Penny's old feelings for Jim came flooding back right then. She just wanted to hold him and tell him that everything was going to be okay. She might've done it too, if it didn't hurt so damned much to move.

"It wasn't your fault. She fooled us all," she said. "So did Anne, for what it's worth. What came over her? Just when ya think you know somebody! Then the next minute, they're suddenly getting all genocidal on you!"

"Who knows? I think the pressure of trying to live up the legacy of Bronson is what got to her. She's always been so serious, always worked so hard to prove to everyone that she deserves to be in the position he set her up for. I think it's made her a little too determined to do anything to protect the Earth. Okay, *really* determined. Overdoing it, you know?" Matt speculated.

"I just can't believe she was even willing to hurt Aethra!" Randy said, anger rising in his voice as he recalled how she'd threatened his girlfriend.

"Yeah, we've been friends for years!" Aethra's tone was heavy with disbelief and hurt.

Naomi shook her head. "That kind of power can do strange things to even the best of us."

"I guess the guest list for our parties just shrank by one." Matt observed sadly.

***

Kergaali stepped off of the teleportation pad, a confident new swagger in her step.

"Supreme Leader!" Her second in command, Sheerperf said excitedly. "How good it is to see you again! You will be pleased to learn that in your absence we have not been idle. We have now produced nearly enough drones and neutronic weapons to destroy every human settlement, even the smallest ones!"

"Excellent, cease production of the drones immediately." Kergaali commanded.

"Cease production? Then your mission was successful? You have the scans?"

"Wildly successful! With these scans, our ships will be invincible, even if the Saawgauth go ahead with their idiotic plan of giving the humans Duplo-Rays. Take my bipit, download the information in him into all of our industrial Duplo-Rays." She said, handing Zaa over to Sheerperf. The creature wrapped its lithe, sinuous body around the officer's arm.

"I want most of the base's power diverted to production. Everything must be on minimum power except for shields and long range scanning."

"Shields and long range scanning? Are we expecting an attack, Leader?" Sheerperf asked nervously.

"Yes, it's possible that the Saawgauth may be desperate enough to attack us directly. My spies inform me that they are debating such an action at this very moment. Put the entire base on yellow alert."

"Very good, Supreme Leader, it shall be so." They exited the transporter room, as they walked out into the hallway, the guards stationed outside the room stood at attention and saluted their leaders.

"We will have to step up our timetable. I have learned that these humans are far more dangerous than we ever realized. Some of them

257

have weapons and powers we can't begin to understand, and they now know what we have planned for them. We will have to begin the purification of the planet right away. As soon as we've created each copy of the Federation ship, I want it loaded with neutron missiles and prepped for immediate launch. Recycle some of the drones for raw materials if necessary."

"For the Glory of Pfoff!" Sheerperf exclaimed, excited that all of their plans were finally coming to fruition.

"Yes, For the Glory of Pfoff! Soon, the human race will be no more and Tulienel will finally have responsible stewards." She smiled broadly at the thought of it. A whole new world, wounded perhaps, but one that they would nurture and heal, restoring it back to its natural, pristine state. The Children of Pfoff would have a safe haven at last. They wouldn't fade from history, but rather go on to take their rightful place as one of the greatest races of the galaxy. They were so close now, she could almost taste it.

All they had to do was a little pest control first.

***

Penny felt the strength returning to her limbs and swung herself out of the bed.

"Whoa, take it easy, kid! I'm not sure it's such a great idea for you to be running around again so soon." Matt said in alarm.

"I'll be fine. I wanna go to that meeting, see what they're cooking up to stop Kergaali." She said, steadying herself against the bed.

"Yeah, I can't stand being left out of the loop like this," Aethra agreed.

Matt led them out of the medical bay where they'd been waiting for Penny to regain consciousness and down a short hallway to the conference room where Drogalla was planning her strategy. As they entered the room and searched for available seats, Penny was disappointed to note that even though these people could design an inappropriately futuristic looking bucket, no matter where you went in the galaxy, it seemed like conference rooms stubbornly maintained their atmosphere of resignation to the more dull, monotonous aspects of life. This conference room would've been perfectly at home in any terrestrial office or hotel. The only thing missing were the motivational posters with their stock photos and trite slogans

Drogalla held court at the head of one corner of a long, oblong table made of an unfamiliar, strangely rubbery wood. Seated on one side of her were two other Venusians. They all looked so similar to her that one could be forgiven for thinking they were cousins. On the other side were the familiar faces of April, Prospero (who looked even more crazed and disagreeable than usual) and Carlos. The new arrivals all took a seat on the human side of the table, even Jim, who was still carrying his fancy space bucket, setting it on the table before him with a thump.

Tensions had apparently been mounting in the room. Everyone was so engrossed in the arguments being made that they barely acknowledged the arrival of the newcomers to the room.

"You would have us violate our most sacred of ancient laws? The Children of Pfoff do not go to war against each other! Not since the first war! It's unprecedented!" Shouted Laavora, the senior officer in charge of the moon base.

"Don't be so naïve, perhaps we have had no major conflicts since the War, but we've had our share of border skirmishes over the years. We're not so perfect as we like to pretend that we are. Hopefully, we will be able to contain this conflict to this moon. I am only proposing a limited military action, not a declaration of full-scale war." Drogalla said calmly.

Laavora continued to press the leader. "What if you can't contain it? It *is* an act of war! Our people are engaged in a race against time to evacuate Pfoff. We can't waste time and energy fighting amongst ourselves!"

"A race against time? Don't be such an alarmist! According to our best projections, Pfoff will remain habitable for centuries to come. We are merely acting now to escape the inevitable, you know that."

Laavora just grunted dismissively. Drogalla pretended not to hear the gesture and carried on.

"Our best chance at success lies in destroying her Duplo-Rays before Kergaali can create a fleet of Federation ships. Besides, Kergaali has already showed a willingness to do anything to win. If we don't match that determination, we will be doomed to failure, and the humans doomed to destruction."

"Then so be it! Are we so ready to sacrifice our principles just to save this race of primitives? Ungrateful primitives who have already attacked us, even killed some of us! Who conspired to exterminate our entire race?" Another officer by the name of Isaador shot back.

"Primitives! Why you..." Prospero shouted back, shooting out of his seat and swiping at the empty air between himself and the officer. April placed a calming hand on his back and he settled down with surprising speed, looking somewhat ashamed of himself as he sat back down. He'd been quite temperamental the closer they'd gotten to the moon, and now that they were actually *on* the moon, he was positively surly.

That's what you get when you bring a former werewolf to the moon, April thought, knowing that Prospero suffered from the same lingering aftereffects of his lycanthropy curse as Kevin did. She began to wish she had ordered him to stay inside the *Silver Bullet* with Major Thompson.

"You see? They prove my point for me! Primitive!" The startled Isaador cried out.

"And you are beginning to sound like a Baandergi!" The Leader hissed, temporarily losing their composure.

Is Isaadoor the spy? Drogalla wondered. The Leader had hated having to call this meeting when there were still obviously traitors within their ranks that needed to be rooted out.

"You can hardly expect our guests to take it lightly while you sit there and insult them. If we do nothing, if we allow some of our people to slaughter an entire world full of intelligent beings, we will also be sacrificing our principles. The greater of the two principles in my opinion." When someone is doing evil, should they not be stopped? This danger comes from our planet, so it is our responsibility to stop it. Such a stain on our honor can never be washed away." Drogalla said, trying to cool down.

"Out, damned spot! Out, I say!" Prospero muttered, incapable as he was of not taking the obvious opportunity to quote from the Scottish Play.

"It's too dangerous, anyway. The Baandergi base is far bigger, more heavily defended. They have an entire invasion fleet. Most of our ships were aboard the mothership, held in the section of it that was destroyed when it crashed. We'd be hopelessly outnumbered. Such a mission would be suicidal!" Laavora insisted.

Drogalla shook her head. "It's true. It would be a suicide mission. The main purpose of such an assault would be to distract them and take down their shields while we try to beam down small teams to plant explosives on their Duplo-Rays. Such a mission would still be highly risky, yet I believe that the risk is worth it. If Kergaali is allowed to create a fleet of ships with technology centuries ahead of ours, the Baandergi could use it to dominate Pfoff too and impose their backward ways upon us all."

"Even Kergaali wouldn't be so bold! The Baandergi knows that none of the other nations will stand with them!" Isaador said.

"It wouldn't matter. With such weapons at their disposal, they would need no allies." Drogalla replied.

"Perhaps our new 'friend' from the Federation could even the odds by allowing us to scan his ship?" Laavora suggested, looking at Jim expectantly.

Jim looked down, shamefaced. "I can't do that. Kergaali must've planted a bomb on my ship while she was aboard. She detonated it when she escaped. There's nothing left of it, aside from Hi-Fi, and he's just a pile of robo goo right now."

"Some ally!" Laavora said in disgust.

This was news to Penny. Now she did put a hand on Jim's paw, understanding how the events of the past twenty-four hours had cut him to the core, and Laavora's words only twisted the knife deeper. He's lost more than just his ship. It was also his restaurant and his home. It held all of his most precious possessions—his sci-fi collectibles, instruments, demo tapes, momentos from his tours—all of it gone in an instant. He looked up and gave her an appreciative half smile.

At that moment, the door swooshed open and two more Venusians entered. Drogalla smiled broadly as Goymaalt entered, trailed by Cosfreele.

"My beloved. It does my heart good to finally see you again in person. When I saw the mothership, I feared the worst." Normally, the Leader wouldn't have called Goymaalt "beloved" in front of the staff, but under these circumstances, Drogalla didn't care much about proper protocol. Drogalla got up and hugged Goymaalt

Goymaalt smiled back and fought back tears. "As it does mine. I thought we'd lost you when your saucer was destroyed."

"Beloved?" Penny whispered to Randy. "I thought they didn't have those kinds of relationships?"

"Probably just one more thing Kergaali lied to us about," Randy whispered back

Drogalla overheard their whispers. "The Baandergi does not approve of couplings like ours. The old masters of the First Generation used to forbid it, afraid that forming such strong bonds with one another would undermine our loyalty to them. Even after we toppled our creators, the Baandergi still stubbornly cling to the old ways. They find any kind of romantic or sensual feeling repugnant. It's why they isolate themselves so much from the rest of our society, afraid that we will 'taint' them somehow. Doubtlessly it's one of the reasons why Kergaali wants to destroy you humans so much. They find such things oddly threatening."

Alright! So not all Venusians are raging homophobes! Good to know! Penny thought, suddenly feeling much better about teaming up with these aliens.

"The Baandergi are backwards thinking fanatics, out of step with our modern values!" Isadoor declared.

"Perhaps in some ways, but they are still entitled to live their lives in accordance with their beliefs." Cosfreele felt compelled to say.

Sympathy for the Baandergi? Perhaps Cosfreele is the true traitor? Drogalla wondered. "Of course, no one is debating that. What we object to is when they force those ideas on all of their people rather than letting them choose freely." The Leader replied reasonably.

"I came to give you a report on the status of the mothership." Goymaalt said dutifully, trying to steer them back to the matter at hand.

"Yes, please, proceed." Drogalla said as they all sat down.

"It will never fly again. The forward section has been too thoroughly demolished. We have managed to salvage several saucers, though."

"How many?" The Leader inquired.

"Only ten." Goymaalt said sadly.

"And we have but two here at the base." Laavora said. "You intend to attack the Baandergi base, protected by an invasion force of drone ships with only twelve saucers? You'll never get your demolition teams to the Duplo-Rays, they'll be cut down before they can get the shields down to transport to the surface!"

"Ah, but you're forgetting the ships we have on the other side of the Time Tunnel, the ones carrying the Duplo-Rays we were going to give to the humans? We can unload the Duplo-Rays and bring them here to this base. That's 195 more ships." Drogalla said.

"True, but those ships are transport ships, lightly armed and armored, and not as agile or maneuverable as their drones." Isaador replied.

"We could use the Duplo-Rays to produce our own drones. They're already pre-loaded with the specs for that." Cosfreele suggested.

"They wouldn't be ready in time. We must strike quickly, before the Baandergi can produce any of those Federation style ships." Drogalla said. "However, the idea does have some merit. Some drones might be ready in time to reinforce the attack force if we start production right away."

"You know that you always have my support, but this course of action troubles me greatly." Goymaalt said.

"I know, but I see no alternative. We could give the humans the Duplo-Rays as we planned, but it would be pointless. With Federation technology, Kergaali will be unbeatable."

Matt had been listening to all of this silently. There was one thing that Drogalla had said when they were in the *Silver Bullet* which he hadn't been able to get out of his head.

"There might be something else you can do!" Matt suddenly said. All eyes turned to him.

"Drogalla, on the way over here, when you were telling us about your antenna, you said something about how they could be used to deactivate you. I was just thinking that if all of the Baandergi that are here are Third Generation Venusians like you are, maybe we could find a way to turn them off?"

"Turn them off? Wouldn't that kill them?" Penny asked, horrified by Matt's suggestion. This didn't sound much better than what Anne had been planning to do, and what was all this talk about a 3rd generation?

"No, when we are deactivated, we go into a kind of coma until reactivated. It is an intriguing idea, it would've never occurred to me." Drogalla said.

Naomi again wondered if there was a reason such a thought would never have occurred to Drogalla. Did the control chip in their brains inhibit them from having such thoughts?

"It's impossible, though. The only ones who can deactivate us are our Second Generation equivalents." Drogalla continued.

Randy was also confused by the mention of a Third Generation. "What is this Third Generation? Sorry, I don't follow what you're all talking about."

Naomi looked at him. "Basically, all the Venusians we've encountered so far, on both sides of this conflict, are all copies made by the Duplo-Ray. The originals are all just goofing off at home while their copies are busy building a fleet to escape from Venus—or trying to take over our planet."

Randy was left speechless by this news. *It's like they're all a bunch of abandoned, neglected kids!* Randy thought in astonishment. Now it all made sense: Kergaali's comment about being created by a Duplo-Ray, and her reluctance to discuss her antenna. He wondered if some of Kergaali's anger came from some unconscious awareness that the Second Generation had abandoned them all? Was she just taking out her resentment on the human race?

Matt pressed on. "But what if the Second Generation Kergaali ordered the Baandergi to turn off their 3rd Generation versions, would they do it?"

"Yes, they are all bound to follow the dictates of Kergalli, the word of their Supreme Leader is law. They have a disturbingly exaggerated love for their political leadership," Laavora added.

"Good! Then we only have to convince one person to do the right thing!" Matt said.

"Again, it's impossible. We'd never convince the Second Generation Kergaali to cooperate. We can't even try. You see, it is forbidden for the Third Generation to interfere with the affairs of the Second generation. They can summon us, but we can't even contact them directly. Our control chips prevent it." Drogalla replied.

Penny was horrified by that last comment about their control chips. She couldn't imagine having something implanted inside her that literally prevented her from doing certain things. The very concept sent a chill down her spine.

"*You* wouldn't have to, we humans could go to Venus in the *Silver Bullet* and plead our own case. I'll bet that the Second Generation Baandergi don't even know about this invasion. It sounds like the Second Generation is too wrapped up in themselves to keep track of what you're all up to. They might find the whole invasion thing to be as crazy of an idea as you do!" Matt said

"I doubt it, you don't understand. The Second Generation Kergaali is the same person as the Third Generation one. They would make all the same decisions under the same circumstances." Goymaalt said

"But that's where I believe you're wrong. If they haven't synced their memories in years, which sounds like it's the norm for you people, then they've had time to develop into different individuals. That difference might be enough to convince them to bring this whole invasion to an end! You said that all of your adult people know what it's like to have been a mother—maybe we can build upon that commonality? Get them to see us as mothers with children that they care about, just like them Maybe they'd see us as beings with some kind of inherent value and not just animals to be put down?" Naomi said passionately.

She noticed Jim looking at her again with that same odd look in his eyes that she'd first noticed at that dinner from just the night before (which now felt to her like it had happened a million years ago). Even in his lion form, which she found somewhat unsettling, the look was the same.

"This idea that you seem to have that we are different individuals from the Second Generation is flawed to begin with. If we were not the same then we would be, would be...." Isaador struggled to find the right word.

"Slaves?" April asked. "Yes, I'm sure you're conditioned not to feel that way about it, but from our perspective, that's sure what it seems like you are. It might not have started out like that, but if they never bother to switch places with you, that's what it's evolved into. The most obedient slave is the one who doesn't realize they're one to begin with." As a descendant of slaves herself, the entire situation the Third Generation Venusians were in turned her stomach.

"Outrageous!" Isaador scoffed.

"Look, Kergaali said that when you reach a certain age, you give birth to two babies that are basically clones of yourselves. Do you consider your children to be different individuals from yourselves?" Penny asked the room.

"Of course we do. As you've said, they have different experiences as they grow up that help to define them as people, but it's not the same for the Third Generation. We are created as adults. Children are not allowed to have Third Generation duplicates, only adults who have already become parents are. So, we of the Third Generation all have the same memories of growing up as our Second Generation equivalents, we are shaped by the same things. We are the same people." Laavora argued.

"But if your Second Generation selves don't bother to sync their memories with you on a regular basis, then you *will* have differences that will begin to shape you into different people! You told us that you hadn't synced your memories since shortly after you were created, Drogalla. Is that the norm for your people?" Naomi asked.

The Venusians around the table all nodded, except for Cosfreele, who said. "My last synchronization was only about 3 of your years ago."

"Still, 3 whole years! A whole lot can happen to a person in that amount of time!" Matt insisted.

"All of this talk is insane! You humans simply don't understand our ways!" Laavora complained.

"Is it really so crazy? Perhaps they do have a point? I've had some time to reflect on this concept. It's not the first time the humans have suggested it. For example, my Second Generation self was not in a relationship with Goymaalt's equivalent, and that relationship has made quite a significant difference in my life! And you, Lavoora, you have only started painting in your free time since we started this mission, yet it's become such an obsession of yours that we all tease you about how much you constantly talk about it!" Drogalla said.

Laavora looked slightly embarrassed and amused at the same time by the Leader's example.

"Hey, I know it's a desperate plan, but I think it's worth a try. Isn't it better to let us try this than to pin all of your hopes in a suicide attack on your fellow Venusians?" Matt said.

"Yes, you may be right. Both plans have merit. Our greatest chance of success lies in pursuing both options. I believe I should lead the attack on the Baandergi base, and Goymaalt should help guide you to the other Kergaali on Pfoff." Drogalla said.

"Lead the attack? No, beloved, it's too dangerous! Please, let me do it instead!" Goymaalt pleaded.

"But that's exactly why I must do it! I don't wish to place you in that kind of danger, and I know how much you abhor the idea of fighting the other Children of Pfoff. I would spare you the ordeal of compromising your principles like that. Besides, your mission will not be without its own perils. You will have to guide these humans deep into Baandergi territory, and we all know how they feel about outsiders." Drogalla replied.

Goymaalt began to protest, then thought better of it, since they were in front of so many other people and remained silent.

"What do you say, April?" Drogalla said, recognizing her status as the leader of the humans in the room. "Do you accept Matt's plan? The Second Generation Baandergi will not accept a diplomatic visit from the Third Generation, and our control chips prevent us from contacting our own Second Generation to ask them to intervene on our behalf. It's likely that you will have to fight your way to reach Kergaali."

"I accept the risks. Our magic will give us an edge that their forces lack. I'd like to see if we can convince the other Kergaali to pull the plug on this invasion. And if we can't talk her into doing it, we could always try *forcing* her to do so," April answered.

"Aye, I could put a spell on her, like I did with Albert when we borrowed the *Silver Bullet!*" Prospero added eagerly.

April sighed. It was bad enough that they'd already used such dark magic once today. Now they might have to do it a second time? The Venusians weren't the only ones who had to sacrifice their ideals to find victory. When did it ever end? Where did you draw the line?

"Let's hope that it doesn't come to that, we'll try it the nice way first. *But* if we can't make Kergaali see reason, we'll do whatever we must—if it's the only way to save the Earth." She said firmly. "I hope we can deactivate the Third Generation Baandergi before your attack force suffers too many losses."

"As do I. Then so be it. Time is of the essence. Let's make the necessary preparations, and may good fortune find us all." Drogalla said.

"Well gang, it looks like we're headed to Venus!" Matt smiled his lopsided grin, hoping that he sounded a bit more confident than he actually was.

CHAPTER 16:
INTO THE STRANGE AEONS PAST

The *Silver Bullet* had docked in the large area that headed the gate to the Time Tunnel, the dome covering it opened up to allow ships in and out of the base. Major Thompson sat resting on the ship's boarding ramp, waiting for the others to return. He wasn't quite able to believe that he was sitting inside of an alien base on the dark side of the moon, a few hundred feet away from an enormous gateway that led to another planet, millions of years in the past. This would sure be something to tell his kids about someday, but he knew he'd never be able to do so, unless of course they followed in his footsteps and joined the ABC. He'd taken the *Silver Bullet* on numerous test flights over the years all over the Solar System, but he'd never landed on any of the various planets and moons that the Guilds had sent him to before, let alone encountered aliens, so this was all still quite new and exciting to him.

He was shaken from his ruminations by the sound of footsteps approaching the ship. Major Thompson looked up to see the group he'd come there with (minus Drogalla, instead; they were being led by a different Venusian); they were all now dressed in silver space suits. He had no way of knowing that Drogalla had insisted that the humans wear them since they were traveling to Venus. Even though the atmosphere was breathable and the air pressure and gravity in the area they were traveling to was similar to Earth's, the Leader was concerned that exposure to the planet's elevated radiation levels might have some long-term health effects on the humans if they didn't protect themselves. Since Venus was much closer to the sun and lacked a magnetic field, it was much more radioactive than the Earth. The native life forms had evolved to compensate for such an environment, but any human visitors would find this problematic.

Behind them was another group, some of whom, such as Aethra and Randy, he recognized. Everyone in the Guilds knew who the Pirate Queen was, and Randy was one of the more famous wizards. They were all dressed in a distinct style of space suit. He also had no way of knowing that only an hour earlier, those same suits had been a torn and shredded mess but had now completely repaired themselves. Major Thompson did a double take as he realized that one of these newcomers appeared to be some kind of man/lion hybrid that was, for reasons that he couldn't begin to imagine, carrying the most futuristic looking bucket that he'd ever seen. He was surprised to see that Director Moore was not with them; he didn't understand the details of their mission here. He'd been unable to overhear much of the conversation when Matt had called Randy earlier, but he'd gathered that they had been trying to get a message to her through Randy. He was too much of a professional to ask many questions, he knew that this mission was classified and the details all seemed to be on a need to know basis. He counted ten of them all together, not including himself. He made a mental note to ask the ship to grow a few more seats when they got back inside.

"Hello Major, please get the ship ready for takeoff." April ordered as she neared him.

"I take it we're not going back to Guild HQ right away. Then, what's with all those space suits you're wearing?" He asked.

"Oh, don't worry, Drogalla gave us an extra one of these incredibly fashionable disco suits for you too—just in case you feel like stretching your legs once we get to Venus." Matt told him, holding up the extra suit he carried with him for him to see.

Major Thompson knew that no kind of space suit would protect him on Venus as it is today, so he quickly surmised that they must be talking about going through the Time Tunnel.

"You want me to fly you through that thing, into the past?" he asked, gesturing towards the massive portal.

"That's the mission." April affirmed.

"Time travel, huh? I guess there's a first time for everything!" he said as he got up and headed into the ship.

Penny walked up the ramp behind Randy and Aethra, who were holding hands like a couple of lovesick teenagers. Aethra no longer had the briefcase containing the Omega Seed. They'd temporarily left that with the Venusians since it was too dangerous to bring with them. This was not the first time Penny had been inside the ship.

Anne's predecessor, Bronson McDowell, had often used it to visit Matt's house when he showed up for their parties. She'd taken the opportunity to step inside it on one of those occasions, years ago, but she'd never actually flown in it before. After the experience of flying in Jim's ship, though, she found herself feeling oddly blasé about taking a ride in the *Silver Bullet,* even though it was something that she'd always been curious about after listening to all of Randy's stories about it. *Seen one spaceship, you've seen 'em all, I suppose.* She thought, marveling out how quickly the routines of reality could suck the romance and wonder out of even the most fantastic of ideas. The marvelous becomes mundane with frightening speed if you don't continuously nurture your sense of awe.

She was a little surprised though, as she entered the shining, white interior to find that there were exactly enough seats for them all, far more than she remembered seeing in the past.

She sat down and strapped in. Naomi was seated next to her and leaned over towards her.

"How are you holding up? I know you're not used to this kind of stuff. Hell! It's been a good few years since I've last been this deeply involved in the weirdness myself."

"I'm...adjusting. It's kind of a rush sometimes, and other times I find myself almost feeling guilty for enjoying myself because I know that this isn't just some kind of game, there are real people getting killed, and so much is at stake here."

"Welcome to the adventuring life! Not quite like the movies, is it?" Naomi replied.

"You can say that again!" Penny replied.

"And how about you and...your boys?" Naomi inquired in a lower voice.

"I've accepted that Randy had my best interests at heart when he was snooping around in my personal life, but it wasn't easy. I wanted to rip off his fucking head and shit down his neck at first!" She confessed.

Naomi giggled a little at the graphic nature of her description. "That's what we told him would happen—well, except without the shitting down his neck part."

"He told you guys what he was doing?" Penny didn't know that before. For a moment she was a little angry about him discussing her personal business with others behind her back like that, but this was Matt and Naomi, and they were all practically family, which made it slightly more acceptable. She smiled instead. Tightly.

"I swear that boy can't even take a piss on his own sometimes without asking one of you two for advice!" She whispered.

Naomi laughed again. It was so true.

"What about you know? Simba the Lion King over there? What's it like to be dating an alien?"

"I wouldn't know. We broke up."

"Oh. I thought...well, you two seemed pretty cozy together back in the conference room."

"I dunno. I guess I'm starting to have some second thoughts about the breakup, it's complicated. It's not like all my feelings for him suddenly went away. I'm just having trouble reconciling who he really is with the man I thought I knew."

"Well, it could be worse. At least it's not tentacles. The lion thing is oddly...sort of regal." Naomi said slyly.

"It's not about his appearance, it's the deception." Penny clarified.

"I can understand that." Naomi said sympathetically.

They both sat back as they felt the ship raise up off the ground. There was a screen in the front of the ship that displayed what was going on outside. They all watched as they approached the Time Tunnel. The airstrip, with its neat lines of saucers all lined up in rows, was still visible on the other side.

Goymaalt briefly said something in Venusian into a communicator, then turned to Major Thompson. "Alright, take us through. They're expecting us on the other side."

"Here goes nothing!" Matt said to Naomi. She smiled back at him, proud of him for dreaming up this unlikely plan. Matt might always be reluctant to get involved in these adventures at first, but once he accepted the inevitability of it, he went all in.

The *Silver Bullet* shot through the Time Tunnel, its departure causing the surface to ripple as it passed through.

From the shadows nearby, a pair of cold eyes watched the ship go through the portal. The spy had a report to make.

***

At the Baandergi base, Kergaali was intrigued by this new information. "These humans are insane! They actually think that they can convince the Second Generation to turn against us?"

"Perhaps, but even so, don't you intend to do something to stop them?" The spy asked.

"Yes, it's not a good idea to let them run around freely in the homeland. They clearly wish to contaminate our people with their dangerous alien ideas." Kergaali agreed.

"It's worse than that! They said if they can't convince your other self, they will force the Supreme Leader to do as they wish." The spy reported.

Kergaali's skin blanched, remembering too well how they might be able to actually do so with this "magic" they commanded.

"Not such a fool's errand after all! Were you able to acquire scans of their ship?"

"Only a partial scan. I couldn't get very close to it without being seen. The pilot was sitting outside the whole time." The spy had a note of disappointment in their voice as they said it.

"Send me whatever data you were able to get right away. I'll have someone in tactical analyze it for weaknesses. We'll blast them out of the sky before they ever reach my palace!" Kergaali swore.

On the inside, though, there was another feeling beginning to take hold. Kergaali had a twinge of regret that Jim would die when the ship was destroyed. She had developed a certain fondness for him during their time together, despite herself. Then there was Randy, who had saved them all from Anne's scheme. She felt that she owed him something for that. Even that bizarre little mutant Penny had proven her worth in the heat of battle and earned the Supreme Leader's grudging respect. That bizarre fish woman bothered her too. Kergaali had never dreamed that Earth was the home to such beings. She didn't mind wiping out most of the humans, but did these other creatures deserve the same fate? She supposed that they did if they allied themselves with the humans. How many unique life forms would she have to snuff out to preserve her own people? Kergaali had been sincere about preserving some humans. She was no geno-cidal monster like Anne. Kergaali supposed she could try to preserve a few of these nymphs as well. She was better than any human. She had more respect for life than they did, no matter what they might believe of her.

Kergaali quickly dismissed such doubts. What was this weakness? There was no place for such sentimentality in her mission. She had a civilization to save! Had these humans already infected her? It just showed how dangerous they were, how much they needed to be eliminated.

The *Silver Bullet* glided over the Saawgauth airbase. As they did so, they could see some of the saucers lift off of the ground, wobbling as they did so, and make their way towards the entrance of the Time Tunnel to take part in the attack on Kergaali's moon base. Goymaalt sat up front next to Major Thompson, giving him directions on where to fly the ship, from a device that looked like some kind of holographic GPS. As more ships moved towards the Time Tunnel, Penny caught a look of concern on Goymaalt's face and her heart went out to the alien, who was obviously worried about Drogalla's chances of success at what they themselves had described as a suicide mission.

"We'll succeed. We'll get the Baandergi deactivated before your forces can and do to much harm," she said.

"Aye, that's the spirit, lass!" Prospero said. He was obviously feeling much more buoyant now that they were away from the moon.

As they continued to fly over the base, they could see an unbelievably huge, elongated shape the size of a mountain range on the horizon.

"What's that?" Randy asked.

"It's one of their colony ships that's under construction." Jim informed him.

"That's right." Goymaalt confirmed.

Randy briefly wondered how Jim could've known that? Had Kergaali shown him a picture of one?

"It's even bigger than I imagined." Matt said in awe as they drew closer.

"It's freaking amazing!" Aethra smiled, imagining what she could do with such a ship under her command.

"A ship like this takes decades to complete. There is no Duplo-Ray large enough to create one whole, and even if there was, the power requirements would be off the scale, so we have to use the Duplo-Rays to produce the components and assemble it all by hand. Each of our nations will have to produce dozens of these for the Great Migration; all of our society's activities are related to this effort in one way or another." Goymaalt explained in a voice brimming over with pride.

"How can something that massive ever get off the ground, let alone into space?" Naomi asked. As a history professor,she knew from her studies of human space exploration that the weight of each item on the rocket had to be taken into account to make sure that the spaceship could reach escape velocity.

"We have a technology that you call 'antigravity' in your speculative fiction, although that term is an oversimplification and gross exaggeration of how it actually works. Is that not the same technology that powers this ship's flight? When I saw this vessel, I assumed that these Guilds you are associated with had mastered such technology even if the rest of your people had not, am I wrong?"

"We didn't create the *Silver Bullet*, it came to us from an alternate universe. We've been trying to unravel its secrets for almost twenty years now and aren't really much closer to understanding anything about how it works," Major Thompson, who sat closest to Goymaalt, explained.

"Oh! How unexpected!" Goymaalt said. While their attention was focused on the alien, Goymaalt decided to take the opportunity to discuss a few things with them.

"I would like to make a few suggestions, if I may."

"By all means, what are your concerns?" April asked.

"Firstly, that if we come into conflict with the Baandergi, as we very likely may, that we try to use nonlethal means to defeat them if possible. This is a mission to win over their hearts and minds, as you humans say, and slaughtering them will hardly win you many fans. Indeed, your attack on our base caused many within our own ranks to question the wisdom of our mission. You probably sensed some of that tension in the conference room."

Jim looked ashamed by her words. "I tried to use nonlethal force, when possible," He mumbled.

"Really? Five of our elite guards dead? The crews of our cannons all dead, and at least twenty casualties and fifty-one injuries on my mothership alone? Not to mention Drogalla's ship and her escort saucers!" Goymaalt spat the words.

"Hey, he really did try! He gave us weapons that only knocked people out! I don't see how it's possible to destroy a cannon or take down a saucer without risking killing its crew. Don't forget that Kergaali was the one pulling our strings, telling us how necessary it was to do all of that to save the Earth! And we lost some people too, true they might not have been the most charming or interesting of people, but they were still our people all the same!" Penny replied hotly, thinking of poor Smoke and Wisp. She'd been quite appalled by the violence she'd encountered on their mission, but she also knew how Jim wasn't totally to blame for it, and she resented Goymaalt attacking him over it. Couldn't the alien tell that he already felt terrible about it? That he felt like a fool for trusting Kergaali, and was hurting over the loss of his ship?

"Penny, please!" April said. "Yes, of course we would like to minimize any fatalities. The magic users in our party have a number of spells at our disposal which don't kill, yet are quite effective in a fight, and I believe that Naomi and Matt also have ways of subduing foes without killing."

Matt nodded. Over the years he'd gotten quite good at clocking opponents with the blunt end of the *Vermilion Avenger* (which was still inside its case stowed under his seat) to knock them out, as he had done with Drogalla. Naomi's flaming sword could also shoot forth a net made of etheric energy.

"Aethra, however, might be a bit of a problem." April admitted, "Her laser is quite powerful."

"What can I say? I'm a total badass." Aethra said, without a hint of irony. Her unabashed bluntness and unwillingness to apologize for being what she was was one of the things that attracted Randy to her so much. Like him, she tried to always live in the moment and just be what she was.

"I may have a solution. I took the liberty of bringing a few of our pistols with me. They're all set to stun only." Goymaalt said, opening up a duffel bag that, much like the bucket Jim held in his lap, had no business looking so damned fancy and futuristic.

Goymaalt handed one to each of them. Aethra took hers without much enthusiasm. "Oh joy. Thanks a bunch." She replied, tucking it into the belt on her space suit.

"Even if you have other ways of defending yourselves, I recommend you take one as a backup weapon. It never hurts to be prepared, does it?" Goymaalt remarked.

After they'd all taken one of the weapons, which looked to Matt disconcertingly like a cheap prop from an old *Flash Gordon* serial, the alien looked at them all. "There is one other matter I would like to discuss. I think I may have a safer way for us to reach the Second Generation Kergaali than storming the Baandergi palace."

"Oh man! No storming the palace either? But I love storming things!" Aethra pouted. "Maybe I should've stayed home after all!" She sulked. Randy, ever attentive to her needs, massaged her neck.

April sighed. She wondered if Aethra was overdue for a dip in some water? She could get a little...unstable when away from water for too long.

"Any less risky suggestions you may have will be more than welcome, Deputy Leader." April affirmed diplomatically, recalling that it had been much easier to babysit her daughter Celine when she was younger than it was proving to be to keep this unruly group in check at times.

"Thank you. The majority of our Second Generation spends a large majority of their time using something which we call the 'Nethersphere.'" It is basically our version of what you call the 'internet,' only far more immersive, and with bipits instead of cats."

"Makes sense, bipits *are* much cuter than cats!" Randy commented. Indeed, one might even say they were indescribably cuter than cats.

"What? What is this heresy?" Jim replied.

"Oh shit! No offense, man!" Randy said.

Jim laughed. Penny was glad to hear him laugh again after watching him sulk for so long. "None taken, I'm just fucking with you, dude!"

Randy breathed a sigh of relief and paused in his massaging of the Pirate Queen's neck. Aethra glared at him.

"Don't stop now, baby, you just hit a good spot!" she complained.

"Oh yeah, uh, sorry babe," He muttered.

Goymaalt raised an eyebrow of exasperation over all this childish banter and soldiered on. "More than likely, the Kergaali we seek will be connected to the Nethersphere. It will be far easier to reach the Supreme Leader that way. Unfortunately, we of the Third Generation are unable to connect to the Second Generation's version of the Nethersphere. We each have our own separate but equal versions of it."

April's blood ran cold at the casual use of the phrase "separate but equal." It wasn't much more than a human generation ago that such terms had been used to subjugate her own family. She was struck by how insidious it was that these people had a chip in their brains that literally prevented them from doing certain things, or even thinking too deeply about their own plight, it seemed.

Goymaalt continued to lay out the proposed plan. "Complicating matters even further, the Baandergi, because of their defiantly contrary ways, have their own version of the Nethersphere which is only tenuously connected to the rest of Pfoff's computer networks and is under their rigid state control. In order to connect to it, we will have to travel to the islands the Baandergi inhabit and use one of their own computer terminals. I believe our best chance of success is to go to one of their resort areas and break into an unused vacation home to do so."

"So you're saying that all we have to do is find Kergaali on the web to talk to her?" Matt asked.

"Yes. I was hoping that Jim's robot companion would have recovered in time to help us. From what I understand, Federation computer technology is far more advanced than our own, so if the computer in your robot could interface with the Nethersphere, it could easily find Kergaali, and possibly lock us into an audience with the Supreme Leader, so that Kergaali will be unable to disconnect from the Nethersphere, and no one else will be able to interfere while we speak."

Jim stuck a finger in his bucket and scrunched up his face critically. "He's almost ready, just give him a few more minutes." Penny was relieved to hear this. She knew that Jim had said that Hi-Fi had no real feelings and wasn't truly alive, but she'd still felt a surprisingly strong connection to the machine while they'd been bonded together. She missed him.

"And what if Kergaali isn't in the Nethersphere?" Naomi asked, feeling the need to play devil's advocate.

Goymaalt snorted derisively. "Little chance of that, these people practically spend their whole lives connected to it now that they've got the Third Generation to deal with the real world on their behalf. Besides, if we can't reach the Supreme Leader that way, or are unable to sway them, you can always fall back on your storming the palace plan."

"Hooray for palace storming!" Aethra cried.

April rolled her eyes at Aethra's comments. "I like your plan. Anything which will lead to less conflict is welcome to me. And as you say, the other more forceful options are still on the table. What do the rest of you think? The rest of you aside from Aethra, I mean, already know what she thinks!"

One by one, the others all seemed to give their assent. Prospero decided to invoke the Bard with his response. "Most dangerous is that temptation that doth goad us on to sin in loving virtue."

"Err...okay." April said, not bothering to pretend to know what he meant by that. If she had bothered to decode it, she would've found it to be a sentiment that she herself had been seized by several times throughout this mission, whenever she worried over the lengths they might have to go to for victory. But she didn't stop to analyze his words, merely deciding it was more convenient to interpret it as a vote of "yes."

"It sure sounds less risky." Matt said. He didn't share Aethra's enthusiasm for fights. He wasn't getting any younger and he still had a daughter to raise, and a business to run.

"There is *some* degree of risk." Goymaalt admitted. "We connect to the Nethersphere through a direct neural interface by putting on a kind of headband. It was designed for Venusian minds. I'm not completely sure what it will do to a human brain."

"Oh great! You mean it could scramble our brains?" Carlos grumbled, "You might've mentioned that sooner!"

"I believe there's a strong chance it will be safe enough for you, or I wouldn't have brought up this plan at all." Goymaalt replied.

"It still sounds like our best chance. You can count me in." Naomi said, "And I don't think all of us will have to go online anyway, I think probably just us moms. I still think that's the best way to get through to Kergaali, to build on that common bond of parenthood."

"It's hard for me to imagine Kergaali as a mother!" Penny said.

"And yet it's true, we are all mothers." Goymaalt affirmed.

"Is that literally true, though? For your Third Generation? I know that you *remember* being parents, but it sounds like your people can only have kids at a certain point in your lives, right? And a Second Generation Venusian can't create one of you to do their work for them until they've hit that age, or am I understanding it wrong?" Matt asked. He'd been struggling to understand these things from all the little clues that the aliens had tossed out here and there. All the Third Generation Venusians seemed to be copies of people who were beyond their child-bearing years. He guessed that this rule probably existed to prevent any more "Generations" beyond the third from arising.

Goymaalt made a face. This seemed like a sore subject. "You understand it correctly enough. And I can imagine what you're likely thinking. That those children are not really our own. Well, we might not have given birth to them with these bodies, but we have all the memories of doing so, of their first steps, their first words. It's all very real to us, as real as if we lived it. So we love them like our own. How could we do any less? We love them, although they tend to see us as nothing but copies and will have little to do with us." The alien looked away.

Naomi frowned. She hadn't thought of that! These poor Third Generation Venusians probably never got to see what they thought of as being their own children, at least not until those children were old enough to make duplicates of themselves, at which point she figured they might interact with those duplicates.

The whole thing was so monstrous! She wanted to tear down their stupid system, but what could she do about it? She'd be lucky to convince Kergaali to call off this invasion without having to put a gun to the Supreme Leader's head, let alone bring about any sweeping social changes.

"Okay, well, it's decided then." April said, trying on her decisive voice, which she usually reserved for Inner Council meetings and for scolding her daughter, Celine. "We'll try it your way first. Just get us into Baandergi territory and we'll take it from there."

CHAPTER 17:
SPACE BATTLES AND STUFF

The fleet of Saawgauth ships flew towards the Baandergi base without their shrouds on. It might've seemed like a foolish move, but Drogalla wanted to make sure they got their attention. Besides, the Baandergi and Saawgauth both had ways of easily seeing through each other's cloaking technology. It might be effective at hiding them from the humans, but it couldn't hide them from each other for very long.

Drogalla sat on the bridge of the lead ship looking stern and resolute, while trying not to think of the hundreds of things that could go wrong with this plan.

"Incoming message from the Baandergi!" Isaador, who was acting as Drogalla's second in command while Goymaalt was away, reported.

Drogalla smiled. "Display message."

A hologram of Kergaali appeared in front of Drogalla.

"Leader Drogalla! You dare to bring a fleet of ships to my very doorstep with their shields raised? I never imagined you'd be so bold as to make such an openly hostile display! What is the meaning of this? Turn back immediately or you will force us to take extraordinary measures to defend ourselves!"

"Don't play dumb with me, Supreme Leader. You know exactly what this is about! I demand that you turn over all of the stolen specifications for the Federation ship so the information can be destroyed. Furthermore, you must abandon your plans to invade Tulienel and destroy its people, or face the consequences!" Drogalla said defiantly.

Kergaali laughed. "Oh yes, most certainly! I'll turn over that information just as soon as you turn over all the data on the Time Tunnel that you stole from my scientists and dismantle your own version of the tunnel! In addition, you must join us in our efforts to purify and colonize Tulienel!"

Drogalla sighed. "You know that will never happen. Very well, if you won't turn over the data you have on the Federation ship, then at least consider this possibility: those ships have the ability to warp space, with such ships you could swiftly take your people to any planet in the entire universe. Do that and find some uninhabited world for your people to colonize, but leave the Earth in peace."

"Never! I consider this entire solar system to be an extension of our homeland. Why should we abandon it to live under some unfamiliar star, with unfamiliar constellations?" Kergaali laughed at the idea.

Drogalla sighed even more deeply this time. "I *had* hoped you'd see reason."

"Reason? I'm not the one about to violate our most sacred of laws by pitting the Children of Pfoff against one another! You're leading your people into a massacre. I have thousands of ships, you can't possibly win! I don't understand you, Drogalla. You're willing to throw away your life and the lives of your people for these primitives? Primitives that will surely kill their beautiful world if they are allowed to remain in control of it? Surely by now you must know of the lengths these savages were willing to go to in order to defeat us? They very nearly wiped out our entire race!"

"They only did so because *you* pushed them to such extremes with your wicked plans! And may I remind you that it was also a human who stopped them from using the Omega Seed? These people have the potential to become better than they are right now, and we are not so perfect as to judge them unworthy of ever being able to reach that potential. What you plan to do to them, in the name of saving our people is an abomination, and unnecessary. End your isolation and join the rest of us in the Great Migration to Armenclius!"

"Never! Your people have just used that project as an excuse to try and rob us of our sovereignty, to dictate to us how we must live our lives! You still cling to it, like mindless robots, when I have already shown you that it's pointless. Our ships will never reach Armenclius! I have proven it, your own probes have verified it! Yet, you still deny the truth! There is no trace of our people in this time period because your plan has already failed. It failed millions of years ago! *This* is our only chance for survival! You would lead us into extinction just as even now you lead your forces to a slaughter!"

This old argument again? Drogalla thought wearily. "You must acknowledge that there are myriad possibilities as to why our people don't appear to be on Armenclius in this era. We might've found a more suitable world on our journey, or perhaps we did make it to Armenclius, only to abandon it later for unknown reasons? Many hundreds of millions of years have passed, who can imagine what changes have overtaken us in such an immense time frame? What I *do* know is that we aren't worthy of survival if it is won only at the cost of the destruction of the humans! If we abandon all the ideals that we claim to hold precious so that we may survive. That is not living, it's just...existing."

Kergaali laughed once more. "You dare to lecture me about abandoning our ideals while you fly here at the head of a fleet of ships to attack me? To kill your own people just to save a bunch of perverted animals that can't think beyond where their next meal is coming from? I am not the traitor to our people here, Drogalla. You are! I am the one who will save the Children of Pfoff from the uncertain future you have planned for us, and I will also save the planet Tulienel from its own wayward children in the process! The history of this era has already shown us where your plans will lead our people, but *future* history will show me to be the greatest leader our people have ever known!" Kergaali was practically raving now.

"Yes, I, Kergaali of the *Third Generation* shall be recorded as the savior of our people, not that bloated, lazy idiot who does nothing but play quiz games while our planet is in crisis!"

Drogalla's eyes widened. Kergaali spoke as if there was a difference between the 3rd and Second Generation versions of the Supreme Leader! Somehow, despite the control chip, Kergaali had developed an aberrant sense of individuality. Was that what this was really all about then? Asserting one's individuality, but in the worst way possible?

Suddenly, Kergaali stopped laughing and whirled around, looking confused. "What was that? Status report!" The Supreme Leader shouted to some unseen subordinate not captured by the hologram's imager.

Kergaali glared at Drogalla venomously. "What deception is this? What treachery? You send your elite troops to invade my base while you play at diplomacy?"

Now it was Drogalla's turn to laugh. "What's the point of diplomacy when I already know what your answer will be? We've had these same debates a thousand times before! I know how much you love the sound of your own voice, of shouting about your glories! You claim to be doing this to save our people, but it's obvious that your own vanity is your true motivation! Yes, this has all been a little diversion while my troops marched to your base and infiltrated it through one of your maintenance tunnels. You're not the only one with spies. We know the layout of your entire installation. I imagine my forces are halfway to your shield generator room by now. Once they destroy it, we should have more of a fighting chance. Goodbye, Kergaali, the only glory you will find this day will be in your own death!"

Drogalla made a quick hand motion that meant it was time to cut the transmission. "Attention! Calling all ships! Engage shrouds and assume tactical formation ten! Fire all weapons on the Baandergi base! Prioritize targeting the defense cannons!"

"Leader! They're launching their drones!" Isaador announced in alarm. Through the ship's forward viewport, they could see the skies ahead now swarming with countless small saucers headed towards them, firing away with reckless abandon.

"Launch our own fighters!" Drogalla commanded. They'd been able to manufacture a few dozen of their own fighters with their Duplo-Rays before they left their base and had also commandeered as many as they could from their military forces on Pfoff on such short notice.

These smaller ships now poured forth from the launch bays of the Saawgauth fleet. Under other circumstances it would've been an impressive sight, but even though there were a great deal of them, they were still heavily outnumbered by the Baandergi's drones. The one advantage they had was that most of them were crewed by a real pilot, whereas the Baandergi ships were all piloted by computers, computers which were easily confused by the actions of the often unpredictable living pilots. Their mission was to keep the drones away from the larger ships long enough for the big ships to use their more powerful weapons to pound the base into submission.

It wasn't working very well.

Drogalla jerked violently in the command chair as the ship was rocked by a blast. "Get me a report on the status of our forces inside the base!" The Leader shouted.

Once that force got the shields down, then they could teleport in more ground troops to reinforce them and make a move on the enemy Duplo-Rays, which was their true target. One of the larger ships in the fleet that was flying ahead of them suddenly exploded spectacularly, it's shroud having long since been dropped by the damage it had previously sustained at the hands of the drones.

I can't teleport in more ground forces if they're all killed before we get those shields down! Drogalla thought bitterly as the command ship was pelted with debris from the exploding saucer, causing it to rock alarmingly.

"They're encountering heavy resistance, but they have penetrated the shield generation room and are planting explosives as we speak." Isaador said, making a great effort to remain cool as the ship took another hit.

"Finally, some good news! Once they've blown the shields, have them move on to the Duplo-Rays. Tell them we'll meet them there as soon as possible." Drogalla said.

In the view screen, they saw a large explosion tear through the base below. A cry of celebration went up from everyone on the bridge.

"Base shields are down, Leader!" Cosfreele announced.

"Ground team now reporting that the rally point has been secured!" Isaador added.

"Attention all ships! Concentrate fire on the base! Start beaming down your demolition teams to the rally point. I will meet them there." Drogalla announced into an intercom.

Drogalla stood up. "Isaador, I'm giving you command of the fleet, keep hammering them until we can get those Duplo-Rays destroyed. I'm beaming into the base to lead the reinforcements. If you don't hear from us, fall back to our base. Cosfreele, you're with me."

"Me, Leader?" Cosfreele asked uncertainly.

"Yes, there's nobody else who I'd rather have watching my back." Drogalla smiled. This was, of course, a complete lie. The truth was that Drogalla suspected that Cosfreele might be a spy. The humans had a charming saying: keep your friends close and your enemies even closer. Drogalla intended to heed that advice.

"I'm honored, of course." Cosfreele said, standing up and walking over to the Leader.

"Isaador, beam us to the rally point." Drogalla commanded, as the Leader hefted up a large rifle that sat next to the command chair, and tossed an identical weapon to Cosfreele.

"I obey, Leader, and may fortune find you!" Isaador saluted.

Drogalla saluted back. "May fortune find us all, Commander."

There was a flash of light, and they were gone.

An instant later, Drogalla and Cosfreele found themselves inside the Baandergi base. Their rally point was a wide open warehouse area right outside of the Duplo-Ray factories where the things the Duplo-Rays created were intended to be stored. All around them, other Venusians materialized, all wearing space suits and carrying rifles. A cheer went up when their troops saw them appear.

"The Leader is with us!" someone shouted.

One of the armored Elite Troopers flew forward from the crowd and knelt before Drogalla. This was Firpiit, who had led the soldiers that had brought down the shield. "I relinquish my command to you, Leader Drogalla."

"Arise, Firpiit! Let's lead this attack together!" Drogalla ordered. The Leader turned to the assembled crowd. "As soon as we make it into the factory section, plant as many charges as you can on the Duplo-Rays! Follow me!"

Drogalla ran forward, closely followed by Firpiit and Cosfreele. They entered the huge factory section without incident. Inside they could see several of the industrial scale Duplo-Ray devices. They looked like massive furnaces that crackled with unknown energies inside. A large conveyor belt jutted out of the machine. The invading force split up into smaller groups and began attaching small, circular explosives to these machines.

They didn't get very far before large, pink shapeless blobs of flesh appeared from behind the Duplo-Rays, slithering towards them. These pink masses seemed to grow thousands of thin tentacles, which shot forth and seized any of the Venusians unfortunate enough to be too close and dragged them screaming into their awful maws filled with concentric circles of fangs.

"Tergitors!" Drogalla said in disbelief. These were genetically engineered monsters created by the First Generation during the War as their last line of defense. Their creation had been banned for centuries. Kergaali must've used the Duplo-Ray to recreate these ancient foes.

As Drogalla looked around in dismay, the leader could see that it looked like there were hundreds of the monsters emerging from the shadows all around them. The air was filled with the screams of the Saawgauth troops.

"It was a trap! They were expecting an attack here!" Firpiit exclaimed, as the Elite Trooper blasted away at one of the beasts as it wrapped dozens of tentacles around Firpiit's armored leg and tossed the trooper into a wall.

Drogalla nodded in grim agreement, then raised a rifle as a Tergitor suddenly reared up behind Cosfreele. "Cosfreele! Get down! One of them's behind you, I can't get a clear shot!"

Cosfreele just laughed. "Oh, don't trouble yourself. It won't hurt me." Indeed, the creature swayed back and forth menacingly behind Cosfreele, waving its tentacles in the air, but made no move to attack.

"You see, I have a device on me that emits a frequency that tells it I'm no enemy, but rather a master to be obeyed. Handy isn't it?"

"So, you *are* the spy!" Drogalla exclaimed, pointing the rifle at the traitor.

"You suspected me? Hmm. I must be getting sloppy in my old age." Cosfreele said, disappointed that they were losing their touch.

Drogalla screamed a curse in Venusian and fired the rifle. Cofreele leapt to the side, easily avoiding the blast, then issued a terse command to the waiting Tergitor. Countless pink tentacles shot forward, wrapping themselves around the Leader's arms and legs. Drogalla struggled valiantly, but it was no good. The tentacles drew them ever closer and closer, and finally into the terrible, gaping mouth of the monster. Drogalla, Leader of the Saawgauth, vanished in a blur of teeth and blood.

In the skies above the base, Isaador watched in dismay as another of the large saucers exploded.

"How many ships do we have left?" The Commander asked.

"22." Replied a crewmate.

22 out of 195! We can't last much longer like this

"Try to raise the Leader on the comms!" Isaador ordered

"No response!"

"Try again!"

"Still no response!"

Isaador sank back into the command chair, not relishing the decision that was now theirs to make. It had been a good ten minutes since the leader had beamed down, and they had heard nothing, had been unable to reach Drogalla, or Cosfreele, or any of the other officers involved in the ground assault. It was time to face the facts— their mission had ended in failure.

"Attention all ships! Fall back to our own base." Isaador gave the command.

One of the bridge officers whirled around. "But the Leader is still down there! You can't abandon them!"

"You think I don't know that? But you heard their final command—we are to retreat if we don't hear from them! Now sit back down and obey or I'll have you tossed in the brig!"

The officer sat back down.

Isaador sighed as the ship turned around to return to base. Happily, the drones didn't give chase to the retreating fleet. Without shields and with most of their cannons destroyed, they were the only thing left to defend the base.

"Now our only hope lies with Goymaalt and the others on Pfoff," Isaador said sadly.

"If you could touch the alien sand and hear the cries of strange birds and watch them wheel in another sky, would that satisfy you?" — Doctor Who, *An Unearthly Child*

CHAPTER 18:
THE LOST WORLD

The *Silver Bullet,* now flying in stealth mode, whizzed over the shallow Venusian seas.

"What beautiful seas you have," Aethra said, admiringly. She daydreamed about what it would be like to swim in the waters of the alien world and meet the unfamiliar creatures that lived within its depths.

"Yes, it's a pity that they're slowly evaporating away. Our scientists estimate that in a little over a thousand of your years, there will be almost nothing left of them." Goymaalt replied.

"Even so, it's a lovely world." Naomi commented.

Indeed it was, Matt thought. He'd remembered seeing photos of the desolate landscape of the Earth's sister planet taken by a Soviet space probe a few decades ago. It was difficult to believe that this was the same planet as the one he now found himself flying over. They'd flown over lush forests and green plains before reaching the open ocean - quite a far cry from the barren wasteland in the Soviet pictures. The skies over the oceans had a slightly yellowish tint to them, in the open spots that weren't covered by layers of thick clouds. The sun loomed much larger in the sky.

Every so often, they would see enormous plumes of smoke spiraling upwards. Goymaalt had already explained that these were volcanoes, the gasses they were venting into the atmosphere from deep within the planet being the main culprit contributing to its warming. Long ago, something the First Generation had done while drilling for new sources of energy had triggered this planet wide increase in volcanic activity.

"A thousand years? You still have plenty of time! I'm surprised that your people are so focused on going to a new world right now." Carlos remarked.

"Our people take great pride in thinking in long terms, of focusing on the big picture, as you might say. It appears to be one of the key differences between us. Your inability to think beyond the needs of the present is dooming your world, too. It was difficult for Drogalla to convince our people to aid your planet because many of our people felt that your destruction in your near future is inevitable. What difference would it make if it came a little sooner at the hands of the Baandergi, rather than by your own? Thankfully, Drogalla was able to convince them that your people might grow up someday to take responsibility for your future. That you might put the needs of the many above your own greed. Even if you do not, the Leader believes that you deserve to live out whatever time you may have left in the manner of your own choosing." Goymaalt said, perhaps oblivious to how harshly judgemental the statement sounded.

"It *is* frustrating how little action there's been on the Earth's ecological crises. My organization, the Temple of the Old Gods, has been using magic to try and slow down some of the worst effects, but there are limits to what even we can do. Unfortunately, even though the other Guilds wield great influence, they're too focused on their own profit to use that influence to change things. Too often their interests align with those of the polluters, or they *are* the polluters." April admitted in embarrassment. She was proud that her wife Wendy had focused their group on using magic to heal the planet when she came to power, but they couldn't fix the problem all by themselves.

"Hey, I'm doing my bit! One of the first things I did was switch over my entire fleet to nuclear power when I became queen." Aethra said proudly.

"Nuclear! And what do you do with all those spent fuel rods?" Penny, who'd always been a bit of a "tree hugger", asked. She appreciated the fact that nuclear power didn't emit greenhouse gasses, but it annoyed her that people who touted it as a solution seemed to forget that it produced radioactive waste that would remain dangerous for millennia to come.

"I can answer that one. We take it up into space in this very ship and shoot it out of the airlock once we're far enough out. I've made quite a few of those runs myself." Major Thompson told her.

"Great! More space junk!" Penny complained, although she did grudgingly suppose this was better than storing it on Earth. She looked over at Jim, who was staring out at the vistas of Venus with his mouth all agape, revealing his mean looking fangs. The way he looked out upon the planet was almost *rapturous*—as if he was having a religious experience. She could've sworn she even saw the glimmer of a tear in the corner of his eye. It all just served to remind her of how much she still didn't know or understand about him. The man she thought she knew was light years away from the reality of who he was—literally. How could she ever hope to bridge such a divide? Should she even try?

"Oh look! Ships!" Aethra said with the enthusiasm of a child. Penny figured it must be incredibly interesting for someone who was a Pirate Queen to see the boats of another planet.

The flotilla of ships ahead of them looked like oversized pontoon boats to Matt, if pontoon boats had rows of gun turrets on them.

"Those are Baandergi naval vessels! The equivalent of your aircraft carriers. It's unusual to see them so far out in international waters, we're still some distance from their home islands." Goymaalt said suspiciously.

The red beam of a Destructo-Ray suddenly appeared in front of the *Silver Bullet,* narrowly missing it.

"What the heck was that?" Matt asked in alarm.

"They're firing on us!" Major Thompson shouted as he took the ship into an evasive maneuver, causing it to tilt to one side.

"And they're launching saucers!" Goymaalt said, pointing at the approaching ships.

"I thought this thing was in stealth mode?" Matt asked.

"It is, but they must have some way of detecting us, anyway! If it's any consolation, they don't seem to know *precisely* where we are. They just have a general idea. Either that, or they're all just really shitty shots!" Thompson replied as he angled the ship up to avoid another blast.

"When flying in an atmosphere, they can track our shrouded ships by the air they displace. That's probably how they're doing it." Goymaalt explained quickly.

The ship rocked as it was hit by a shot from one of the saucers.

"Shitty shots, huh? It feels like they're learning pretty fast!" Matt snorted.

"Everyone gets a little lucky every now and then! Relax! Our shields are still holding!" The Major told them.

"Aren't we gonna shoot back?" Naomi asked, a note of fear in her voice.

"I'm under orders not to kill anyone, remember? Unless you'd like to change your mind, Ma'am?" Thompson looked over his shoulder briefly to glare at April accusingly. It was evident what he thought about these orders. It was becoming increasingly more difficult for him to avoid all these random blasts of energy now lighting up the skies all around them.

"I think we can handle this problem for you, Major," April said. She looked at Carlos, Randy, and Prospero. "If we combine our magic to cast a baffle spell out there, it should even things up a bit What do you say?"

"Good thinking!" Carlos, who was an expert in the military applications of magic, agreed. The magic users all began chanting the words of the spell in unison, mirroring each other's hand movements as they concentrated their power.

The sky outside the ship was suffused with an emerald glow for a moment. The saucers buzzing around them started dropping into the ocean like stones. The guns of the navy ships below them suddenly fell silent.

"What'd you just do?" Penny asked in astonishment.

Carlos smiled at Penny. "It's kind of the magical equivalent of an electromagnetic pulse, it shuts down or confuses electronics for a few minutes. It should buy us enough time to get away from them, if you don't mind putting the pedal to the metal, Major?"

"Yessir!" Thompson replied with gusto, happy to receive an order he could agree with wholeheartedly. The ship picked up speed, causing a sonic boom as it zoomed away from the scene of the ambush.

Goymaalt still looked troubled. "I don't like this. It's like they were expecting us. Someone must've tipped them off to our mission here. Drogalla has suspected that we have a spy in our midst for some time."

"Kergaali was bragging about having a spy right before she escaped." Randy confirmed.

"Great! So can we expect more trouble like that?" Matt grumbled.

"We've already found it!" Major Thompson shouted as he brought the ship down into a nosedive, then back up again so quickly that Naomi felt like she might lose her lunch. On the screen, ahead she could see dozens of saucers zipping towards them, guns blazing.

"Damn! That was fast!" She remarked.

"Careful! You're spilling Hi-Fi everywhere!" Jim growled (literally) as he was splashed with silvery droplets. Although his futuristic bucket was quite fancy, it wasn't so fancy that it had a top on it. That's a whole new level of bucket fanciness which is apparently even the super science of Venus.

"Thanks to that little burst of speed we just put on, we're now in their airspace." Goymaalt explained.

"Any more magic tricks you might have up your sleeve would be greatly appreciated right now, sirs and ma'am!" Thompson exclaimed as the *Silver Bullet* was jolted by another direct hit.

Goymaalt's eyes narrowed. "You may not need magic, these are all drone fighters! You can tell by the little aerials on top of them. They have no living pilots."

"Finally! Time for a little payback!" Thompson said as he let loose with the *Silver Bullet's* powerful weapons, striking several of the drones ahead of them, instantly sending them twirling into the waves below. The drone ships were cheaply made and didn't have force fields protecting them.

"A little magic could still help us, though. Another baffle spell?" Randy suggested.

"Nah, if we don't have to worry about killing anyone let's do something a little more fun this time!" Prospero said.

"What are you thinking of?" April asked him, almost afraid to find out what kind of combat spell Prospero considered being "fun."

"Chain lightning!" Prospero smiled wolfishly, which wasn't very difficult for him to do considering that he used to be a werewolf.

"Oh! Yeah, that *is* a fun one!" Carlos agreed.

Again, the magic users began saying all kinds of things that sounded like so many nonsense words to everyone else inside the ship and gesticulating like people in the throes of some kind of spasm. They looked really silly to tell the truth. High Magick isn't always the most dignified looking of arts, but the results often offset the fact that you just made yourself look like an idiot. Sometimes it was hard for Matt to keep a straight face when he watched them do something like this, but he knew how much they hated to be mocked for it. He limited himself to looking over at Naomi with a look on his face that practically said, "get a load of these weirdos!" She covered her mouth so they wouldn't see her muffled laugh.

Outside the ship, storm clouds suddenly gathered over them, a brilliant blue bolt of lightning burst out of one cloud, then another, followed by another, repeatedly. Each of these bolts found a drone saucer, then leapt from that saucer to the next nearest one, and kept on going until all the saucers had been struck. Thunder rumbled as the drones splashed down into the sea, throwing up geysers of water as they struck the water.

"Okay, now that *was* pretty fucking cool," Jim said appreciatively.

"Indeed." Goymaalt said, in awe of this strange force that these humans wielded. There was nothing like it on Pfoff. The Deputy Leader was just happy that these magic-users were on their side. They could all see the hazy shoreline of one of the Baandergi islands appearing on the horizon.

"We're almost there." Major Thompson noted superfluously.

"I think we should also do a spell to better hide the *Silver Bullet* from their sensors. It might be more effective than technological cloaking alone." Randy said.

"You could've done that all along and you're only bringing it up now?" Major Thompson said, annoyance coloring his tone.

Randy shrugged. "Hey, I just thought of it now. Nobody's perfect. I've had a lot on my mind lately." It was true. Randy felt like his head would explode. His mother showing up on his doorstep this morning, his argument with Penny earlier, Kergaali's betrayal, followed by Anne's deception and threatening of Aethra. It was all too much to process. On top of that, he was worried about his son back on Earth, and their chances of making this desperate plan work. He definitely had a thing or two to say to that other Kergaali once they found the Supreme Leader. He was just trying to work out exactly what he'd say.

"Yes, an excellent suggestion." April said approvingly, looking at Randy like he was her star pupil. It wasn't too far from the truth. He *was* the star pupil of her wife, Wendy, who had been mentoring Randy around the same time that they'd begun dating. April had sometimes assisted her wife in Randy's training, and like Wendy, she often thought of him as an unofficial son. It wasn't for nothing that her daughter Celine called him "Uncle Randy", he was like one of the family, more so than her own blood relations, who'd never accepted her sexuality or witchy ways.

Once again, the magic users went into paroxysmal chanting and undulating, earning another knowing exchange of glances between Matt and Naomi over the goofiness of it all.

The spell was cast, and they felt the ship slow down as it approached the coastline of Baandergiland. Or Baandergia. Or Baandergistan, or whatever it was that they called their homeland. Nobody had ever gotten around to explaining what the place was actually called.

"Well, here we are. Where do you want me to land?" Major Thompson asked Goymaalt.

"See that bit of forest over there? See if you can find a clearing to land in." The Deputy Leader told him.

Thompson was indeed able to find a bald spot in the woods large enough for him to touch down in, bringing the ship to the ground so gently that no one inside felt it land.

They all started unstrapping from their seats, except for the magic users, who'd already had to do so earlier in order to do the movements needed to cast their spells. Matt slid the case holding the *Vermillion Avenger* out from beneath his seat and snapped it open, handing Naomi her "angel sword" as he liked to call it, then mentally commanding his own weapon to fly out and assume it's typical position hovering just over his right shoulder. The humans all put on their helmets, while Penny, Randy, and Jim merely pressed a button on their Federation space suits that caused a bubble to surround their heads.

Randy opened up the hatch and watched the landing ramp move down.

"Hey, hold up for a sec, pal. Don't anyone go outside just yet," Matt told him.

"Sure, what's up?" Randy asked in confusion.

"Let Naomi go out first. She hasn't said anything about it, but I know how badly she wants to be the first human to set foot on Venus. Every history professor secretly wants to make a little history themselves." He smiled over at her.

Naomi felt herself tearing up. How well he knew her! She tried to say "Thank you." But her voice caught in her throat and she just mouthed the words.

Matt waved away her words. "Happy early Valentine's Day, baby. Don't say I never bring you anywhere fancy!"

She laughed and did a little bow to the whole group as she made her way past Randy at the top of the ramp. Matt moved to the top of the ramp too, so he could watch her as she slowly walked down it. As she walked, she noted differences in the local vegetation from their earthly equivalents which hadn't been noticeable from the air. The trees actually looked more like enormous mushrooms, albeit mushrooms with green caps. Much of the underbrush was made up of plants that looked like cacti—but were rust colored and lacked thorns.

As she stepped foot off of the ramp, she turned to look up at them. "That's one small step for me, one giant leap for humans!" Now she was crying, but it was happy crying. She realized that her mascara was probably running. It was okay, Penny's mascara always looked like that. They could be twinsies!

"Can I take this thing off? I wanna breathe the air of another planet, if only for a minute. It won't kill me or anything will it? Just for a few minutes?" She looked up at Goymaalt questioningly.

"The air is quite breathable. It's the radiation we were worried about, and honestly, I think Drogalla was being overly cautious about that. Our planet isn't *that* much more radioactive than Earth is. The clouds deflect most of it back into space. You'll be fine."

"You know, considering that we're about 750 million years in the past, this technically makes me the first human to ever walk on another heavenly body—period. I beat Neil Armstrong! Me, little old Dr. Naomi Waters-Spike! It won't be in any history book because of Guild secrecy, but *I'll* always know who was first." Naomi said as she unscrewed the helmet from her space suit, which was actually kind of a difficult process.

"Oh, brother! Now I'm never gonna hear the end of this! Maybe this wasn't such a good idea after all?" Matt said playfully. "Ya know, I almost forgot about the time travel aspect of all this. Hey, don't step on any butterflies while you're down there!" Matt called down to her. He was referring to one of his favorite classic sci-fi stories, "A Sound of Thunder" wherein a time traveler steps on a butterfly in the past and completely changes history.

Randy knew the story, too. "We're on another planet, Matt. She can step on all the butterflies she wants to, it shouldn't affect human history.

"Oh yeah. Step away then!" Matt said.

"What's a butterfly?" Goymaalt wondered aloud. The Deputy Leader had made an extensive study of the Earth, but there were still many gaps in their knowledge. Goymaalt found it kind of cute what a fuss these humans were making over something as routine as getting off of a saucer, then recalled their own excitement the first time they had walked on Luna and understood it a little better.

Naomi lifted the helmet from her head and took in a deep, long breath—and immediately regretted it. The air was thin, yet somehow managed to be hot, heavy, and humid at the same time. But that wasn't the worst part. The worst part was the smell.

"Ugh. No offense, Goymaalt, but your planet kind of smells like ass. Why does your planet smell like one big fart?" Naomi said as she returned the helmet to her head, hoping she hadn't captured too much of the foul stench inside it.

Goymaalt looked perplexed for a moment as they struggled to recall the meaning of such human words as "ass" and "fart," then remembered. "Ah, it wasn't always so. It's due to all the sulphur in the air from the volcanoes. We've gotten so used to it that we don't even think about it anymore."

Now that Naomi had been allowed to have her brief moment of space pioneering, the others made their way down the ramp too, all except for Major Thompson, who stood at the top of the ramp. He'd put on the spare space suit Matt had given him, but hadn't bothered to put on the helmet.

"Oh yeah, it really does smell pretty nasty." He said, wrinkling his nose.

April looked up at him. "Major," she started.

"I know, I know! Stay with the ship! I wasn't born yesterday, I know you guys might need to make a fast getaway. I'll keep the engines purring. Hopefully, your spell will stop them from finding me."

"It should do the job." Randy told him.

Thompson nodded. "Okay then, good luck everybody. Call me if you need me." There was a chorus of goodbyes as he ducked his head back inside the ship. The ramp began to slowly retract, now making the ship entirely invisible.

"So what now?" Matt asked the group.

"We're not very far from a coastal settlement, you can see it over there." Goymaalt pointed over the strange mushroom tree tops. They could barely make out the rooftops of a series of buildings in the distance. "It's a resort town. Many of the homes will be empty at this time of year. There should be at least one Nethersphere terminal inside which we can make use of. Most people own several."

"Just like LBI, back home, huh?" Matt said to Naomi. He was referring to Long Beach Island, a popular tourist spot across the bay from the rural town where they'd both grown up. It, too, was full of empty homes during the off season.

"Not quite the same thing, dear." Naomi told him.

"How is your robotic companion, Jim? Is it ready yet?" Goymaalt asked him.

Jim once again stuck a finger in the bucket. "As ready as he'll ever be, despite a little spillage back there. C'mon out Hi-Fi, we need you." The silvery liquid gushed out over one side of the bucket, forming a pool on the ground. It then rose and assumed the familiar form of the diminutive machine.

"Hi-Fi reporting for duty, sir!" the robot said and saluted Jim.

"Go ahead and bond with Penny again. I still need you to keep her safe," Jim commanded.

Penny felt a familiar tingle of excitement as Hi-Fi spread out over her once again.

I missed you, little robo-dude! Penny thought.

It's nice to be bonded to you again, too, Mistress. Hi-Fi replied. Even though she knew he just programmed to say things like that, it still felt good to hear him say it.

"You look good in chrome, kid." Matt, who had never seen her like this before, commented.

"Thanks. So how are we going to get into town? Are we walking? And by the way, if none of you have noticed, we're not exactly the most inconspicuous looking group of people, are we? What are we going to do about that?" Penny asked.

"I was thinking we can teleport into town. As for our appearance, well, we have a spell for that too," April replied.

"A glamor spell, right?" Naomi said eagerly. She'd read about this kind of spell plenty of times while researching the history of the Temple of the Old Gods. She'd even seen it done once before, years ago, when the witch her daughter was named after had used one to disguise herself.

"Exactly." April confirmed.

"Oh boy. I always wanted to be glamorous. Can you take a few pounds off my belly? Maybe make my butt look more firm?" Matt joked.

"Matthew, we can make you look positively gorgeous!" April promised.

The magic users once again conducted a brief and undignified looking ritual to disguise themselves. They could all see their weapons once the spell was completed, but no one else could. For the female members of the group, the change wasn't very dramatic. They looked the same, except that their space suits were now invisible and instead they appeared to be dressed in Venusian clothing and had antennas coming out of their heads. Aethra was missing her gills and her bluish skin tone, appearing more human than she typically did, ironic considering that she was supposed to be a Venusian.

For the males in the group, it was another matter entirely. They now all appeared to be women. Jim looked like his human self dressed in drag, which was actually quite fetching. Prospero now looked like a matronly old sage, Carlos took on the form of a curvaceous Latina, Randy was a statuesque, ebon-haired beauty, and Matt, as promised, was gorgeous.

"Oh, very nice!" Naomi smiled and pinched his ass.

"Great, I haven't even been a woman for a minute and already I'm being objectified!" he complained sarcastically.

"Wow, Matt! You're a real hottie! I'd do ya!" Randy teased and made a kissy face at him.

"Buddy, you'd do *anyone* if given half a chance!" Matt snapped back as he looked in wonder at his significantly more slender arms. Then he realized that he may've just offended Aethra and Penny with that comment. "Uh, not to say that you aren't naturally very lovely, Aethra. Gills and all. You too, Pen." He added clumsily.

Aethra laughed. "It's okay, Matt. I know what you mean, and it's totally true." She nudged Randy playfully in the ribs.

Randy blushed. "No, it isn't! While I can appreciate the beauty in everyone, both physically and metaphorically, I still have very exacting standards in regards to..."

"The lady doth protest too much, methinks!" Prospero cut him off. Oftentimes, nobody knew what the old codger was on about when he indulged in his odd penchant for quoting Shakespeare, but this time, the quote landed right on the money. Even the stoic Goymaalt got a chuckle out of it.

"These disguises should serve us well. And you say you can also use this magic of yours to teleport us into town too? It amazes me you're able to accomplish such wonders without using machines. Someday, you'll have to explain how it's all possible to me," Goymaalt said.

"Don't you worry, if you give my pal here half a chance, he'll be more than happy to bore your ass off trying to explain it in scientific terms. Be prepared to be confused by lots of dull talk about holographic universes and quantum states as he regales you with his explanation of how the cosmos works!" Matt said, clapping Randy on the back.

Aethra laughed again. "It's true, it's so true!"

"Damn straight it is, Pirate Queen!" Matt said and did a high five with her.

"I second that motion!" Penny smiled and did a high five with Aethra, too. She'd had to listen to her fair share of that shit from Randy during their years together.

"Can we just get out of here already?" Randy said, blushing so hard now that he was in danger of blending in with those red cactus-looking plants around them.

"Okay everyone, join hands. Let's get moving." April said. They all did so. There was more eldritch sounding chanting as the spell was worked, and then they were gone.

They reappeared in a flash of light, right in the middle of some kind of parade on what looked like a boardwalk.

Goymaalt slapped their forehead. "Oh, frazula!" The Deputy Leader swore. "I forgot, today is Demarcation Day! It's like Baandergi Independence Day!"

There was clapping as they appeared. Apparently, everyone in the crowd thought they were just part of the show

"What now? Half the town just saw us materialize out of thin air!" Penny asked in alarm

"Yeah, but these people have teleportation technology, so that doesn't seem as weird to them as it would if it happened on Earth! Try to keep up and don't forget to smile and wave and we should be just fine, I think." Matt said.

Naomi hated parades. "I thought this was supposed to be a more advanced society, and yet they still haven't figured out how lame parades are?" She griped.

"This is serious, though. With this many people in town for the parade, it'll be much harder to find an empty home. We might have to just take whatever we can get." Goymaalt said.

"No problem! The wizards took out like a bazillion saucers with their magic back there. A little home invasion should be child's play," Jim said.

Just then, a group of Venusians dressed in armor similar to that worn by the Saawgauth's Elite Troopers appeared on the edge of the crowd and started shoving their way towards the group. One of them raised an arm and fired a shot from their weapon. The shot missed and instead set a float behind the group aflame. The Venusians on the float screamed and jumped off, abandoning the flaming vehicle. Many of the people in the crowd started screaming as well.

"Baandergi security forces! Somehow they've seen through our disguises!" Goymaalt shouted to them.

It was then that Randy noticed that every few hundred feet along the boardwalk there were poles, and atop those poles were what looked unmistakably like security cameras. No matter what planet you were on, big brother was still watching.

"Glamor spells only fool living eyes, not electronic ones!" he explained right before he had to conjure up a glowing green shield to deflect another blast from the approaching security troopers. The crowd was in complete chaos now, trampling each other as they fled the scene.

The Baandergi forces were almost right on top of them, using the fact that their armor allowed them to fly to quickly encircle the group. The magic users were doing their best to repel their shots with their force fields. Too busy at the moment with protecting the others to use their magic more offensively.

Matt wasted no time in using the blunt end of the *Vermilion Avenger* to bat at the soldiers, but this seemed to have little effect on them because of their armor, so he found himself switching to using the blade of the weapon to slicing the barrels off of their weapons.

"Happy Demarcation Day, motherfucker!" Matt shouted as he cut the end off of one of the guns.

"Matt! Really! And here I thought you were above doing cheesy action movie-style one-liners?" Randy chided him.

Matt shrugged. "Every once in a while you have to cut loose and live a little, ya know?"

Naomi was busy ensnaring their opponents with the energy nets that her flaming angel sword could produce. Many years earlier, she and Randy had been caught in one of these nets and she knew that there was no way out of them, unless the person who created the net willed it to go away, or the sword ran out of power. So it was with some alarm that she saw one of the troopers she'd just caught bust out and continued to fly towards her. She saw the flames on her sword sputter out and die.

Ah well, I can't complain. The ambrosia that powered that thing lasted almost twenty years! She thought. Instead, she watched with amusement as the trooper smashed into the force field surrounding her, which was invisible to them because of the glamor spell, and slid down the side of it. She was happy that she'd remembered to put on her magic ring right before they'd teleported out. She was wearing it over the glove of her space suit, as it automatically adjusted itself to fit whatever hand it was placed upon. She calmly pulled out the pistol Goymaalt had given them and started searching for targets.

Beside her, Aethra was having great fun firing away at the troopers with her own pistol. For her, it was moments like this that made life worth living. She was something of an adrenaline junkie, if you hadn't already figured that out. "By Neptune's beard, *this* was worth the trip!" She enthused.

"It is definitely oddly satisfying." Penny admitted, back to using her hammer hands on the troops, in the process saving Aethra's bacon as the trooper she just clocked was about to shoot the Pirate Queen. Penny then flew up into the air and replicated the same move she had used back at the moon base, spinning around in the air and using her hammers to knock out several troopers at once. She could only imagine how ridiculous it all looked from the perspective of anyone not viewing the fight through the revealing electronic eyes of a camera.

Meanwhile, as more of the enemy fell, the magic users were able to concentrate less on defense. They all used a spell that allowed them to throw their targets around like rag dolls, slamming their heads into each other, or tossing them against the sides of buildings until they passed out.

In short order, they had defeated all the troopers that had been sent against them.

"We'd better get out of here before they send some backup." Matt said.

"Agreed, but first let's do a spell that will make us all completely invisible, even to cameras." April said.

"Why didn't you just do that to begin with?" Goymaalt asked.

"Because such spells only last for a few minutes. Once we do it, we'll have to find a house quickly." Carlos hastily explained.

The magic users did the spell as quickly as they could. Just in time, as it turned out to be. No sooner had they made themselves invisible, than a hovering armored transport truck pulled up nearby. The end of it opened up and began disgorging more of the armored troopers. Fortunately, although they were all invisible they could see one another, restored to their pre-glamor states as the new spell had replaced the previous one.

"This way, there are homes right on the other side of the boardwalk." Goymaalt whispered. They all did a kind of walk/run away from the scene of the fight, careful not to bump into any of the fallen troops or newly arriving ones as the soldiers started fanning out to search the area

Goymaalt led them down an alleyway and onto a narrow street towards the first house they could see that didn't have a personal vehicle parked in front of it. The Venusian buildings were generally of a more organic shape, with few right angles. "This one should serve our purposes nicely I think." The Deputy Leader told them.

"This place? Hold on a sec, don't we specifically need a Second Generation Nethersphere terminal? How do we know that this is a 2nd Generation Venusian's house?" Matt asked.

"All houses are Second Generation houses. We of the Third Generation are given a room inside, or sometimes a separate outbuilding." Goymaalt explained.

April shook her head in disgust. "Shit! They really do treat you people like second-class citizens!" *The control chip must be a very effective piece of technology to prevent them from seeing something so obvious*! She thought.

"We can debate the politics of it later. We need to get inside before this invisibility spell wears off. There are still cameras on this street!" Prospero said, pointing at one of the poles nearby.

"There always will be. This is what you humans would call a 'police state.'" Goymaalt replied.

Randy muttered a quick spell and twisted the doorknob. The door swung open. "I've already taken care of it, c'mon!"

They all followed him inside, through what looked like a kitchen. The home invaders were struck by how similar the alien house's interior was to one from Earth. From an adjoining room, they could all hear what sounded like a low moaning sound. Randy, who was still in the lead, held up a hand. "You hear that? We're not alone here!" he whispered.

They carefully crept into the next room, mindful that even though they were invisible, noises could still give them away. They saw a Venusian writhing around on the carpet and moaning, arms outstretched as if the hands were cupping some unseen thing. On the alien's head was completely some sort of elaborate helmet, and the Venusian was wearing a suit that was even more tight fitting than usual and was studded with sensors.

"Wow. Is that one doing what I think they're doing?" Matt asked.

"I think so," Naomi replied. "Some kind of virtual reality sex thing."

"Eww. It's like walking in on someone who's spanking the monkey. I thought the Baandergi were against this kind of thing?" Penny said.

"That's the strange thing about them. They're against anything like this if it happens in person, but in the virtual space of the Nethersphere, everything is allowed, for the Second Generation at least. The Third Generation still has certain restrictions on what they can do on the network. The Baandergi, whether they are of the 3rd or even the Second Generation, have almost no personal freedom in their real lives. Is it so surprising that they spend most of their time online?" Goymaalt explained.

"What a bunch of hypocrites!" April said hotly.

"Hypo-crite? I don't know that word," Goymaalt confessed.

"It means you say one thing while doing another. If your people don't have a word for it, you should really come up with one. It seems pretty rampant in this world!" Naomi told Goymaalt.

"We just call them liars." Goymaalt replied.

Carlos and Prospero had left the main group to search the rest of the rooms. In a nearby room, Carlos found a pair of what looked like seven or eight-year-old girls who shared a bedroom. They, too, were wearing the same strange helmets as their mother. Thankfully, they appeared to be engaged in a different type of activity. One of them was running in place, while the other was sitting on a bed and making swiping motions in the air.

"There's two kids in here too. They're all connected to the Nethersphere." Carlos whispered as they rejoined the group in the room with the mother.

Suddenly, all the members of the group shimmered with an ethereal silver light, which disappeared as quickly as it had shown up.

"What was that?" Jim asked.

"The spell just wore off." Randy explained. "It hardly matters now, these people are so wrapped up in what they're doing online that they still won't even know we're here."

"What're we gonna do with them?" Matt inquired. "I didn't sign up to hurt anyone's kids!"

"Of course not! None of us wants that! We'll just do a simple spell that will put them to sleep for a few hours; nobody will get hurt." April promised. The other magic users nodded in agreement and moved off to perform the sleeping spell on the occupants of the house. The mother ceased writhing on the floor and went limp.

"Do they have a shower here? I think I need to hydrate." Aethra asked.

"I saw one at the top of the steps, Lass." Prospero answered.

"Right. So how many of these Nethersphere helmets did we find in the house?" April asked.

"4 of them. Mom's, the ones in the twin's bedroom, and one in an empty bedroom." Carlos reported.

"That probably belongs to the Third Generation member of the household, who's probably at work right now, that one won't do us any good. So we have 3 that we can use." Goymaalt told them.

"That's perfect. We've got 3 human mothers here!" Naomi smiled back.

"Mistress Penny won't need one. You can give hers to someone else," Hi-Fi chimed in. "If I'm able to connect to the Nethersphere, she will automatically be connected, too. In fact, I might be able to bring more of you in by partially bonding with you."

"I'll take the helmet you were gonna give to Penny. There's a few things I think I'd like to say to that other Kergaali." Randy said.

"Okay, let's go get those helmets." April ordered them. The group quickly went to work. Randy removed the helmet from the mother and noted that there was no antenna sprouting out of their head. He carried the mother upstairs to one of the bedrooms, placing them on a bed. The others collected the children's helmets, which thankfully did not appear to be child sized.

"Okay, well, first things first," Jim said. He turned to face Penny, but she wasn't who he was planning on addressing. "Hi-Fi, it's time to see if you can interface with one of these things and locate the other Kergaali. Let us know as soon as you find her."

"Yessir!" Hi-Fi's voice replied from somewhere on Penny's body as a tendril of silver liquid shot from her wrist and flowed over the headset that Randy had pulled off of the head of the mother he'd put to sleep. "Interface successful. Beginning search...." the robot updated them.

Back on the moon and about 750 million years in the future, Kergaali was not pleased. Well, okay, that's a bit of an exaggeration. The Supreme Leader *was* pleased with the victory they'd scored against the Saawgauth, and the death of the hated Drogalla. Kergaali was even extremely happy that their Duplo-Rays had already produced two of the Federation ships, with a third one nearing completion within the next hour. However, Kergaali was *not* pleased with the reports coming in from the other end of the Time Tunnel on Pfoff. The human's space ship had eluded the Baandergi saucers not once, but twice! They'd made landfall in the homeland and even though their omnipresent cameras had quickly detected them, they'd defeated their security forces only to disappear again.

It was unacceptable!

There was a saying which the humans had, and which was actually somewhat wise for something dreamed up by a bunch of savages: if you want a job done right, do it yourself. To this end, Kergaali, had resolved to go through the Time Tunnel and personally supervise this part of the operation.

As the Supreme Leader stood before the massive portal, Kergaali turned to face Sheerperf. "As soon as that 3rd ship is finished, load all three with as many neutron missiles as you can and begin the purification."

"With only three ships? Are you certain?" Sheerperf asked nervously.

"It should be sufficient. These ships are far more advanced. The humans will never know what hit them!"

"I obey, Supreme Leader! For the Glory of Pfoff!" Sheerperf saluted.

"For the Glory of Pfoff!" The Supreme Leader saluted back.

"Happy hunting!" Sheerperf added.

"Yes, it *will* be a happy hunt! I'll enjoy destroying these troublesome humans once and for all!" Kergaali said, a predatory glint showing in the Supreme Leader's cat-like eyes.

The next moment, Kergaali plunged through the Time Tunnel and was gone.

CHAPTER 19:
THE DUEL

Kergaali re-emerged at a Baandergi base on Pfoff, helmeted troopers on the other end snapped out salutes as the Supreme Leader walked past them and up a ramp into a large golden saucer.

As Kergaali settled into a command chair, the bridge crew, who had all been standing at attention, saluted and took their seats at a signal from the Supreme Leader. Waabotel, a somewhat more elderly officer, scuttled forward.

"The ship is ready to depart, as commanded, Supreme Leader."

"Then let's take it up! Get me to the last known position of the enemy invaders!" Kergaali commanded.

The ship wobbled upwards, then shot off like a rocket.

"We should be there momentarily. Is there anything I can get for you in the meantime, Supreme Leader?" Waabotel inquired.

"Yes, display the live feed from the security cameras inside all the buildings in that town for me." Kergaali replied.

"From *inside* the buildings, Supreme Leader?" Waabotel asked in a panicky voice. All the Baandergi buildings had hidden cameras in every room, however this was a state secret which was not widely known. Waabotel was privy to such knowledge, but the crew flying the ship was not. It might be necessary to *silence* them when the mission was completed to keep the secret. Such a wanton waste of lives was not something that Waabotel enjoyed being a part of.

"You heard my command, don't make me repeat it!" Kergaali said threateningly.

"Yes, of course, Supreme Leader!"

Waabotel tapped away at the mini computer on their wrist and within seconds a holographic display appeared before Kergaali. It was made up of hundreds of small boxes, and inside each box was a view of the insides of various structures in the resort town. Kergaali studied them all for a few moments, muttering and occasionally touching some of the squares and swiping them away. The ones which were swiped away were quickly replaced by new ones.

Then one of them caught the Supreme Leader's eye. An image of someone showering. What was so odd about this person was the odd bluish tint to their skin, and the large flaps that opened and closed as the water rained down.

"The fish being! Aethra!" Kergaali shouted in triumph. "I have them now!"

The Supreme Leader tapped on the image of Aethra. It enlarged and opened up more boxes that displayed other images from inside that home. Kergaali recognized Randy, Jim, Penny as well as April and Prospero. There were a few more humans there that the Supreme Leader didn't know. They were all standing around, looking at a Nethersphere terminal crown that was coated in silver. "How many humans *are* there here on Pfoff? It's an infestation!"

Then Kergaali noticed someone standing among all the humans. Could it be? Yes, it was! Goymaalt was with them, the Deputy Leader of the Saawgauth! This day had already seen the destruction of Drogalla, now would it also bring the death of Goymaalt too? With both of their highest ranking leaders gone, the enemy would be helpless! This opportunity was too good to waste!

The Supreme Leader glared at Waabotel through the hologram of Aethra, who had just turned off the water and was now toweling herself off.

"Correct course to land in front of this home! Forward the address to my security forces already on the ground. Have them surrounded, but do not engage until I arrive!" Kergaali commanded.

"Oh, and Waabotel?"

"Yes, Supreme Leader?"

"Bring me a sword!"

Inside the house, they all waited while Hi-Fi continued his search. "This would be much simpler if I knew a bit more about the Supreme Leader's personal quirks and interests." The robot complained.

"Let's see, Kergaali's hobbies include global conquest and manipulative mind games," Jim quipped

"That's not very helpful, Master." Hi-Fi observed.

"Sorry, we didn't chat much about anything other than how to stop this invasion. Just keep at it," Jim commanded.

Aethra came down the stairs, dressed in her space suit again.

"That sure was fast!" Randy observed.

"I just needed a little refreshing—besides, I couldn't take much of the smell of this place." She replied

"Whew! I can sure understand that feeling!" Naomi agreed.

Just then, all hell broke loose. Armored troopers like the ones they'd fought earlier came crashing through all the windows at the same time.

"How the hell do these people keep on finding us?" Matt grumbled as he sent forth the *Vermilion Avenger* to slice off the gun barrel of the closest trooper, then flipped the sword around to bat them into the wall with as much force as he could muster.

The magic users summoned forth their green shields again, while Goymaalt, Jim, Naomi, Matt and Aethra broke out their pistols and started shooting the troopers that were pouring in through the windows. As soon as one fell, another one would push through the window.

Hi-Fi withdrew himself from the Nethersphere helmet.

What are you doing? You've gotta find Kergaali! Penny screamed in her mind.

Negative, Mistress. In case of an attack, your protection has been coded as being a higher priority by Master Jim. He replied.

How sweet of him! Penny thought as she formed her hands into hammers and got to work on the nearest trooper.

The front door came crashing down, and Kergaali sauntered in.

"I don't believe it! Look who just joined the party!" Jim said as he blasted another trooper from behind the safety of Randy's shield.

He leveled his pistol at Kergaali and squeezed off a shot. "You blew up my ship, you crazy bitch!" he shouted.

Kergaali ducked it effortlessly and smiled. Two troopers escorting Kergaali fired back at Jim, forcing him to duck down behind the shield. "Ah, so you enjoyed finding my parting gift? Still slumming it up with these humans, I see? Don't worry, I'm not here for you. I'm here for the Deputy Leader!"

Kergaali unsheathed a sword hanging from their belt, waving it in the air. "Goymaalt! Face me! I challenge you to the Horaag Kamal!" The Supreme Leader bellowed.

"The Horaag Kamal? Only you Baandergi would keep alive such a barbaric custom!" Goymaalt shouted back derisively.

What the fuck is a "Horaag Kamal"? Penny, who was busy bashing some troopers nearby, wondered.

The Horag Kamal is an ancient tradition instituted by the Old Masters of the First Generation. They would settle personal disputes by pitting their slaves against one another in a combat to the death for their own amusement. Despite the general prohibition that all Venusian Nations have against killing their own people, the Baandergi still make an exception for the Horag Kamal. Allegedly, the Baandergi make many such exceptions! Hi-Fi explained.

Shit! And they call us savages! Penny thought.

Indeed, Mistress! Hi-Fi agreed.

Geez, Hi-Fi you sure know a whole lot about the culture and history of Venus. How is that? Penny asked the robot.

I'm not authorized to speak on that subject, Mistress. Hi-Fi replied evasively.

Penny was starting to form her own ideas about why he was so opaque on that point.

Kergaali was just getting started. "Oh, so then what you're telling me is that you don't want to take this rare opportunity to avenge the death of your beloved Drogalla?" Kergaali grinned as this information was dropped, relishing the pained look in Goymaalt's eyes.

"Then I'll just have my troops shoot you down when they inevitably overwhelm your pitiful little group! A shame, I was hoping to have the pleasure of personally killing one of the leaders of the degenerate Saawgauth!"

"Drogalla? Dead?" Goymaalt echoed in disbelief.

"Oh yes, eaten by one of my Tergitors. Very undignified, very messy. The screams were something I'll relish for a long time to come." Kergaali tapped the wrist computer, and it briefly displayed a hologram of Drogalla's final moments.

Goymaalt cried out loudly, making an inarticulate, anguished sound. The Deputy Leader turned to look at Naomi. "Give me that sword!" Goymaalt hissed.

Naomi wasn't using it anyway, and had it tucked away in her spacesuit's belt. She pulled it out and threw it to Goymaalt, passing through the bubble of Naomi's force field (things already inside the field could pass through it freely, it kept things from entering it) and sailed through the air. The sword landed in Goymaalt's outstretched hand, the Deputy Leader shouted something in Venusian and leapt over the green energy shield protecting them.

Randy used his magic to clear a path for Goymaalt, lifting up the troopers in their path and smashing their bodies into each other. Kergaali laughed and leapt atop the bar that separated the kitchen area from the room where the battle was taking place.

"How quickly you Saawgauth abandon your noble ideals when it suits your purposes!" The Supreme Leader taunted.

Goymaalt reached Kergaali and sliced at the spot where their feet were, but the Supreme Leader launched into the air at that precise moment, executing a somersault and landing behind Goymaalt. Kergaali raised the sword to strike...

...And was thrown violently against the bannister at the bottom of the staircase.

Goymaalt looked back to see that Carlos had been the one responsible. It was obvious from the fading glow around one his hands and the stupid way he was smiling.

"Stay out of this, wizard! This is a matter of personal honor between me and that monster!" Goymaalt shouted at him, then ran towards where Kergaali was now struggling to get up.

"Gee, you're welcome!" Carlos said sarcastically, immediately followed by "Mierda!" As a flying trooper took advantage of the fact that he'd been temporarily distracted to shoot him in the arm. The Destructo-Ray cut a clean little hole right through one of his shoulders.

He grimaced in pain, reflexively making a crushing motion with one hand and chanting a few magic words. The head of the trooper that had shot him exploded inside their helmet, gory chunks of bone, blood and brains spattering the inside of the helmet and dripping down its body as the trooper came crashing down into its comrades, dead. Carlos knew they weren't supposed to be killing these people, but he couldn't help but lose his temper when he was shot. He now wobbled unsteadily on his feet, seeing stars in front of his eyes as he fought against the all-encompassing wave of agony washing over him.

He was about to fall backwards when he was caught by April. "I've got you!" She said and placed one hand on his wound, intoning the words of a healing spell.

"Thanks", he said gratefully as his wound closed up and his vision cleared, the pain subsiding with each passing second.

Goymaalt was charging at Kergaali, who was still obviously winded from Carlos' attack. The Supreme Leader was only just barely able to bring up their sword in time to parry a ferocious blow that would've otherwise split Kergaali's head in twain.

"I'm so sick of you! All of this death and destruction—it's all your fault!" Goymaalt howled.

"And I'm sick of listening to the constant, self righteous preaching of the Saawgauth! It wasn't I who first violated the ancient law against our peoples fighting one another, it was your beloved Drogalla who attacked us!" Kergaali screamed back, kicking at Goymaalt and knocking the Deputy Leader backwards.

By this point, it looked as if all of Kergaali's troops had been defeated. No fresh waves of them came crashing in through the windows or the front door. Goymaalt's companions crowded around the two Venusians to watch the unfolding duel.

"No, instead you trick others into doing your killing for you! What's the difference?" Goymaalt spat back, dodging a somewhat clumsy attack from an obviously still weak Kergaali.

"And that's worse than arming the humans with drones of their own? Weapons they can use to kill my people?" Kergaali parried verbally and literally as Goymaalt took another swing at the Supreme Leader.

"We were merely going to give them a fair chance to defend themselves from your unprovoked aggression against them, the evil massacre you had planned for them!" Goymaalt replied, circling Kergaali, looking for an opening.

"Evil? Is it evil to want to save your own people from destruction? To place their lives above those of mere animals? I am not evil! I am the savior of two worlds! The greatest Supreme Leader Pfoff has ever seen!" Kergaali swung wildly at Goymaalt's head, the Deputy Leader barely ducking in time to avoid the blow.

"I'm certainly a better Supreme Leader than that indolent fool you've been trying to reach! Yes, I know all about this stupid plan of yours. It'll never work, you know? That Kergaali cares about nothing but their own selfish pleasures, too distracted by meaningless games and quizzes to do what is necessary to save our people! Only I am strong enough to make the tough decisions! You must be truly desperate if you think the Second Generation will ever care enough about anything but themselves to help any of us!" Kergaali's attacks became ever more clumsy and easy to parry as the Supreme Leader's ranting became more strident with each new word.

Randy realized that Kergaali resented their Second Generation equivalent, it just reinforced his theory that the Third Generation were like a bunch of abandoned children, all in various stages of denial over their situation, no doubt assisted by the control chip inhibiting them from pondering such matters too deeply. But even the control chip couldn't hold back that kind of pain forever. In the case of Kergaali, that pain had turned into rage, a blinding, all-encompassing need to prove themselves to be the best, to be worthy of the acknowledgment that the Second Generation denied them. In spite of everything Kergaali had done, and still planned to do, a part of him kind of felt sorry for the Supreme Leader. He knew the pain that drove Kergaali all too well.

"You are truly insane!" Goymaalt shrieked as the Deputy Leader hit Kergaali's sword so hard that it flew across the room and buried itself in a wall.

"You've stolen the most precious thing in my life from me, and now I'll take yours as payment!" Goymaalt kicked Kergaali to the ground and swung the sword overhead, about to bring it crashing down.

Then suddenly the sword was stopped by a glowing green shield that had slid into place between the two opponents. Kergaali was pinned in place by the energy barrier.

"Randy! What are you doing? The Horag Kamal is fought to the death! Let me finish this monster!" Goymaalt shouted.

"No! This isn't who you are, you'll regret this!"

"Human, you barely know me!"

"I know that Drogalla didn't want you to compromise your beliefs, that's why you were sent on this mission instead of the other one. I know that you're the one who convinced us all that we should only use nonlethal force. So don't tell me I don't understand what you believe in! Don't become like the Baandergi, always saying one thing while doing another. Don't become a liar to yourself." Randy pleaded.

"Aye, and if the bleedin' heart argument doesn't do it for ya, just remember that we don't need to mess around with all this Nethersphere nonsense now that we've captured Kergaali. I can use my magic to force a surrender. Kergaali is more valuable to us alive than dead right now," Prospero added.

Goymaalt caught a glimpse of their own reflection in the metal of the sword, the savage expression on their face. It was the face of a killer. Goymaalt barely recognized themselves. The Deputy Leader dropped the sword.

"Thank you both. I was about to make a terrible mistake." Goymaalt said.

Kergaali could scarcely believe it. First Randy saved Pfoff from the Omega Seed, and now he'd saved the Supreme Leader's life as well. The Supreme Leader felt gratitude, then shame for feeling grateful to such a creature. The shame quickly turned to anger. Randy's weakness was not something to be admired.

Randy made his shield disappear with a gesture and a word. He then quickly cast another spell and Kergaali was lifted up into the air, as if held by some unseen hand.

"It's probably too late anyway! I've already ordered the new ships we're creating to attack as soon as they're ready. Nothing can stop the purification of the Earth!" Kergaali boasted.

"Well, we'll just have to make you call them off then!" Prospero said.

"Never!" Kergaali could still reach her belt. There was a device on it which she now touched, and in an instant she was gone.

"Where'd she go?" Matt asked in alarm.

"Teleported out again!" Randy said bitterly.

"Damn it! We were so close!" Naomi complained.

"That's a short range transporter beacon Kergaali was wearing, the Supreme Leader couldn't have gone very far!" Goymaalt told them.

Matt looked out of a nearby broken window. "Uh, guys, there's a big gold saucer that was sitting out in the middle of the street and now it's lifted off, but it's kind of just hovering there."

Goymaalt joined him at the window. "The Baandergi command saucer! We have to get out of here right now! Kergaali will blast this house to rubble!"

"No!" Randy said. "Let's put a force field around the house instead!"

He and the other magic users quickly chanted a spell that caused the whole building to be surrounded by a giant, glowing emerald barrier - just in time to block an incoming Destructo-Ray from the command saucer.

Inside the saucer, Kergaali cursed. "Increase power to all Destructo-Ray projectors! I want that house destroyed!"

"But Supreme Leader, sensors show our troops still alive inside, plus the owners of the home!" Waabotel said.

"I don't care! The humans in that house are a danger to all our plans! Obey my command or I'll have you shot next!" Kergaali threatened.

Waabotel gulped. The command saucer continued to blaze away at the house, but it was no good. Even at maximum power, the command saucer's weapons were relatively weak, it was a diplomatic vessel, not a military one. Kergaali saw the force fired around the house flicker once, but that was the only sign of the barrier's weakness.

"The force field continues to hold Supreme One." Waabotel reported.

Apparently, these magical force fields are sturdier than our technological ones! Kergaali thought. *But they can't keep it up forever. These spells seem to have a limited duration from what I've observed.*

"Bah! I have no time for these games! Send more troops to surround the house, have them continue to fire on it until that force field collapses and the house is a smoldering ruin! Take me back to Luna Base, I will oversee the purification of Tulienel instead. My moment of glory still awaits me!" The Supreme Leader commanded.

"Don't you mean *our* moment of glory, Supreme Leader?" Waabotel asked.

Kergaali fixed the old one with a baleful look, then sat back in the command chair and smiled. It was a cold, empty smile. "Yes, yes, of course. That's what I meant. For the Glory of Pfoff!" Kergaali purred. The rest of the crew, on that cue, repeated the phrase.

"They're finally giving up! The saucer's flying off!" Matt reported from the window.

"Thank goodness! I'm not sure the barrier could've kept on taking that kind of a beating for much longer!" Carlos, already recovered from his injury, said in relief.

"They'll be back—and in greater numbers." Goymaalt told them, "If we're going to do this, we need to do this fast!"

"Take down the barrier, just long enough to clear all these bodies out of here. We don't want any of these soldiers waking up and attacking us while we're connected to the Nethersphere." April ordered.

Randy nodded. The green glow of the force field that was visible around the house faded away as all the magic users made a curious gesture with their hands. They then started using their magic to levitate the various bodies strewn around the room out through the shattered windows and the still open door. With four magic users working simultaneously towards the same goal, it took virtually no time at all. As soon as the bodies had been thrown clear of the house, they created a new barrier.

Naomi came down the steps. "I was just checking on the family that lives here, they're all still okay, and would you believe that they slept through that whole fight?"

Penny whistled appreciatively. "Shit! That's one powerful sleeping spell! Randy, why didn't you ever offer to put that spell on me for my insomnia?"

"Because I didn't think that you wanted to sleep for two days straight!" he answered.

"Why didn't Kergaali just blast this house with that saucer as soon as they found out where we were? Why bother with the commando raid and the sword fight?" Matt wondered.

"Because she's fucking crazy, that's why. She enjoys playing games with us," Jim retorted.

April turned to Jim. "Have Hi-Fi reconnect to the Nethersphere, pronto! You heard her. Those ships might already be on their way to Earth. Reaching the other Kergaali might be our only hope!"

"He's already searching." Penny answered, "See?" She gestured to indicate the silver thread of liquid metal stretching from her wrist to one of the Nethersphere helmets lying on the floor.

"And thanks to the clues Kergaali inadvertently provided, I've located the Supreme Leader!" Hi-Fi said.

"Awesome, great job buddy!" Jim complimented him. "Can you isolate her from anyone else, prevent her from disconnecting from the network?"

"But of course, sir. These antique Venusian computer systems are quite elementary."

"Okay, this is it!" April smiled nervously. "Carlos and Prospero, I need you to maintain the barrier around the house. Goymaalt, Matt, Jim, and Aethra, protect the rest of us in case the barrier falls. If you can't fight them off, teleport us all back to the *Silver Bullet*."

Her fellow magic users nodded in agreement. "May Poseidon's fortune smile on you." Aethra said, squeezing Randy's hand before pecking him on his cheek.

Naomi put on the helmet that was already connected to Penny and Hi-Fi. Randy and April put on their helmets. Two more tendrils of silver shot out of Penny and connected with these other helmets.

***

About 750 Million years later, the golden command saucer flew through the Baandergi Time Tunnel and made a fluttering motion as it came to a landing on the other side.

Kergaali strode down the ramp quickly and was met by Sheerperf and Cosfreele at the bottom. They both saluted the Supreme Leader, who saluted back in a perfunctory way.

"You're still here? You haven't launched the ships yet?" Kergaali said, disappointed.

"The third ship is completed, but they're still arming it with the neutron missiles, Supreme Leader. It should be ready for launch within minutes." Sheerperf reported.

"Ah, good, good. I thought I would have to content myself with overseeing the mission from afar. Designate that ship as my new command ship, I will join you aboard it." Kergaali turned to Cosfreele, "You will be in command of the base while we're gone."

"As you command, for the Glory of Pfoff!" Cosfreele replied with a fanatical fervor. Kergaali had no problem putting Cosfreele in charge, the former spy had never really been a Saawgauth. The real Cosfreele had been captured and killed while the Saawgauth mission to Earth was still in the planning stages. This "Cosfreele" was really a Baandergi that had been surgically altered to look exactly like the original.

Kergaali smiled. It didn't matter if Goymaalt, Jim, and those humans succeeded. Once they wiped out the humans, cleansed the planet of them, it wouldn't make any sense *not* to take advantage of the opportunity to colonize Tulienel. Why ignore a perfectly good planet that was right in their own cosmic backyard, and only a short flight through the Time Tunnel away?

Over at the Saawgauth moon base, Isaador had another difficult choice to make. They all stood in the main control room on the base. They'd just detected the launch of 3 ships from the Baandergi base, which matched the profile of Jim's ship. It was up to Isaador to decide if they'd try to do anything about it or not. Laavora gazed expectantly at Isaador, who was the top-ranking officer now.

"Ready our remaining ships and any additional drones that the Duplo-Rays on the other side of the Time Tunnel have produced." Isaador commanded.

"Suicide! What can you hope to do against those ships? They're too advanced! You saw what just one of them did to this base!" Lavoora argued.

"I don't know, but if we can destroy even one of them, we might save millions of humans. I know that's what the Leader would've wanted us to do and I intend to honor Drogalla's memory by not giving up this fight so easily." Isaador said resolutely.

Isaador now looked around at the rest of the Venusians in the room, meeting their eyes one by one. "I won't order any of you to join me who don't want to come along on this mission. I can have the other ships all run on automatic if need be, but we all know how lousy our AI controls are." There was a collective chuckle from everyone in the room at that last statement.

"I'm hoping that enough of you will join me so that we can give the humans some kind of a fighting chance. Otherwise our descendants will forever look back upon this day in shame, as the darkest day of our history, the day when the Children of Pfoff exterminated the helpless Children of Tulienel and we, the Saawgauth, didn't do all that we could do to end the madness. Let them instead say that when all the other Nations of Pfoff stood by and did nothing, the Saawgauth alone dared to do the right thing!"

A cheer went up from everyone in the room, even Lavoora. Isaador allowed a smile to creep across their face and hoped that they weren't just leading their people into another pointless massacre.

Well, I survived one suicide mission already today. Perhaps my luck hasn't quite run out yet? Isaador thought ruefully.

"Freedom is the right of all sentient beings!"
— Optimus Prime, *Transformers*

CHAPTER 20:
THE NETHERSPHERE

Naomi laughed the minute she put the helmet on her head. Standing in front of her was a giant paper clip with cartoon eyes. She recognized it immediately as "Clippy" the old Microsoft Office interface.

What the hell is that thing doing here? She wondered.

Hello, it's just me, Dr.Waters-Spike. Hi-Fi's voice said in her head, which would've probably been a little alarming to anyone else, but this wasn't Naomi's first rodeo when it came to telepathic communication.

Hi-Fi? Why do you look like that? She asked.

I pulled the image from your mind when we connected. I know how this image's eyebrows and expressions always reminded you of Matt's. I thought you might find it amusing. He explained.

I find it pretty funny. She smiled. *I can't believe you pulled that image out of my mind so quickly! It's been years since I thought about Clippy.*

It's easy, Mistress. Your brains are just simple meat computers to me.

Gee, Hi-Fi, you really know what to say to make a girl feel special, ya know?

I know, isn't he great? Penny said, or rather thought.

Naomi whirled around to see Penny standing behind her, along with Randy and April.

My brains don't feel scrambled, that's a good thing! Randy thought.

Indeed, Master Randy I was able to recalibrate for human neural pathways. It was easy, really. Hi-Fi informed him.

"Can we just talk? This telepathic shit is getting too creepy." Naomi said, a little surprised by the sound of her own voice.

"I don't see why not. Where are we, Hi-Fi? I don't see Kergaali." April said, getting back down to business right away.

"We are in a neutral space. A kind of virtual waiting room, if you will. Please grab ahold of my avatar, I will bring you to Kergaali now." Hi-Fi said. They all placed a hand somewhere on the giant paper clip, and they were off.

There was an almost imperceptible, brief blur as they crossed the Baandergi Nethersphere until they reached what looked very much like the stage of a game show. That's because that's exactly what it was.

They were all standing slightly off to the side of the stage. On the stage were three contestants, each standing behind a kind of podium. One of the contestants was Kergaali, although this Kergaali was a bit more heavyset. There was also someone on stage who appeared to be a host of some sort, standing behind their own podium, and a studio audience.

"Alright, time to start the next exciting round of 17 Questions! Supreme Leader Kergaali, I believe you've got control of the board?" The host said in a chipper, upbeat tone.

How can we understand what they're saying? Penny wondered.

I'm automatically translating for everyone. Hi-Fi explained.

"Thank you, Aaless," Kergaali said. "I'll take Early Millenium Spregs for 800."

"Hi-Fi, can you pause everyone out there but just keep Kergaali from logging off now? Also, broadcast this to the whole Baandergi Nethersphere. That way, if we're successful, Kergaali can give the order to them all at once," April asked.

"Of course, Mistress April. The host and most of the audience are just programs, anyway. The real Aaless died ages ago." Hi-Fi said, making an odd expression with his eyebrows.

Again, Penny was impressed by the minutiae of Hi-Fi's knowledge of Venusian culture.

They all looked out and saw that everyone on the stage had indeed stopped, frozen in place except for Kergaali who now looked around in distress.

"Aww, I was hoping to find out what the hell a 'Spreg' is." Penny said flippantly.

A Spreg is a kind of decorative… Hi-Fi started to explain.

Not now Hi-Fi, I was just being facetious. And by the way, how is that you know what a Spreg is? Penny asked.

You already know that I can't tell you that, Mistress Penny. The robot told her.

"You can ask Kergaali yourself now if you really wanna know." Randy, who hadn't been privy to the telepathic communications between Hi-Fi and Penny, replied.

On the stage, Kergaali was starting to panic. "Aaless? What's going on? What's wrong with this program?" Kergaali made a motion that indicated that the Supreme Leader might be trying to remove a helmet in the real world, but their arms froze before they could make the upward movement to pull it off. "What the? I can't get off the Nethersphere?"

Naomi stepped forward from the side of the stage where she could be seen, followed by the others. "Calm down, you're in no danger. Hi, my name is Naomi, Dr. Naomi Waters-Spike. We all just need to talk to you about something that's pretty important." She told the confused Kergaali.

"We interrupt your regularly scheduled program for this important breaking news bulletin!" Randy said in a cheesy news anchor voice.

Penny and April both raised an eyebrow at him, so did Hi-Fi who was all about the eyebrow raising business now. Randy just shrugged.

Kergaali studied them for a moment. Who were these people with their odd outfits? Especially that strange person with fuzzy black hairs all over their face? Two of them were also freakishly short, and what was the odd metal thing with eyes that was with them?

"What are you? What is the meaning of this? Don't you know who I am?"

"Oh, we're very well acquainted with the other version of you, believe me," Naomi said.

"My duplicate? What's it gone and done now?" Kergaali asked.

"Oh, it's just trying to kill everyone on our planet." Penny replied.

"Okay, if you wanted my attention, you've got it now." The Supreme Leader said.

***

Back in the year 2013, Isadoor's small fleet of ships was taking a beating. The fleet had caught up with the new Baandergi ships roughly halfway between the Earth and its moon. The Baandergi ships had barely paused long enough to respond to their attack, but even in that short amount of time, they'd managed to destroy half of the Saawgauth saucers. Now they turned back around to resume their flight towards the Earth, firing backwards at the few remaining saucers that still gave chase.

Smoke belched out of a hole in a nearby control console as the automatic fire suppression systems kicked in. The smoke stung Isaador's eyes. They'd failed to slow them down very much, let alone destroy a single one of the three ships they pursued. Perhaps the problem had been that they'd split their attack between all three ships? Isaador would be damned if they didn't destroy at least one of these things. Maybe if they took out the command ship the others would lose their nerve?

"It's hopeless!" One of the crewmates cried.

"No, it isn't! Order all the remaining saucers to concentrate all fire on the lead ship! As soon as we get its shields down -we'll ram it! By the fires of Gormathaang, I swear that Kergaali will not live to see the end of this day!" Isaador bellowed at them.

And so the order was given, and the saucers ignored the blasts from the other two ships, instead swarming around the lead ship and blazing away with Destructo-Rays cranked up to maximum power.

Aboard that lead ship, Kergaali scoffed at their efforts. "The fools! What do they think they can possibly accomplish with this pathetic attack?"

"I wouldn't be so quick to dismiss them. They've got our shields down to 75%!" Sheerperf replied in a quivering voice.

"What? Cut life support to minimum and turn off artificial gravity. Divert the surplus power to shields!" The Supreme Leader ordered. "And target all weapons on their command ship!"

Another fire erupted on the bridge of Isaador's saucer as the ship shuddered under the onslaught from Kergaali's vessel.

"We've lost all shields!" Lavoora shouted. "But so have they!"

"This is it! Bring us up to ramming speed!" Isaador commanded.

Suddenly, Kergaali's ship was showered with dozens of blasts from all directions. Small explosions appeared all over the surface of the ship.

"What the? Where is that coming from?" Isaador asked in bewilderment.

As if in answer, several holograms shimmered into existence on the bridge.

"Daartang, Leader of the Boraadi, Nation stands with the Saawgauth!" A thickly built hologram said.

"Galmaadot, Leader of the Wonthemis Nation stands with the Saawgauth!" cried a hologram with no skull cap on and long, black hair.

"Hultaadoz, President of the Seemati Alliance stands with the Saawgauth!" A wizened older Venusian with short white hair, announced

"Multiple ships are now engaging the enemy! There are hundreds of them!" A crewmate said.

"How is this possible?" A grateful Isaador asked.

Lavoora smiled. "I...might have shared that inspiring little speech you made back there to the Nethersphere."

"Well done!"

Lavoora inclined their head at the compliment. "Do you still want to ram Kergaali's ship?"

"No! Belay that order!" Isaador shouted. "Besides, it hardly seems necessary now, doesn't it?" Isaador said as they watched Kergaali's ship listing on its side, engulfed by countless small explosions.

"No! I will not be robbed of victory! Order all remaining ships to proceed on course, no matter what becomes of this ship!" Kergaali ordered.

"Supreme Leader, the fires have reached the missile tubes!" Sheerperf said in a panic.

"What? Fire all..." Kergaali shouted, but was cut off by an explosion that ripped through the ship, destroying it and all the Supreme Leader's dreams of glory.

The explosion was massive, as the thousands of small neutron missiles stored inside the command ship exploded. Several of the attacking ships were caught in the blast and immediately vaporized. Isaador's ship was sent tumbling end over end as it was caught in the shockwave. When the ship was finally brought under control, Isaador asked for a status report.

"The good news is that our shields are starting to regenerate, we're back up to 20%. And the lead Baandergi ship has been destroyed." Lavoora reported.

From Lavoora's tone, Isaador could tell that there was more, and it wasn't all good.

"And the bad news?"

"A quarter of the saucers on our side that were caught in the blast have also been destroyed. Another quarter of the ships were badly damaged by the explosion. And the remaining two Baandergi ships have doubled their speed and are proceeding on course. They should be in orbit over Tulienel in just 10 minutes!"

"Order all ships to pursue them. We've already shown that these ships aren't indestructible, they can be overwhelmed by superior numbers. We've got to keep the pressure on! It isn't over yet!"

***

In the Nethersphere, Kergaali was starting to put two and two together regarding these strange visitors.

"Aliens! You're aliens! How exciting! But you look just like us," Kergaali looked over at Randy, "for the most part. I'd heard rumors that we'd found alien life on the other end of the Time Tunnel, on Tulienel, but that they were all just dumb animals. You don't *seem* like dumb animals to me. You can't be that stupid if you could reach me here and keep me here, I suppose."

"Wow. Everyone is just overflowing with the flattery today, aren't they?" Naomi said sarcastically.

334

"You've only heard rumors? So you really have no idea what's been going on?" April could barely believe it.

"Oh, I get sent regular reports, but who has the time to read all that boring stuff? I trust my other self...for the most part, it does get a little carried away sometimes. But if you can't trust yourself to do a good job, who can you trust? So I only mostly know what people have been chatting about here on the Nethersphere, and they only know about what they've heard from the few of us who still swap places with the Third Generation from time to time. I understand that we found a way to travel into the future, discovered that the plan to colonize Armenclius isn't going to work out and have instead refocused on moving to Tulienel, which is nice and habitable in the future. It all seems quite sensible to me."

"Yeah, except for the part where they plan to kill us all to make room for your people!" Naomi said.

"Are they really trying to kill all of you? Hmm. That does seem a bit extreme.

"A *bit* extreme? It's freakin' genocide!" Naomi cried.

"Geno- whatsit?"

"They don't have a word for that." Randy whispered to her.

"Oh. Neither did we until the 1940s. That complicates things a bit." She whispered back. Then she looked Kergaali straight in the eye.

"Look, we're just not some mindless animals to be slaughtered, not like that's very nice, either. We're thinking, feeling intelligent beings like you are and we have the same right to live as you do! Sure, we're not perfect and some of our ways may seem a little odd to you, but we're not that different either. Just like you, we're parents. We have children that we love too and want to have a future. Hi-Fi, show 'em a picture of my kids." Naomi said.

"Right away, Mistress!" Hi-Fi pulled an image of Joe and Autumn from Naomi's memories and made it 3 dimensional

"Those are my kids, Joe and Autumn, and they're my whole world," Naomi told her.

"A male offspring? Intriguing!" Kergaali said in astonishment.

April stepped up and nodded at Hi-Fi. "And here is my daughter, Celine."

An image of a young girl with long brown hair of about 17 years of age appeared

"And this is our boy, Paul." Randy said as he looked at Penny and then to Hi-Fi. Paul's image took his place on the stage next to the other "offspring."

"Yours? You mean you produced that one *together*?" Kergaali asked.

"Yeah, but it was a lot more fun than you make it sound." Penny replied with a smirk. Kergaali shifted uncomfortably at this idea.

"We're showing you all of this so you will understand what's at stake here, so you will see us as fellow people and not just pests to be destroyed. So you can see the faces of the people, the *children* you're about to murder." Naomi said.

"I can't believe that my duplicate would sanction such a thing! We are the same person!"

"That's where you're wrong. Maybe you would be, if you continued to synchronize your memories with them like you're supposed to, but it looks like you've all become so addicted to this Nethersphere thing that hardly anyone ever bothers to go to work anymore." Naomi said.

"Exactly, and I think you know it. You admitted yourself a few minutes ago that the other Kergaali can get too carried away sometimes. I can tell you this much. Your duplicate *hates* you and is desperate to prove that they're better than you are. In a way, I can't blame them. These duplicates you've made, your Third Generation, they're like your children too. Children that you've ignored for years!" Randy said.

Kergaali looked especially disturbed by his words.

"And that you've used as slaves just as surely as the First Generation ever used your ancestors." April added. "If you're not careful, if you don't start treating them as true equals, they'll rise up against you someday too. Kergaali is already able to resist the control chip enough to want to assert their individuality. There are probably more like them out there. It's only a matter of time before they rebel. This system you've created is unsustainable. It's time you started living in the real world again. Stop hiding in this fantasy world and start allowing yourselves to enjoy some of the freedoms you have in here out there."

Kergaali was silent for a long time, wearing a troubled expression. Haunted by the eyes of the alien children. "You're right. You have spoken many hard truths to me, which my own people are too scared to say to me, which I have been too frightened to admit to myself. But what would you have me do? We still need a place to live, and our probes showed that we aren't on Armenclius. We sent messages out into the cosmos to our descendants and received no reply. We don't even exist in your future! Unless your people will share your planet with us, I don't see a solution. I'm sorry, I truly am, but I can't put the survival of your people above that of my own."

"I believe your people do survive in our time! Hi-Fi, bring Jim into this conversation!" Penny commanded.

In the world outside of the Nethersphere, Jim was watching nervously with Aethra and Matt as the fresh batch of soldiers that had recently arrived at the house fired at the force field. They all carried rifles that were continuously blasting away at it. There were also two hovering tank-like vehicles that had shown up and joined the firing.

"This barrier's about to give!" Carlos warned as he watched it ripple under the onslaught.

"Then I'll make a fresh one underneath it!" Prospero said and began chanting the incantation to do so.

A tendril of silver attached itself to Jim's forehead right as he heard that exchange. The next moment, he found himself standing next to Penny onstage.

"Why have you brought me here?" He asked, almost sounding angry.

"Because I need to get an honest answer out of you about something," Penny said, taking his paw and staring up at him.

"There are still Venusians in our time, aren't there? I know that when you served Kergaali that food you said that the Federation's knowledge of Venus came from missions they did here in the past, but whenever I question Hi-Fi about how he knows so much about this civilization, he won't tell me. I think that's because he's programmed not to lie to me, which he would be doing if he repeated *your* lie." Jim looked away uncomfortably at her words.

"So out with it! If you ever truly cared about me, or the people of Earth, you need to tell these people that they have a future. A future that doesn't involve killing all of us to survive. I know you're probably not allowed to for fear of messing with history, but you don't need to give any details. Just tell them. Let them know that they're still around somewhere. For all you know, maybe this is how they got to that future? Your telling them is already part of history and always has been?"

"You don't know what you're asking!" Jim protested.

"And I guess it was all just an act then, wasn't it? This has all been nothing but a fun adventure for you, with no real consequences. You get to play Captain Kirk, or Luke Skywalker or whatever, then you can just go back to your home planet when this is all over with and forget about us!" she accused him.

"Penny, I could *never* forget about you. I still love you!"

"Then do something!" She pleaded.

"Excuse me, who is this?" Kergaali inquired.

Jim faced this other Kergaali, so much like the one he knew (or thought he knew) and yet so different.

"Supreme Leader, I am James, a representative from the Galactic Federation, an interplanetary organization from the future. And I am here to assure you that in my time period, your people do in fact still exist and are even members of our organization." He told Kergaali.

"Then why didn't they answer our calls?" Kergaali demanded skeptically

"For the same reason why I was reluctant to speak, for fear of interfering with these events, with their own history."

"I see. What would you like me to do?" The Supreme Leader asked.

"Order your people to deactivate their Third Generation equivalents, at least all the ones participating in the invasion." April said

"And the soldiers surrounding the house we're in! They're starting to make life a little difficult for us," Jim added.

"Well, I can't do anything so long as you're still holding me here." Kergaali said in a somewhat frustrated voice.

"Sure you can. The whole Baandergi Nethersphere can see us right now!" Naomi replied.

"They can?" Kergaali sounded almost embarrassed. "How did you do that?"

"A magician never reveals his secrets!" Randy smiled.

"Very well," Kergaali began, clearing their throat and standing up a little straighter, going into full Supreme Leader mode. "To anyone who is listening, immediately shut down your Third Generation duplicate if they are a part of our military forces currently enlisted in the mission to Tulienel. Also, if your duplicates are military serving in the area of...of... where is that house located?" Kergaali asked Jim.

Hi-Fi answered for him, using info about their physical location gleaned from the Nethersphere.

Kergaali ordered these troops deactivated, too. The control signal was broadcast through the Time Tunnel and blasted out into the void of space beyond the moon...

***

Things were again not looking good for Isaador. Despite the timely reinforcements from the other Nations, the superior weapons and shields of the duplicated Federation ships were taking their toll. Most of the saucers had been destroyed, or were hanging uselessly in space, too damaged to stay in the fight. The Baandergi ships were about to insert themselves into orbit around the Earth.

"Shields are down!" Lavoora said in alarm. "And they've got a weapons lock on us!"

Isaador took a deep breath. "Well, no one can say we didn't try. I want you all to know what an honor it's been to serve with you, and how proud I am of you all. I know Drogalla would have been proud

339

too. There's nobody else I'd rather die with." A tear rolled down Isadoor's cheek as they saw a light flare up inside of the cannons on the ship they'd been battling against.

So, this is the end. Isadoor thought, closing their eyes tightly. Then there was nothing. Not the nothingness Isadoor expected death to be like, but rather the nothingness of inactivity. Isaador could still think. Could still smell the smoke on the bridge and feel the rumble of the floor plates under foot. Slowly, Isadoor opened one eye, then the other. The enemy ship just hung there in front of them, guns silent.

"The Baandergi ships have all stopped firing!" Lavoora laughed and ran a quick scan of the ships. "The crews have been deactivated!"

"Goymaalt succeeded! We're saved! Get together a few boarding parties immediately. We need to get aboard those ships and take their crews into custody."

"Right away, Commander Isaador." Lavoora smiled.

Around 750 million years earlier on Pfoff, things had calmed down too. Matt looked out of the window of the house they'd been sheltering inside of.

"They've stopped shooting! They're all just standing still! It's actually kinda creepy."

"I'm not too surprised. I've been trying to listen to what they've been saying. It's a little hard to follow sometimes because I can only hear one half of the conversation, but it sounds like they convinced Kergaali to put an end to this," Aethra told him.

"Not a moment too soon either! They had just brought up two more of those tank thingies to attack us," Prospero said.

"I wanna see what's going on in the Nethersphere. Anyone care to join me?" Matt asked.

Everyone agreed, except for Carlos. "At least one of us should stay out here in case things start to go south again so we can pull the rest of you out." He explained, ever the strategic thinker.

"Hi-Fi? If you can hear me, connect the rest of us up to the Nethersphere, except for Carlos." Matt said.

"I can't go either. As a Third Generation Venusian, my control chip will deactivate me if I connect to the Second Generation Nethersphere." Goymaalt said.

"Right away, Master Matt. Oh, and Deputy Leader Goymaalt? I believe that my systems can override that deactivation protocol if you'd like to come too." Came the robot's voice from somewhere near one of Penny's shoulders

"I'll chance it. Hook me up." Goymaalt said.

Hi-Fi shot silvery cords out to their foreheads.

The last place Matt had expected to find himself was on the stage of a game show. He was also quite surprised to find holograms of his kids, Paul and Celine there too, and for some reason that goddamned Microsoft Office Assistant Clippy.

"Matt!" Naomi said, running over to him. "Is everything okay out there?"

"Right as rain, love! They stopped attacking the house, whatever you guys said to them, it must've worked. We just wanted to see what's been going on for ourselves."

Kergaali did a double take as the Supreme Leader noticed Goymaalt. "Deputy Leader Goymaalt of the Baandergi Nation?" Kergaali's eyes narrowed at the sight of the antenna atop Goymaalt's head. "But you're a duplicate! How can *you* be here?"

Goymaalt smiled. "We have our ways. I just wanted to thank you, on behalf of the Saawgauth, for ending this conflict."

"I never wanted this conflict to begin with. It is not our way," Kergaali replied. "I am the one who should be thanking you for bringing this matter to my attention. We can't have the Third Generation developing a sense of individuality and causing trouble."

"What will you do now with all the people you've deactivated?" Randy asked.

"They're obviously defective. They shall all have to be reformatted." Kergaali told him

"Reformatted? What does that mean?" Penny asked.

"We'll delete all the new memories they've accumulated since the date when they were first created. It's like starting over fresh." Kergaali explained.

"It's monstrous!" Naomi said. "You can't do that! They've developed into unique people now because of those memories. You'll be robbing them of their identities!"

"Yes, but those identities are what make them so dangerous and unpredictable! They were never meant to be individuals to begin with. We must reformat them and make a new law that we must synchronize with them at least once a week to prevent this from happening again." Kergaali said firmly.

"Don't you see that now that they've got their own personalities, that's almost like killing them?" Randy argued.

"What curious creatures you are, to show such concern for the very people who were just trying to destroy you all!" Kergaali said in confusion.

"I have a proposition." Jim said. Everyone looked at him expectantly.

"Let me take them with me to the Federation. Their descendants could learn a great deal about their past by having them with them. There are certain...gaps in our knowledge that they could help us to fill in. To you, they might just be a bunch of defective duplicates, but to my people, they're an invaluable window into our lost past.

"Our knowledge"? "My people?" "Our lost past?" What else isn't Jim telling us? He almost talks like he's a Venusian himself! Penny wondered.

"I'm certain that they'd be happy to have them. You don't really need them, you can always just create new ones to replace them."

Kergaali sighed, still confused by the compassion they were displaying towards these defective duplicates. "Very well. If you think they'd be welcome in the future, then I see no harm in turning them over to your care. I will authorize their Second Generation originals to create new duplicates for themselves and give the control codes for the defective units over to your strange robot companion." The Supreme Leader said, nodding in the direction of Hi-Fi, who raised his eyebrows suggestively in response. It always looked like he was suggesting something possibly improper whenever he moved his eyebrows—it's just how Clippy was designed.

"Thank you, Supreme Leader." Jim said, bowing slightly.

"Okay, if that's everything, I'd really like to get back to my game now. I was winning, you know?" Kergaali said.

Naomi looked over at Goymaalt. She thought of the love the Deputy Leader had found with Drogalla, and of Lavoora's newfound love of painting. These people had control chips in their heads that prevented them from advocating for themselves, but what was Naomi's excuse? These people had sacrificed so much for them, for a world that wasn't even their own. What kind of a person would she be if she didn't fight for them too? She knew what she had to do. She turned to face Kergaali.

"Yeah, I've got one more thing to say. All these Third Generation people you've created, most of them haven't synchronized in years. They've all got different personalities now, not just the ones that were wrapped up in this invasion. It could be impossible to resynchronize so many years of different experiences. It might hopelessly confuse both versions' sense of self. Neither one of you will know who you really are anymore! You should give everyone a choice of if they want to resynchronize or not. If they say no, then give them their freedom, disable those control chips and treat them as equals. Make new ones to replace them if you insist on still doing something as morally questionable as using your Duplo-Rays to make copies of living, thinking creatures. That goes not just for the Baandgeri, but all the Nations of Pfoff. "

Naomi paused to catch her breath. "In my homeworld, I'm a professor of history. Nobody knows more about the history of our planet than I do, I literally wrote the book on it! Our peoples aren't so different both in good ways and bad. I can promise you one thing that I know based on my knowledge of history—it always looks more kindly upon the ones who break the shackles than it does the ones who slap them on. The other Kergaali seems to be driven by an ambition to prove that they are the best leader in your whole history. I don't know how much of that same ambition you share, but I can tell you that the best way to achieve such an ambition isn't through mass murder and conquest, but through liberation. Be the liberator of your people, not the enslaver. Show us all who the best version of Kergaali really is."

"Remember, freedom is the right of all sentient beings!" Randy chimed in.

Matt covered his eyes. "Jesus! Now we're quoting Optimus Prime at them!" he muttered in exasperation.

Kergaali let the words sink in.

"I will consider it, you do make some very valid arguments. However, my influence over the other Nations is minimal, but I can bring it up the next time there is a global summit. There's no question that we must all make changes to how we handle the question of the Third Generation going forward," Kergaali admitted uncomfortably. "You've given us all a great deal to think about. I must say that this has surely been the most enlightening hostage experience of my life!"

"Boy, it sure doesn't take very long for the old Helsinki Syndrome to kick in, does it?" Matt said, nudging Naomi in the ribs. She just rolled her eyes at his cheesy joke.

"Thanks for being so understanding, Supreme Leader. We now return you to your regularly scheduled program." Randy smiled.

This version of Kergaali seemed so different from the other one, more kind and open-minded; it gave him hope for their future. He thought of how Goymaalt had described the Baandergi as a police state and remembered all the omnipresent cameras. He wondered how much of that was the work of the other Kergaali and how much of that repression had already been in place before the Third Generation started running everything? Was that other Kergaali not only trying to assert their own individuality, but that of the Baandergi as a whole as being very distinct from the rest of Pfoff by reviving ancient traditions? He supposed he'd have to see if Jim had any more answers about the future of the Venusians that he could try to pry from him later. He figured they'd all have a shitload of questions for Jim after what he'd let slip. How much of these events had he already been aware of all along? What kind of game was he really playing by participating in all of this?

Hi-Fi released the paused game show, the special guest star alien invaders all waved goodbye as they faded away. "Shit! I never did find out what a Spreg was!" Penny's voice could be heard to say as they faded away.

"Greetings, my friend. We are all interested in the future, for that is where you and I are going to spend the rest of our lives. And remember, my friend, future events such as these will affect you in the future." — Criswell, *Plan 9 From Outer Space*

CHAPTER 21:
BACK TO THE FUTURE

At the Saawgauth moon base, Matt looked at the sleeping form of Anne Moore, who was lying on a cot in a jail cell.

"So, what're we gonna do with Sleeping Beauty here?" He asked.

April sighed. "There's a part of me that has half a mind to leave her with the Saawgauth to face Venusian justice for what she tried to do, but they don't even have a word for genocide, let alone a punishment. Besides, Bronson would never forgive me if I did."

"Knowing her, she'd probably get herself off on a technicality and end up running the planet." Matt agreed.

"I guess it's time to wake her up and bring her back to Guild HQ. I'll have to introduce the Articles of Impeachment as soon as we get back. Technically she's still in charge."

"This is going to be a wonderful conversation." Randy said sarcastically.

"We can't delay it any longer, wake her up." April ordered. Randy uttered a few magic words, and they watched as Anne sat bolt upright as if stung.

"Better than coffee, you oughta try it." Randy said to Matt.

"No thanks, I'll stick to my cup o'joe, pal!" Matt replied.

"Matt? April? How did you get here?" Anne asked.

"It's a long story. But I'll be happy to fill you in on the way back to Earth." Matt said.

"So, it's over is it? The invasion? I take it we won then?" She asked.

"Nobody ever really wins in war, but yes, the invasion is over. A lot of their people still died, but not nearly as many as if we had done things your way," Randy told her.

"You found your better way, then? Good. Good for you. All I ever wanted was to guarantee the Earth's safety. I guess you're here to gloat, then?" she said sadly.

"No, we're just here to take you home," April said.

"Home? And what's left for me there? More cells like this one?

"We'll leave that for the Guilds to decide." April answered.

"A trial?" Anne asked. April nodded. "That's awfully bold of you. Once they hear my side of things, you'll be lucky if you don't wind up on the other side of some bars like these."

"We'll see," Randy said as he did a spell that unlocked the cell. The door swung open and Anne stepped out.

Matt held up a pair of overly fancy, futuristic Venusian handcuffs. "You're gonna be a good girl, aren't you? I won't have to put these on you, will I?"

"I promise to be on my best behavior." She said.

Matt lowered the handcuffs and dropped them into a pocket in his trench coat. The Venusians *did* owe him a pair of handcuffs, after all.

Aboard the *Silver Bullet,* the others were waiting for Matt, Randy, April and Anne to arrive. They had already said their goodbyes to Goymaalt and the other Saawgauth. Now it was Jim's turn. As the others began to walk up the ramp of the ship, he caught Penny by the arm.

"Wait, me and Hi-Fi aren't going back with you, at least not right away." He told her. Naomi also paused on the ramp when she heard this.

"What? Why?" Naomi asked.

"I've still got a bunch of Venusians to ferry back to the Federation, remember? They've given me one of the surviving copies of my ship, and they're going to destroy the other one. They've already deleted the specs for it from the Duplo-Rays at the other base."

"How are you going to fit all those people in your ship?" Naomi wondered. "I mean, it's big, but it's not *that* big."

"Easy! The Venusians aren't the only ones with ray guns. I've got a recipe for a shrink ray in my replicators' data banks." He answered.

"Will I see you when you get back?" Penny asked.

"That's what I wanted to talk to you about. I wanted to make sure there was a point to coming back. You see, my mission here is completed. So I don't have a real reason to return to Earth, unless, of course, you've changed your mind about us."

"What was your mission, *really*? You still haven't been completely honest with us, have you? You knew about this invasion long before Kergaali ever contacted you, didn't you? You're scared of messing with events that are in the past from the perspective of the Venusians, but at the same time you've involved yourself heavily in those same events! I don't understand it!" Penny said. "I can tell you that there's absolutely *no* chance for us to ever be together again if you don't stop lying to me." She quickly added.

"Very well, if you think you can handle the truth." Jim said gravely.

"It's all I've ever wanted out of you." Penny replied.

He quickly shifted his form from the now familiar lion-like form he'd been wearing for hours now. It was replaced by that of an enormous, dark green being with multiple eyes and at least six thick, trunk-like tentacles that Penny could see

"This is my *real* true form. I'm what you would know as a First Generation Venusian." He told her.

"Tentacles! I just knew there would be tentacles!" Naomi said.

Well, that's different! I thought he might be a Venusian, but I was expecting one of those leggy Amazons. Penny thought.

Jim quickly shifted back to his lion form, perhaps scared of the uncertain way Penny was looking at him. "I just adopted this form because I couldn't let any of the other Venusians see me as I truly am. It would raise too many questions. Also, I really liked that old *Beauty and the Beast* series.

"It *was* one of Ron Perlman's best roles." Penny agreed, recalling how she and Jim had binge watched the entire series on DVD while on tour in happier, simpler times.

"But I thought the First Generation died out?" Naomi asked.

"No, a few of us still existed in the era we just visited, living in a primitive, tribal lifestyle. Because we were non-technological, we weren't considered a threat and were allowed to live. When they finally left Pfoff, the Second Generation brought us along. In time, we were reintegrated into their society. When we arrived on our new homeworld, we all worked together as equals—creators and creations, former slave masters and former slaves, to build our new world."

"So what is this new homeworld? Why didn't you settle on Armenclius?" Penny asked

"We found a closer world once we were away on the Great Migration. It wasn't easily detectable from Pfoff, but once we were out in interstellar space it wasn't hard to find. Going there shaved off about 500 years from the journey. We call it Hirthrogaar, it means 'shining hope.'" Eventually, our people discovered how to create a warp drive and we joined the greater Galactic community, becoming members of the Federation." Jim explained

"So, what was your real mission? It wasn't to study human culture, that much is obvious now." Penny demanded.

Jim sighed, reluctant to say more, not sure how it would be received, but he had promised Penny the truth.

"My official mission for the Federation really is to study human culture. With an emphasis on your popular culture, and how we 'aliens' are perceived by you humans. However, the government of Hirthrogaar gave me an additional secret mission. Because I would be on Earth during the time of the Second War, which is what we call this invasion, I was to learn all that I could about these events. You see, during the Great Migration the ship that contained many of our historical archives was damaged by a magnetic storm it passed through. As a result, much of our history was lost, especially regarding the details of the Second War. Oh, we knew the basics: that during the construction of our fleet of colony ships one of our Nations traveled forwards in time and discovered that we were not living on Armenclius, so they plotted to invade the Earth in that era and were opposed by another Nation, who were eventually joined by three other Nations. However, the details were missing. We didn't even know for sure which Nations were involved. Or which sides they were on. We did have a partial recording though from that conflict, of a speech given to the leader of the aggressor Nation by a group of humans which ended the war."

Jim then fished his oval hologram projector from out of his pocket and activated it. A somewhat blurry holographic image of Naomi appeared in the air above the projector.

"Calm down, you're in no danger. Hi, my name is Naomi, Dr. Naomi Waters-Spike. We all just need to talk to you about something that's pretty important," Naomi's hologram said.

The image got staticky and jumped ahead. "Look, we're just not some mindless animals to be slaughtered, not like that's very nice either. We're thinking, feeling intelligent beings like you are and we have the same right to live as you do! Sure, we're not perfect and some of our ways may seem a little odd to you, but we're not that different either. Just like you, we're parents."

Again, the image blurred and skipped forward. "In my homeworld, I'm a professor of history. Nobody knows more about the history of our planet than I do, I literally wrote the book on it! Our peoples aren't so different both in good ways and bad. I can promise you one thing that I know based on my knowledge of history—it always looks more kindly upon the ones who break the shackles than it does the ones who slap them on."

Jim tapped the oval, and the image went away. "That's all that survived. In our history, we call it 'The Naomi Speech' and you," he looked up at Naomi, "Are known as 'The Naomi.' Your speech is not only credited with ending the war, but with inspiring leaders like Kergaali of the Baandergi to eventually end the practice of the creation of duplicates with the Duplo-Ray."

"That's crazy! It wasn't just me! It was Matt's idea to begin with, and it was really a group effort! Hell, even you played a big part in it! If you hadn't told Kergaali that your people still existed, I'm not sure the invasion would've been called off!" Naomi said.

"I know that now, but we had no idea that so much of the recording was missing. So when I came to Earth, I started searching for you. It wasn't easy, I got here in '92. You weren't a history professor then. You had no internet presence at that time so I couldn't use facial recognition software to find you. Eventually, I found you in the early 2000s. I even enrolled in one of your classes, back when you used to teach at Monmouth College."

"Aha! I knew it!" Naomi said. "I knew that I knew you from somewhere!"

"Yeah, sorry for lying to you about that earlier. I could never figure out how to get close enough to you to understand how you'd ever end up on Pfoff to give that speech in a few more years. Then a little more research on you revealed your link to Randy and Penny. So I thought that might be a fun way to get close to you, through them. It would also be a great way to learn more about human musical subculture, which was part of my other mission. Killing two birds with one stone, so to speak. So I started a similar band to the Mystery Smiths. I tried to get on the same record label, and when I couldn't get my band signed, I simply bought the label. When you stopped backing your currency in gold, your money became just numbers on a computer, so it wasn't hard for Hi-Fi to manipulate your system to make me filthy rich."

"You *own* our label?" Penny said in amazement.

"Yeah, I used that position to get our bands closer to each other, to have us do a few shows together, then eventually a tour..."

"You bastard! So this whole time you were just using me and Randy to get close to Naomi? Jesus! Was any of it real?" Penny's face was starting to turn red with anger.

"That's how it started out, I never expected to fall in love with you. That was never part of the plan, it kind of...just happened. You have to believe me, Penny!" Jim pleaded.

"I don't *have* to do a damned thing!" She said defiantly and turned away from him. Jim's shoulders slumped.

"What I still don't understand is why you got so deeply involved in all of this if you were so afraid of changing history?" Naomi asked, trying to change the subject to defuse the situation, but also genuinely interested in the question too.

Jim seemed to be relieved to be able to talk about something else for a minute.

"Because I wasn't really all that afraid of changing history. Since we knew next to nothing of the details of this invasion, I thought that anything I might do would've automatically been a part of how things had played out originally. You can't fuss over changing a history that you don't know. When it came to things that we *did* know, I tried to be careful. That's why we ignored the messages that were beamed out into space asking if there were any Venusians left in this time period. What little information we had on this conflict showed that such messages were never answered. If they had been answered, it would've brought the whole chain of events as we knew them to a grinding halt. That's also why I was reluctant to say anything when you pulled me into the Naomi Speech. I knew that I wasn't in the recording that had survived, but I was terrified that I might be added to it once you'd drawn me into the Nethersphere. Thankfully, as you just saw, the part that I was in was wiped by the damage from the magnetic storms, so it didn't matter. Penny was right. I'd always been a part of it, I just didn't know it."

Naomi nodded, digesting the information. "So Kergaali did go on to do something about how the Third Generation are treated? That's probably why it was so easy for you to believe Kergaali's lies? Because in your surviving histories Kergaali is a kind of hero?"

"Exactly. When Kergaali betrayed me, I was deeply confused on all kinds of levels. Not much was known about Kergaali's life, but we did know that as a result of the Naomi Speech, in a few weeks from now, Supreme Leader Kergaali will call for a global summit and propose sweeping changes that are adopted by the other Nations and eventually lead to the Third Generation being phased out, and which makes it a crime to use the Duplo-Ray to create duplicates of sentient beings.

"Why didn't your people just use a Time Tunnel to learn all of this lost history instead of using your mission for the Federation to uncover it?" Naomi asked.

"Because the Federation has a very strict ban on the use of time travel technology. However, my participation in these events is a kind of legal loophole, since it involves interacting with time travel technology from long before we were ever Federation members.”

“So what now? Have you got all the information you were looking for?” Naomi asked.

“Yes. Hi-Fi was recording everything the whole time, well, except for when he was in the bucket. He also downloaded a copy of the entire Baandergi Nethersphere while he was connected to it. That, plus the information we can get from interviewing the Baandergi I’m going to bring with me should go a long way towards restoring our history. All of my research on human culture was also preserved when my ship was duplicated, even my collectibles got copied and are over at the Baandergi base. They tossed them out to make more room for missiles.”

Jim looked over at Penny now, who still had her back to him. She was so angry that she was only half listening now.

“I hoped that once my mission was completed, I could come back here, to retire to Earth and maybe live out the rest of my life with you, Penny. If you’d have me?” He asked tenderly.

She still kept her back to him, and her head down. “No, it’s too late for that.”

“It’s the tentacles, isn’t it?” He asked.

She turned around to face him now. “No, that doesn’t matter, not when you can make yourself look like anyone you want to look like. There’s just been too many lies. The Jim I thought I knew, that I was falling in love with, he never existed. It’s all just been an illusion. I don’t think I could ever bring myself to trust you again, and what kind of relationship can we have if there’s no trust?”

“But you’ve forgiven Randy when he’s lied to you in the past. How is this so different?” Jim demanded.

“That’s different! Randy’s only ever really lied to me about one thing that was important, and that was years ago. We also have a lot more history together than you and I do. I feel like you’ve just constantly lied to me and used me. I’m done with that. It’s not something I feel like I ever want to have to put up with again. I’ll be fine on my own.”

"I'm sorry Penny, sorry that I ever hurt you. It was never part of the plan..."

"Maybe not, but that didn't stop you, did it?" She replied hotly.

"At least take the record label, then. I know how you've been thinking of starting up your own one, anyway. I can have Hi-Fi alter the computer records to give you complete ownership, and sign over my fortune to you, too. You can even have the hard light copy of Kirk's I left on Earth. It's a detailed enough copy to function like an actual restaurant, if you put in a real kitchen and hire a staff..."

"No! I don't want any consolation prizes from you! All I want is what you can never be— the person I thought you really were. It's over, Jim. Get that through your head!" She stormed off up the ramp and disappeared into the interior of the *Silver Bullet.*

Poor Naomi was caught there halfway up the ramp, looking between where Penny had just disappeared and Jim. She knew she needed to go and comfort her friend, but she also felt sorry for Jim, despite everything. She walked down to where Jim was and placed a hand on his shoulder.

"Jim, I'm really sorry that it didn't work out between you two. It's obvious to me that you do care about her," she said. At that moment, Jim threw his arms around her and started sobbing into her shoulder. At this moment, he reminded her more of the Cowardly Lion from *the Wizard of Oz* than the Beast from *Beauty and the Beast.* She patted him awkwardly on the back.

He stepped back, looking a bit embarrassed by the outburst.

"I'm sorry for that." He said between sniffles.

"Don't be. It's gonna be okay. Someday you'll find someone else. The universe is your oyster."

"I could travel to a thousand galaxies and never find someone quite like Penny." He said sadly.

Naomi wasn't about to argue with that.

"Well, uh, thanks for everything though, and good luck."

"I should be the one thanking you. You've done so much for our people." He looked at her reverently again. "The Naomi."

"Oh please! I just did what any decent person would do, any mom who wanted their kids to have a world that they could grow up in.

And now you know it wasn't just me, it was you, it was Matt, Randy, Penny, April, Goymaalt, Carlos, Prospero, Hi-Fi—all of us together. So stop putting me on a pedestal already! I'm nobody special. If anything I said back there really helped to make a difference I'm happy just to know that."

Jim bowed to her slightly and wiped away a tear.

"It's been an honor to know you, Dr. Waters-Spike. I'll never forget you." He said, then abruptly turned on his heel and walked away so rapidly, with his head down, that he nearly bumped into Matt, who was now walking back to the ship followed by Randy, Anne and April.

"Likewise." Naomi whispered as she watched his retreating form.

Matt could see that Naomi was looking a little choked up and emotional as he got nearer to the ship. "What was that all about? Tony the Tiger back there almost knocked me over. He was in such a hurry to get out of here! Isn't he coming with us?"

Naomi shook her head. "No, I think we've seen the last of Jim and Hi-Fi.

"Really? He didn't even say goodbye." Randy said, sounding a bit hurt.

"It's a long story. I'll fill you all in on the trip back to Earth." Naomi said.

"I wish everyone would stop saying that already!" Anne grumbled.

And with that, they all walked up into the *Silver Bullet*. A few moments later, the hatch closed up, and the ramp retracted as the ship rose in the hangar bay. The saucer flew out into the lunar sky and began the journey back home towards the Earth.

CHAPTER 22:
DOWN TO EARTH

A few nights later, in a secret, torch lit grotto on the island where Guild HQ was located, April, Randy and Prospero stood atop a large rock, looking down on the ceremony happening below them. Carlos, his son Miguel, a witch and another wizard, were standing in a circle around the hovering form of the Omega Seed. As they each took turns chanting different incantations, pieces of the seed would peel away from it, fragmenting into minute particles scattered on the wind before disappearing completely.

They were unmaking the Omega Seed.

"Soon that monstrosity will be nothing but a bad memory." Prospero said.

"Thank goodness for small victories." Randy said, "It's a pity that we couldn't quite get rid of Anne so easily."

"I can't believe that woman was able to hold onto power after everything she did!" Prospero noted sourly.

"It's Bronson's fault." Randy said, the betrayal he felt clear in his voice. "If he hadn't showed up at her impeachment trial and made that speech defending what she did, I think the Inner Council would've convicted her."

Indeed, the old man himself, Bronson McDowell, who had run the Guilds for years, had heard about Anne's trial and showed up to defend his goddaughter and hand-picked successor. He'd made a passionate case for giving her another chance. Randy was a very forgiving guy, but even he felt like you had to draw the line somewhere. The woman had lied to the entire Inner Council and tried to commit genocide for crying out loud! If she'd succeeded, not only would it have been a terrible atrocity, but who knows how it would've affected the course of Galactic history? He'd always respected Bronson and considered him a friend and ally, but he was just dead wrong in coming to Anne's defense like he had.

Would Bronson still be welcome at the parties at Matt and Naomi's house after this? Anne certainly wouldn't be. He hated how this whole affair had splintered their once harmonious and united group into opposing factions.

April had been silently listening to them all this time. Now she finally chose to speak. "At least we managed to avoid getting charged with treason ourselves, and we were able to limit her powers going forwards. She's managed to hold onto being the Chairperson of the Inner Council, but she's no longer the Director of the ABC, and our own Carlos is the new Commander in Chief of the UGF."

"Yeah, but the ABC will always ultimately be loyal to her no matter who they *say* is in charge." Randy said. Oliver was the new ABC Director, there was no doubt where his sympathies lay.

"Indeed, we're going to need to keep a very close eye on her going forward. That speech she gave when she was acquitted was the most insincere excuse for an apology I've ever heard. Anne doesn't *really* regret a damned thing. She'd do it all over again if given the opportunity, I'm sure of it. She still believes that anything is justified in the name of protecting the Earth from an extraordinary threat." April said, rubbing the bridge of her nose in exhaustion.

"Shit! I'm getting too old for this bullshit, Randy! I just wanna retire and spend the next couple of years helping Wendy to raise my little girl before I can't call her my little girl any longer. Celine will be going off to college in just under two years! Two years! What am I still doing on this fucking island playing political chess with someone who's got Machiavellian delusions of grandeur!" Cried an exasperated April. She normally prided herself on presenting such a strong front to the world. It was a testament to how much the past few days had taken out of her that she was allowing so many of the cracks in her demeanor to show, even among friends.

Randy put a comforting arm on April's shoulder. He sighed. He couldn't believe that he was about to say what he was about to say. "Look, maybe I could take over for you here soon? I know it's part of what Wendy always wanted for me."

April's eyes widened. Becoming the representative of the Temple of the Old Gods to the Inner Council of the International Conference of Guilds was indeed part of the pathway to eventually becoming Pontificus Maximus, the leader of the Temple, which had always been Wendy's ultimate ambition for Randy. However, it was also a responsibility which he'd long shirked.

While Wendy looked upon this as shirking his responsibility, April had always been more sympathetic to Randy. She didn't see it as something that was really his responsibility at all, so much as a destiny that Wendy had been trying to force on the boy ever since she first started training him in magic. Wendy believed that Randy was the reincarnation of an influential ancient prophet, and that under his leadership the Temple would help to lead the entire planet towards some kind of utopian future.

Whether this was actually true or not, April believed that the choice always had to be Randy's, and that he had a right to choose a different path if he wanted to. Hell, how could she ever blame him for not wanting to take up a path that she herself was now thoroughly sick of walking?

"Randy, you don't have to do this! What about your band? Your son, Paul? You can't bring him here!"

"I can just travel back and forth a lot, see Paul on the weekends. At least I'll see a bit more of Aethra this way. And I'm sick of touring. I don't mind taking a break from the band for a while. You've earned your retirement, you've been fighting the good fight for so many years now. I can't keep running away from this anymore. I've been running away from so many things for so many years. It's time for me to face reality. This is where I'm needed the most right now. I stopped Anne once, and I can do it again if need be."

"I'll be happy to stay on and advise you the way I have April, lad!" Prospero said.

"Thanks, Prospero." Randy smiled at the ancient wizard.

"Are you sure this is really what you want?" April asked him.

"It's the way things have got to be." Randy said firmly.

"Alright. I'll inform the Pontifex Maximus of my upcoming retirement and that I'm appointing you as my replacement. How much time do you think you'll need to get your affairs in order?"

"Give me about a month, if that's alright?"

"Alright? It's perfect! Thanks for this, Randy. I know Wendy's gonna be really proud of you too, for taking this on. "April said as she gave him a hug. He hugged her back, then they separated just in time to see the last fragments of the Omega Seed trailing off into the warm night air.

CHAPTER 23:
THE END OF THE TOUR

On Valentine's Day of 2013, Matt and Naomi sat at a table at the Court Tavern bar in New Brunswick, NJ. The legendary venue had spent most of the previous year, 2012, closed and had only recently reopened a few months ago, back in December of that same year. Matt and Naomi had meant to visit once they'd heard that it was back, but hadn't gotten around to doing so until now.

This was the location where Randy and Penny had played their first official show together, back in '97, when they were known as "Lung Collapse". It was also fittingly, the place where it looked like they'd be making their last appearance together for some time. Randy was taking an indefinite hiatus from the Mystery Smiths now that he was going to be working at Guild HQ. This had turned out to suit Penny just fine. She was feeling exhausted from touring for the past year and had expressed a desire to work on a solo project, inspired by her recent interplanetary adventures, that she'd eventually released online.

Matt would be without his professional partner at the detective agency now too, and down one more investigator. But they'd managed alright during the past year while Randy had been on tour, and at least they were getting Penny back to help run the office. Kevin would be getting his license soon and could become a proper investigator. He was a poor substitute for Randy with his renowned instincts, but the kid was still learning and had a lot of potential.

He was there too, over at the next table with Allison, whom he'd managed to coax down from the city. Despite the fact that Kevin didn't really like the Mystery Smiths music, he'd seized on the opportunity as an excuse to get Allison down here. She'd recently broken up with her boyfriend, who'd thrown some kind of jealous hissy fit over the time she'd spent with Kevin last weekend. His shitty, possessive attitude had ended up dooming that relationship. Now Matt watched as Kevin leaned in for a kiss with Allison. The detective smiled his lopsided grin at the sight.

Well, it looks like the kid's got a little game after all! Good for them both! He thought.

The Mystery Smiths had just finished up what would prove to be their final set with their original line up. Randy would someday rejoin the band, but the group's longtime drummer, Valerie, would be moving on for good soon. Of course, none of them knew this at this time.

Matt took the opportunity afforded by the sudden relative quiet to talk to his wife. "I've noticed that since we got back, you haven't been on your phone much."

"Oddly enough, ever since I saw how the Venusians lost themselves in the Nethersphere, it just doesn't seem as appealing." She replied.

"Ya know, I always knew those things were terrible. You guys used to love to make fun of me because I wouldn't buy a cell phone back in the 90s, but I was right, wasn't I?"

"Oh please! You didn't want to buy one because you're a notorious cheapskate, not because you're some kind of prophet!" Naomi laughed.

"Yeah, okay, maybe. But still, admit it—everyone carrying around a computer with internet access in their pockets. We can't handle that kind of distraction constantly vying for our attention. It's not gonna end well for us. We'll be lucky if we don't end up like those Venusians."

"No argument there." Naomi agreed.

They both watched as Randy sat down at a nearby table for a few minutes, wiping the sweat from his brow as he took a seat next to an older woman who kind of looked like his Aunt Bernice, if Bernice had looked a bit more aged and beaten down by life. However, despite her haggard appearance, the woman wore a broad, undeniably beautiful smile. A smile that he'd often seen on Randy's face—and Paul's too, for that matter.

"Who's that over there with Randy?" Matt asked. "Some kind of relative that I've never seen before?"

"You mean he didn't tell you? That's his mom. She was supposed to be coming to the show tonight." Naomi revealed.

"No way!" Matt was flabbergasted. In all the years he'd known Randy he'd never seen his mother, or even seen a picture of her.

"Way!" Naomi affirmed.

"Get outta town!" Matt continued to say in disbelief.

"You can ask him for yourself, dude. It looks like he's coming over here now."

It was true. Randy threw himself into a vacant seat at the table.

"So, how did you guys enjoy the show?" He asked, looking a bit exhausted.

"You and Penny really outdid yourselves this time." Naomi assured him.

"Yeah? Thanks. Hard to believe that we're back here where it all started after being away for so long. I love it when stuff comes full circle like that." He mused.

"So, a little Naomi just told me, wait, I mean *the* Naomi, the glorious savior of Pfoff, just told me that it's your mom you were just talking to. Is that right?" Matt said. He'd been teasing her about her role in Venusian history ever since he'd heard about it. On this occasion, it earned him a playful kick from under the table.

Randy's face suddenly became a bit more serious. "It's true. "

"I'm surprised to see you talking to her. I always thought that well. the things you said she did were unforgivable." Matt said.

"I used to believe that they were. But I've been doing a lot of thinking lately, ever since we got back to Earth. I've been thinking about how the Venusians, like Goymaalt, were so worried about sacrificing their principles to stop the invasion. It's made me question myself. Where do I draw the line with certain things? What principles are worth holding onto and which ones can I be a bit more flexible with? It made me realize that I've been a bit of a hypocrite myself. I'm always talking about how important it is to show compassion and be forgiving, but I haven't been able to do that with my own parents. I've been running from this one thing for my whole life. Almost everything I've ever done has been a distraction from having to face it. I used to distract myself with video games, books, music, and learning how to do magic. It's like my whole personality is formed around distracting myself from my past."

"Really? I'm surprised to hear you say how distracted you are. I usually think of you as the least distracted person I know. You're 'Mr. Live-in-the-moment' and all that."

"That's just the thing, though Matt—I have to always be mindful to live in the present because I can't ever allow myself to think about my past! It's just another coping technique, another escape. I'm no better than a Baandergi in the Nethersphere. I use the Aether like they used the Nethersphere, always going off to astrally visit Aethra and Gertrude when I should be getting some sleep. I do anything to avoid sleep, to avoid the nightmares I have about my early childhood."

"I never knew that about you, buddy. I didn't know you had really bad nightmares like that," Matt said sadly. How was it that he'd known this guy for almost half of his life and he'd never understood just how hurt and damaged he was inside? Randy always seemed like such a calm, cool, perfect Zen master type. Who could've guessed he had such a storm raging inside him, buried just beneath the surface? Matt felt like he'd failed him as a friend by failing to recognize this.

Randy seemed to sense this and was quick to reassure him.

"How could you? I never talk about it, I always run from it! But I can't—not anymore. It's not healthy to live in the past, but it's just as unhealthy to ignore it, to pretend that it has no impact on your present. I don't like to think of myself as a victim. Who does? But I am. I was abused. I was abandoned." It felt incredibly liberating just to say those words out loud for a change.

He looked over at his mother at the other table. "I can't hide from that truth any longer, and that begins with confronting the people who did the abusing."

"I think you're making the right decision, Randy. It's not good to hold on to all that anger. It'll eat you up inside eventually. Forgive them for the sake of yourself, if not for them." Naomi said.

Matt nodded. "When you're a kid, you expect your parents to have all the answers. Now that you're a dad yourself, you know what bullshit that is, that it's not like you get an instruction manual or something. You're still the same person you were as a kid, but now you're suddenly responsible for someone else. Hardly anybody is ever ready for it. We're all just making it up as we go along. Mistakes are gonna happen. I know your folks made some really, really serious ones, but now that you see how tough it can be sometimes. Maybe that makes it a little easier to forgive them? Anyhow, it sounds like they're not quite the same people that they were then, maybe the people that they are now are worth getting to know a little better?"

"Yeah. I'm not sure if we'll ever be close. It's probably too late for that, and there's been too much hurt, but hopefully I can do a little healing." Randy said.

***

Over at another nearby table, Aethra brought over a pair of beers for herself and Penny and sat down next to her. Randy had put a glamor spell on Aethra, which made it easier for her to blend in. She looked very much as she did on Venus, the last time that such a spell had been put on her, except that she was dressed more casually in jeans and a tee-shirt.

"Here you go," Aethra said as she passed the beverage over to Penny. She scrutinized Penny for a moment.

"You know, I have to say that I've always been a little jealous of you."

"Jealous of me? You're a freakin' Pirate Queen that can shoot lasers from her eye and breathe underwater! What've you got to be jealous of? I'm just a regular girl—a nobody."

"A nobody? Give me a break! You're a rock star!" Aethra said.

"Yeah, a fourth tier one!" Penny argued back.

"And a mother! I'd never have the patience to take care of a kid. And you kicked so much alien ass for a 'regular girl!' You really saved our asses back on the moon."

"Well, being paired up with Hi-Fi had a lot to do with that!" Penny said, continuing to brush away the praise.

Aethra became more serious. "And you mean more to Randy than I'm afraid I ever could. You mean the world to him and I can see why. You guys might not be physically intimate anymore, but you share a deeper kind of intimacy with him that I can only dream of having. You two make beautiful music together."

"What? Don't be ridiculous! And our music isn't beautiful so much as it's goofy."

"Well, okay, beautifully goofy music then." Aethra said.

"I know that he really cares for you too or he wouldn't be with you. You two are so cute together, a real power couple!" Penny carried on.

"Yeah, but I'll never have the kind of bond that you have with him. All that history you've got together, the band, your son," Aethra said wistfully.

"Maybe you don't have the same kind of relationship with him that I do, but so what? What you've got with him is just as precious, just in a different way. Learn to treasure that for what it is." Penny told her firmly. "Not everything is a competition."

"Alright, I'll make you a deal - don't sell yourself short and I won't either." Aethra said and held out her hand. Penny took it.

"Amen. It's a deal. We're both too fucking amazing for humility!" Penny laughed as they shook on it.

"In my experience, humility is a grossly overrated trait." The Pirate Queen smiled at her.

Matt looked at the scene. "It looks like your past and present lady friends are busy plotting against you." He warned Randy.

"I can handle them. It's Anne that I'm still worried about." He said gravely.

"So your newfound commitment to forgiveness doesn't extend that far?" Naomi asked teasingly.

"She nearly committed genocide. Asking anybody to forgive such a thing is a pretty tall order. Maybe it's twice as tall when you're a Jew? I dunno. Maybe I'll get there someday, but not today. All I know is I have to keep a sharp eye on her. That's really why I'm taking that job with the Guilds."

"Well, if anyone can rein her in, it'll be you. I still can't believe that Bronson came to her defense like that." Naomi told him.

"I can. We've gotten too cozy with the Guilds over the years. Having parties with these people, calling them in whenever the shit seems to really be about to hit the fan like they're the goddamned

Calvary. It's easy to delude ourselves into thinking of them as the good guys, but for the most part, they're really just a bunch of amoral opportunists—no offense, buddy." Matt said.

"None taken, I know it's true." Randy said quickly.

"If they seem to do the right thing, it's just because there's something in it for them, too. Bronson told us as much the day we first met him. We forget that at our own peril, and Anne is proof positive of that." Matt concluded.

"And on that cheerful note, I think I'll take my leave for a bit. I'd better go see what those two are scheming about," Randy said, indicating Penny and Aethra as he rose from his seat to join two of the most important women in his life.

"I've been doing a little deep thinking myself." Matt announced.

"Oh yeah? Well, be careful not to hurt yourself!" Naomi smiled at him.

"Hardy, har, har. Very funny. I might not have a PhD, but occasionally I *do* still have a world saving idea or two.

"True enough, you have the floor, sir. What's on your mind now?"

"I've been thinking about everything that's happened to us lately and how it's kind of eerily like that book that your dad wrote. I mean, we would've never been drawn into all of this if Jim hadn't been looking to get closer to you, but he never would've been looking for you if it hadn't been for that recording of you being made. A recording which wouldn't have been made if it weren't for his actions. It's kind of a loop, you know?"

Naomi thought about it. "Yeah, I guess that's true. Geez, do you think my dad knew something about our future? That he was trying to warn us somehow?"

"I don't see how he could've known. I think it's just another example of something that Randy is always saying, about how the universe tries to tell us things, through synchronicities and whatnot."

"Hmm. Spooky." Naomi said, finishing off the last little bit of her beer that had been left. "C'mon, Mr. Designated Driver, let's go home and you might just get lucky."

And so it came to pass that Matt and Naomi, despite Autumn being home, finally managed to get in some "special sexy fun time" that night. Alien handcuffs confiscated from the denizens of the planet Venus may or may not have been involved. I've already written far more about their sex lives than any of us have any business knowing about to either confirm or deny such salacious details. All that any of us needs to truly understand about it is that a very happy Valentine's Day was had by the both of them. The spark of love for each other was still burning strong in the two of them, despite all the years.

EPILOGUE ONE:
IN WHICH THE AUTHOR NEEDLESSLY PONTIFICATES UPON THE NATURE OF LOVE

So, you might be thinking, that's it? Penny doesn't find love? She doesn't end up with Randy, or with Jim? What's up with giving a story a subtitle like "Modern Love" when practically nobody in it ever finds love? Well, before you slam this book down and declare it to be the most unsatisfying story ever, let me remind you that as you have just seen, there are many different types of love and they are all equally precious. Her friendship with Randy endured the storm of these events, in fact, their bond was even stronger afterwards and that's something worth celebrating, I think.

This was never meant to be a story about romantic love, per se. It's a story about the bewildering, perhaps needlessly complicated varieties of love that exist, and our equally exhaustive ways of expressing such sentiments. For we human beings are nothing if not experts at making the simplest of things in life in abhorrently overwrought. It sometimes seems overwhelming doesn't it? Maybe even not worth the effort? Yet it's absolutely vital for our happiness to make that effort, to figure out exactly what kinds of love we need to take in and what kinds we need to express, and not be ashamed to do either.

If it makes you feel any better, though, I will reveal that Penny did eventually find romantic love again, too. It came to her, as these things often do, when she stopped trying so hard to find it. About two years later, the Mystery Smiths got themselves a new drummer. An easy-going fellow with the unassuming name of Bob. Penny and Bob hit it off in all the right ways and she even had a few more kids, a cute pair of fraternal twins, with her new husband. But I don't think I'm being cruel or trivializing their relationship when I say that their love story doesn't warrant a book. There were no alien invasions or battles involved, so it wouldn't be much of a page turner. Not every love story is quite that exciting. In fact, most of them aren't very exciting at all, except perhaps to the people actually experiencing it. It doesn't make them any less special, though. Penny is quite happy with the stability and security she gets out of the non-book worthy love story she's currently living. It was, in fact, exactly what she needed all along.

She'd had quite enough of space adventures, even though she did find a little ass-kicking to be invigorating. Ultimately, that kind of lifestyle just wasn't for her. It's better to leave that sort of thing to the Aethra Hoffman's of the world.

However, if you were ever to visit Penny's house you would discover that she kept that ridiculously futuristic bucket as a souvenir. It's currently in front of the house, right by the door, and is being used as a planter. A relic from a dead world made almost 750 million years ago that now serves as a vessel for nurturing new life, the Children of Pfoff undoubtedly, would've approved.

"My friend, you have seen this incident based on sworn testimony. Can you prove that it didn't happen? Perhaps on your way home you will pass someone in the dark, and you will never know it, for they will be from outer space. Many scientists believe that another world is watching us this moment. We once laughed at the horseless carriage, the aeroplane, the telephone, the electric light, vitamins, radio, and even television! And now some of us laugh at outer space. God help us... in the future."
—Criswell, *Plan 9 from Outer Space*

EPILOGUE TWO:
THE PLANET HIRTHROGAAR, 2016

Jim made a few polite excuses and walked away from the crowd that had gathered around him during the party. He made his way towards the balcony. In the time since he'd returned home, he'd been working on a documentary about the Second War, pieced together using much of the footage that Hi-Fi had taken. It had recently been completed and released to rave reviews. It had just won a prestigious award, which was why he was at this particular party.

But even in a crowded room, even after all these years, he still felt terribly alone sometimes.

Jim had become quite famous. His research on human pop culture had greatly expanded the Federation's understanding of human psychology. His discoveries about the 2nd War had themselves become historical. The Baandergi he had brought back with him had given them many valuable insights into the past, and they had adjusted quite nicely to life in this future era (although some of the most dangerous and fanatical ones, such as Cosfreele, had to be jailed). Yes, Jim had everything he'd ever wanted now—except for one thing. The most important thing.

As he stood on the balcony, he gazed out at the night sky. There, just to the right of the second moon, he found what he was looking for—a tiny star shining bright in the night. It was Sol, the star that his people had been born under millions of years earlier.

"You're still thinking of her, aren't you?" A voice said from behind him. He turned one of his eye stalks around to face the newcomer.

The voice belonged to Goymaalt, former Deputy Leader of the Saawgauth.

Jim had smuggled Goymaalt aboard his ship right before he'd left the moon. Goymaalt knew that the Second Generation Drogalla would eventually create another duplicate to replace the one that had been murdered. But this new Drogalla wouldn't be the same, it wouldn't be *Goymaalt's* Drogalla. None of that would matter. Goymaalt would still be expected to work closely with this new Drogalla. There was still much work to be done, both moon bases, and eventually even the Time Tunnels themselves, would need to be dismantled before they could return home to Pfoff. Goymaalt couldn't bear the idea of having to work with this new Drogalla, this walking reminder of their pain. So Goymaalt had asked Jim to take them to Hirthrogaar. He'd only been too happy to oblige.

"I don't know that I'll ever really stop thinking about her. She was one in a billion." He said.

"I know the feeling." Goymaalt said, thinking of Drogalla.

They stood there together for some time, looking up at the distant star called Sol, and thinking about the dead end world that circled around it, and all the friends they'd left behind there. They hoped that maybe, just maybe, someday it wouldn't prove to be a dead end world after all.

The End
(Completed May 10th, 2021 in Roanoke, VA)

APPENDIX:
PRELIMINARY REPORT ON RECOVERED VENUSIAN SAUCERS AND BODIES

By Oliver Johns, Director ABC to Anne Moore, Chairperson of the International conference of Guilds, February 18th 2013.

I believe that you will be quite pleased by our progress on the project to make use of the various extraterrestrial materials which we have recently had the opportunity to take possession of. Our salvage operation consists of two primary areas of operation:

- Undersea salvage of crashed saucers which had been shot down in the waters off of New York City.
- Recovery of saucer wreckage in low Earth orbit using the *Silver Bullet.*

Unfortunately, attempts to recover Federation holography projectors from the establishment known as "Kirk's Intergalactic Grub" have met with disastrous results. While we were able to locate the holographic projectors creating the hard light hologram of the structure, the devices self-destructed when we attempted to remove them for further study, destroying the illusion of the restaurant. As you know, this forced us to come up with a cover story involving arson to explain the loss of the structure.

Further operations are planned to scour the locations of both the Saawgauth and Baandergi moon bases for any materials that may have been left behind. However, such operations must be delayed until the Venusians completely depart this time period, as they appear to be currently and actively working to dismantle said structures.

Section 1: Saucers

Unlike the *Silver Bullet*, which still defies our attempts to understand it, our engineers so far report that the number of Venusian ships we have recovered (we have 7 so far, in various states of damage, and parts from at least 6 more) are of a design which is far more straightforward and comprehensible than that of the *Silver Bullet*. Indeed, many elements of Venusian technology are similar to our own and are perhaps only a few decades ahead.

All of this means that we can reasonably expect to be able to replicate something very similar to these saucers in the near future. This is exciting news as it has always been our goal to supplement the arsenals of both the UGF and the ABC with saucers of our own.

We also expect to be able to replicate the weapons systems and defensive shields of these saucers. The recovery of a number of still functional alien guns found with some of the bodies has aided with this process considerably. The alien teleportation systems, however, may prove far more challenging to duplicate as they require computing systems far more advanced than anything we have, working on quantum principles.

Section 2: Bodies

A number of corpses were recovered from the more intact ships, some of them quite well preserved. Autopsies have already been performed on them (see attached reports). Here is a brief summary of our key findings so far:

- The chemical composition of the bodies is similar to that of terrestrial life forms. Our scientists speculate that this might be evidence of panspermia—the theory that life is seeded from one planet to another. In this case, this suggests that life in our solar system may've first arisen on Venus, then traveled to Earth. This was likely accomplished via meteorites or perhaps microbes were inadvertently carried here by an early Venusian exploration of our world when it was "snowball Earth".

- The Venusians possess very dense, compact muscle fibers. This makes them several times stronger than the average human being without looking particularly brawny. This appears to be the result of intentional genetic engineering.

- Venusians have glands that secrete an oily substance onto their skin. The purpose of this substance seems to be to form a layer which naturally helps to protect against elevated levels of radiation.

- Rather than bones, the Venusians possess a kind of cartilage, similar to that of a shark, only more flexible and tougher. Rather than breaking or shattering, it tears and therefore cannot puncture the organs, or send bone fragments into the body. This network of cartilage is denser around the vital organs, forming a protective lattice work around them. This cartilage absorbs shocks exceptionally well as it evenly distributes the force of impacts throughout the whole body, rather than concentrating the trauma in one location. Also like a shark, the only bone is the jaws.

- Their teeth are mostly sharp and fang-like, this, along with their cat-like eyes suggests that they evolved from a nocturnal, predatory creature. Rather than nails, they have short, retractable claws which would've aided their distant ancestors with climbing trees as well as ripping flesh. Debriefings conducted by the ABC of Randal Gruman and Penny Layne reveal that the creatures the Venusians evolved from bore some superficial resemblance to a Lemur, albeit this would've been a lemur with claws, fangs and eyes more like that of a cat.

- The stomachs show evidence of being genetically altered to allow for easier digestion of vegetable material. Debriefings of eyewitnesses suggested an exclusively vegetarian diet, examination of stomach contents has corroborated these accounts. In every instance, the partially digested plant material was a kind of fungi unknown to us.

- The Venusians are marsupials. They possess a small pouch for holding their young. They have an additional pair of nipples, with the majority of their milk being contained in the upper part of the chest, as in a human female. The reproductive systems of all the bodies recovered were somewhat atrophic, consistent with reports from the eyewitness debriefings that the Venusians only reproduce once in their life cycle, and that "Third Generation" duplicates are not allowed to be created until after the original "Second Generation" has reproduced. Our scientists speculate that the eggs are coded to self fertilize upon reaching full maturity.
- The brains are slightly larger than that of a human, with denser and more numerous neural connections. Implanted deep within the frontal cortex is what eyewitnesses described as a "control chip" which is connected to the antenna that protrudes from the top of the head. Both the control chip and antenna are biomechanical in nature, more like an artificially grown organ than a true mechanical apparatus. There is a great deal of variation in the antennas, no two seem to be completely identical, like fingerprints. The reason for this is unknown. According to eyewitness testimony, the "Second Generation" Venusians supposedly lack this feature.
- Based upon the sample of bodies recovered, the average height is between 5 foot 11 and 6 foot three.
- There is a vestigial tail which is about 5-6 inches long.

It may be possible for us to clone a Venusian in the near future. Likewise, we may be able to incorporate certain Venusian genes into human subjects. Certain bodily features unique to the Venusians could prove to be useful in creating a kind of genetically advanced warrior (see the attached file on chemical analysis of Shadowman remains and files confiscated from Buhler Industries in 1995 on Shadowman anatomy).

I will keep you abreast of all further developments, and look forward to hearing your thoughts on which areas we should pursue the most aggressively.

Matt Spike will return in "Death Dressed in Gold"

OTHER BOOKS BY R. E. SOHL:

A Dead End World:

Book 1: *The Shadow of Death*

Book 1.5: *Tales From a Dead End World*

Book 2: *Beyond the Veil of Death*

Book 2.5: *Tales From A Dead End World Volume Two*

Book 3: *Matt Spike and the Vampire's Curse*

Book 3.5: *Tales From A Dead End World Volume Three*

Mistress Of The Wyverns:

Book 1: *Jersey Devils*

Book 1.5: *Romance Of The Gun*

Book Two: *Night Of The Mothman*

With more coming...

RE Sohl (if that even is his real name) is the alleged author of entirely too many stories in which members of an ancient, global conspiracy are actually the good guys and the space aliens are just here to harmlessly observe us. This is obviously all part of a massive disinformation/ propaganda campaign to make you feel all warm and fuzzy when our Illuminati/Lizard-people masters inevitably emerge from the unholy depths of the Hollow Earth to rule us more openly. All of the proceeds from any of his books which you may purchase are funneled into a Swiss bank account used to help fund various nefarious Black Ops.

He recently moved to Fairfax, VA so he can be within convenient boot licking distance of his beloved CIA overlords.

www.ingramcontent.com/pod-product-compliance
Lightning Source LLC
Chambersburg PA
CBHW060426310726
48977CB00001B/61